BEHIND CLOSED DOORS

Behind Closed Doors

LOVE HURTS

K.F. Johnson

One Ironwoman Publishing

Contents

1	Brian & Brenda	1
2	Brian	11
3	Brenda	24
4	Brian	36
5	Brenda	54
6	Brian	70
7	Brenda	87
8	Brian	102
9	Brenda	117
10	Brian	133
11	Brenda	150
12	Brian	161
13	Brenda	180
14	Brian	194
15	Brenda	208
16	Brian	220
17	Brenda	231
18	Brian	241
19	Brenda	255
20	Brian	265

vi | *Contents*

21 Brenda   275

22 Brian   284

23 Brenda   294

24 Brian   305

25 Brenda   314

Enjoyed This Book?   323
About The Author   324

One Ironwoman Publishing
Grayson, GA 30017

Cover Design by Christine N. Davis
ISBN: 978-1-954469-00-6

1

Brian & Brenda

SIBLINGS

BRENDA

I buttoned the top two buttons on my silk nightshirt and quietly crept out of bed. Teddy usually slept like a log anyway, but I didn't want to chance waking him. I slid on my stuffed lion head bedroom slippers and stood by the bedside looking at him. I loved looking at his 6'4", cocoa brown, muscular body lying in my bed. The moonlight spotlighted his muscular form like a perfect Adonis. Love had me doting on everything about that man from his unblemished and beautifully structured face, all the way down to his crusty and ashen feet…regretfully.

I ran my fingers through my hair, sighed, and made a slow, quiet stride to the kitchen. Once again, I'd allowed that sexy Mandingo of a man to work his way into my bed after I'd pledged not to. He had me dangling on a string for the past three years jockeying for a commitment, yet I routinely let him back in to my heart; and clearly, back into my bed.

My fantasies ate, slept and drank the thought of Teddy and me living together in marital bliss. The reality was that I'd have to get him to agree to exclusivity first, which was harder than getting Tiger Woods to admit he's black. I repeatedly had inner lectures with myself about the never-ending cycle I was in. Unfortunately, the content of those lectures blurred once I was in his presence, loving his mannish ways and under the spell of his charm.

There was no question my body was satisfied, but my heart wasn't so lucky.

I opened the refrigerator and was startled by the cold and wet nose of my Min Pin Zeus on my ankle. I looked down to see him wagging his little nub and pawing at my calves, begging to be picked up.

"Hey baby. Mommy can't pick you up right now," I whispered as I improvised by stroking him with the bottom of my foot.

I rifled through the scarce remains of the week's groceries and settled on the bowl of grapes on the bottom shelf. I pulled the bowl out and noticed the message light flashing on my answering machine from my peripheral. I leaned my back up against the counter, turned the volume up just enough to be heard at close range, and hit play. The machine started:

"You have seven messages. First message 5:24pm:

'Hey Brenda baby what's going on? This is John, and I was calling to see if you wanted to have dinner and maybe catch a movie with me on Thursday. I know how busy you are sometimes… (Laughter)…and if I don't ask now, you'll be too busy later. Hit me up when you get in if it's before 1 o'clock. I got a long day tomorrow. Bye.'

I smiled and popped a few grapes in my mouth as Zeus tried to coax me with moans and groans to share. John was a new guy I'd been seeing who had a lot of potential. Being a detective for the Fulton County Police Department posed a problem for coordinating date schedules at times though so we usually communicated via email and telephone. So far, he was holding his value.

"Second message 6:23pm:

'It's Dexter. Call me back when you get a chance. I wanted to see if I could get a little taste of that brown sugar before I leave out for Cali on Tuesday. Give me a buzz when you get in. Peace.'"

Dexter worked in the advertisement department where I worked and traveled in different cities on assignment often. We'd dated now and then in the last year and had done the bump and grind a few times. He certainly was not on a level where he could call and request 'a little taste of my brown sugar' though. Who the hell did he think he'd stepped up his game enough to be?

If it wasn't for that pretty boy face, and his sexy body, he'd be unbearable. Between his overbearing arrogance and occasional lisp, I'd gag myself with a dirty dish towel before dealing with him on a regular basis. Lucky for me, I didn't have to work in the office very often. He could hold his breath waiting on that call.

"Third message 8:04pm:

'Hey girl, it's Rhonda. I swear if your ass doesn't come into the new millennium soon and turn your cell phone on I'm gonna hurt you,'" my best girlfriend joked. "'and this tired ass 1992 answering machine needs to be donated to the Salvation Army too. I need to talk to you and your primitive behind can't be reached. Call me!'"

I giggled while chewing a mouth full of grapes and rolled my eyes. I didn't like the idea that people always seemed to have access to everybody all the time, these days. I cherished my alone time, so I rarely kept my cell phone on me unless I was on a project for work, or some urgent call was expected. My friends and family hated that they didn't have me at their fingertips, and I loved that they hated it...Oh well.

"Fourth message 8:22pm:

'Hey sexy it's Keven. If you get in before 10 o'clock, call me cause...'"

Zeus yelped startling me into a clumsy frizzy where I dropped some grapes and inadvertently bumped my knee on the cabinet door near where I was standing. "What the hell?" I scolded while he wagged his nub and looked past me.

I turned around to Teddy standing by the kitchen entrance wrapped in the sheet from my bed. He looked at my answering machine and leaned his elbow on the adjacent kitchen counter.

"Checking your messages in the middle of the night eh? That's not looking too good on me. Am I gonna have to lay it down on you again so you can keep your attention where I'm at?" He asked casually.

The messages continued to play, but I quickly turned the volume down on the machine wearing an uncomfortable grin.

"It wasn't a sneak move or anything. I was just checking them while I got some grapes since I didn't get around to it earlier," I answered trying to sound as casual as he did.

"Umm hmm. Well, you're my woman tonight so come back to bed and forget about the other dudes trying to get at you."

"Just for tonight huh?"

"No, not just for tonight baby. You know what I meant. You're always gonna be my woman in my heart though."

"Just not the only woman, right?" I asked with attitude.

Jealousy had been eating at me like the Ebola virus, and it was increasingly more difficult for me to have a conversation that didn't lead to a sarcastic remark about our in-exclusivity. It increased the amount of arguments we had too of course, but I couldn't help it.

Teddy sighed and came to stand directly in front of me. He licked his soft, sensual lips, took a few grapes from the bowl, and fixed his eyes on me in the dim light from the streetlamp outside.

"Do you ever hear me talking about other women? Or see other women's things at my place when you come over?" He asked.

"I don't have to see you shit to know you shit," I responded crossing my arms in front of me.

"Your potty mouth is ridiculous Brenda. I thought we were too deep for this at this point. Whether I'm seeing any other women or not, me and you are still, me and you. I know you're not sitting here acting like you're not seeing anybody else right? Especially when I just caught you picking up messages from a gang of guys. You don't see me pouting and catching an attitude with you. It's because I know we don't get down with anybody else the way we get down with each other. Why do you like to argue all of the time?" He asked popping a grape in his mouth.

I wanted to scream, 'Hell this is the problem, for Christ's sake!' Why wasn't he catching an attitude about me seeing other dudes? If we're supposed to be so deep, then why didn't he have a problem sharing me? I'd tried being laid back about him dating other women, but I only succeeded in pretending to be okay with it. In the end, my jealousy and resentment eventually surfaced like the Loch Ness Monster on his ass.

"Why not? I mean be real with me Teddy," I said exasperatedly. "How long are we supposed to keep being each other's...I don't know...number one booty call?"

"Well, I don't know what you want to call me, but I don't think of you as a booty call baby," he replied pulling me close to him. "You know if the situation provided it would just be me and you."

"If the situation provided for what?" I countered removing myself from his embrace. "There's nothing you're doing now that couldn't be done if we started seeing each other exclusively. Nothing except you messing with other women, that is. You're almost 30 years old Teddy. You're not tired of playing Casanova Lion King to a tribe of females yet?"

"Brenda, I don't like to do things unless I can put 100% into it and I can't do that right now. I'm trying to build and keep my real estate business a float baby. It's a recession, and the time and effort I'm investing in my business are what you're gonna be wanting and I can't give that to you at the moment. I want to give it to you, but it wouldn't be fair for me to pretend like I can do what I know I can't. Once I've got that straight then..."

"That's just stupid Teddy. If I knew that was where your time away from me was being spent, then it wouldn't be a problem. You know how busy I get once I'm on a project for work, and I don't have a lot of time so I can work with that. You always try to pull the timecard out on me."

"Brenda," he said sternly looking into my eyes and shaking his head. "Are you listening to what I am telling you or are you hearing what you want? I said I-am-not-ready. I'm committed to my business right now and that's as much as I can handle right-now. I'm not in the mood to talk about this same stuff over and over again while you run this guilt trip on me knowing what's up."

"Really," I replied feeling the knot in my throat as I held back tears. "Well how about you screw your business next time you want to get off because I'm tired of getting screwed." I said storming from the kitchen back to the bedroom.

***

BRIAN

The air was stifling, and the music reverberated through the walls of JAGUARS while scantily clothed females danced seductively with the nights designated drink lackey.

"See now that pretty little piece of ass might actually make a brother think about hanging his players robe up. If she has half a brain in her head to compliment that body," I said watching a sexy long haired Beyoncé clone on the dance floor. "I love my job," I continued, wearing a big grin while I served a drink to a customer.

"Yeah right. You haven't stuck with just one female since I've known you Brian. I don't even think you're capable," Donald, my young bartending understudy commented.

I kept smiling and started making another drink order. "Yeah," I laughed. "Right, right. That's true. There's no reason to buy when I can lease homeboy."

A frown suddenly took his face hostage as he scratched his bald head and deposited some cash into the register. "Huh? What's that mean?"

"My man, you're a little too old to still need an explanation for such simple things. It means, exactly what I said. Okay, listen…women are just like cars," I began. "Let me break down my philosophy to you," I said in my imitation pimp voice as I checked myself out in the mirror above the drink racks.

Every curl in my low fade was still in place. My cocoa brown skin was still flawless, my muscles were still bulging through my black tank top and my hazel brown eyes were sparkling with the same shine as always. I smiled at myself and gave a complimentary wink at the reflection of a beautiful dark skin sista' sitting at the bar who was also admiring my good looks.

"When you first buy a car, it's the best thing since sliced bread right?" I spoke in a moderately low tone. Loud enough for him to hear, but not so loud that I was shouting. The loud music sometimes made it hard to have a normal conversation between two people without talking to the entire club, but I'd of course mastered the technique.

I put my index finger up, signaling Donald to pause the conversation while I made a big brawly dude standing at the bar a Long Island Iced Tea. Once I was done and grabbed his money, I returned back to talking.

"Okay so like I was saying. Eventually, no matter how good or fly the car you have was when you first bought it, it's gonna get old. It's gonna start showing defects, needing extra attention it didn't need in the beginning, and soon the thrill of having it wears off. In most cases, it ends up costing you more to keep it, than to just trade up for a newer and better model, for probably half the drama. Now replace the cars in my analogy with females. You will get the same results; hence, it's better to lease, not buy," I grinned. "If you never committed to keeping it in the first place, you have less drama when it comes to replacing it."

"Well, I don't think that's true. Some cars hold up forever, like vintage cars. Some women never lose their shine," he stated.

"Believe me my man. Once they start getting comfortable, they start trippin' about things they didn't trip about before. Nagging, getting fat, they stop doing their hair and nails, and lastly…but most importantly… they stop givin' up the ass on a regular basis. At the end of the day, you're never gonna get your money's worth, so the better option is to lease. If you don't already have a fleet of chicks, when one trick starts messing up, trade up. Plain and simple."

He laughed like a school kid looking at a playboy magazine. It was obvious that my mission had not been accomplished. "Sounds pretty cold-hearted B. I mean everybody changes, and if you just get rid of them every time they do, you're always gonna have to switch up," dumb Donald responded.

He was still thinking like a punk. I had given him yet another invaluable piece of information from my "Playboy Diaries" (as my sister Brenda liked to say whenever I talked about my dating views), and it was being wasted on dumb ears.

I shook my head at him as I took another drink order. "You think like a woman," I replied.

"Why?" He exclaimed in a high-pitched tone which pretty much answered his question right there. "Because I look for love in my relationships? I just don't want to..."

I cut him off because I couldn't take the bitch-ass-ness he let come out of his mouth any longer. "Forget about it Donald. I know this is all over your country ass head. You talkin' about you're looking for love and what not. You can't handle my level of play."

He sucked his teeth and began tending to an agitated Chinese looking girl who was jockeying for a space at the bar to order.

I noticed the chunky light skin woman with long black braids I'd served earlier rolling her eyes and sucking her teeth at me whenever I looked her way. I frowned and thought, 'What the hell is wrong with Ms. Fat Ass?' She practically inhaled the Hennessy and Coke I'd served her a few minutes earlier and slammed the glass down on the bar in front of me.

"I need another one Mr. Know-It-All" she snarled at me. "Since you know so much, I assume you know what I had before."

I did indeed remember what she'd ordered before "What's all the attitude about?" I asked as I began refilling her glass.

I was hoping this woman wasn't about to make me get ugly with her ass. No, let me rephrase that, because it's physically impossible for me to get ugly. I'll just say, before she made me, act ugly.

"My attitude is about all that bull crap you're back there saying to that boy and e'rything," she spat in a drunken southern drawl. "Oh yeah, I heard you back there. Uh huh, you didn't think anybody heard you, but I heard you. That's real trifling how you're talking about women."

Donald's eyes grew to the size of golf balls when he heard her reply.

I smirked. "Sweetheart, I'm not sweating if you heard what I was saying or not. It was a conversation between me and my boy." I finished her drink and looked to her for payment. She gasped over-dramatically and slid a ten-dollar bill towards me.

"Oh, so you're just an asshole then? Are you trying to say you don't even care what I think? Even with me being a woman? Cause I know you wouldn't be saying that!" Ms. Fat Ass continued.

All I was trying to do was teach Donald's bamma ass how to handle chicks instead of beating off every night. Now I had to deal with this mouthy freak. No good deed goes unpunished.

"Sweetheart, you enjoy your night," I responded trying to save her the humiliation she was potentially asking for by going down this road with me.

"Don you owe me for this," I said as I turned and walked toward the other end of the bar to another customer. "Your sorry Michael Jordan with an f'd up grill ass is over here cowering. Like that chick is gonna do something to you," I snickered.

"Whatever man. I'm not c... c... cowering over here. I... I," he paused and took a deep breath. "I'm just shy around some women. Especially big angry ones."

I laughed out loud at that. This guy is the wimp of the week.

"I... I... I just haven't found one that I like. I... I... I... take it slow. You know cau... cau... cause you gotta be careful these days you know? I got game," he continued trying to puff out his chest. "I just like my women to be r... r... really lady like. I gets mi...mi...mine."

He had so much sweat dripping from his brow by then that it looked like he'd just escaped interrogation under a bright lamp.

"Yeah, ok Stuttering John, slow down. Don't get all nervous, I'm just clowning you dude," I said laughing and considering Ms. Fat Ass's case closed. I pulled my vibrating cell phone from my pocket and hit "ig-nore" before putting it back.

Donald's 21-year-old behind always seemed to be scared of dealing with women. Not the typical guy of that age in my book. He moved his country ass from Oklahoma to Atlanta earlier in the year and I took him under my wing when he started working at JAGUARS a few months ago.

Really...I thought he was more liable to have his next intimate en-counter with a hand job than a female. In fact, I was beginning to won-der whether the ladies were ever really on his agenda when he came to Atlanta in the first place. He was pretty soft, and Atlanta is popular for a lot of things that include *soft men...*

2

Brian

INTRO TO A PLAYBOY

"Uh excuse me…," Ms. Fat Ass began again while I was serving another customer. Her attitude was still clearly sour as she leaned over the bar resting her enormous breasts on it. "But I just gotta say this to you because you're really pissing me off right now. Your Denzel Washington wanna-be ass doesn't-have-a-clue!"

Her sloppy slurring was beginning to spawn spit with every word, and my patience was wearing thin. I didn't like loud, unattractive women on a regular day, let alone one that was getting in my business and on my nerves where I work.

"Settle down now. It seems like you might have had too much to drink already so why don't you just let this go right now," I coaxed.

"Settle down?" She hollered attempting to wag her long nailed finger close to my face. "I'm not one of these little hussies up in here that're always up in your face about something. I'm a strong, black, independent, woman, and I don't take any shit! In fact, I think you owe every single one of the ladies in here an apology for what you just told this guy. Women ain't like no, God-damn cars. We are to be respected and…" she went on.

I looked at Donald, who was doing his best impression of a scared little bitch and tongued the inside of my cheek as I mulled over my next move. The club was packed, and the music was loud, so I doubted more than the people within immediate ear shot heard what was going on. I didn't care. I never liked women to jump bad with me. This chick had already met the criteria for a bitch slap when she initially started with her nosey comments.

I took a deep breath and started to say something when I felt something whiz past my ear and heard it land on the shelf behind me. "What the hell?" I yelled jumping slightly to the side.

"Pay attention to me pretty boy!" the braid bound bitch taunted holding a piece of ice in her hand; which I presumed was akin to what had just flown past my head. "I'm talking here! I'm sick of y'all pretty-boy's feeling like you can ignore everybody!" She spat out.

"Bitch do you know I will smack those braids out of your head?!" I yelled back at her as I thrust towards her.

She was startled by my sudden move and nearly fell off of her seat jerking away from me. "You better get your drunken ass together before I come across this bar on your ass. You'd better learn how you're supposed to talk to a grown man! Somebody damn sure better check your ass before I get to you," I warned as I saw one of the bouncers approaching me with Donald in tow.

It figured his punk ass would feel like we needed to bring in reinforcements. People near the bar scurried out of the line of fire as the bouncer, who we called Tiny reached the bar and stood behind Ms. Fat Ass. "What's the problem Brian?" He asked.

"This woman is throwing ice at me and getting belligerent. It's obvious she's already lit, but I'm not gonna have her throwing shit at me," I answered. The mere thought of a close encounter with a scar on my face was enough to send me into a rage.

"No wait! Wait a god-damn-minute-now! This guy's the one who's in the wrong!" She protested looking around for support from the people who gave enough of a shit to gawk at her ignorant display. "I mean he's standing back there talking a bunch of bull about women! He's threatening to hit a woman, and he's being..."

"Alright miss, you're gonna have to come with me," Tiny said with an annoyed expression beginning to move her away from the bar. Ms.

Fat Ass started to struggle some, but once he tightened his grip on her arms, she stopped fighting.

"This club is some bull! Your bartenders are some sexist ass holes! Wait! I gotta get my friend! Waiiiitttt!" She yelled as Tiny shuffled her through the crowd.

I shook my head in aggravation as I moved toward another customer.

"What can I get for you?" I asked a pretty butter scotch colored chick in a skimpy black dress. "Pretty lady," I followed.

"Wow, well I don't want whatever she had," she said motioning in the direction where Ms. Fat Ass was drug. "Your girlfriend?"

"Not in this lifetime," I replied. "She's drunk."

"I hope so with the way she's acting. You must've really upset her."

I didn't answer, but I leaned on the bar gazing at her. She was undeniably a stunner.

"Ok so...I was hoping for something strong and sweet, but feminine. Any suggestions?"

She unleashed a sultry smile and leaned closer to me so I could take in the scent of her sweet-smelling perfume.

"Sex on the beach?" I replied with my own showstopper smile. She looked as if she was ready to give me her application for the missionary position. So far, she was a good candidate for the job.

"Excuse me?" She asked revealing a full set of pretty pearly whites. "That's a drink I hope."

"Yes, unless you were open for more," I joked.

"Uh...no, I think I'll stick with the drink," she said as she wiped an imaginary dust particle from her cleavage and moved a lock of her long curly weave behind her ear.

I made her drink with a little extra liquor and sat it in front of her and waited. "Try it."

She took a sip, smiled and said, "That's the best Sex on The Beach I've ever had."

"Ah well, you obviously haven't been to the beach with me before," I replied.

"Natalie," she said extending her hand with a giggle. "Let's get to where I know your name first before we get intimate so soon."

"Brian," I said shaking her hand lightly and looking toward another customer motioning me at the end of the bar. "Hold that thought baby," I told her as I walked away to answer the call.

When I returned she handed me a business card. "My cell phone number is on the back. You should call me sometime. Maybe we can go out somewhere where the music isn't too loud to have a normal conversation."

I smiled and nodded putting the card in my pants pocket.

She winked at me, smiled and began to dismount the bar stool holding the drink in her hand.

"Call me," she said again.

"Yeah, I will but, I think you forgot something," I replied.

She chuckled girlishly. "I don't need your number honey. I'll get it when you call."

"No baby, it's not my number, it's my bill."

The seductive smile she wore melted like an iceberg. "Oh, did I forget to pay that? I thought maybe you'd let this one ride on the house. Just this once, while we're getting acquainted."

"Oh yeah?" I laughed. "Naw sweetie, you're pretty and everything but you're gonna have to hustle these other dudes who came to spend their money for the free drinks. The drink is $9, and you can keep the tip if you wanna feel like I gave you the hook up."

"So, you can't just write this one off if I promise to make our date worth it later?"

"Sweetheart, you're makin' yourself look pathetic begging for a drink. It's only $9."

She mumbled something that I'm sure was nasty under her breath, reached into her pocketbook, and pulled out a $10 bill. "On second thought, you can lose the number I gave you. You're clearly not the caliber of man I thought you would be."

"Not a problem sweetheart. I lost interest as soon as you showed your bum side." I answered in the same snide tone she was carrying with me.

I had already forgotten her name. Ms. Freeloadin' Freak rolled her eyes and propped her free hand on her hip. "If this is how you were talking to home-girl they just shuffled out of here, I can see why she was flippin' on your classless ass."

"And you're being classy by trying to bum a free drink? They call it bummin' a free drink for a reason," I said taking her money and walking to the cash register in back of me. "Change?" I asked turning back around, but she had already made her way through the crowd and disappeared.

I looked toward Donald who was watching like I was his favorite reality TV show, prompting me to walk closer to him so that only he could hear. I didn't want another "Ms. Fat Ass" incident. "Don't let these freebie freaks make you lose your job homie. Only chumps let a woman sucker them into doing things that only benefit her. Especially if you haven't even test driven her ass yet."

Donald cracked a nervous smile, "Test driven her ass? Still like a car huh?"

"Always is," I replied grabbing a glass to start my next order.

Maybe Brenda was right; I probably did need to write this stuff down. I'm a clever dude.

***

It was 3:25am and the lights signaling the clubs closing had been on for more than a half hour alerting the stragglers that their money had expired. I wiped down the top of the bar while Donald collected glasses off of it and brought them back to the sink.

Jimmy, the owner and manager of the club, approached and sat at the bar directly in front of me. He could barely fit all 300 pounds of his 6'3", white, bald headed ass on the stool, but he made do. He looked much more like a bouncer than an owner, and when necessary, he performed as one too.

"Hey there playa-playa," he called attempting to sound hip but sounding more like a character in a SNL skit instead. "Tiny tells me you had a little incident tonight. Now I know you're a ladies' man and all that there…but you gotta keep it under wraps while you're behind my bar now bro."

His southern twang was thick and screamed, 'You know you're a red-neck when…' every time he spoke.

"It was under control Jimmy. This wasn't one of my women acting up. This was a woman who didn't know how to hold her liquor or mind her business. It wasn't anything I could have stopped before it happened," I replied.

"Oh okay. I just didn't want another one of those nights like that time last month when that ghetto girl, no offense," he said putting his palms up. "Nothing racial or anything, but she was acting really ghetto; even if she woulda' been a white girl."

I might have taken offense had he not been 100% on point. That chick Monica wigged out on me and another female in the club when she saw us talking. I was bedding Monica fairly regularly at that time. I guess she'd assumed I was her man by then. The poor chick was not only sadly mistaken, but was corrected when the girl she confronted punched her in the face repeatedly until she fell out. Sometimes people need to put more thought into who they mess with.

"You know what I like about you though?" He asked chuckling as though he was already telling himself a joke.

"What's that?"

"You're an equal opportunity employer wit' them there ladies you entertain. A lot of fellas just date black women, or white women, or the Chinese, or whatever. You…you get you a piece of everybody and they always look good. Even the ghetto ones," he belly laughed.

"That's a requirement," I replied pulling my keys from my pocket.

"Back when I was your age, I pulled in the beauties too, but I didn't go for anything but white girls. I saw some other types I wanted now, don't get me wrong or anything, but it wasn't so acceptable back in my day. Watching you and these different gals though, makes me wish I'd took a dip in another pool sometimes though," he continued raising his eyebrows. "And I suppose that one over there, staring at you with that 'come hither' look in her eyes is waiting on you too then?"

I looked in the direction he was motioning toward and saw the petite, green eyed, redheaded sex pot I was about to bring to the layer leaning on the wall by the Exit sign.

"You would be right," I answered smiling.

"Umm umm umm! And she looks like a firecracker too. Alright then. I'll see you tomorrow." He said stretching his hand across the bar and shaking my hand.

"Later," I said

She smiled as I approached her and kissed me on the lips when I arrived. "Oh my God, my feet are killing me right now," she exclaimed. "The things we women have to go through to look sexy for men."

"Well judging from how good you look in your outfit, the trouble was well worth it," I said putting my arm around her shoulder as we left the club and headed to the parking lot. "So, did you and your girls have a good time tonight baby?"

I couldn't remember her name for a damn thing, but it didn't matter; I usually didn't. I couldn't remember this girls name, but I remembered how Charlie Brown had loved "The Little Redhead Girl" in the PEANUTS comic strip and that was gonna be how she would be known to me.

I'd met her and her sister while I was hanging with my home boys at a sports bar the night before. For a white girl, The Little Red Headed Girl was built like a sista; big boobs, fat ass, small waist and thick thighs. Her hair was a deep red and fit her complexion and green eyes perfectly. It wouldn't be long before I found out whether the curtains matched the drapes.

"Yeah, we had a blast. Thank you for the V.I.P. status for me and my girls. You really helped make my last night out nice."

"Well, that's good. You're leaving for L.A tomorrow right?" I asked, opening the door for her to get into my Navigator. Getting her and her people V.I.P. status didn't cost me anything, but she was about to pay for that favor regardless.

"That's right!"

When I got in on the driver's side she was beaming with excitement.

"I can't believe I'm about to be a real model now. Oh my God it's been what I've wanted since I was little and now, I'm signed to a big modeling agency who thinks they can get me a lot of work."

I smiled thinking about the work I had for her later on that night. I put my hand on her thigh while I drove and took a deep breath. "I hope you don't mind just going straight back to my place instead of Waffle House or something. It's late, I've had a long day and I'm not really feeling like stopping anywhere. I have some baked Ziti I made last night at the crib if you're hungry."

"You made? You cook?"

"Yeah girl. Don't let the good looks fool ya. I went to culinary school too. I'm a damn good cook. I might even be opening up my own restaurant in ATL soon."

"Is that a fact? That's cool. I never would have thought you would be the chef type. You seem like the 'I Kong, You Jane' kind of guy," she said imitating her version of a rough jungle voice. "That's sexy. So, do you eat, as well as you cook?" she asked while guiding my hand between her legs to feel her smoldering box.

My dick got hard just thinking of the sex game I was about to get into with her at my place. "I'm a picky eater. Sometimes I need a little persuasion to try something new."

"Persuasion? Like what?" she questioned as she pulled my fingers from fondling her twat and put one in her mouth.

"Oh shit!" I shouted as the Navigator swerved between 2 lanes. How was I expected to focus when she was doing stuff like that? I love it when I pick a good freak!

We were both startled and began nervously laughing once I had my ride back under my control.

"Keep your eyes on the road honey," she said seductively raising her already short black dress to expose the hot pussy I was just petting. The sheer material was so light that I could see her nipples getting hard under the dress.

"See now you're trying to get me in an accident with all of that," I scolded, nearly catching whiplash from the numerous times I turned my head back and forth looking at her bare body.

"How close are we to your place?" She questioned as her left hand wandered to the zipper on my jeans and began to work it open.

I was thinking how unnecessary it would be for us to make it to my place at all if she was about to unleash my "lion" from its cage. I was gonna pull over and give this chick what she wanted right then and there! "We're almost there."

"Okay," she said as she pulled my dick from my underwear and brought it out for inspection.

"Damn girl...you about to make me pull this thing over and fuck you right here."

"Uh uh. I want to go back to the privacy of your place. I can keep you interested until we get there though," were the last words she spoke before plugging her mouth with my fully erect meat.

"Oh yeah," I moaned with my eyes half closing for a moment before I turned onto the last straight away before we reached my apartment complex.

She was making slurping sounds while her hand and mouth exercised my rod till it was throbbing with pleasure and I was about to erupt. "Oh yeah girl...just like that...just like that," I moaned pulling my Navigator into an empty parking spot crookedly in front of my complex. I put my hand on the back of her head and guided her in the last strokes it took for me to bust in her mouth.

She immediately tried to pull up, but I kept the pressure on her head a few seconds more before letting her up.

"Dammit Brian!" She shouted, wiping the evidence of my pleasure from her mouth with the back of her hand. "What the fuck? You could have at least given me a heads up that you were about to cum first. Asshole."

"Heads up," I said laughing. "Man, I'm sorry girl. I couldn't speak at the time. You had me locked up to where I couldn't even get any words out my mouth," I lied. I could have said something first, but why would I when I wanted her to take it in her mouth? Common sense.

She scowled as she picked up her purse from the floor where it had fallen. "So, are we here?"

"Yeah, this is my spot."

"Nice," she said looking at the complex through my windshield as she opened the door to get out.

I put my still fairly erect meat back into my pants and let my shirt hang down over my open zipper as I got out. What was the point of closing it when I was going to open it right back up in 50 paces? "Right here," I directed as I lead her to my first-floor apartment.

"I hope you know I don't do this all of the time," she informed me as I opened the door for her to enter my place. "I mean I'm not a slut or anything. I just figured, it's my last night out and I'm about to move to another city so…"

I didn't listen to whatever else she was jabbering about since I was sure none of it would have any significance to me. The Little Red Headed Girl was more than likely about to experience curbside assistance once daylight broke anyway. Her historical Hoeing activities held no interest for me.

"You know what I'm saying? Brian?" She called as I paused for a moment to thumb through my mail at the door.

"Yeah baby, don't worry about all of that. I'm not with you to judge you tonight; I'm trying to give you something to think about on your plane ride tomorrow."

"Technically, it's tonight since its Sunday already. My plane leaves this evening."

"Tonight then," I replied pulling her into my arms and cupping her ass with both hands. There was too much talking going on, and not enough sexing!

***

I kissed and licked the nape of her neck sending chills through her body and causing her to moan with pleasure. I let my fingers slide the G-string panties (that I didn't even know she was wearing until that point) off of her butt and down her soft firm legs.

She was kissing and licking my neck and ears while her hands worked my pants and underwear down to my ankles. We did an erotic dance to my bedroom as we undressed and fondled each other on the way.

Once our bodies hit the bed it was like somebody called 'Action!' in a porno flick. Her mouth was immediately wrapped around my dick again...right where I wanted it. Say what you want about white women, but the ones I've gotten with always sucked me off with the skill of a prostitute in a room full of dicks. No hesitation, no phony 'I don't usually do this' crap, just straight dick sucking paradise.

It was at least 2 hours before our escapade was over and I'd penetrated damn near every open hole she had. A few used condoms and wrappers were strewn on the floor along with things we'd knocked from their resting places all over the room.

Nature's cruel alarm clock chirped outside of my window just as I started to doze off to sleep. I found myself thinking about pulling the bug spray from my kitchen cabinet and spraying their loud birdie asses just when The Little Redheaded Girl began babbling too.

"Oh my God Brian...you're amazing. I thought you looked like you'd be able to f..."

"Woman it seems like it's impossible for you to shut up if you don't have something in your mouth. Shut up already and sleep," I barked putting the pillow over my head.

"Excuse me? Shut up? Not a morning person maybe? Sheesh!" she said in a pouty voice.

She was silent for a handful of minutes before rejoining her loud bird buddies in aggravating the hell out of me again. "So, should I try to make arrangements to come see you again the next time I'm back in town? I'm supposed to come back a couple of times this month..."

I lifted the pillow off of my head and looked at her disgustedly. "Listen Baby, I don't do the after-sex chat. You can either lie down till I wake up, or you can get the hell out. Make a choice."

"Are you fucking kidding me right now? Uhhh...I am not some little tramp that..."

"Alright you're gonna have to get your stuff and bounce. You have diarrhea of the mouth and I'm not in the mood for this shit right now," I interrupted sitting up in the bed. "It was good fucking you but you're running your mouth too much. I hope you have a safe trip to L.A. Yadda, Yadda, Yadda...it's time for you to go."

Her green eyes became cat like slits as she picked up a pillow from her side of the bed and hit me with it. "Motherfucker," she hissed snatching her dress from the floor and began dressing.

I snickered to myself and propped her weapon of choice behind my head and laid back. This white girl had a lot of balls, but if she wasn't careful, I was gonna shove them down her throat.

"Are you laughing?" She asked as she stood searching for her underwear. "Cause this shit ain't funny. If you're joking, you need to call your own bluff right now because I'm mad about this. I didn't think we were gonna get married or anything, but you don't have to be such an asshole. I don't deserve to be disrespected."

She paused and looked my way, waiting for me to respond to her blathering. To her dismay, I didn't break character. I was really too tired and drained to entertain the drama with her and I was hoping my silence would speed up her desire to get the hell out of my place.

"Black son-of-a-bitch! You ain't a Player. You ain't no Baller! You ain't shit!" She spat with her hands back on her hips glaring at me.

"Black son-of-a-bitch huh? Listen lady, that black mess isn't fazing me because you loved this big black dick a minute ago. You better go' head with that tough white girl attitude before you get your feelings hurt." I said getting out of the bed and going over to my dresser to get some boxer shorts. It was beginning to look like this might not end as smoothly as I'd hoped. I didn't want to be butt ass naked when I tossed her ass out my front door.

"You better stop hollering at me before I knock your teeth down your throat first of all," I stated slipping on my boxers.

"Second, FUCK YOU!" She screamed walking out of my room into the living room. "You wasn't about nothin' in bed anyway; I was faking it the whole time! It's a shame you got all that size and don't know what to do with it. I'm an actress, remember? I can fake it really good and you can't tell the difference. Your dick is a dud and…"

"I thought you were supposed to be a model but whatever girl. You earned your Emmy then bitch. L.A. will be lucky to have you," I broke in.

She slid on her thigh high boots, stomped over to the coffee table and grabbed her purse off of it. She dug in, pulled out her cell phone and turned to me with a fire in her eyes that Drew Barrymore would have killed for in FIRE STARTER.

"You know what Brian? You are a callous, self-centered prick," she proclaimed going to my door and struggling with the locks to get out.

I walked up behind her and turned the locks the correct way and body checked her out of the way so I could open the door. She stumbled a little and cursed me, "Bastard!"

"Yeah, yeah. Get out," I said unaffected. I was too sleepy for this bull-shit.

She turned toward me in the doorway and opened her mouth to speak but I was done with her talking. "Out," I said palming her face and pushing her out of the door before closing it.

"You God damn bastard! Don't you ever put your hands on me again! You bastard piece of shit!" she shrieked kicking on the other side of the door.

I went back to my bedroom and flopped across my bed. Finally, I had some peace and quiet I thought…and then the birds started chirping again. Damn it!

3

Brenda

MEN LEAVE… OR DIE

I got into my bed and pulled the blanket up over me since Teddy still had the bed sheet wrapped around him. I closed my eyes trying to prevent the tears from escaping and turned my back to the doorway. He entered the room, and I could feel his presence standing over me.

"Brenda. Brenda?" he called again nudging my blanket covered shoulder. "Come on now…don't be like that. You know I love you and I want the best for you. I just don't want to sell you promises I know I can't keep. Would you rather I pretend like I'm ready and then mess everything up? Wouldn't that make things worse for us? I don't want you to end up hating me baby."

I threw the blanket off of me furiously and abruptly turned to face him. "Cut the bullshit Teddy. You know and I know that it's not just about your business. You just want to have your cake and eat it too and I'm tired of catering to you. It's not like I haven't been here with you all of these years while you do what you want to. You need to remember that I have other options too…just like you do."

"Yeah, I know you have other options, and you exercise those options too so you cut the bullshit. I'm not blind or stupid; I can see that you're a good woman. But Brenda, my eyes are on the prize right now and I can't be sidetracked by jealousy or attitudes because I came home late or didn't call when you thought I should have. It seems like every other month I gotta re-explain this stuff to you again and it's…"

"You damn right you do because every time I try to break it off with you and move on with my life...here you come with the sweet talk, and the flowers and I get dragged back in!" I protested. How dare this jerk try to make me out to be some kind of desperate woman who can't get a grip! Even if there was an inkling of truth to it...I was who he made me to be!

Teddy walked around to the other side of the bed and got in with his face twisted into a frown. I hated that even during the argument he was looking sexy as hell. "Oh, come on! So, you're trying to play like you're a victim in this? Please baby girl... like I said, we do this every other month. I have a closing at 8 o'clock and I've gotta get some sleep so let's pick this same old bullshit argument up later."

"I don't give a rat's ass if you have a closing in the morning or not. I know you have a God damn closing in the morning with that same bitch you've been screwing..."

"Whoa! Whoa! What the hell are you talking about? You don't even know what you're talking about!" He yelled back.

"Ohhhh yes I do. I know exactly what I'm talking about. You and that bitch have way too many deals going on together. I've seen how she looks at you and at me whenever I have come up on y'all trying to..."

"You are something else. You need help woman. I work with her Brenda! She's an agent! She brings me buyers for the properties and..."

"Yeah, that ain't all she brings you!" I shouted swiveling my neck and getting up on my knees in the bed so we were face to face. "Since you're claiming to be so open about everything and we're not exclusive," I taunted. "Why not just admit it then? I know you're fucking that bitch too. It's funny how you have so many female business partners all of the time. No wonder you can't get your money straight when you've got so many women you're juggling to spend it on. So, what now? Huh? What, you gonna act like you're not banging her too?"

He stared into my face breathing hard and angry with balled up fists. If his complexion could have achieved it, his face would have been flushed with anger. He turned away from me, licked his lips as he always did when his nerves were getting to him, and lay back in the bed with his back propped up against my headboard.

"So, this is what you spend your time thinking about?" He asked calmly.

My blood was boiling to the point where I could almost feel it traveling through my veins. Oh no he didn't try to act like all I have time to do all day is think about his antics! And furthermore, what the hell was with his calm? Well, he wasn't the only one who could reel it in when need be.

"Hardly," I replied attempting to sound and appear just as calm as he had. "Are you going to answer the question?"

"Why? You seem to already think you have all of the answers. Is it really necessary for me to actually answer the questions at all? I just don't get why you can't leave well enough alone. If you could stop trying to put more on this relationship than it could hold, we would be just fine. Stop rushing everything. If it's gonna happen, it will happen."

"Play it again Sam," I said feeling that knot creeping up into my throat again.

"What?"

"You're a broken record on this subject Teddy. 'Stop rushing Brenda,' you say. 'If it's gonna happen, it will happen.' And you think that I've spent 3 years messing with you to go for another undefined amount of time waiting for you to grow up? I am 27 years old Teddy," I said looking at him and no longer controlling my tears as they streamed down my cheeks. "I'm ready for marriage...a family. I can't just keep playing the field while I wait for you to come to your senses and wife me. I'd like to be able to have my kids at an age when I can actually play with them too you know."

He went dead silent; and this time, his silence spoke louder and said more to me than any words could have. I knew what was coming next...and my heart sank.

He studied my face like I was a long division problem, and he didn't have any paper. "I don't want to hurt you baby. It doesn't make me feel good to see you crying and to know you're hurting because of me.

Maybe I'm being selfish for trying to keep you in my life when I know you want things I can't give you yet. Yet," he emphasized. "I know it's not fair for me to expect you to hang on until I'm ready. But every time I try to let you go, I can't."

Teddy groaned as if the words brought him pain, and Zeus, who was lying down by my bed, growled and barked in response. My tears had now drenched the top of my silk top and I got out of bed to get some tissue.

I went into my connecting master bathroom and pulled several squares of tissue from the box on the sink. My heart and head hurt at the thought of losing him, and the realization that he'd never really been mine in the first place. I didn't want to end up being a weak woman who'd settle for half a man over having no man at all...like my mother. I sat on the side of the tub, wiping the tears from my cheeks and blowing my nose. How much longer was I gonna keep up the back and forth before I got the backbone to end it permanently?

I don't know how long I stayed in there thinking and regaining my composure, but when I emerged from the bathroom, Zeus was asleep on the floor while the other dog, lay sleeping in the bed.

***

I lay motionlessly in the bed with my eyes closed, pretending to be asleep as Teddy leaned down and kissed my forehead on his way out in the morning. It was a bittersweet kiss that I both savored and despised. I hated that the truth was, if he had woken and said he changed his mind and wanted to be exclusive now, I would have gone for it. Was I really that needy? Damn...I really am my mother's daughter...I hated being weak minded for a man.

I rolled over on my side when I heard my front door close behind him and Zeus jumped up onto my bed. He walked tentatively over to me and cuddled up against my chest. Knowing he was not supposed to have his little butt in my bed, when I opened my eyes and looked at him, he licked my neck and then rested his head on it. I couldn't help but laugh. At least my baby loved me.

Just as I was starting to fall back to sleep my phone rang. I reached back with one hand and felt on the bedside table until I found the cordless phone and put it to my ear.

"Hello," I said in a groggy voice. When the phone rang again, I realized I hadn't pushed the TALK button yet and pushed it with my thumb. "Hello," I repeated.

There was loud sobbing and the faint sounds of voices in the background. "Bren...Brenda...he's," I heard my mother weeping on the other end. "Your father is...he was just...he's..." she continued.

I popped up in the bed and shrieked, "Ok mommy calm down. What happened? Did he hit you again?" I don't know why I was so undone when receiving her weeping calls was practically common.

She started to bawl even harder until she finally blurted out. "Your father is dead. He...he drowned in the pool last night, or this morning. Early this morning."

I was silent as tears began to race down my cheeks, one behind the other. I wasn't sure I'd even understood what she said. "Dead?"

"We... he didn't come in after the party and... I didn't know," she began. "He didn't come to bed. But he doesn't always come to bed anyway. I didn't know he was still in the pool all that time Brenda...he was in the pool when I went in but..." she broke off into spurts of hard crying again.

"Oh my God," is all I could manage as my entire body felt like Jell-o. Zeus repositioned himself onto my lap and was leaning against me trying to console me in his own little dog way.

"Brenda...I can't do this right now. The police are asking me a lot of questions and... I just... I need some support. Can you come home?" she asked trying to contain herself.

"I'm coming now," I answered getting out of bed. "I'll be there in a few minutes."

I hung up the phone and scrambled around my bedroom slipping on sweatpants, a T-shirt, socks and sneakers. Did she say the police were asking her questions? Why were the police there? I was crying, but I honestly wasn't sure what I was crying about. Granted, I'd just learned my father died, but the reality of it was that he was not that good of a father or person.

My father spent more time drinking, womanizing and traveling than he did putting in daddy/daughter time. He was really just an older, meaner version of my brother Brian who unfortunately had a lot of my father's personality traits to match his good looks.

I grabbed my pocketbook and car keys off the top of my bedside table and headed out the front door. Five minutes into the drive I was going to call my brother Brian but realized I'd left my cell phone on its charger in the kitchen.

"Shit!" I said out loud banging my hand on the steering wheel. The one time I actually would have wanted to use the damn thing and I left it in the house.

My thoughts were muddled with grief, relief and confusion as I turned onto the highway. My father had drowned in the pool after the party she'd said? But he didn't even like to swim so why was he in the pool? Yeah, he liked to get into the water every now and then and could be found with a drink in his hand soaking in the Jacuzzi on the regular...but he rarely did the pool.

This almost didn't seem real. I had wished him dead more times than I could count throughout my lifetime; especially after he'd humiliated or beaten me, but he'd been an un-prickly thorn in my side the past few years. I barely ever saw or spoke to him anymore since I'd moved out seven years ago.

I pulled my black BMW into my parent's driveway and sat staring at the gurney being wheeled out through the front door with a white sheet draped over the body on it. It felt like an episode of CSI, except I didn't have a script on what to say or do next.

There was one police car parked next to the ambulance where two EMS men were unloading my father's remains into the back of it. I got out of my car slowly, attempting to wipe any evidence of my tears away from under my eyes as I approached the open door.

I could hear my mother talking through whimpers as I entered the house and I followed her voice into the kitchen. The only way to get to the backyard and the pool was to go through the kitchen or through the side gate outside of the house, so I guessed that was why she was in there.

"It was late, and I went upstairs to bed at…I don't know…maybe 2 or 3 0'clock," my mother was telling one uniformed officer as they sat at the kitchen table together. "We just had a pool party with a couple friends over. My best friend Jenny and her friend Avis. He was still on the float drinking a beer when I went inside. Everybody was already long gone from the party and it was late. I was tired and he didn't want to get off of the float, so I left him."

"So, he was awake when you went in…" The brawny, clean shaven, dark-skinned officer asked. He paused from taking notes when I entered the room, and my mother followed his gaze to me.

"Oh Brenda!" she exclaimed jumping up from the table still dressed in a long nightgown and house coat.

My mother stood 5'9" with an almond complexion, in full make-up. Her freshly tapered, short curly salt and pepper hair was brushed neatly to the back. She was probably no more than 15 pounds heavier than me, and men seemed to think she resembled Dianne Carroll. Maybe I actually was in an episode of CSI because my mother had never gone to bed, or woken up looking so put together in all my life. Where were her favorite flannel pajama pants and the variety of animal printed T-shirts she'd been wearing to bed since my brother wore Underroos?

"Are you the daughter?" Officer "good-body" asked standing up and revealing the sensational physique originally hidden behind the table-top.

"Yes," I answered pulling away from my mother's embrace and taking his seat.

My mother sat back down and dabbed an already soaked tissue to her eyes. "I can't believe it," she told me reaching across the table to touch my hand. "I'm so glad you came. God forbid I had to go through this…this…this mess without you. Have you spoken to your brother yet? I just couldn't make the call a second time."

I didn't answer and looked suspiciously from her to the officer who was watching me intensely. What was with the show she was putting on? My mother and I were on speaking terms, but we were not close. My brother had all but exiled her from his life several years ago and I reserved my communication with her for holiday's and birthdays.

I don't know, maybe I was judging her too harshly considering she did just find her husband of nearly 30 years dead in her backyard. Still, who but my mother would find it necessary or even think, about being fake under these circumstances. I guessed years of practice pretending she had the perfect marriage and family might have put her button on autopilot.

"I'm sorry to have to put you through this right now ma'am but it's routine whenever we are called to the scene where someone... where there is a deceased victim. I just need the information for my report to corroborate the coroner's findings. It's best to get the details while they're still fresh in your head," the officer explained compassionately motioning as though he were going to put a hand on my mother's shoulder but rethought it.

I'm sure it was inappropriate for me to be lusting after a policeman taking the report at the scene of my father's death, but this guy was fine. If it was another day, another time, I would have flirted enough to persuade him to get to know me a little better. I could see by the way he kept looking at me that he was thinking the same thing. Ummm ummm ummm, bad timing can be a bitch sometimes.

"I understand," my mother said as fresh tears welled up in her eyes. "This is all just such a shock and... I don't know. I told you everything I remember and everything I saw. The EMS guy said he probably passed out drinking on the float and...and somehow fell off it into the pool."

"The EMS guy gave you a probable cause?" The officer asked surprised.

"Well, I was wondering if that might have been what happened and he agreed," my mother answered dabbing at her tears.

"Why was he in the pool though? He doesn't even like..." I started.

"He's been taking swimming lessons and... I mean he was. He was spending more time in the pool now instead of just sitting in the Jacuzzi like he used to. He spent most of his time in the pool with everybody almost all night. It was his idea to have the pool party, in fact. I think his new girlfriend must have encouraged it," she said bitterly.

The officer's eyebrows went up as quickly as mine did. Not because I was shocked by what she said, but I was shocked that she was speaking of it. Especially now.

"Was the girlfriend here too?" He asked.

"No, she's out of town," my mother quickly said with a slight roll of her eyes.

"So, there was just the four of you at this party?"

There was a long pause before she answered. "Yes. I consider anything other than me and my husband to be a party."

I put my hand to my forehead and glanced at the digital clock on the range oven.

8:46 Am. This was already one of the longest days of my life.

***

The officer questioned my mother further on the events of the evening, asking whether there were any altercations during or after the party, the full names and contact information for Jenny and Avis, whether he had any known health problems that could have led to his death, and whether she heard any noises in the night or had any ideas of her own about how he'd died.

He advised her that she may be contacted by the coroner's office once the official report on the cause of death was in and that she may also receive a routine follow up call from the police department. He left his card, expressed his sympathy for our loss and left.

I watched her walking around the kitchen, putting coffee on the brew and searching the refrigerator.

"What do you want for breakfast Brenda? It's been years since we've had breakfast together," she said whisking a hair that had fallen into her face back away from her eyes.

For as much as she'd been told she favors Dianne Carroll, I was beginning to wonder whether she was an actress like her too. She certainly turned perky all of the sudden...after the officer left.

"Are you okay?" I asked blandly.

She wasn't being real with me and I knew it. I watched her day in and day out almost all my life and I knew when she was turning her phony on. But why now? Maybe she didn't want to seem weak? No that couldn't be it. She wasn't worried about looking weak to me or my brother when she stayed with my father regardless of the women he pissed on their marriage with, the times he put his hands on her or me and Brian.

"So, is that really what happened mommy?"

"What do you mean?" she asked with her back turned to me as she began making breakfast.

"What you told the police. Is that all true?"

She spun around like she had wheels on the bottoms of her feet. "Of course! Why would you ask me that right now?"

"Because you are acting weird," I responded calmly, looking her straight in the eyes. She turned back around to the oven. Suspicious!

"Brenda what do you expect? I just saw your father lying dead in the backyard. Am I supposed to act normal at a time like this? I'm trying to keep myself together."

She couldn't look me in the eyes. Liar.

"I noticed. You seem to be managing that a lot better now that the officer is gone. One minute you're crying a river and the next you're all perky trying to make breakfast."

My mother turned slowly back around towards me with her face tense and flushed. "So, what are you saying? You think I did something to him?" She questioned. "How can you be so ugly to me right now? You're sitting here analyzing my every move after I've just lost my husband? Am I supposed to follow some sort of mourning protocol? Where are your tears for your father? Why aren't you balling?"

"Mommy I'm not saying you did anything to him. I'm just saying that you're acting strange. If I'm wrong, I'm sorry. And I have cried for him; not that he deserved my tears. He wasn't a real father to me when he was alive anyway. Let's be honest about that," I shot back feeling a knot in my chest again.

"Let's be honest about what? He was your father and he just died. I am your mother and I just lost my husband. What else needs to be discussed right now? I swear you and your brother are always trying to turn..."

"Listen Ma, you called me to come over," I interrupted her.

"Brenda...are you staying for breakfast with me or not? I know what kind of father Robert was to you and I also know what kinds of pain and suffering you kids went through with him. I have my own pain about that. I'm not pretending I don't know the truth child," she argued. "But why can't you just forget that for a minute? A second? The man is dead...good or bad...he is not coming back. What's the point in speaking ill of him now? I don't have the energy to deal with any more than is already on my plate with this. I'm going to have to make funeral arrangements and all kinds of stuff and..."

"Okay mommy, okay, okay. All of this came out of the blue and I... I don't really know how I feel about it at this moment. I was crying on the way here, but now I'm just kind of blank. The whole crazy way you said he died and with everything he's done I'm just trying to let it sink in," I explained getting up from my chair. "I'm gonna go call Brian in the office upstairs."

"There's a phone right there on the wall but if you want to go upstairs and talk, that's up to you. Are you staying for breakfast with me or not?" I couldn't tell if her voice was more annoyed than upset, but it was definitely a combination of both.

"I'm staying," my words trailed off as I climbed the stairs to call my brother. I wanted to talk to him in private, but I wasn't gonna miss the opportunity to eat her home cooking...since I was already there. One thing we couldn't deny was that my mom was an excellent cook.

"Thank you," she sighed. "It's like pulling teeth to get a simple answer or some respect from my own kids. I think I've earned my respect by now." I heard her complaining loudly amongst the clanging of pots and pans behind me.

My mother was a catalog model in her younger years and for a little while when her and my father met, but she'd confessed to me once that her secret passion had always been cooking. A lot of people didn't expect for someone so attractive to be able to throw down in the kitchen like 'they grandmamma 'nem', but my mother was from South Carolina. She could make your mouth water from the smell of her food alone.

Olivia Andrews was the type that cooked when she was sad, mad or stressed which was damn near all of the time. How she remained thin is still a mystery to me. I've never seen her lift a finger to exercise. Unfortunately, she didn't pass that gene down to me and if I ate too many pieces of fried chicken, my butt started spreading like the bird flu.

When Brian was younger, he used to be up under her all of the time, and as a result she taught him the tricks of her trade. As chauvinistic as my brother is, I wouldn't have expected him to get into something so traditionally noted as being a female duty; but he's a surprisingly talented cook and even went to Culinary School. In fact, he'd been trying to persuade our aunt to go into a restaurant business with him as of late.

Brian and my mother used to be inseparable when he was younger; a complete 180 knowing their relationship now. You'd practically have to staple Brian to my mother's back to get him to spend any time with her or even talk to her without a specific reason. Things done changed in the words of The Notorious BIG.

4

Brian

FROM BEGINNING TO END

Cassidy and R. Kelly's song HOTEL startled me awake playing from my cell phone because I was receiving an incoming call. I knew without even looking at the time that it was too early for anybody to think I was going to answer the damn phone. I grabbed it from my bedside table and silenced it without opening an eye and attempted to go back to sleep. About a minute later my voicemail tone blared from the cell phone I was still holding.

"Who the God damned hell?" I grumbled aloud.

I was able to doze back off to sleep eventually but soon enough the loud voices of what sounded like church bound loud mouths assaulted me through my open window.

I sat up in the bed, wiped the sleep from my eyes and looked at my cell phone to see who wanted to talk to me so badly. My parent's number? Of course. It was probably my neurotic mother calling with some of her foolishness. I scratched the top of my head and pressed play to listen to the voicemail message as I glanced at the clock. 10:48am.

I was surprised to hear my sister Brenda's voice instead of my mom, but I chalked it up to the fact that she damn near never has her cell phone with her. It was a waste of money for her to have a cell phone at all if you asked me. She said it was important to call her back but didn't say why. I hate when people do that. How about you tell me what the emergency is, and I'll be the judge of how important it really is.

I was surprised she was over there at all though since she rarely went, even on the holidays. Good old RA (my father's nickname) had likely flipped the script and smacked my mother around for the billionth time; followed by my mother crying a river to Brenda to get some sympathy and attention. My parents liked to act like they were Cliff and Claire Huxtable in public; but in real life, they were more like Ike and Tina Turner.

My sister lives one floor above me and I'm glad she didn't sashay her high-strung ass down to wake me up when they called with the drama.

I pressed the CALL BACK button and stretched out for a minute while the phone rang the elder Andrews line. By the 4th ring I was about to hang up as I walked into the bathroom to take a leak when someone picked up.

"Hello?" Brenda answered on the other end of the phone as I balanced my cell on one shoulder and situated myself to release the dragon and take a piss.

"What's up girl? What did your dysfunctional momma and daddy get their old asses into this time?" I asked sarcastically.

"Brian...Umm...what are you doing right now?"

"Pissin' in the toilet. What's the emergency?"

"Pissin'? You are so disgusting," she complained.

"Look girl, your little early morning phone call woke me up from getting my beauty sleep so what the hell is the emergency for the last time before I hang up on your ass?"

She was oddly silent and the only thing making noise was the tapering off sound of my urine stream into the toilet.

I shook off, flushed, and began to say something else when she said, "Daddy drowned in the pool in the backyard this morning."

I stopped in my tracks and tried to process what she was saying. "What?"

"Daddy...died. They had some kind of four-person party at the house last night and it's looking like he fell in the pool off of the float drunk or something, and drowned."

My heart was racing like I'd just drank a Red Bull and I felt tears attempting to burn their way from my eyes. "Oh," was all I could muster.

"Are you okay?" She asked with a sniffle.

"Yeah. I'm gonna be alright. I just wasn't ready to hear that. You caught me off guard. A four-person party? Sounds like an orgy to me. So, did he hit his head or something on the side of the pool? Wait a minute...what was he doing in the pool?"

"It was not an orgy fool. You know how much he drinks so who knows what all happened. The police were here asking mommy a bunch of questions and they took his body to the coroners to determine the exact cause of death."

"The police. What did they need the police for?"

"I think they just came out when the ambulance came and it's some kind of routine thing from what the officer I talked to said."

Her voice was quivering as she spoke, and I heard her muffle the phone for a few seconds while she blew her nose. "Mommy's acting kind of strange though."

"Strange like what?" I asked frowning and wiping a tear from the corner of my eye. My hands were starting to tremble, and I didn't know why.

"She's just...not right. I can't describe it but its Stepford Wife-ish. It seems like she's holding back or being phony about something. Like..."

"What's strange about that? She's always been phony with her overly dramatic ass. What did she do? Throw herself in the pool next to him and beg God to bring him back to life for her? She's a fucking Drama Queen Brenda. What better time to go over the top than right now?" I replied angrily walking back into my room and getting back in the bed.

"Yeah," is all she said in a low tone.

"So, what's happening over there now?"

"Nothing really. They were moving his body out when I got here and, mommy cooked so I stayed for breakfast. She was telling me that daddy has a girlfriend. One he told her about and that had him taking swimming lessons. She said he was doing a lot of stuff with the woman and didn't even bother coming home much anymore. Can you believe that?"

"And her ass just took it as usual. Where's the grieving widow now with her acting ass, and why are you still there?" I questioned with my eyes closed pulling the pillow up over my head. I felt a headache creeping up on me and all I wanted to do was go back to sleep. It was too early for all this.

"She's in her room. What do you mean 'Why am I still here?' I'm here because our father just died, and our mother probably shouldn't be left alone right now. Regardless of everything we're mad at them for Brian, daddy is dead. She loved him and we need to try to do the right thing by her. You should be here too," she replied annoyed.

"You must still be watching those old Cosby Show reruns because something obviously has convinced you the real world works like that. She's probably gonna be sleeping better now than ever, knowing that he's not coming back home ready to whip her ass at every turn," I answered. "That's probably why she's acting weird. She probably wants to jump up in the air and click her heels together, but she knows she's supposed to be in mourning."

"Brian. Seriously," she sighed.

"So what? We're supposed to just act like she wasn't the weak link that kept our dysfunctional family glued together and be the loving children she doesn't deserve? Maybe if she would have ever had the guts to try to make him go to rehab or something, or to leave him it wouldn't be like this. You know what Bren; I'm going back to sleep. He's still gonna be dead when I wake up so there's no reason to rush now. "

"Really Brian? Why don't you drop the tough guy act for a damn second? I know if I'm feeling upset, then you gotta be feeling worse. At least you were his favorite." She murmured clearing her throat.

"It was just a matter of time before his drunken ass killed himself anyway Brenda. Only difference is that he drowned in the pool instead of in the bottle like I thought. I am upset but what am I supposed to do about it? Run over there and listen to her blathering and putting on her best Scarlett O'Hara performances for people when they come by? Girl you know I don't play that game with her anymore and I'm damn sure not playing it today."

"She told the officer about his girlfriend too you know."

I started laughing out loud. "Ho-ly shit. So, once he's dead she has no problem letting the cat out the bag but when he was alive she avoided the subject like the plague."

"Yeah, well she said it without a flinch so I guess she got tired of pretending."

"Ha!" I laughed again. "Her crazy ass has been pretending like those other women didn't exist since I can remember. I doubt she's tired of it now." I rubbed my hands across my eyes. "The jokes just keep coming girl, I swear."

I had to keep laughing...before I started crying.

"You're not fooling me with all this fake laughing Brian. I know you like you know me, and I know this is an act. Obviously, your mother is not the only one good at acting," Brenda said aggravated.

"This whole thing is funny if you really look at it."

"Do tell," she responded drably.

"You don't remember the summer when we first got that pool and we kept trying to get him to float? Mommy was like, 'Robert, stop acting like a child and get in. All you have to do is float. Everybody can float.' And he told her, 'The only way you gonna get me to float in that pool is face down, cause you gonna have to kill me first!'" I chuckled. Brenda was silent. "I guess he showed her," I belly laughed.

***

When I hung up, I got out of bed and headed to my living room to veg-out in front of my 52". I sat on the couch flipping channels between SPORTS CENTER and CNN but there wasn't anything impressive on to watch. My sister was mad I wasn't coming to the house, but she'd get over it. I was estranged from my parents for a lot of years now...by choice. My dad was a weekend drunk with a mean streak and a taste for every beautiful woman that crossed his path. He used to be a pilot for Pan Am Airlines and when they folded, he picked up drinking for a fulltime job.

Once he landed a job as a private jet pilot for a major entertainment company, he cut back his drunken tirades to weekends and holidays. My mother's dumb ass stayed with him no matter what he did. I guess she stopped giving a damn that he was gone more, and for longer periods of time after a while. When he was home, he would complain, they argued, he drank, beat her ass, and left for "test runs," or all of the above.

I laughed to myself about the "test runs." That was the lame excuse he'd give my mother for why he had to leave the house for long periods of time when he was back in town. He was doing test runs alright…testing running different chick's pussies. I couldn't blame him though. My weak ass mother wasn't giving him any reason to stay home. All she cared about was her looks, shopping, and "appearances." Phony bitch reminds me of a lot of these model type women out here. They got everything on the outside but their usually dumber than barbells, and their sex is as boring as watching paint dry. Excluding The Little Red Headed Girl of course.

Since there was nothing on TV, I decided to take a shower and start my day off. The water beating against my face triggered my eyes to start watering uncontrollably. I knew I wasn't crying. When I got out, I wrapped a towel from the rack around myself and got out.

The view from my patio was great for being on the first floor since the property was elevated with a drop off from the back. I went out the sliding glass doors in my bedroom to see how hot it was and took a deep breath of fresh air as I gazed out.

"Nice view huh?" A stunningly beautiful brown skin woman with short light-brown hair, wearing a white tank top and blue jeans spoke from the adjacent patio.

"Very nice," I replied to who I saw across the divider rather than outside. My cousin told me there'd be a new tenant moving into the apartment next door, but I guess I'd been too busy to notice when it actually had taken place.

"I know we're on the first floor and everything so the shrubs might hide a lot but, do you always come out on your deck half naked?" She asked with a big wide toothed grin.

Shining my pearly whites back at her I said, "Sometimes I do, when I want to check the weather."

"I see. So, then you have some sort of weather radar when you're half naked? FYI, they have forecasts on the weather channel all day long if you have cable. You know…for those times when it might be raining out or something," she answered while her eyes took me in from head to toe.

It's was times like these that I appreciated the hard work I put in to keep my body in shape. I bet she wanted to put her lips on me so bad I could almost feel them.

"Well, when it's raining I usually learn that from looking outside. I do like the hands-on weather predictor approach though. Did you just move in?" I asked making sure to let my grip on my towel loosen some.

She smiled, shook her head in amusement, and took a sip of something from a mug. "Yes, I just moved in a few days ago. Should I assume you live there since you're so…comfortable?"

This chick was sexy as hell. She didn't have on anything spectacular, yet she looked better than a lot of the women that spent their entire pay checks on their wardrobe. "I do," I answered.

"And your girlfriend doesn't have a problem with you giving all of Buckhead a free peepshow when she's not around?" She asked with a sly smile.

My grin widened at her blatant inquiry of my relationship status but before I could answer she said, "Wait, let me rephrase that. If you have a girlfriend, I doubt she'd like you showing all of Buckhead your jewels."

We both smiled and her cheeks flushed as she set her mug down on the table on her side of the patio. Her nipples were standing at attention, and in turn, challenged my dick to stand and solute them. I definitely intended to get to know my new neighbor a lot better.

"So, you really want to know if I have a girlfriend huh? I'm Brian," I said leaning across balconies to extend my hand.

"Umm no that was not my point. I'm Nadia," she said shaking it. "But I think we might need to continue this convo' a little later when your family jewels aren't flapping in the wind."

I hoped she was as interesting as she looked because she'd soon find out that my dick was too big to be flapping. It had been a long time since any of Atlanta's double X chromosomes presented any challenges I cared to pursue. I like a challenge.

"Hey," my cock blocking cousin Kelly said appearing at the patio door dangling her keys. "I couldn't wait to get outta… Oh hi," she said in Nadia's direction as my grin shrunk.

"Hi," Nadia replied stiffly, looking like somebody turned out the light on her smile when Kelly approached. Competition.

Kelly was a shapely 5'7" with looks that could kill a Mockingbird and most women reacted similarly whenever she was around.

"This is my cousin Kelly," I clarified. "Her parents own the building."

"Oh okay. Nice to meet you. I'm Nadia," she said.

"Nice to meet you too. You getting all settled?"

"It's coming along pretty good. Actually, I need to get back to unpacking and making my house a home," she answered grabbing her mug.

"That's good. I live on the second floor, so you'll probably see me a lot. There are only 3 apartments to every floor, so you were actually lucky we had anything available. The Buckhead area is pretty popular," Kelly told her.

"Alright well then I'll catch up with the two of you later," Nadia said as she headed back inside her apartment.

"Yeah, you do that," I called behind her, brushing past my cousin and back into my room. Leave it to her ass to come out while I'm getting to know the dime next door. Dressed in long gray sweatpants, a tight pink shirt that read YES THEY'RE REAL across the front and white Nike sneakers, she looked like a kid with her hair in a ponytail.

"Look girl…didn't you have enough time to put on something decent and some make-up? What you got your black ass down here for anyway? I told you to stop using that damn key like you live here. I'm gonna take it back if you keep walking up in my crib all unannounced," I scolded.

She sucked her teeth and threw her keys at me. "Negro please. Don't nobody want to walk in on you and your damn skanks gettin' it on in here. I know you usually already kicked them to the curb by this time in the morning so stop getting all huffy."

"One of these days you're gonna come in here and I'm gonna pop you with that 9 milli," I said laughing as I started to get dressed in blue jean shorts, and a yellow short- sleeve shirt.

She rolled her eyes and strutted over to pick up the key's she'd recently flung at me. "That is-not-funny Brian. You better not pull that gun out on me. I'll start calling first or knocking before I come in," she said.

I responded with a frown and a disbelieving expression while I dressed. "What you need to do is keep that damn key out of my lock at all unless it's an emergency. It's an emergency key Kelly. Keep that in mind."

Kelly rolled her eyes and sucked her teeth. "Give me a break Brian I'm still getting used to living alone since me and Keenan broke up. Stop acting like an asshole. Or rather… stop being and asshole."

"Why don't you bug Brenda like you do me?"

"That girl's out more than you are or she's usually entertaining some dude. Y'all are definitely two peas in a pod the way y'all keep a revolving door on your bedrooms. The only difference is that she's trying to snag Teddy in between them."

"You sound like you don't approve," I returned as I laced up my yellow and white Nike sneakers.

She sighed and flopped herself down onto my bed. "I'm not judging her or anything. I'm just saying that she has a lot of dates for somebody who claims to want to settle down. Plus, that dude Teddy she's all over, something about him that I just don't like."

"Yeah, well I can cosign that. I keep telling her ass to stop messin' with him, but I'm guessing his pipe game is irresistible. I know that's what keeps the ladies coming back to me, regardless of how good or bad I treat them," I bragged.

"T.M.I. Brian. I'm *soooo* uninterested in how you handle your chicks in bed. I'm just saying..." she sat up, twirled her ponytail around one finger and looked down at the floor. "I got laid off from my job and I lost my man all in one month. Can a sista get some sympathy please?"

"Oh, stop wallowing in pity girl. Keenan was a slack ass idiot who you were always busting with other girls, and you hated your job anyway. Hell, it could always be worse. You could've woken up dead like my father did," I said with a smirk as I brushed my waves into place.

Kelly's face turned Medusa stone cold and she asked, "What? You're kidding right? That's not even halfway funny Brian."

"I'm not kidding. He drowned in the pool at my mother's house this morning. Ding Dong the Warlock is dead."

"Oh my God. And you're walking around here like it's just another day? Seriously Brian. You're being serious? Uncle Rob drowned for real?" I could hear the tears caught in her throat as she spoke, and I truly wasn't in the mood.

"Kelly, I don't even know why you're about to cry. You know he wasn't shit just like I do. Life goes on. Well at least mine will. "

***

Kelly was getting on my nerves, crying and trying to coax me into showing some emotion for my father's passing that I wasn't feeling. After shutting her down, I got my duffle bag and escorted her out of my apartment on the way to work off some steam at the gym. The church-goers traffic was pretty thick and although I was hungry, I knew I'd be waiting for eons to get a meal anywhere at this time of day.

I was feeling in the mood for some old school NOTORIOUS B.I.G and started blasting "F' The World" in honor of my father's passing.

I remembered one of the few times he suffered consequences and repercussions for his bad behavior. My dad had just returned home after a week of being gone on flight duty and was in the shower. My mother took that opportunity to toss his briefcase looking for evidence that he'd been seeing other women. Of course, she found what she was searching for; receipts from a lingerie store, and a string of condoms in his shaving bag. I was downstairs in the den watching football with my home-boys Ike, Paul and Jerry from school just before I heard the eruption upstairs.

I left my boys and went to see what was going on, half expecting my mother to be pinned up against the door with my father's hands wrapped around her throat. Instead, she was in the doorway of their master bathroom looking like Diana Ross in MAHOGANY, wearing a long kimono style robe, make-up streaming down her face, her hair all over her head and screaming bloody murder at my father. "...and what the hell do you need condoms for when you're out of town Robert?! I guess I should be grateful you're at least using protection, but do you really need this many?! I swear I should shock the shit outta your ass with this god damn stun gun and get it over with!" She yelled unfolding a string of condoms and tossing them in the bathroom.

"Woman you don't know what the hell you're talking about! I told you to stay outta my stuff anyway! How you know they're mine just because they're with my stuff?! Your crazy ass betta not have that damn stun gun nowhere near this shower. I know that!" My father's words echoed as I heard the water turn off and my father abruptly jerked the shower curtains back.

"I'll be damned if you're gonna just keep doing this to me Robert," my mother sobbed shaking her head back and forth almost as though she was talking to herself. "I've put up with WAY too much of your mess and been married to you way too long for you to keep treating me like this. You told me you were finished with these side hos' out here! You come home mad and putting your hands on me for every damn thing under the sun if you think I've been with another man! But you can do whatever and whoever you want? I don't think so!"

"Ma, calm down," I told her knowing that when my father got out of the shower he'd be explaining with his fists.

"No Brian. No! I don't...wait, what did you say?!" She yelled to my father diverting her attention away from me and back to whatever he had just yelled from the bathroom.

"I said...you better listen to the boy before I knock some sense into your ass!" He repeated appearing in front of her almost as quickly as a ghost. He had his robe all half-assed thrown on and still had suds on his face with water dripping from him. "You must've been hangin' around your big mouth, nosey sister with all this going on here!" he continued flailing his hands at his sides.

My mother flinched but held her ground. "You said you would stop," she said defiantly in a guttural tone.

"And I did," he replied mimicking her tone while drawing an intimidating distance to her face. "Who says those ain't old?"

"Well, which is it then? Not yours, or old?"

"It's none of your damn business is which one it is. If it's in my stuff, then it's not your business to question me about it, Olivia."

My mother stepped back from him and lifted the hand she was holding the stun gun in slightly.

His eyes looked down at the stun gun, and then back to my mother's face. "You better be ready to draw your last breath if you shock me with that," he told her.

"I got company downstairs," I interrupted hoping to bring this whole thing to a close.

"Did you buy me some lingerie?" My mother asked him, ignoring my comments.

They were at a staring stale mate for a minute as my father decided how he would answer that. "Maybe I did," he finally said.

They were both breathing hard as hell; my dad looking like the lion about to pounce on his prey, and my mother looking like the cornered elk.

I watched them with disgust and fascination, hoping they could find a way to wrap it up quickly and without bloodshed.

"Maybe you did," my mother repeated robotically with tears streaming from her eyes.

"You don't wanna go here Olivia. Now I said I'm not sleeping with any other women, and that should be all you need to know. You must've forgotten who the man of the house is. Do I need to make myself anymore clear?" My father asked getting into her face again.

The next thing I knew there was a buzzing sound and he jerked backwards into the bathroom. I heard him making gagging sounds as his body hit the floor with a thud.

"You must have forgotten who the woman of the house is. Do I need to make myself clearer?" My mother replied calmly, still holding the stun gun out in front of her and expressionlessly watching him struggle to fight off the pain.

I stood by the stairs smirking and peering in at him writhing on the floor. I bet that Motherfucker wasn't ready for that! I was glad she had at least shown some backbone for a change but that was about all of the change I was gonna get. Of course, once my father got hold of his faculties he was looking for payback. By that time, I had already told my boys I'd catch up with them later and led them to the door, so RA (The nick name me and my sister gave our father which stood for his initials and how loud he would yell when he was angry) was good and ready to settle the score.

He and I ended up ultimately facing off that night once he realized my mother wasn't going to relinquish her stun gun for the evening and he decided that I was trying to disrespect him in his own home by telling him to 'Keep his hands off of my mother.' We ended up in our worse fight ever where I chipped a tooth, and he broke his left index finger.

After that day I decided that I wasn't going to keep fighting for my mother if she was going to keep sticking around for the same bullshit over and over again. Realistically, if a woman stays with a man she knows is cheating, and lets him man-handle her, she's getting exactly what she set herself up to deserve.

I knew the stuff my father was doing to my mother mentally and physically was bad, but I was also starting to understand that in life, you can only do what other people allow you to do to them, therefore; it's up to them to set the boundaries.

She was weak and the weak are devoured.

***

My cell phone started vibrating in my pocket and I answered it with my Bluetooth as I pulled it out to see who was calling.

"Hello?" I answered.

"Hey Boo!" an excited female said on the other end. "So, you finally decided to answer a call from a sista huh? What's been cookin' good lookin'?"

Black Fox's name was on the caller ID and I smiled. I might have just answered the call to what…or should I say who I was gonna do that night to get my mind off of all the drama going on.

"What's up girl?" I asked steering around some old ass lady who couldn't decide which lane she wanted to drive in. "What's going on?"

"Not a whole lot; I was just talking to my friend who asked about you and I told her, 'I haven't seen him in forever.' You didn't go out and get you a steady, did you?" She asked in a silky, sexy voice.

I laughed out loud. "Hell no Baby girl. You know me better than that. I don't "go steady" sweetheart. That's for people in the 6th grade. I've just been on my usual grind and trying to get this restaurant idea of mine off the ground. What you ladies at THE MAN TRAP missing me? Or is it just my doggy style?"

"Speaking for myself, I miss the doggy style. I'm hoping most of them can't speak to that though," she said seductively. "I was starting to think that maybe you had gone and wifed some other female or something. You know how rumors can be in the A-town. I heard some different things about where you were," she said giggling.

Black Fox was a brown-skin mediocre looking female who transformed into a clone of the actress Vivica Fox when she was made-up. Hence the nick name "Black Fox" which she acquired working as a stripper at THE MAN TRAP. I never bothered to ask her real name and I really didn't care to. I already knew everything I needed to know about her; she could slide down a pole like a seasoned fireman (any pole), and the sex was good. More importantly, she never seemed to want anything more than my dick…and that was all I wanted to give her.

"Come to the source when you hear a rumor about me baby. Hold on a second," I said as I switched to the other line to answer another incoming call. "Hello?" I answered.

"What up man?" my friend Doe-Boy asked on the other end.

"What up Doe. I'm on another call right now. Let me hit you back okay?"

"Yeah okay. Hit me back for real too. I wanna let you in on some stuff."

"Yeah, okay mom… I'll call you back," I joked before switching back to Black Fox's call

"I'm back," I said reentering the conversation. "So anyway Fox, speaking of that good pussy, you gonna let me get some tonight?"

Fox wasn't like a lot of the chicks at THE MAN TRAP who claimed to be working their way through college or doing it for other seemingly good reasons. She simply liked the fast money, the late hours, and she had booty popping skills.

She'd said once, 'I get to sleep late, dance, make money and be every man's fantasy for 4 hours a night. I pay all my bills and get extra cash to blow. My mother's been working 50-hour weeks for 20 years and she still barely keeps her lights on. You tell me who lives better?'

"Shiiiiiiiit. Whenever you decide to bring your ass over to my house, I'll be ready to give you what you want. I don't know about tonight though cause baby I'm working midnight to 4 tonight so if you want some you gonna have to get to me before then or when I get off."

"I gotta work tonight too. I'm talking about when we get off. I get off; you get off, why not get off together?" I joked as I pulled into the parking lot at the gym.

"That sounds like a plan to me."

"Aiight then. Later," I said to her as I said hanging up.

Once I got inside the gym, I went into the locker room and stopped at my usual. Before I'd even opened the locker door, this cocky and stocky brown-skin cat from New York named Supreme came up beside me.

"What up my man? You haven't been in here in about a week. You ready to get that ball run up on your ass today though huh?" he prodded with a jagged-toothed grin.

I really hated that 5% nation motherfucker with his phony ass name acting like everybody from the south is dumb as a box of rocks.

"Run up on my ass? Get outta here wit' that homo talk dude. What, you been lookin' for me?" I replied not looking his way.

"Ain't nobody talkin' homo to you faggot! No, I ain't been lookin' for you, but your baby's mom's is. She's been comin' up here on a regular. You must not be doing your baby daddy duties to her satisfaction," he continued with a cynical laugh.

"Dude what the hell are you gossipin' about? I don't have a "baby's momma" first of all, and secondly, why you ridin' my jock so close?" I asked running my tongue across my teeth in aggravation.

Supreme smirked and slung his bag over his shoulder. "I'm a man, I don't gossip. I relay information. That chick Gwen has been up here talkin you up."

"Well, you got a real bitchy way of relaying information if you ask me then. You my receptionist now?" I teased.

At that point, a few of the guys that were straggling around the locker room started looking our way.

"Why you getting all defensive with me B? I'm just trying to give you a heads up that the chick has been around here a lot, and this is how you do me? Aiight then. I see what's up wit' you," Supreme said shifting the useless toothpick he always had in his mouth from side to side.

"I don't know what you heard but I don't have a baby momma like I said. Maybe you should save the gossiping for the chicks," I said heading out into the gym area.

Gwen a.k.a. "Stalker Channing" was a piece of pool-side pussy I made the mistake of doing at a party one night. She wasn't on the same level as the females I kept in my flock, but she got the pipe anyway with

Vodka and circumstance as her wingmen. Now the Ho claimed she was pregnant.

"Yo' don't get disrespectful. I'm just sayin'," he said wiping his nose. "I wasn't really interested in what the gossip was anyway son. She told wifey and everybody in earshot you been dodging her calls. I saw her…" he paused for a second thinking. "… like, like Wednesday, I think. What's today? Sunday? Yeah, yeah it was Wednesday."

For somebody who wasn't interested in what she was saying, he sure knew a whole damn lot. Typical gossiping motherfucker. It seemed like every bitch in Atlanta either went to his girlfriend, or "wifey" as he called hers', salon. I'm sure I was often the topic of their yapping like little schoolgirls. Atlanta's black social scene is pretty small for a big city. If you're anybody in the ATL, everybody either knows you, or knows of you. Just like that game 360 degrees of Kevin Bacon, they could make 360 degrees of Brian Andrews. It was my gift and my curse.

"Yeah, well don't believe everything you hear. That chick is delusional. One fuck does not a daddy make. And stop calling me son. Your daddy maybe," I laughed. "But not your son." I said.

He stuck his middle finger up at me. "Okay, I'm just trying to let you know how your business is being played out in the street, but if you don't want to hear it…that's on you," he retorted walking toward the exit in pace with me.

"Yo, I got it covered. I'm good," I interrupted.

"That's cool, wit' yo' country ass."

I blocked his babbling Big Apple Ass out in my head. Dude had diarrhea of the mouth if there ever was any. As usual, the haters lined the walls waiting to get a basketball game in while the courts were still in full use. A few of them mean mugged me as I passed while another group tried acting like they weren't a bunch of flaming sissies.

I swear, an A grade dude such as myself has the equivalent of the 'Mo' Money' Mo' Problems' syndrome. The better I look; the more people hate. Can't win in Atlanta for the most part. A lot of brothas either want to be you, or they want to be with you, and I'm not down with that punk shit.

Of course, there's always one renegade faggot who doesn't give a damn, and Derron was the one who hung out at RUN-N-SHOOT all the time. He was a light-skin Puerto Rican who played in, what looked like 9th grade nut huggin' gym shorts, and wore his hair in a slicked back curl. He never dared open his mouth to me, because I'm sure he knew I'd bust his jaws wide open if he did; but he was definitely a repeat staring offender.

"Why is your attention all over here dude?" I asked him with a frown before completely passing him.

"I'm just looking your way. Not at you," he claimed sucking his teeth and looking away.

"Yeah, well you just make sure that's true," I warned.

5

Brenda

PREPARE TO BE UNPREPARED

I walked upstairs and down the long hallway to my old bedroom, which was now converted to my father's office. I didn't see why a pilot for a private airline needed a home office, but he had one anyway.

Pausing in the doorway, I observed the changes to the space which had once been my haven. It brought back some bittersweet memories. Two huge bookcases full of books I doubted my father had ever read covered both sides of the walls. My father's high school and college football trophies were on the tops of both of them and a huge oak desk frolicked in front of the window facing the doorway.

I sat down in the thick leather chair behind the desk, tracing my fingers over the framed picture of my parents with Brian and me at Six Flags Over Georgia. I was probably 13 when that picture was taken, and it was the last one I could remember taking with all of us together. I wondered why he'd even bothered to put it up since he was never really the family type.

I took the cordless phone from its cradle beside the desk top computer screen and dialed my brother's number. I knew there was a 50/50 chance he would ignore any calls coming from my parent's number, but I didn't have a choice at the moment.

The phone rang a few times, and then went to his voicemail.

"Hey Brian, it's your sister. Call me back as soon as you get this message. It's really important. No joke. I'm at mommy and daddy's house and I don't have my cell phone with me so call the house number if you get this message before 10:30. Bye."

I took a deep breath and sunk back into the chair as the weight of the past 24 hours began to sink in. I caught a glimpse of a hole that was almost completely covered by the bookcase on my left. Almost. It was midrange on the wall, and I winced and rubbed my right shoulder as I vividly recalled how it got there. Courtesy of my dear-old-dad.

My father was rarely home, even when he was in town, but you never knew whether it was Dr. Jekyll or Mr. Hyde who was coming to dinner when he came in. Drinking Daddy was malicious and scrutinized every step and breath I took. Sober Daddy seemed to only be aware that he had a son, unless Brian had gotten on his nerves too.

I basically skated between being the girl he loathed and the girl he ignored. I have very few memories of him being caring or nurturing to me...although there were a few.

When I was 14, I was sitting on my bed (which at the time was positioned up against the wall where the hole is) talking on the phone to my best friend Rhonda. My music was up loud, apparently too loud for me to hear my father's yells to turn the radio down.

I was in the middle of a sentence when suddenly my room door flew open and my father stomped in and yanked the radio volume dial down. "God damn it Brenda what the hell is wrong with you?! Are you deaf?! You didn't hear me yelling up here to turn this down?!" he screamed.

"No," I answered cautiously.

Oh shit...

"I bet you didn't! Runnin' your mouth on the phone with the music up to 10!"

He approached my bed huffing and puffing; I assumed it was due to him flying up the stairs like a bat out of hell. He stared at me with anger in his eyes.

On the other end of the phone Rhonda kept saying, "Hello? Hello Brenda?"

"Get off the God damn phone too! Phone bill is already high as George Clinton and you don't have a nickel to put on it either. Hang up!"

"But I just got on the..."

"I didn't ask you when you got on the phone Brenda. I said get off of it," he growled at me.

My stomach was doing nervous flip flops and I felt the beads of sweat forming on my forehead. He was drunk...I saw it in his eyes and smelled it on his breath.

"I gotta go...I'll call you later," I told Rhonda as I hung up the phone in silent prayer that he would leave me alone after that. But he didn't.

He continued to hover over me like a stealth bomber waiting to drop a bomb on me. After what seemed like several minutes...I climbed off the bed on the opposite side from where he stood. I wasn't sure what the stare down was leading up to, but I was hoping to get out of the room before it got there. He still didn't move, but his eyes followed me like a horror movie wall painting as I walked gingerly by him.

Suddenly he reached out and grabbed my arm with extreme force and jerked me close to him. I let out a yelp and started to pull away, but his grip tightened, and he jerked me closer in.

"You know I'm really sick of you and your mother walking around here like you don't have any rules to follow," he spat at me with the stench of vodka attempting to choke me. "You hear me?"

"Yes...you're hurting me daddy. I didn't even do anything," I begged with tears streaming down my cheeks as I tried to keep my balance standing on my tippy toes since his grip had me slightly lifted from the floor.

"Your mother's a weak, do-nothing, tramp and you're gonna turn out to be just like her if you don't learn to respect what a man tells you. I'm gonna break your defiant attitude against the rules." The disgust in his voice hurt as much as his grip on my forearm.

I didn't know what he was talking about or why he was talking about it, but I did know that I hadn't done anything for him to be snapping off the handle like this at me.

"Defiant how? You only tell me the rules after you tell me I broke them," I answered. I suppose it was the first time I'd spoken up to him while he was tormenting me, but it wouldn't be the last.

The fire in his eyes grew as he flung me backwards with so much force that I landed on the bed awkwardly, causing my shoulder to slam into the wall through the one space in my bedpost where the wooden pole was missing.

I don't know what came first; the cracking sound, or the pain in my shoulder, but I let out a shriek that could have gotten me a part in the next SCREAM movie series. In the middle of my screams, I looked at my shoulder and saw how displaced it looked...then I blacked out.

When I came to, I was looking up at a bright panel of overhead lights and a pretty Spanish looking woman with her dark hair in a ponytail, a stethoscope around her neck, and wearing blue scrubs.

"Okay she's awake," she called out to people I couldn't see as she laid her hand gently against my cheek. "Brenda? Can you hear me? You're in the ER at Piedmont Hospital. Do you know what happened to you?"

I didn't answer her. Hell yeah I knew what happened to me. What I didn't know was what she knew or what would happen to me if I told her what happened.

"Is my arm okay?" I asked as the pain made sure I remembered that too.

"No, I'm afraid not. You may have a concussion and your shoulder is fractured. I'm going to take you into the room to take some tests and x-rays to check for other injuries before the doctor comes to see you again. Your father said you were doing some sort of wrestling with your brother and jammed your shoulder into the wall?"

I couldn't tell if her questioning look was one of belief or disbelief of my father's version, but I hadn't decided what my version was going to be yet, so I kept quiet.

She just sighed and smiled slightly when I didn't respond. "You're going to be alright honey."

It actually took nearly 3 months for me to be alright in reality. I had to have my arm in a sling to keep my shoulder immobilized, physical therapy and pain meds for the rest of the summer. Even now I sometimes have stiffness in my shoulder...

I guess my father was stronger than he thought and probably panicked when I passed out from the pain. Wrestling with my brother. Yeah right.

Now, as I looked at the hole I thought, he wasn't ever any kind of father to me, but he was a Motherfucker!

***

On the outside, Robert Andrews seemed to be a handsome, charming, well-put-together man. He had a beautiful former model wife who kept up her looks with age and he was making good money as a Pilot for the now defunct Pan Am Airlines before he started flying for Private Paradise, a company that supplied pilots for private planes. My early memories of my father are good but from the age of 8 up, there's very little that I can attribute to being positive about our 'relationship." That's around the time he became a heavy drinker. Although my mother was usually the target of his rampages, by no means were my brother and I excused from anything he felt we deserved.

My senior year in high school, my mother's uncle passed away and she went to Miami for the funeral. Brian was in Daytona for college spring break and my parents let me stay home alone. There was initially a lot of crap about me not going with my mom to the funeral, but I managed to get out of it. Instead, I spent most of that time hanging with my friends since my father hadn't slowed up his extracurricular activities enough to actually look after my 17-year-old ass.

That Friday night I got in after midnight and accidentally crept in on my father having sex with some skank on our kitchen counter. They were startled and my father nearly knocked Skankarella onto the floor trying to keep his footing and save his dick from snapping off at the same time, while she fumbled to pull her dress back down.

"Girl..." he began to say as he said glancing at his watch. "What are you doing coming home this late!" he yelled. "I thought you were staying at Rhonda's."

I was almost speechless and too disgusted to even attempt a response through my neck rolling glare. Almost!

"Yeah, I can tell you weren't expecting me or anybody else to be here tonight," I replied snidely. Over the previous year I had slowly begun not to give a damn what my father said since it was usually negative and sometimes abusive. I also recently started fighting back which seemed to have slowed the frequency that he made attempts.

"What? Well then why are you traipsing your young ass in here at the crack of dawn like you grown and paying bills in this house? I know your mother isn't stupid enough to have approved of this-here," he spat in an alcohol tainted tone.

"I'm sure she wouldn't approve of this-here either!" I said defiantly.

His face twisted as he began approaching me yelling, "Who the hell are you talking to like that you little bitch?! I'm your God Damn Father and you better not forget it whether you like it or not before I knock your block off! I put the clothes on your back, pay your bills, and give you a roof over your head, and you got the nerve to come in here talking to me like you're doing for me?! Who-the-hell-do-you-think-you-are-talking-to?!"

"Rob!" the steamy slut screamed as he backhanded me causing me to stumble backwards.

"Get off me! You just mad cause your shady ass got cau..." I began to yell to him weeping before my sentence was cut short by the force of another slap across my face. Falling back into the hallway and holding onto the wall for stability, I started to run.

"You better shut your damn mouth! You don't judge what I do you little bitch! I take care of you! You don't take care of me!" he yelled grabbing me by the neck and pinning me against the wall with all his force. He snarled through baited alcohol drenched breath as I struggled to escape his clench and catch my breath with tears streaming down my face.

"No! Don't Rob you're gonna kill her!" his side trick exclaimed.

He loosened his grasp around my neck, but didn't remove it or his hand pressing against my chest. "So, what are you gonna do now? Tell your mother?" He asked leaning into my face with an eerily low tone.

The combination of fear, anger, lack of oxygen and the stench of musty vaginal juices on his face sent me into a violent bought of vomiting. Luckily the first heave didn't miss my father's face. Linda Blair couldn't have done better herself. My father sprung back from me like I'd tasered him (which I wished I could have) and I weakly scurried further down the hall to the half bathroom slamming the door behind me and rushing over the toilet.

"Damn it!" I heard him yelling. Once my insides were practically empty, I rested my head on the wall near the bowl where I sat on the floor. Feeling dizzy, sick, sore and afraid, I started crying. Why did this have to be my life?

I heard my father and the woman quarrelling somewhere in the hall. Skankarella's government name was Dana and she must have been a flight attendant, or worked for the airlines in some way because she was worried my mother was going to come for her 'The next time she saw her,' she'd said. I figured she must have been around my mom before if she expected there to be a next time. My father didn't attempt to come in after me or say anything else, and fortunately when I emerged, they were gone.

I went to my room and packed enough clothes for a few days and stayed at Rhonda's house until my mom came back. I was lucky that Rhonda's parents loved me like one of their own cause they never sweated me being there the whole time except to ask when my mom was returning home. Because my dad was a pilot and gone most of the time, I think they just assumed he was out of town for work and I was lonely.

My father never acknowledged the situation after that, and I didn't bother to tell my mother because Brian convinced me that she was only going to do what she'd always done. Nothing. She always took her lumps and disrespect like milk and cream in her coffee, so having her as an ally was as good as being alone.

Brian and I knew she would do anything to keep her cushy lifestyle and the public perception that she and RA were living the perfect life. Why any woman would stand for letting themselves and their children be verbally ridiculed and physically abused is a mystery to me. My resentment of the entire situation only grew stronger over the years and as I got out on my own I, like my brother, distanced myself more and more from my parents.

Brian once said, 'She's been a doormat all our lives and if it wasn't for her, I wouldn't have been a doormat for Gabrielle's tramp ass. Best believe that won't happen to me again. Now I can see why daddy's been messin' around on her weak ass all these years.' That was on the heels of the discovery that his college sweetheart had broken his heart and consequently transformed my cool as hell, funny, cute and loving brother Brian into the 'cold, cruel, womanizing, fuck you later, Brian' of today.

As adults, I usually avoided my father or limited communications with him. How somebody can be so charming with everybody, but his family baffled me, but he seemed to manage it with skill. I'd eventually become numb to his existence. I greeted him indifferently at family events and begrudgingly spoke to him on holidays and birthdays. I guess the reality of it was that I never stopped putting on the facade my mother nurtured, and Brian showed glimpses of my father's personality traits more and more as we aged.

***

When I got back from my parent's house I was greeted by an excited Zeus at the door. "Hey baby," I said to him putting my pocketbook and keys down on the coffee table and headed into my kitchen. I grabbed Zeus's dog food in the big bag by the refrigerator and filled his bowl to capacity before returning the bag. I took a deep breath and tried to work the tenseness from my neck as I headed to my room. I had barely gotten 4 paces when the doorbell rang. Assuming it was probably Brian coming upstairs to check on me, I walked lazily to answer it without bothering to check the peep hole.

"Hey there lady!" Edwin exclaimed with a huge grin to greet my blank stare.

What the hell...I hate pop ups!

"Umm...Edwin what are you doing here?" I asked exuding my unpleasant disposition.

"Well Sunshine," He said smiling nervously while darting his eyes past me into my place. "I thought I would come by and surprise you. Take you out for lunch and maybe later to dinner somewhere nice. I brought you these..." he said springing 6 wrapped yellow roses from behind his back. "I didn't just catch you getting in from church, did I?"

My facial expression didn't change, and I didn't make a move toward the flowers at all. "No, you didn't. The flowers are nice, but I don't like people coming over out of the blue and of all times this isn't a good one."

"Oh, my bad. You got company?" He pried still attempting to analyze the inside of my apartment behind me. I stepped out into the hallway and closed the door almost entirely.

"Like I said, this isn't a good time right now."

Edwin was a broker who worked for the same company I did, but in a different department. Unfortunately, his interest in me far exceeded the expiration date on my interest in him, which was roughly 3 months ago. He stood 5'9" with a muscular build, thin rimmed glasses and a dark chocolate complexion. When I met him one morning in the elevator wearing a nicely fitted suit and hat, he seemed like a sleek new prospect.

Of course, later I discovered that underneath the hat dwelled a large, lumpy and ill formed bald head which harbored endless ideas on how to infringe on my time. At first, we were hitting it off well. We had a number of dates and talked on the phone about twice a week until he began randomly coming by my office and calling me as much as twice a day. He even showed up at the movie theater I mentioned I was going to with a friend and tried to pretend it was a coincidence.

"Oh okay, is it because you need to straighten up? Because I'm not picky like that. I mean there's no rush. I certainly wasn't trying to rush you by popping up. I did call your cell phone First but you didn't pick up or call me back and I was already headed out this way so I just thought…I might as well keep coming right?"

"My father died this morning Edwin. I'm not really in a social mood right now."

"Oh wow!" he exclaimed. "I'm so sorry. I didn't know. What happened? Oh man. You shouldn't be alone at a time like this Brenda. Let me comfort you."

Comfort me? More like smother me. Damn this dude was persistent.

"It was an accident in the pool," I replied impatiently. "Honestly, I don't really want to talk about it, and…" I started as Zeus whimpered and scratched on the other side of the door.

"Oh yeah, yeah I completely understand." he cut me off. "You probably don't even know which way is up right about now. I've been in your shoes before and I know your instinct is to want to be alone, but actually, the best thing for you is to be around other people to help you work through it and not get depressed. I lost my father when I was 12 and it was one of the hardest days of my life," he preached attempting to move in and hug me as I cringed away.

"Edwin! What is wrong with you? I said no! Keep the flowers, keep the lunch and leave me alone. You've been doing too much for a while now and you're obviously blind to the fact that we're not on the same page. You pop up on me at work, pop up at my house, and call me like 50 times a day…" I barked exasperatedly. "C'mon man! What I gotta do for you to get the picture that I need you to fall back?"

"Fall back?" he repeated as though I were speaking Swahili. "I have been falling back Brenda. I don't get angry with you when I have to call you 4 different times before you pick up or return my calls. I haven't even made any moves on you to try to make love to you again after that magical night we spent together a few weeks ago. I've been letting you go at your own pace because I know women sometimes have guilt for sleeping with a guy too fast, or whatever other insecurities you gals carry. I'm trying to be sensitive to your needs Brenda but you're not making it easy on me."

Oh-my-God! We had one 30-minute sex session which I certainly wouldn't classify as magical and consequently had not bothered for a round 2. No wonder he was still single.

"Look I gotta go," I said turning and opening the door to go back inside and began to close it.

"Wait a minute!" He yelled using his foot as a door stopper. His contorted face quickly smoothed itself back out into a nervous smile. "Okay I'm sorry for pushing you at a time like this. I'm being insensitive and I apologize. At least take the flowers, accept my apology and promise me a phone call sometime soon?"

I didn't smile, didn't take the flowers and didn't answer. I simply stood there with pursed lips in a ready-to-close-the-door-stance staring blankly at him.

"Okay. As you wish. I'll just call you later then an..."

My neighbor Lina came out of her apartment already talking, "Hey Brenda girl I've been meaning to come by and talk to you about something. Oh I... I'm sorry..." she stuttered in a southern bell way when she pretended to just notice Edwin at my door. "I heard your door but didn't know you were out here talking to such a fine young man. I'm Lina," she continued tip toe sprinting over to shake his hand. Her ginormous, un-bra'd, implanted breasts were practically bursting out of her flimsy shirt as her elbow length blonde weave swirled around her.

I rolled my eyes at her antics watching Edwin do his best to force his eyes from her jugs to her brown, aged, and smoker wrinkled face. She was probably one of the oldest strippers still on active duty at nearly 50 years old.

"Hi. Nice to meet you," Edwin said beaming.

Seriously? He was such a lame.

"What beautiful flowers. Didn't mean to interrupt anything," she replied bashfully posing so that her booty cutter shorts struggled even harder to keep her ass inside. "Going on a date?"

"He was just leaving and I'm going inside," I answered drably.

"Do you want to take your flowers before you go in?" He asked.

"Oooh girl! Cause if you don't want them, they would look great in my living room. I love flowers," Lina offered with a Cheshire cat grin.

"You can have them then Lina. Enjoy the rest of your day Edwin," I said curtly, closing the door and locking it.

Trying to get rid of him was like trying to detach a leech. I felt drained and pissed all at the same time.

***

I was lying across the couch reading a new Omar Tyree book and trying to keep my mind off of all of the recent turmoil in my life and my father's morbid demise when my doorbell rang.

It had been a few hours since Edwin popped up and I was hoping it wouldn't be another unwanted guest making a surprise visit. I bothered to look through the peep hole that time and saw my cousin Kelly who lived in the apartment across the hall from me.

She nearly fell in when I opened the door since she was leaning on it.

"Real bright," I teased going back to my plush spot on the couch.

"Girl, leave me alone," Kelly laughed coming inside and flopping down on the couch beside me. She stretched her lanky legs out beneath my coffee table and began fussing with her ponytail.

"So. Are you okay?" she asked hesitantly. "Brian told me Uncle Rob died last night and I wanted to come by and see about you."

"Well," I said scratching my head and letting out a deep sigh. "I don't know yet. I have a lot of mixed emotions about it. Sort of, hot and cold."

"Yeah, so does Brian. He's acting like it's just another day but... I don't really think I believe it's hit him fully yet. Can't be," she said looking confused.

"To be honest, I don't even want to talk about it. Where is my brother anyway? I at least thought he would have come up here to see me when he saw I was home."

"He went to the gym about an hour ago. Speaking of leaving, I saw your new guy leaving here this morning. I think he might even be interested in Amanda's apartment on the first floor. You know because she's moving out in a few months," she joked in obvious agreement to my wanting to change the subject.

"What new guy? Teddy? He is not new, and that's probably the last time you're gonna see him anyway." I claimed.

"No girl. The new dude that's been coming by. Bald head, glasses and dark skin? You know I know who the hell Teddy is," she said rolling her eyes.

"Edwin? He's only been here once before and that was to drop me off. Since when does seeing a guy twice around my place make him my "new guy"?"

"Really? I'm pretty sure I've seen him like 4 or 5 times around here and I thought at least 2 of those times he was coming out of your place..." Kelly answered perplexed.

My heart was beating fast and I was beginning to feel a little panicked. Edwin had never been inside my apartment before and he's only dropped me off once. All of our other dates ended up at his house or we drove separately. She had to be mistaken that she'd seen him more than that. Didn't she?

"If you ever see him around here again and I'm not talking to him, call me. That mo-fo better hope you're wrong cause if his ass is stalking me, I'm gonna let Brian put some lead in him."

Kelly stared at me blankly and started petting Zeus who was now leaning his head atop one of her stretched out legs.

"I feel like I should be consoling you right now, but I don't know how to do that when you're holding everything in Brenda. You know you can let out a good cry and have my shoulder to lean on if you need to, right?"

"About Edwin?" I chuckled. "There's nothing for me to cry about when it..."

"No not because of that. Because of Uncle Rob," she interjected.

"You have a very different father than we had Kells," I replied with a sigh. "In fact, I'd probably cry more if Uncle Donovan died than I ever will over my father."

Kelly continued petting Zeus and asked, "So how's your mother taking it?"

I thought about it for a second. "I don't know girl. How is a woman in her position supposed to handle it? She's coping, I guess. When I got over there this morning she was crying and talking to the police, but by the time I left she seemed like she was back in her Elizabeth Taylor mode. Superficial and glammed up."

Kelly's eyebrows furrowed, "I talked to my mother about an hour ago and she was on her way over there to make sure Aunt Liv was okay. What's the story again? That he fell asleep in the pool?"

"Girl don't get me to lying. What's the story is right," I said without a thought. "She says he was drunk, and she left him out on the float after some pool party they had last night and when she went out there this morning he was dead in the water."

"I thought he didn't like the water, or was it just the pool? I remember how he used to get all pissed whenever anybody tried to coax him in the water at barbecues and stuff."

Funny how everybody that knew my father knew he didn't like the water and it was the first thing that came to mind when they heard how he died. "Yeah, my mother said he'd been taking swimming lessons or something and didn't act like that anymore. Anyway, I know I said I didn't want to talk about it when you asked about it earlier."

"Oh..." Kelly answered as my cordless phone began to ring on the end table.

I motioned to Kelly to pass the phone to me, which she did. I looked at the number on the Caller ID and recognized Athena's work number.

"Hey chick, what's up? Why are you at work on a Sunday?" I answered and questioned all at once.

"You know I hate having to come in on a Sunday to finish up work that should have been done through the week" Athena complained, "but my new assistant wouldn't know her ass from her eyeballs if I didn't point them out to her. What you doing today? Wanna go with me to the mall at around 5 o'clock?"

"I don't know. I've already been out early this morning checking out my mom, and right now I'm feeling like staying behind these 4 walls for a minute. My father died this morning. Drowned in the pool."

"Oh my God girl!" Athena gasped. "I'm so sorry to hear that. I'll be over there after work to see you."

"I'm cool," I replied almost with a laugh. Sad as it was, I really didn't need much consoling. I was actually pretty relaxed.

"Are you sure? Maybe you should call Teddy and see if he can come over and stay...."

"Girl we broke up last night," I said cutting her off. "For good this time too."

I heard her hard and doubtful sigh and immediately rolled my eyes in response.

"Uh…okay. And this would be the 134th time you did this? Or is it the 135th?" she teased. "I'm sorry girl, I know this isn't the time to be cracking jokes, but you know you and Teddy do this like clockwork."

"I'm not a basket case so the jokes are fine...but I am serious this time though. For real. We're broken up for good this time. Finito!"

"I hear you talking but I'll just wait and see. I do hope he's to the curb for good though. He's just one of those dudes who wants to partake of the plethora of the single or foul living Atlanta female population while keeping you in wait. You can't keep a man if you never had him…and sorry to say it to you honey…but that man is not ready to be had."

My heart hurt to hear the confirmation in Athena's voice that echoed what I already knew. Reality really does bite. "Anyway, I was calling because I want all us girls to meet at SILK tonight for some drinks. I got some news, and I don't want to tell it 4 different times but I can just tell you now if you're not up for going out," she said.

Athena, Rhonda and I had been friends since our first day of Pre-K, and along the years we added Belinda a.k.a. Lottie in Junior High and Yvette in High School. We're sort of the black version of the show SEX IN THE CITY except some of us aren't quite that successful, skinny, or model-esk. All of our mouths are just as sassy and some of us have just as much sex.

"Some news huh? Finally, gonna make Quame' a daddy?" I probed.

"Damn I hate trying to surprise people who know every damn thing," she joked. "Yes girl. A bun is in the oven."

"Yeah, okay I'll be there. Just know that I'm not good at planning baby showers so you're gonna have to get Rhonda or Lottie to do it. Both of them already have kids so…"

"Alright well let me get back to work before I have to cuss Jennifer out for not putting a meeting on my schedule with a client, I see going into the meeting room right now with her stupid self," she interjected hurriedly.

"Bren you sure you don't want me to come over there?"

"I'm fine. Congratulations girl," I replied looking at Kelly who'd fallen asleep. "I guess when one life leaves, another enters."

I knew Athena like I knew the back of my hand and her face had been looking a little plump the last month or so. Her and her husband Quame' had been trying for a child since they got married less than 2 years ago.

It seemed like everybody was moving in the directions they wanted to go, and I was stuck in the same spot. Career wise, I was up to par with the rest of my girls. Being a Market Researcher for BRONSON & BRONSON was definitely bringing me the finances I needed to live a good lifestyle, but I wasn't quite as happy with my personal life.

I decided that the reason I was feeling like that is because I'd been selling myself short dealing with Teddy like he was my man in an open relationship, instead of taking it at face value. We were not in a "relationship", especially when we were in bed more than out of it together. Teddy's game was the same from day 1 and I kept playing, thinking I could change it.

Not anymore… GAME OVER!

6

Brian

SITUATION ABORTED

I'd talked to my boy Nate on my way leaving the gym and told him about my father's passing, so he invited me over for some drinks to chill & get my mind off of things. When I pulled in his driveway beside his black Coupe Deville, he was already exiting his house barefoot, dressed in a long T-shirt, swim shorts and holding a beer in each hand. "Hey B. Yo' man I'm really sorry for your loss," he said giving me a big bear hug. Although I am 6'0", Nate is 6'6" and has been called "Too Tall" since 6th grade. His bear hug made me feel like a midget. Not to mention the unwelcomed chill I felt from the cold bottles pressed against my back.

"I was just getting ready to get in the pool when you called," he said handing me a bottle.

Nate was my college roommate and if there was anybody more like a brother to me than my other best boy Ike, it was him. I hadn't opted for Ike's house because I assumed Tara would be there. I'd already had a big enough dose of bitches for the day and I knew she'd runneth my cup over.

"Your new pool is pretty nice. Looks like you've been making sure to get all the use out of it you can huh?" I said opening and taking a swig from the Heineken.

"Yeah man," he replied as we walked around the back of his house to the pool. "You know me and the water go together like white on rice."

I nodded knowing he used to talk about wanting to be on the Olympic swim team when we were in school. He was one of the top swimmers on our college team, but he never made it past that. Now he taught algebra and coached the swim team at a local high school.

He took his shirt off and walked over to the edge of the pool before diving in. He swam a quick lap as I sat and got comfy in one of his lawn chairs. Nate surfaced a few minutes later at the edge of the pool facing me and wiped the water from his eyes.

"You comin' in? I got some extra trunks if you need 'em," he offered.

"Nah I'm good. I don't feel like messing up my hair," I joked.

"Ah shut up fool," he laughed. "So, um... Did you wanna talk about your pops or..."

I shook my head, "No not at all. I didn't talk to his ass when he was alive and now that he's dead I don't have much else to say about him. Dude everybody is bound to die sometime. I guess this time was his."

Nate's expression was blank. "Man, you a cold brother. So, you don't feel nothin'' about it? I know he wasn't the father of the year, but he was your father. At least he stuck around. Mine didn't."

I sipped my beer in silence. No need to repeat what he'd already heard me say. After a few moments of silence, he pushed off and started swimming again. When my beer was done, I went back around to the front of the house and let myself in to get more. I maneuvered my way through his hardwood floored bachelor pad into the kitchen and grabbed 3 beers with one hand by the bottle necks and tossed my empty bottle in the trash on my way out. As I approached the pool again, Nate's phone began ringing.

"Your phones ringing," I said sitting one beer down by him on the side of the pool and going back to the chair I had risen from.

He sucked his teeth and opened the beer, "Probably just Joyce again. We had a fight about some ex-boyfriend of hers that keeps coincidentally popping up where she is and I'm not. I hung up on her ass about an hour ago."

"You hung up on her? Like a little girl? I swear you still haven't grown any balls since we were in college."

"Brian you talk more shit than a little bit. Everything somebody does that isn't what you would do is like a bitch or a girl. You got a complex about your manhood man. You need to check yourself." Nate said shaking his head as he drank his beer.

"I don't have a damn complex. Look, if you want to let some woman run you and drain you dry of the few little chips you make teaching those kids then go ahead. I'm just trying to teach you how to keep your life stable. I don't know how my two best boys let their women turn them into the biggest pussies I know," I said leaning forward with my elbows on my knees.

"Pussy? Yo' chill out with that B. I know you had a rough day but you about to let your mouth write a check your ass can't cash. Plus, you acting like you're the guru of dating or something. You trying to "teach" me," he snickered. "I'm doing alright all by myself. You just worry about them females you mess around with bringing you drama."

"Never happens man. You know I'm speaking the truth. I get just as much, if not more ass as you and Ike, without even half the drama. Y'all invest too much faith in females I'm telling you."

"Is that so? You call getting your car keyed, chicks flippin' out on you at your job and stalking you less drama?" He laughed before taking another sip of his beer. "Bruh, and don't forget I was a witness to just how pussy you can go back when you were with Gabrielle. That's why your ass is so bitter now. What's that Tara called you...oh yeah...a 'womanizing, woman beating, woman hating asshole.'?"

"Woman hating and beating? I'm the last one to hate a woman, but if not letting them walk all over me is what she means, then so be it. Plus, you know anything Tara says about me is because she can't have me anyway. Point blank," I rebutted with a smirk.

"Yeah, well I'm gonna leave that alone because I don't want to get on Ike's girl like that but about you..." Nate let out a belly laugh. "I can't believe you're sitting here playing like you don't handle women with disrespect. It's true they keep coming back for more punishment, don't ask me why, but still...I'd fuck a dude like you up if he was dating my sister."

"You act like I go around punching bitches in their faces or something. Not that a lot of them wouldn't deserve it with the mouths they have on them," I half joked. "But seriously, I love women and women love me. As for your sister...she could only dream of the day I'd let her ride this dick," I taunted taking a sip of my beer and wiping sweat off my forehead.

And while we were on the subject, I was serious about his sister Rene. That drunken old Trollope had tried on many occasions to get me to let her wrap her grubby little cougar cat around my dick in the years I'd been friends with Nate. If it wasn't for my higher than her, standards and her linebacker sized husband, she might have succeeded by now.

"You know what? Now that I think about it... Gabrielle is the only woman I can remember you dating that you didn't treat like a booty call. You're probably still letting that mess that happened with her run your life after all of these years' man. Seriously, all bullshit aside, you never plan on letting another woman back in?"

"Dude what are you babbling about? I never said I was doing or not doing anything because of that bitch. You are the one who thinks you got me all figured out. You, my sister and my cousin watch too many talk shows with all of this relationship counseling," I said reclining back in the lawn chair.

"Man, you are talking to your boy right now. You trying to tell me you'd be content just screwing random chicks for the rest of your life?"

What's not to like about that?

***

As much as I hated to admit it, the subject of Gabrielle always hit a sore spot. We were together from my sophomore year in college until nearly the end of my senior year. She wasn't the first girl I'd had a serious relationship with, but she was the first and only girl I'd ever fallen in love with. A short, dark skin cup of coffee with a perfect petite little shape and shoulder length hair, she had me at "Hello". She looked like a 5'2" version of Beverly Johnson the model. Her major was Political

Science, and I was impressed at how someone so beautiful could be so smart and opinionated at the same time.

Gabrielle was the complete opposite of my mother in every way. Stubborn, confident, and outspoken. I was young then and didn't know better than to let my emotions allow a woman to control me. We talked about, marriage, kids, everything was all planned out and I thought I had been blessed. Life wasn't that simple though, even in college.

Senior year, Gabby started getting too busy to spend time with me. She blamed it on the intensity of schoolwork and when I called she was always busy or just about to start studying. My boys tried to warn me that she was up to something and called me "pussy whipped", but I didn't believe she'd ever do anything like that. We were in love, the sex was off the hook, she was beautiful, smart, and all mine. That was all I needed to know...or so I thought.

One weekend my boys and I went on a road trip to Tuskegee to watch our college play in a football game. We left Thursday night, were skipping classes on Friday and planned to come back Sunday night. Everything went as planned until Saturday when the dude that drove us got word that his little sister was hit by a car and was in critical condition. We were back on the road to school within hours and arrived about 9 o'clock that night.

Gabby lived 3 blocks from campus and since all of the fella's I rode with lived on campus, I decided to go to her house. Though she had a roommate, I had the key to her place because I often crashed there in between classes and was there when she got home. I let myself in, dropped my duffle bag at the door and walked to the back of the apartment to her bedroom. I didn't even think twice about the noise I heard coming from her room. I figured it was the television since I could see the light from the T.V flickering through the crack in her bedroom door. Either she thought I was her roommate, she didn't hear anybody come in the house, or she didn't give a damn; but when I opened her room door, I almost passed out.

My future wife was on her knees in front of a guy I knew from Spanish class. Keith, Kevin or whatever the fuck his name was had his dick buried deep in Gabby's throat. She was moaning and sucking feverishly like it was a Tootsie Roll lollipop and I just stood there with my mouth hanging trying to process what I was looking at.

"Oh yeah baby," he said putting his hand on her head and pushing her down further. I could feel the pain and anger overwhelming me; my vision was becoming blurry from the tears welling in my eyes and I wished I had a gun to blow both their brains out.

"Fucking bitch!" I finally managed to yell, startling her as she fell back onto her naked ass. The dude looked surprised but not particularly upset or afraid.

"Oh my God Brian...," she exclaimed out of her dick sucking lips while wiping her mouth.

"I swear to fucking God, if I ever see your face again I'm gonna punch you in it!" I yelled as I turned and walked back down the hallway toward the door. I picked up my bag and till this day I think I remember hearing that dude laughing, but I was never quite sure about that.

I felt so humiliated and angry. I couldn't understand how my mother stayed with my father knowing that he was out fucking around on her all of the time after experiencing pain like what I'd felt. I walked for hours and at some point, Gabby started paging me and leaving messages on my pager voicemail. I never called her back, but I did listen to the messages when I got back to my apartment; which I walked to, even though it was more than 10 miles from campus.

"Brian I'm so sorry," she'd said crying on the voicemail. "Please call me back. I know I fucked up but I just...I don't know I was weak. You weren't paying enough attention to me or something, I guess. Baby, please call me back when you get this. I love you. I'm worried about you. We can work this out. I kicked him out as soon as you left, and I'll never see him again if you say so.'"

If I say so? What the hell did she think I would say if I ever forgave her ass? 'Oh yeah Gabrielle you can still be friends?' That bitch had lost her mind! She claimed to love me. Really? Not as much as she seemed to love that dick! Every time I asked for a little head, she acted like I asked her to eat my ass or something; yet she sucked that brotha off like he was Carvel ice cream in a cone.

Word got out amongst our friends in different versions of the story, but Ike and Nate were the only ones I told the full story. Nate was the one that went to her place and got everything of mine for me since I refused to ever go back there. When she called me, I cursed her out until she hung up and I avoided her like the plague in person. I couldn't focus on school and ended up failing most of my finals for the last semester. All I had to do was take two classes over to graduate, but I wasn't in the mind set to do it.

Three months after the breakup, Gabby came to GROOVE THEORY, the club where I was bartending then. Her first mistake was fucking around on me. Her second mistake was thinking there was any way in hell we could reconcile or even be friends. I left at about 2 in the morning and she was sitting on the hood of my Mazda 626. When I walked up, she leapt off of the hood and began shifting from foot to foot nervously ringing her hands.

"Brian, before you say anything, please hear me out." She'd said holding her hands up defensively before I'd reached my car. I stopped at the driver's door and stared at her with disdain in silence. When I didn't say anything, she continued. "Okay first, I'm sorry. I really miss you and I know I fucked up royally. I can only imagine how mad you still are, but I'm hoping you've calmed down a little bit since the last time we spoke. I'm really sorry to bring it to you like this but it's the only way I can think of to get where I can talk to you and you can't hang up on me." She paused again and seemed to be awaiting a response.

She was wearing a Morehouse College shirt that used to be mine, tied in a knot in the back with blue jeans and sneakers. Her hair was pulled back in a ponytail and she wasn't wearing any makeup except some lipstick. I hated that she was still beautiful to me.

"Umm, I don't even know how I can ever make you trust me again, but I'm willing to do whatever it takes to get our love back. I know I fucked up and I don't know what I was thinking. Maybe it was the stress of all of the classes or me just getting scared, but I know now that I can't live without you Brian. I need you in my life and I'm begging you to give me a chance to make it up to you. I'll do whatever you need me to do to prove I can be trusted again," she said reaching out in an attempt to grab my hand.

I pulled my hand away from her disgustedly and put my key in the car door to unlock it without a word. I needed to get out of there before I did something we would both regret.

"Brian please!" she yelled immediately and started the waterworks. "What else can I say? What else can I do?"

I opened the car door and started to get in, but she grabbed my arm and pulled me back toward her. "Baby, look at me," she said turning my face toward her. "Can you say you don't love me anymore? I mean really say you don't love me anymore?"

I can't explain the blanket of anger that covered me when she touched me; I can only say that it was the most rage I've ever felt at one time. I took my hand and mashed her in the face so hard that her head snapped back, and her balance was challenged.

"Bitch don't you ever put your motherfuckin' hands on me again," I said in a low murmur between my teeth.

I turned to get in my car again and she screamed out, "Don't do this! I love you!" The crying grew more intense and she was so frantic that she was literally trembling.

"And what the fuck does that have to do with me?!" I yelled at her as my anger exploded. Her eyes grew huge as saucers as I quickly started to approach her.

"I catch you sucking the flesh off another man's dick and you expect me to think you love me?! Bitch please!" I yelled smacking her hard in the face.

She hit me back and suddenly it felt like I was watching myself from the outside. I had her by the hair, and I was hitting her as hard as I could with an open hand while she unsuccessfully attempted to fight me off. I felt empty inside and my hands were moving as if they were on autopilot.

I spent two nights in jail, got fired from my job, and my father made sure to talk major smack to me for having to bail me out to anyone who would listen. He was a funny son-of-a-bitch sometimes. I didn't even bother to go back and forth with him while he was ranting and raving either because he and I both knew that he was no one to ridicule me for hitting a woman. His anger was about the bail money, not what I did.

Surprisingly enough, Gabrielle didn't press charges against me and back then they didn't prosecute if the "victim" didn't want to. Some victim she was...

Later that year I decided to enroll in culinary school and put off getting those last few college credits until my head was back in it. That's the year I realized that women should never be more than a place to rest your dick unless you're willing to live the rest of your life at their mercy.

Fool me once, shame on me; fool me twice...never.

***

I sat and shot the shit with Nate for most of the day and we'd moved the pool talk into the house where we watched ESPN and clowned each other's favorite teams.

"Alright dude well I'm gonna get ready to leave," I told him after I checked my watch and saw it was already after 7pm.

"Nah you not ready to leave right now. You gotta chill for a while with all those damn beers you just had. You gotta work tonight?" He asked rising from his armchair and disappearing into the kitchen.

"Man, I haven't had that many drinks. I'm supposed to work tonight but I'm probably calling in. I'm not in the mood for catering to a bunch of loud mouths."

"Well, I'm not gonna send you out there drunk driving to get killed on my watch," he called from the kitchen. "I'm gonna order some pizza and call the fellas over to watch the Marciano vs. Chile fight."

"Oh yeah I forgot that was tonight," I answered leaning back on the black leather couch I was resting on. "Alright I'm in."

My cell phone started ringing and I pulled it from my pocket to view the Caller ID. It was Gwen's stalking ass ringing my phone for the third time in a day. Time to curb this fool's enthusiasm.

"What are you calling me for?" I answered nastily.

She was silent at first, which I assumed came from her shock that I'd actually answered at all. "Uh...Brian?"

"Confused about which potential baby father you're calling?"

"See now why you wanna start off the conversation with me having to curse your ass out? I haven't said two words to you and look how you answer the phone," she returned snippily.

"What do you want? You've been calling my phone non-stop like an idiot so spit out whatever it is you called to say."

"Well maybe if you would answer the phone when I called in the first place, I wouldn't have to call so many times. Don't trip because you're the one who's playing phone games. Just answer the damn thing next time. You got me running all around Atlanta trying to talk to your ass and it doesn't even have to be like this."

"First of all, let me set you straight before we go any further with this conversation. I'm not your man, this baby you're having may or may not be mine and I know that. Stop telling people that you're having my baby when you don't know whose fucking baby you're having. Secondly, I don't have your ass running around nowhere. You just don't have sense enough to know when to give up." I stated.

"What do you mean I don't know whose baby it is? Are you insinuating that I'm some kind of a freak or a Ho and I don't know who my baby's father is?"

"Cut the bullshit Stalker. I didn't just meet your ass yesterday. You've been kickin' it around my sister's circle for years and your reputation isn't a secret to anybody. You spread your legs like whipped butter from what I've heard and that's why I hadn't messed with you before. You caught me when I was drunk at the right time and you got lucky. Now you trying to run it like you're carrying my seed and I'm not feelin' that."

"Go to hell Brian. I-am-not-a-stalker first of all," she whined. Had I called her that out loud? "I don't know what your sister has been saying about me either but, I am Rhonda's friend, and your sister wouldn't know what the hell I do anyway since I don't talk to her like that. And what do you mean I got lucky? So, what… I'm supposed to be happy you gave me the time of the day now? Pu-lease," she protested loudly. "This is your baby, and you need to just accept it and talk to me to figure out what we're gonna do about it. I can make this hard, or I can make this easy."

"Bitch, you don't know what hard is unless it's a dick. Believe me, I can make it hard. Keep running around talking sideways about me like some teenager and you will find out though. If it is my baby, I don't want it so what else is there to talk about. We're not gonna be together and I don't want no bastard babies out here with my name on 'em."

Nate came back and sat in his armchair but the frown on his face said that he didn't approve of my conversation.

"Well Brian, this may come as a surprise to you, but you don't run the show over here. Whether I have the baby or not is not just up to you. In fact, it's really just up to me…so if you want me to do something your way, I'd expect you to be a lot nicer to me than the fucked-up way you've been acting," she said snidely. "It's my body and it's up to me."

Stalker was a 5'5" brown skin chick with thick thighs, a small waist and A cups. Her face was nothing to write home to mother about, but she was a decent looking female who tried to spice up her appearance with expensive clothes. Without the bells and whistles, she would've been completely invisible to me.

"Woman, are you really trying to act like you don't have a rolodex of numbers to surf through for your baby daddy's name? Come on now. I live here sweetheart. Your reputation precedes you. Frankly, I don't give a damn what the facts are. I'm telling you I'm not feeling you having my baby and I'm not trying to be dealing with you on any level." I told her furiously. "What you need to do, is focus…like I said before… on either aborting this pregnancy or finding the real baby's father. Point blank…period."

"Okay yeah, so it could possibly be somebody else's… but I'm almost 100% sure it is not. I'm not trying to game you. You're not rich or anything so what makes you think I'd be trying to trap you into being my child's father? You're a bartender for Christ's sake! You got good looks and you're good in bed but that's it! Everybody talks about you like you're Billy D. Williams or somebody but you're really just an asshole off the ass. This isn't about you. This is about an innocent baby!"

Stalker might be a moron, but she did have some of her facts straight. I am good looking and I do lay a mean pipe. All that other crap she was spewing…rubbish from a scorned woman.

"Sweetie you're in your late 20's working at Express as a fulltime job and making less money than the average high schooler. Believe me baby; in your world…I am P. Diddy. See now if you got other guy's as possibilities…why the hell you putting my name out there then? That's the bogus shit that…"

"Since you can't use any vocabulary that's bigger than 4 letter words, I'll just do me and not worry about what the hell you want. This is my body." She said breathing so hard into the phone it sounded like a bull on the other end.

"Look, I'm tryin' to be a laid-back dude about this but you gonna make me act out on you," I said balling up my fist.

"This is you laid back? So, what; are you threatening me? You gonna do something to me Brian? You trying to fuckin' control what I'm gonna do with my body? Fuck you! The way you're talking to me…to hell with you! You can find out if I'm keeping it or not in 6 months' then motherfucker! I'll show you who can act out!" she yelled as she hung up on me.

I bit my bottom lip and pressed END on my cell phone, but I kept staring at it anyway. I wanted to ring her neck for playing Russian roulette with my seed. What kind of low self-esteem bitch would want to have a child by a man who doesn't want her?

Dumbass.

***

Doe-boy, Floyd, Nate and Mitch roared as I slam dunked the ball into the basket with my tongue out while rubbing my bald head...or rather my Xbox character did. It was a massacre for Floyd as my team beat his 108 to 72. "Yeah boy! Who's next? Who wants to test the champion? I told y'all deez nuts were too big for you to fuck wit!" I yelled throwing the game remote onto the couch and jogging around the circumference of Nate's living room.

They'd all answered Nate's call to come over and watch the fight but until it started, we were playing Xbox. I was a little surprised to see a couple of them get out the house at all.

"Aw this is some bullshit! I told you I hurt my thumb at the lumber yard yesterday. Rematch! Rematch!" Floyd yelled shaking his right hand as though he were trying to shake a feigned ache away.

"Yeah right Floyd! Take your beat down like the bitch you are and move out the way so a real man can get in here and make Brian pick up his face off the floor!" Doe-boy said grabbing the remote from Floyd and sitting on the couch in game playing position.

"Oh, dude you don't want none of this do you?" I said playfully mocking him. "I mean do you really want me to take yet another one of y'all out before you gotta run home to your women?"

"Aw shut the hell up you pretty boy motherfucker! I'm about to kick that ass up and down the court so you can go to work and drink yourself under the bar tomorrow night," Doe-boy replied pushing buttons to select his players.

"See now you trippin!" I said taking my seat and grabbing the remote. "You haven't beaten me in anything since I've known you, unless you cheated that is."

"Punkass. You swear everybody cheats whenever they win something you crybaby ass b-e-yotch! Get ready to lose punk!"

"Yeah, whatever fat boy!" I said as we began to play.

"I'm telling you that my thumb got hurt. I couldn't even move the remote right. You saw how I was struggling Mitch," Floyd whined as he sat down on the couch beside where Doe and I played.

Mitch sucked his teeth, took a swig of the Vodka in his cup and said, "Yeah brotha I saw you struggling alright. Struggling not to get your ass kicked! Looks like you lost the battle."

Everybody in the room laughed and Nate chimed in, "Damn take your loss and move on punk!"

Floyd shook his head and gave Nate the middle finger. "Don't front like I didn't just beat you like a runaway slave yesterday buddy. You damn sure didn't take it like a man...punk!"

"Ooooohhh," Mitch egged. "Oh, he beat you in your own house Nate? Damn you must be losing your mojo!"

"Nah Joyce has it in her pocket...right next to his balls!" Doe-boy said as he attempted to force a turnover from my team.

Again, everybody laughed and Nate smacked Doe-boy in the back of the head as he walked past the couch where we sat. "Every one of y'all dudes is pussy whipped one way or another except for Brian; so, all of y'all need to cool out about who's got my balls." Nate said sitting at the card table.

"Hey, I'm not pussy whipped!" Mitch insisted. "In fact, I practically have to beat Melissa off me. I think she's dick whipped, poor girl. She didn't know who she was messing with when I got at her!" He yelled sitting at the table adjacent to Nate and pulling a deck of cards from the shelf by the table.

"Yeah, little dick Willie probably did surprise her since you always boasting about how you lay it down!" Floyd joked.

"Ha-ha very funny motherfucker!" Mitch frowned. "You should be one to talk when your girlfriend has been Jo-hand-a Hancock for the last year!"

Doe-boy paused the game and let out a roaring laugh that caused him to nearly choke on the gum he was chewing. Floyd rolled his eyes and exhaled annoyed as he stressed his supposed thumb injury again with a shake of his wrist. "Whatever," he replied.

"So, Brian what's the deal with Gwen and the pregnant rumor?" Mitch asked as he and Nate began playing Blackjack.

I shifted my head to try and loosen the crick in my neck and restarted the game for Doe-boy and I. "Why's everybody all on my dick about that?" I answered.

"Dude ain't nobody all on yo' dick about nothin'. I just asked a question. If she's all up in the barber shop running her mouth about it, it's public information. I'm just trying to find out if it's true so I can start preparing to take the little motherfucker to the strip joints," Mitch joked slapping a card down on the table.

Nate took a swig of beer before saying, "Man that woman is an idiot."

"I told you not to mess with that girl, but you didn't want to take my advice. She got something about her," Doe-boy said squinting and shaking his head. "I can spot a bitch with loose marbles a mile away. I told you not to dick that chick down B."

"To be real with you I don't know if she's pregnant with my kid or not," I said beginning to think about it. "What I really want is for her ass to shut up and just abort it if it's mine."

"Who's Gwen?" Floyd asked oblivious to the conversation.

"The chick he hit out at Rhonda's party a while back. You know, cute, thick, wit' a lot of make-up on? She was wearing that low cut blue thingy," Doe-boy said rubbing his chest like they were women's breasts.

Floyd still looked confused but didn't respond.

"Well, you better make sure she doesn't then because child support is a bitch. Take it from me my man. I pay $1050.00 a month for 2 kids from my X-wife and that in itself explains why I'm still driving that damn Ford Escort I've had since before power steering." Mitch said.

"Yeah, they don't play in Georgia about that shit. What I want to know is why you still sleeping with chicks without a condom? I mean we grown ass men. That's your favorite saying and you running around like a little boy wit' your dick out." Doe-boy said as one of the players on my team fouled his player.

"Man, sometimes you just don't get to the condom. I mean if I'm gonna fuck a chick in the pool...what, I'm gonna wear a condom in there? If we walking to the car and she decides to give it up in the alley on the way…what I'm supposed to say? 'Oh girl…I would do it, but I need a condom?' Please. I wear them most of the time, but sometimes you just gotta do what you gotta do." I explained.

"Aw now see you playing games with your life B. Some stuff is a game, but this isn't one of those things. I'm being real. If you don't have one, fuck it, it ain't that important or go get one. If you getting the ass as regularly as you claim, you don't have to be pressed to get it when you not ready." Doe-boy continued.

"Look man my luck isn't that bad for one thing, and for the other, I'm not playing games. 95% of the time I'm strapped, but like I said, sometimes you gotta do what you gotta do."

"Or who you gotta do," Floyd joked.

"Sounds like you might have to do jail time sooner or later from the way you were talking to her on the phone. Brutal," Nate interjected.

"You won't think it's funny if Gwen does turn out to be pregnant and has the baby anyway. You definitely won't see anything funny in getting AIDS or something. You don't know where she's been or who she's been getting it in with. Don't be stupid man. Strap it up all the time unless you're exclusive." Mitch said getting up and walking down the hall into the bathroom.

It was quiet, less the sound of the game Doe-boy and I were playing and the music coming from the radio.

"Look I don't need a sex-ed class from you 4 stooges. I keep telling y'all that I'm a grown ass man. Furthermore, I'm the only one of y'all who's getting any ass that isn't attached with handcuffs to my wallet. Y'all need to be asking me for the key to my success! I know what the fuck I'm doing and I'm no idiot. My jimmy is just fine and of all of y'all, me and Nate are the only ones who don't already have Bay bay's kids running around here. All of y'all Dr. Phil asses can stop the session now. Thanks, but no thanks." I protested.

"If you say so man," Doe-boy said. "All I know is no matter whether you wear a condom or not, it's not going to save your ass from the beat down I'm putting on your ass tonight!" Just then he scored the winning basket at the buzzer and the game was over.

I'd never lost to him before and the odds that I would have lost this game were slimmer than Laura Flynn Boyle. Lady Luck is a Bitch too!

7

Brenda

EVERYBODY'S BUSINESS

I took the day off of work on Monday. I just wasn't in the mood to go in and I did have a legitimate excuse with my father dying so... I might as well use it. I didn't do much the entire day but lie around, watch T.V., and order take out Chinese food. My brother finally brought his raggedy behind upstairs to my place and we talked about everything that was going on, including my suspicions about my mother's weird behavior but, he didn't seem too concerned one way or the other.

By Tuesday I was ready to go in and feel productive. I had a couple of big clients who were embarking on some large purchases and I needed to be present to make sure that everything that needed to be done was getting the attention it needed. I was thumbing through the files in my bottom file cabinet searching for notes I'd taken for a similar purchase on a different client when there was knock at my office door, which was open. I looked up to see Edwin in the doorway smiling like he was posing for a Dentyne commercial.

"Well, aren't you a beautiful sight for sore eyes," he said. "I didn't think you'd come in today."

I looked at him with a blank expression seeing as I'd heard no question to respond to.

"What are you doing for lunch?" He continued.

"Working. I'll probably be out the rest of the week, so I have a lot to catch up on and a lot to prepare in advance," I answered shifting my attention back to the files I was sifting through.

"Okay. Well, what about dinner?" He asked approaching my desk and looking as though he was about to take a seat in the chair beside it.

"Edwin I'm really busy and I don't have time for small talk," I said curtly.

His bright smile faded, and he straightened up like a soldier at attention. "Be straight with me Brenda. Is this entire attitude you're giving me predominantly about bad timing or are you blowing me off?"

I rolled my eyes and looked up at him. "Edwin, I thought I made myself clear when you popped up at my house. And another thing," I said positioning myself with both hands on my desk. "My cousin tells me she's seen you at my place pretty often. What the hell are you doing lurking around my building?"

He was uncomfortably silent as his eyes darted around my office for a few seconds. "I'm looking for a new place and I like your area. I've been trying to make up my mind if I wanna live over there is all. It doesn't have anything to do with you."

"Really," I said tonguing my teeth. "Okay well like I said, I have a lot of work to do. Thanks for checking up on me."

Suddenly his toothy smile returned. What the hell kinda side show actor was this guy?

"You're quite welcome. You know I still care for you. I'll just give you some space," he said exiting my office.

I shook my head at how weird his behavior was and caught a glance of a red light flashing inside my pocketbook under my desk. When I reached inside, I saw that it was my cell phone alerting me that I'd missed 2 calls and had 1 voice message. It also looked like the battery was about to die soon. I'd left my charger in the house so there was no chance in reviving it. One missed call was from my mother and the other was from my friend Rhonda. I figured Rhonda was confirming that we were going to SPA CIDELL after work, but I had no idea what my mother wanted. After scrolling my phone for my mother's number, I called her back from my office phone.

A man picked up on the third ring. "Hello?"

I was shocked into silence. Had I accidentally dialed the wrong number? "Uh... Hello can I speak to Olivia? This is her daughter."

"Oh wow, sure you can. Hold on a minute," he replied jovially. I heard him put the phone down and a few moments later my mother came on the line. "Brenda?"

"Mom who was that?" I asked immediately.

"Oh, that's just Avis. I was umm... having some problems with the air conditioning over here and with your father gone I needed someone to come and fix it for me."

"With my father there you would have needed someone to come and fix it," I said dryly. Who was she trying to fool?

"Umm... hold on a second honey. He's leaving and I have to let him out," she said abruptly putting the phone down.

I pressed my ear closely to the phone to try and hear what they were saying since I heard them talking to each other in low murmurs and I could swear I heard her say, 'I love you too' before I heard the door close. My mother came back on the line and said, "Okay I'm back. So... I was calling you because I was going through your father's things to donate and I found some bonds he had in a lock box. I figured you'd probably know what to do with them or how to cash them in right? I mean I don't see that he's ever signed them or that it says who the bonds were specifically for or anything. There's 5 of them and 3 of them are for $500. The other 2 are only for $200 each but they look old. I'm guessing they should be worth at least twice that by now. Even with the economy. What do you think?"

"You're already going through his stuff to donate?"

"Well," she seemed off guard and nervous. "Well yes. I'd just rather start the process now before it has time to really sink in that he's gone, and then it will probably be too hard for me to even do it at all. I just can't believe he's gone," she whined beginning to sob.

Nothing she said made a damn bit of sense. It would be harder for her to "start the process" later rather than now when it's supposed to all be fresh in her mind? Not to mention that she did find a dead body in her pool. Some grieving widow.

"Mom I'm at work right now. Were you planning on cashing them today?" I asked snarkily.

She took a deep breath and cleared her throat. "No. I... I was just asking Brenda. I mean it's not like I'm hurting for money or anything. I was just surprised to find them, and I was wondering about them and their worth. I'd probably just give them to you and Brian anyway. I guess I'll have to call the insurance company soon and let them know he's died too."

"Yeah, I guess you should," I responded. 'Right after we hang up like you already planned,' I thought to myself. "I have to go Ma. I just called to see what you wanted; I'm working."

"Alright then I'll just put these bonds in a safe place, and you can look at them whenever you come over next. I'm hoping that will be tomorrow though, because I need some help with getting the house ready for all of the people who will probably be coming by."

"Will do," I said as I noticed a call from Rhonda coming in on the other line. "I gotta go Ma. Bye."

"Hello?" I answered clicking over to the other line.

"Holy hell the world must be ending! Did you just answer your cell phone on the second ring?" Rhonda clowned.

"Smart ass. How about my mother is already getting my father's stuff ready to donate and getting his finances squared away," I groaned.

"Wow she doesn't waste time huh?"

"It damn sure doesn't look like it," I replied as the beeping from my dying battery began. "But hey listen, my battery is dying. I'll be by your job to get you at 5 o'clock okay?"

"Yeah okay. Meet me at the front of the building."

"Alright later," I said hanging up just as the screen began to shut itself down while it ran out of juice.

Suddenly I wished I'd taken Tuesday off too.

***

Rhonda and I sang along to an old Michael Jackson's greatest Hits CD like we were American Idol contestants as we drove down Peachtree Street. "Say you wanna be starting something… you gots to be starting something…say you wanna be starting something…" I belted out as I pointed at her and she pointed at me. Suddenly she turned down the volume and pulled her cell phone off of her waist.

"Hello?" She said through her earpiece. "What's up girl? (Pause) No, chilling with Brenda on our way to get our nails done (Pause) umm," Rhonda said looking at me as though she was contemplating something. "Umm, I don't know if that's a good idea (Pause) I know but I don't feel like any foolishness between you two today and you know how I feel about it (Pause) yeah at SPA CIDELL so we can get massages too."

"Who's that?" I asked frowning.

"Listen girl, it's a free country but let the record show that I was against it. (Pause) okay (Pause) later," Rhonda said hanging up her cell phone and looking at me cautiously.

"Who was that?" I repeated.

"Gwen."

I sighed and rolled my eyes. "And once again your big mouth has told the bitch where we're going. Why does she always want to be where she's not wanted? I mean if y'all want to hang when I'm not around, that's on you; but that chick knows I can't stand her." I said aggravated. I was in a good mood until before that little interruption.

"Listen I don't know what is up with her. I think she just really wants you to like her. Maybe she admires you. She talks about the things you do all the time; because you know I brag on my girl. You're a Financial Advisor making big doe that's about to quit your job…eventually, started writing your book and you're a fly girl like me. What's not for her to envy?" Rhonda said playfully pushing me.

"Girl please. First of all, stop telling that trick my business. Second of all, she does not admire me and she's probably just trying to get at Brian." I groaned. "She's a leech and she just wants to hang on so she can suck what we have out of us for herself. Plus, you really just brag on a bunch of malarkey anyway because I haven't written a damn thing yet."

"Brenda you know I can't hold water, so I don't even know why you trip every time you find out I told something. You and I have been girls forever but Gwen's my girl too. Y'all don't have to knock heads for everything do you? Anyway, you know I never give up any important information though, just the bullshit."

"No, it's not just the bullshit you give up. That skank has been telling people she's gonna bleed Brian dry when she has the baby; and she keeps talking about where she's gonna move to and stupid stuff like that. That's all gotta be coming from you running your mouth about his money. I bet the bitch wasn't even gonna have the baby till you opened your trap. She's not fit to be anybody's mother with a past like hers. Every time I turn around, she's trying to be up in my face and acting like we're cool too. She's your friend, not mine."

"Brenda damn, I said I was sorry about that; I'm not gonna keep apologizing for telling her about the money because you will get over it," she said snidely as she grabbed her pocketbook from the dashboard and put it in her lap. "Gwen is good people if you look past some of her mistakes. Everybody didn't grow up with good role models. I know you don't want to have her in your family, but it looks like that's what is gonna happen, so you might as well get over it."

"You-are-a-freaking-trip," I said as we pulled into the parking lot for SPA CIDELL. "You got a lot of nerve talking to me about getting over something when you threatened Paul's ex-girlfriend with her life. If he was gonna get back with her because she was pregnant, no big deal. If it was gonna happen it was gonna happen, right?" I replied.

"That's different. Paul is my man and Brian is your brother."

"So," I said raising my eyebrows.

"So, if he has to pay child support it doesn't affect you. It also doesn't affect you if he wants to have more kids or whatever. You're just gonna be the aunt. I'm gonna be the stepmother to whatever little rug rats are trotting around with his genes. I couldn't let that bitch have his baby." Rhonda retorted.

I half laughed. "Oh, so it's like that?"

Rhonda huffed. "I'm just saying if you get to know Gwen and stop dissing her all the time, you might like her. You don't even give the girl a chance."

"Hell, I gave her a chance all the times we hung out with her and she played us out by acting like a slut. I don't need her bringing me down. If my family is gonna be out in the world I don't want drama every time I go to see them. Gwen is a drama queen and a liar. Who would be thrilled about somebody like her raising a child? Her ways of thinking are warped, and damn it, let's be real; so is my brother's. I'm not looking forward to him bringing any babies in this world with anybody, but she's at the bottom of the totem pole," I said as I took my key out the ignition and turned to look at Rhonda face to face. "We been friends for over 2 decades Rho; you know what I'm about and I'm not about this shit."

"Brenda you can't manipulate everything to be the way you want it to be. Gwen is my girl, but you know you and me are like sisters. When it comes down to it, I have your back no matter what happens, but I just don't think she's as bad as you do. She really doesn't have any female friends except me; so that's probably why she's trying to get close with you too. Why can't you give her a break?" Rhonda said.

"So, you're surprised you're her only female friend? She's always talking about what chicks are jealous of her and whose man she stole and what not. What female is gonna deal with her and keep her in their circle when she acts like that? She doesn't have any loyalty and her morals are low Rhonda. If she shows up and she comes at me wrong, it's gonna get ugly."

Rhonda sucked her teeth, rolled her eyes and said, "Oh boy, here we go."

We both got out the BMW and walked side by side to SPA CIDELL. Soon we were in our long white robes, lying on massage tables in a room with soothing music and the sounds of water trickling around us.

Our masseuses came in and we disrobed down to our waists and turned onto our stomachs. My masseuse was a tall, dark haired, buffed Italian looking man with huge hands and a beautiful smile. "I am Antonio. If you 'ave any questions, or I putting too much pressure on where I press, you say, 'Antonio, no there.'" He said mispronouncing some words in a sexy Italian accent.

"Okay," I said smiling as I turned my head toward Rhonda lying on the table next to me and made a crazy face.

Rhonda smiled back at me as her masseuse began kneading the cricks from her neck. She mouthed the words, 'Mine's name's Furio. Like on the SOPRANOS.' We both snickered and I closed my eyes with pleasure as Antonio loosened the tension from my right shoulder.

"Feel good eh?" He asked.

"Very," I replied.

***

After 45 minutes of a greatly needed massage, Rhonda and I continued on to get our pedicure and manicure in another part of the spa. They handed us chilled water in wine glasses, and we sat down on soft lounge chairs behind manicure tables to get our treatments.

"Man, I needed that," I said to Rhonda as she nodded in agreement.

"I know that's right. I'm not even sure if Paul can make me shiver like my man Furio. I might have to give him my number," she joked.

I chuckled as the manicurist began on my hands. "What color?" The pretty blonde woman asked.

"Champagne's a good color," I said selecting a nail polish from the rack. "What color you getting?" I asked Rhonda.

"Umm, I'm getting a French manicure. I'm trying to make this thing last all the way until the wedding next weekend. I'm wearing green to the bachelorette party and purple to the wedding so I didn't want anything that would clash."

"Oh yeah that's true," I said rethinking if I was going to switch colors. I was wearing a pink dress to the bachelorette party but the dress I was going to wear to Ike's wedding was canary yellow. I decided champagne would carry me over with both.

"Man, I can't even believe they're getting married, can you?" Rhonda asked me.

"I know; it's crazy. Who would have thought anyone who is even remotely close to my brother would be getting married," I laughed.

"I know that's right! And to Tara of all people. That girl was a tyrant in college and she's a tyrant now. I don't even see how they stayed together this long." She replied as I saw Gwen walking in from the corner of my eye.

I exhaled deeply and licked my lips in dismay.

"Good afternoon ladies," Gwen said as she sat down on a lounge chair near us with her manicurist.

"Hey," Rhonda said looking at me sheepishly. I didn't respond.

"I figured I'd come down and get my nails done with you guys too. It's about time for these things," she said playfully as she held up her hands with chipped fingernails.

"Yes it is," Rhonda answered.

"So, I heard y'all talking about Tara when I came in. Isn't her bachelorette party coming up? Where is that gonna be?"

"Don't answer that or she might pop up there uninvited too," I said snidely.

Gwen squinted her eyes at me and said, "I would not crash a bachelorette party. I was just asking. And yeah, let me get that bright orange color too miss," she then said to the manicurist who was going through the nail polish bottles. "This won't hurt my baby will it? The fumes I mean."

The manicurist shook her head no with a big smile as she directed her attention to Gwen's slightly plump stomach. "Oh, when's your baby due?"

"October," Gwen responded now with a huge smile as she rubbed her belly.

I rolled my eyes with disgust and let out a sigh.

"Did Brian tell you that already Brenda? I think it might be a boy, but I haven't confirmed it with the doctors yet."

I looked at Rhonda and inhaled deeply again. This bitch was really pushing her luck.

"So anyway, like I was asking, where's the bachelorette party gonna be? Me and my girls will probably go to JAGUAR that night. I doubt you'll have to worry about me crashing. I heard that some Falcon's player is supposed to be having a party at JAGUAR that night." She said looking at me with a smirk. That bitch knew Brian worked there; who the hell was she trying to fool? Dumb ass broad wasn't gonna see him there anyway though because he was gonna be at Ike's bachelor party.

"Yeah, I heard about that on the radio," Rhonda said. "Who you going with?"

"Oh, my cousins are coming in from Ohio so I'm trying to show them around. I'm pregnant, not dead. And you know what else?" She asked but no one answered. "I am so hungry; must be the baby kicking," Gwen said looking my way again as she rubbed a hand over her stomach. "It's so crazy carrying around another person inside your body. I love him already."

I felt like slapping those hazel contact lenses out of her eyes. It was obvious she was trying to get a rise out of me with all the baby references. I wanted to yell, 'Look bitch, all this lovey dovey baby talk is really over the top for somebody who's had as many abortions as you have. Everybody in here can see your belly through that tight ass jeans suit so give it a rest!' But I didn't.

"How many months are you supposed to be again?" I asked her.

"I'm 4 months. The doctor said I'm actually carrying pretty small right now but oooh my bladder can't tell," she answered grinning.

"Humph," I said looking at Rhonda and rolling my eyes.

"What you don't believe me or something? You don't see this evidence? Oh, but then again you don't have any babies so how would you know anyway?" she responded nastily. "Brenda you really need to chill out. I didn't come here to start nothing with you. You're the one who doesn't like me. I've never been anything but nice to you."

"Listen don't try to play me about having babies already because we both know this is just the first one you actually decided to let live. I don't like you and I don't pretend to, so why do you keep trying to be around me? Don't tell me I need to chill out. You need to stay out of my face. Hang with Rhonda on your own time," I spat.

"You're always monopolizing her time so that's hard to do; plus, we are all supposed to be adults. You should be able to hang out with her and other people without being jealous."

"Jealous? Bitch don't flatter yourself. Nobody is jealous of you; I just can't stand you and I don't want your trifling behind around me all the time."

"I'm not saying you're jealous of me, I'm saying you're jealous of my friendship with Rhonda. Rhonda can have more than one best friend you know?" she said.

"Best friend?" I said looking at Rhonda. "You are delusional." I replied smirking as I looked back at Gwen. "And pitiful too. You might wanna stay your club hopping ass home sometimes now that you're pregnant too. You don't have any class, do you?"

"Class? What... and you do? It's real classy for you to be sleeping with however many guys you want to, but you have the nerve to be looking your nose down at me? Get the fuck outta here with your judgmental ass."

"You don't know a damn thing about me trick. You're just talking out your asshole instead of taking a dick in it."

"Listen you two, I don't want my friends to fight; can't we all just get along?" Rhonda said trying to be funny. Neither of us laughed. All 3 manicurists looked uncomfortable and mine had now finished with my manicure and pedicure.

"I'll just set up the fans to dry your nails now. Thank you for coming to SPA CIDELL. You have a wonderful day," my manicurist said as she smiled and exited.

As I sat drying my nails, I admired the job and said to Rhonda, "Yeah this is a pretty color."

Rhonda smiled, probably assuming the drama was over. "Pretty ugly," Gwen said under her breath.

"Grow up slut," I said not even looking her way.

"Takes one to know one," she retorted.

Rhonda's smile faded just as my patience had.

***

"Did Rhonda tell you I was looking to buy a house? I ran into your boyfriend Teddy a while back so I'm gonna use him for my agent. He is your boyfriend, right?" Gwen continued.

I closed my eyes to try to mentally calm myself from reacting to her with a slap in the face. "No, he's not my boyfriend bitch, so I really could care less if you're dealing with him."

"Why're you so defensive? I just said I was gonna use him for my agent. You're really the jealous type huh?" She chuckled antagonistically. I think it's time I get a nice place for me and my son. Oh, I can't believe it's anything else by how strong he's moving around. What you think about the name Omarion? Omarion Andrews. That has a good ring to it doesn't it? It's the name of the boy who used to be in that singing group B2K. He's cute." she rambled.

So, this retard actually thought Brian was going to give that child our last name? And on top of everything else she was naming the kid after some dude in a singing group? Ghetto chick.

"You okay? You getting sick or something?" Gwen asked me.

"Gwen," Rhonda called to her in a low voice.

"Sick of you. Yes," I replied.

"What? I'm just trying to make small talk with her, and she keeps turning it nasty. Since her brother isn't taking any interest in his child, I thought maybe the rest of his family might want to but I'm not gonna kiss anybody's ass. You'll be the ones to blame if our families can't get along with your bourgeoisie acting selves."

Rhonda was now drying her nails under fans like I was, and her manicurist left the room.

"You know just because me and your brother aren't talking, it doesn't mean we can't try to be cordial Brenda. If you just stop trippin' and get to know me, you'll probably find out that you like me. We didn't get a lot of time to know each other before all of this went down and I really think we could all be cool. I mean I don't have anything against you except how you've been judging me without even really knowing anything about me," Gwen harped.

"Gwen, why don't you just stop talking to me? I'm having a good time with my friend and I'm not feeling like dealing with this right now." I responded in a frustrated tone. "Why are you so pressed to make friends with me?"

"I'm not pressed to make friends with you. I just don't want my child not to know his aunt and his father. By the way, my condolences on your father's death. I'm sorry to hear about his passing and that he won't get to know his first grandchild. I'm trying to be the mature one here."

"You're trying to be the mature one?" I asked confused. "Mature about what? Mature that you're a Ho who goes home with every Tom Dick and bigger dick? Chick that is why I don't like you. I didn't like you before you got with my brother and I don't like you now. You know you're just having this baby because you think you're gonna get some money out of Brian. You could give a damn about the baby. You killed a slew of 'em before; so, what makes this one any different? If the time comes that I need to interact with you to see my nephew, we'll handle that then. Not now." I nearly shrieked.

"Brenda!" Rhonda said getting up and stepping in front of the table and lounge chair where I sat. Gwen had gotten up in the middle of me verbally pelting her and started for me. I stood up but didn't move from my place. The bitch was going to be in for a rude awakening if she came any closer; I hated to hit a pregnant woman, but there were plenty of places to hit her other than in the stomach.

Rhonda flung her shoulder length jet black hair. "Y'all gonna make me mess up my nails," she whined.

"You know you talk a lot of shit and I might just need to kick it out of you today," Gwen said pointing her finger over Rhonda's out-stretched arms.

"You would want to back it up. Pregnant women get smacked too." I threatened.

One of the huge masseuses came into the room and said, "Ladies, I think you need to calm down now. If you're done, we're going to need you to leave. This is a spa, not a boxing ring." A thick blonde who looked like he'd just gotten back from the surf said. I rolled my eyes at him and began walking toward my locker to get my clothes out and change.

"Yeah, you keep walking," Gwen called after me. I gave her the middle finger without turning back.

When I got my things out, I went into the nearest bathroom to change and was followed quickly by Rhonda.

"Damn," she said as she entered holding her clothes in her hands.

"Why y'all gotta act like little kids in here? They probably won't even let us come back anymore."

"Rhonda please," I said impatiently. "You're the one that told the bitch where we were going, and you know I can't stand her. She's the one who started up with the mess so don't come at me with that y'all stuff. We trying to enjoy our day and here she comes with the drama."

"You didn't have to be so mean to her either though. I know she was trippin' a little today but damn, she was trying to be your friend at first. You don't always have to be so mean Brenda. How much of that crap did you think she was gonna take?" Rhonda asked as she finished changing into a green halter top and hip hugger green shorts which showed her butterfly belly ring.

"Damn trying to be friends with me. I don't want to be her friend and she knows that. You can't force me to be friends with her and neither can she," I complained as I finished dressing in blue jean shorts and an orange sleeveless shirt that tied in a knot in the back.

"I'm not trying to force you to be friends with her; I'm just saying that you can be civil around each other. You gonna act like a bitch after the baby is born too? You know she's not gonna let you see the baby then."

I put my hands on my hips and looked at Rhonda in disbelief. Act like a bitch? How the hell was she gonna put all of this on me when Gwen was the one who barged in on us?

"Whatever Rhonda. You ready to go or are you leaving with Gwen?" I said in a snotty tone.

"What? Bitch stop trippin'. You know I'm not leaving with Gwen, and don't be mad at me for telling you like it is. I'm your best friend and if I can't tell you like it is, who can?" She said as she slipped on some green sandals.

I sucked my teeth at her as I grabbed my pocketbook and slipped on my orange sandals. "Come on bitch."

"You know sometimes I don't know if I'm rolling with Brenda or Brian," Rhonda said chuckling menacingly.

I didn't laugh.

8

Brian

THERE'S NO FUN IN FUNERAL

By the time Thursday came around I was ready to bury all of the conversation about my father just as much as I was ready to bury him. Luckily my mother required very little help from me in handling the funeral and burial since they had already planned ahead. I had to admit that my sister may have been on to something when she said my mother was acting strangely about his death.

The grieving widow seemed to be having a hard time staying in character if you ask me. I called her Sunday evening, and she could barely get the words out of her mouth for the entire 12 minutes I stomached her without loud sobbing. Brenda told me that some dude had answered the phone when she called her on Tuesday, and she thought she'd heard her say she loved him. Of course, I always suspected my mom was "getting it in" somewhere else since my father was clearly not living up to his side of the wedding vows; but I don't know if I would have expected her to get back into it before his body was even buried. Brenda's conversation with me rang back in my mind:

"She's got something up her sleeve Brian," Brenda had said on the phone. "She's got some strange dude over there 2 days after daddy dies and she's all anxious to get his stuff out of the house and move on. Isn't that a little fast?"

"Alright let's be real Bren...who could blame her if she really isn't sorry he's dead? Are you?" I asked getting comfortable watching ESPN in my living room at the time.

"I don't know if I'm sorry or not, but I don't like being played for a fool and I feel like that's what she's trying to do."

"So, you would expect her to pull you to the side and be like, 'Don't tell anybody but he actually didn't drown, I held him down'? Just let the idea go either way. Let her continue playing the role she sees fit and worry about you. She'll get what's coming to her just like he got what was coming to him."

"I'm not saying I'd expect her to come clean but...I just want to know if she's lying or not. Did you know that the so called "party" they had only had 2 other guests? Jenny and the same dude that she claimed, was fixing her air conditioning? Avis," Brenda said in a detective like tone.

"Oh yeah?" I replied blandly. In my world, 4 people does not a party make; unless it's an orgy, but then maybe my mother saw it differently. Jenny was my mother's best friend though and I don't recall too many occasions where my father would have willingly socialized with my mom's friends and not his own. Not surprisingly, Jenny was not a big fan of my father's due to his treatment of my mother.

"I'm just saying. What's up with that? Daddy...hanging out in the pool with mommy and Jenny and some random guy who's now all up in her face? Riiiight. And... he's the dude who answered the phone when I called yesterday."

Now as I stood staring at the closed casket, I wondered if my father had somehow crossed the last line Olivia Andrews could tolerate before his demise.

"You okay?" My uncle Tony asked putting his hand on my shoulder.

"Yeah, I'm good. I just don't usually do funerals," I answered with a half grin.

"I hear you. Me either," he said pulling a cigarette from the pack in his jacket pocket and putting it behind his ear. "I'm gonna need a smoke when this is over. I never expected to be burying my baby brother."

We stood silent for a few minutes until he looked down at his watch and said, "Well I suppose they're about to get this party started now huh? There are a lot of people out there. Can you imagine if we would have actually had the wake like your Aunt Linda wanted? It would have been chaos in here," he solemnly joked.

I had to agree with my uncle there. I wouldn't have expected my father to have so many mourners at his funeral. I guess not as many people as I thought actually knew the real him. Of course, the majority of them were strange women I'd never met, but then he never was much for introducing his jump offs to family.

We were getting ready to walk down the aisle when the doors to the church auditorium opened and people began to pour into their seats as directed by the Funeral Director and his team. My mother, her sister Tonya, my sister, my Uncle Tony's wife Charlene, their two kids, and my dad's sister Linda were escorted to the front row directly in front of the casket. My uncle sat between my Aunt Linda and his wife and I took a seat at the end next to my sister.

I put my arm around Brenda while she stared intensely at the closed casket with tears welling in her eyes and breathing quickly. It was funny how one minute she was numb and unfeeling about his death, and the next minute she was tearing up. I knew where she was coming from though because my feelings were almost as jumbled up. Minus the tears of course.

"I don't want to sit in front of a corpse Brian," she whispered. "Especially his. I don't know if I can sit here when they open it up."

"I got you sis. It's not gonna be that long. Close your eyes and lean on my shoulder if you need to," I told her.

I know sensitivity has never been my strong suit, but whether my sister knew it or not, she was the only person on earth I loved almost as much as I loved myself. She was the only one who knew me inside and out, and who loved me no matter what I did or said. Sometimes we were the only ones each other had when my parents were busy playing "JERRY SPRINGER" vs. "THE COSBY SHOW" in our house. She was my baby sister and like all baby sisters, she was often a pain in the ass, but she was my pain in the ass and I didn't like seeing her in pain.

"Okay," she said taking a deep breath as the Funeral Director opened the casket revealing my father's still body.

Looking at him lying in the casket in a dark blue suit with his hands clasped across his chest stirred something uncomfortable up in me. Brenda took a deep breath, put her hand on my leg and buried her head in my chest. I saw and heard my mother sobbing She reminded me of Wanda from the old sitcom GOOD TIMES with all of her tissue dabbing and "Oh lord!" hollering. My Aunt Tonya was trying to comfort her and my Uncle Tony was doing the same with Aunt Linda who was crying silently while tears streamed from his own eyes.

I turned my attention to the preacher who began speaking from the pulpit until I noticed someone else come and sit at the end of the pew next to my Aunt Linda. I could tell by the dude's hazel eyes and near perfect features that he was related to us on my father's side, but there was definitely something wrong with this cat. He was wearing a dark blue long-sleeved suit with blue gators; a single gold necklace with a diamond cross, 2 diamond earrings in each ear, and his long hair was pulled back in a ponytail. I couldn't be 100% sure because of the distance he sat away from me, but I would've bet my soul he had eyeliner on. It was official. Either this was Prince…. or Cuz was a fuckin' homo.

I wondered why this dude would be so bold as to sit in the immediate family pew with us when I didn't know his ass from Adam? It seemed like my Aunt Linda was familiar with him though because she left my Uncle Tony's embrace to lean on the other dude. He looked down the pew at me and nodded but once I got a full glimpse of him, I was nearly paralyzed. He looked exactly like a young version of my father.

***

I could barely pay attention to the funeral proceedings as my thoughts were consumed with trying to figure out exactly who this dude who looked like a gay version of me or my dad was. If he was my Aunt Linda's son, she'd damn sure kept him a secret until this point. I didn't like the looks of him or the looks he was giving me for that matter. There was something sneaky and disrespectful in his eyes and I was gonna find out what it was all about before the day was out.

My mind was still homing in on that dude when I felt Brenda's pull as she and everyone else stood to begin the viewing.

"Oh lord! I can't do this alone!" My mother cried out holding one tissue wielding hand in the air and stumbling a bit as we began to pass by the casket.

Brenda shot me a look that could only have been read as "Oh brother" and I kept my arm around her shoulder while we walked. The kids were crying as were all of the women in our row and I could hear other people throughout the church sobbing loudly as well. Instead of looking at my father's lifeless body in the casket, I was watching the mystery dude comforting my Aunt Linda. Who the hell was this guy?

Once my Aunt Tonya was able to drag my mother's wallowing ass from the auditorium with the help of my Uncle Tony, we all stood out in the lobby area of the church. My mom and Aunt T went into the ladies' room together as people began to approach the rest of us separately to give their condolences.

"Who's that guy with Aunt Linda?" I asked Brenda when people weren't surrounding us.

"Who?" She asked confused.

"The guy with Aunt Linda. Does she have a son we don't know about or something? Why was he sitting with the immediate family?"

"I didn't see him. Where is he?" She questioned, scanning the crowd for the two of them.

"Right there," I answered motioning to the area in the lobby where he stood talking to my aunt and accepting condolences from funeral goers with her. "Who's he supposed to be?"

"I don't know but if I didn't know you were standing right next to me, I would have thought that was you standing over there after some kind of...I don't know...metro-sexual make-over."

I wasn't amused. I was really disturbed that he looked so much like us and I didn't know who he was. I had an idea, but I was hoping my superior intellect was a little off this once.

"Let's go find out," Brenda said grabbing my hand and pulling me over to Aunt Linda and the mystery dude before I had time to protest.

"Hey Linda," Brenda said as she hugged her. "Are you okay?"

The tears were still drying on her cheeks when she brushed her hair away from her face and said, "No I'm not okay. I don't understand how my big brother died in a pool when he didn't like pools and I don't understand why that witch of a wife of his didn't want to have a wake for him. She thinks everybody is buying her bullshit tears for him, but I know the truth. I know what she's really about and I'm not just gonna stand here and let her pull the wool over everybody's eyes like she's so distraught over him dying. She's nothing but a fake," Linda spat out.

Brenda's eyebrows went up and I couldn't hold back the chuckle. Aunt Linda never liked my mother and I'm sure the questionable circumstances surrounding my father's death didn't get her any further down on my aunt's shit list.

"O-kay," Brenda said slowly. "And you are?" she asked extending her hand out to the mysterious hazel eyed guy.

"I'm Julian," he replied quickly with a half-smile.

"So how are we related to you Julian?" I asked.

He looked at Linda whose expression I couldn't read and said, "I'm your brother."

Brenda's mouth hung open as her eyes darted back and forth between Julian and Aunt Linda. My head began to throb.

"Older or younger?" I continued. I guess my mind knew it when I saw him sitting at the end of the pew with Aunt Linda, but I needed to hear him say it to make it real.

"Umm, I'm older than Brenda but...I think I'm younger than you are. I just turned 28," Julian answered nervously adjusting one earring in his ear.

"You knew about him?" Brenda questioned Aunt Linda with an air of pain and disgust.

"I've always known about him, yes. It wasn't my place to tell you something your father didn't want me to talk about," she replied snuffly. "Your mother could have said something if she wanted to. She knew before I did."

"You've gotta be fucking kidding me right now," Brenda answered as she pushed past us and headed towards the bathroom.

I slid my hands in my suit pants pockets and asked Julian, "You live here?"

"Yeah, I live here. My mother still lives in the neighborhood too."

"What neighborhood?"

"Where your parents live...lived," he said pronouncing his S's like a snake was translating his words for him. "Believe me, it wasn't my choice to keep it all undercover. I don't like to hide stuff because it always comes back on you in the end. I feel that way anyway. I'm straight forward with everything I do," he replied. Forward is probably the only thing his ass was straight with. "I guess our father thought it best we didn't meet," he continued pronouncing our like it was 2 words, ow-er and I could barely contain my anger.

I took a deep breath from my nose and ran my tongue over my top teeth before speaking...loudly. "Well, I think this is a really bullshit way for you to introduce yourself to us. Aunt Linda that's some disrespectful mess for you to have our father's long lost bastard son come sit on the front row with his widow and his children like that too. I know you don't like our mother and neither do we, but what the hell are you thinking about when you pull some crap like this at a funeral?"

People started to look our way and my best friend Ike came up beside me with his fiancé' Tara. "Yo' Brian calm down. Come out here and talk to me for a second."

"I didn't ask to be born and I have every right to show up at my own father's funeral and sit with the immediate family. I am immediate family whether you like it or not!" Julian shot back.

"Obviously he didn't want everybody to know one of his sons was a faggot ass faggot conceived by a jump off, so you should have played your position in his death, just like you did in his life mother fucker!" I yelled.

"Brian, stop it!" My Aunt Linda screamed. "You don't know what you're talking about and your being just as hateful and as..."

"Shut-up," I interrupted her coldly. "I bet your shady ass orchestrated this whole damn appearance to get to my mother. You're definitely your brother's sister. Even at her husband's funeral you're still trying to show her how much you hate her. And you wonder why me and Brenda don't mess with y'all side of the family," I taunted as Ike tugged my shoulder trying to force me to come with him.

There was a lot of ruckus going on around us. People gasping, questioning what was happening, random people telling me to 'Calm down' or saying 'Now that kind of talk is uncalled for!' but this bullshit needed to be handled.

Julian cut his eyes at me like many a woman had done right after I had called her a bitch, "Yes I am a homosexual. I am not ashamed by that and if it offends you, I'm sorry to hear that but if you call me a faggot again, this faggot is gonna kick your ass like you stole something. I can assure you that my sexual preferences had nothing to do with why our father kept me a secret," he rebutted stepping in front of Aunt Linda.

"Motherfucker, step up then! If there's a real man in there let his ass out!"

That's when the sissy hit me.

***

"Stop it! Stop fighting!" I heard my mother and other people shouting as Julian and I went toe to toe. "For Christ's Sake this is your father's funeral!"

My Uncle Tony and Ike were trying to break up the fight but getting between us was like playing hot potato. We were jabbing, moving and tagging each other like a welter weight boxing match. I had to give it to the little booty snatcher, he had some skill.

"This is disgraceful!" Some miscellaneous voice yelled before Ike was finally able to drag me to an opposite corner while Uncle Tony shielded Julian from a further ass whoopin'.

"You are just a closed-minded son-of-a-bitch Brian! What gives you the right to judge me? I have every right to be here for my father's funeral!" Julian yelled as tears ran down his face. "I didn't come here to fight you or insult you. You started this," he continued bending down to pick up an earring I'd ripped from his ear.

I wanted to bitch smack him for every non-masculine movement he made. My blood was boiling, and this fucker was standing here crying? Real men don't fucking cry in a fight!

"Linda why would you do this at your own brother's funeral? You think he would have wanted this? To have his family humiliated by you bringing his...his...love child to flaunt in all of our faces at his funeral?" My mother shouted to Aunt Linda through what I thought might have been real sobs this time.

"Well, you flaunted yours around our family while he was alive!" Aunt Linda spat back.

My mother gasped and said, "Keep talking and your brother won't be the only dead Andrews in here today."

"Whoa now ladies," Pastor Johns said coming between the women. "Now this is a house of God, and this is a time for mourning. All of this nonsense is not appropriate in this place, or at this time. We should all be heading towards the burial site right now instead of bickering. Olivia if I may, please let me escort you outside to your limo."

My mother didn't divert her knife wielding glare from my Aunt Linda's face for a moment as she replied, "Yes I know that Pastor but his little sister is apparently intent on making sure that she runs my husband's name in the ground before it's all said and done."

"Julian is his son Olivia. He has just as much right to be here as your kids do," Aunt Linda stated venomously.

"Who the hell are you to say what right he has to be here? Maybe if your ass spent more time worrying about your own business instead of medaling in your brother's, you would have a man and some kids of your own. What kind of sister do you think you're making yourself look like? Huh? You look pathetic!" I spat.

"Pathetic?" She hissed at me before returning to my mother. "You really want me to tell everybody Olivia? Should I let your son know..." Aunt Linda began just before my mother shoved Pastor Johns aside like he was a paper weight and smacked the rest of the words out of Aunt Linda's mouth.

They started tussling, grabbing hair, smacking, clawing and screaming grunt like words to each other. Julian pushed past my uncle and stepped in trying to push my mother off of Aunt Linda. Regardless of how I felt about my mom, I wasn't gonna stand there and let this dude or any other lay hands on her.

I broke free of Ike's grasp and caught Julian with a right jab causing him to tumble backwards into some miscellaneous chick that was at the funeral. From that point I was on him closer than those tight ass suit pants he had on, punching and choking him when I felt someone pulling me off of him by my neck. I instinctively tried to fight off whoever was dragging me backwards, but they were too strong and I was growing weak from all of the energy I exerted on my faggot ass brother.

"Be still boy!" My Uncle Donovan yelled at me. "Stop fighting or I'll choke your ass asleep!"

My Uncle Donovan was my Aunt Tonya's husband and once I heard his voice, I stopped struggling. He was a retired Linebacker who played for the 49ERS from 1984 to 1988. He stood about 6'4" with closely cropped salt and pepper hair and the build of a soft industrial refrigerator. He'd set me straight enough times through my life that I knew when it was between him and me...resistance was futile.

"Let me go Uncle Donovan. I'm calm," I protested trying to regain my footing as he pulled me outside of the church stumbling down the steps.

"Alright I'm gonna let you go. Don't you go running back in there Brian or I'm gonna put your ass to sleep," he warned.

"I'm cool, I'm cool!" I yelled as he slowly released his hold on me.

Once I was stable, I rubbed my neck where Uncle Donovan had me in the hold and glared at him. "Was that necessary?"

"What the hell do you think? What's a grown man doing fighting? In a church? At his own father's funeral?" He scolded shaking his head as he brushed away the wrinkles from his suit jacket.

"What you think I'm the one who started that crap? So, you missed the little faggot throw the first blow on me the first time huh? You didn't see that motherfucker and Aunt Linda trying to go in on my mother?"

"I saw a bunch of fools proving themselves. What faggot? Your new brother?" He said with a slight laugh.

"Ain't shit funny about that Unc. Really, I'm not laughing at all about that," I scowled.

"Grow up man. Y'all kids knew your dad was out screwing around all the time. I'm surprised a little tribe didn't show up here to claim him as their daddy. He looks like him. What's his name again?"

"Who?"

"Your new brother. What's his name?"

"Man Unc. Fuck his name! I'm not claimin' that ass muncher as my brother. He's long lost for a fucking reason."

"Stop cursin' when you're talking to me Brian. You know I don't like all that. Plus, we're at a church. How many people gotta remind you of that boy?!"

"Yeah whatever," I said touching the side of my left eye to see if it felt as bad on the outside as it felt on the inside.

"You being a dick about it isn't gonna change anything so you might as well just get over it. From the looks of things, your mother already knew about the guy anyway," he said pulling a box of tic-tacs from his jacket pocket and tossing some in his mouth. "You and your mother got in a fight at a funeral. I told Tonya your mother wasn't as timid as she claimed. I know the look of a caged lion when I see it and your mother had that look a lot. No matter how many times she got back with your father after they fought; I knew she had to snap out on him sometimes."

"This wasn't the time or place for it though Uncle Donovan," I snarled.

"Maybe not, but how many people in there do you think were actually surprised about it? Nobody ever bought the "good husband" act except your mother and even she wasn't convinced. God only knows how many of those women in there right now have a secret to tell about him. Listen Brian..." he said with a deep chew. "Your mother is not as innocent as she may seem. I'm married to her sister and I hear a lot they don't think I hear. No telling what else goes on that even Tonya doesn't know about."

"I never thought she was innocent. I'm not stupid. No woman is innocent," I answered. I took a deep breath and wiped the sweat from the top of my head but when I looked at the back of my hand, it wasn't sweat; it was blood.

"This mess with Julian ain't over though," I proclaimed.

***

I went and sat in the limo to wait for the family to ride to the burial site. My Aunt Linda was originally supposed to ride with me, Brenda, my mother, my Uncle Tony, his wife and their kids. There was only enough room for 8 people and if she tried to squeeze my long lost and tossed brother in with us, I was going to commence to whippin' both of their asses.

My Uncle Fred went to get my mother and the rest of the family while I sat to stew over the events and what my Aunt Linda had threatened. What secret did my frigid old aunt know about my mother that was so dirty my mother would knock the piss out of her for? The hatred between my aunt and my mother was rooted deep beneath the surface. As the story was told to me, my mother was the one who "stole" the love of my Aunt Linda's life (some photographer dude) away from her before my father took my mother away from him.

My mother was modeling at the time and met him on a shoot for a magazine. My aunt claims she and the guy were exclusive and that my mother slept with him even though she knew that he wasn't single. Let my mother tell it, my Aunt Linda was making it out like their relationship was bigger than it really was. She claims the dude told her that he was just casually dating and since my mom only knew my Aunt Linda in passing, as a make-up artist on set, she didn't see him as off limits.

I guess my mom and Aunt Linda got in a couple of heated arguments on the set and again at another public place before the dude put my aunt out to pasture. Months later, my dad stopped in to talk to my aunt on the set of a different photo shoot that my mom also happened to be doing, they started hooking up. Apparently, they were hooking up unprotected because they were headed for a shot gun wedding less than 6 months later and I was the little bundle of joy they got in return.

My aunt never stopped holding a grudge against my mom and my mom's usual tendency to bask in my aunt's discomfort only fueled the embers.

I reached in my back pocket and pulled out the mirror half of a broken compact case I got from my sister. A brother like me always had to be prepared. I still couldn't believe that fucking faggot tried to jump bad. Apparently, he's used to dealing with a bunch of pussies instead of a brotha like me. The motherfucker…correction, fatherfucker…fights like a bitch! As I looked at the cut on my head and under my left eye, my blood started boiling all over again. The asshole was probably trying to scratch my eyes out like most bitches do when they fight.

The other little marks on me would probably fade in the next 24 hours or so. He just didn't know how lucky he was about that. I definitely needed to give myself a facial to make sure I was gonna be back to normal. I'm the type of guy who tries not to treat the little fruit loops any different than the rest of the brothas I run into. Sometimes they take it too damn far though. I'm no homophobe but I'm not feeling their fruity pebble asses talking smack to me or trying to get at me.

The limo door opened, and my sister Brenda stepped one black pump fitted foot inside and held her hand out for me to help the rest of her get in. With her hair back in a tight bun, a sleeveless black dress and barely any make-up on, she looked like a pretty schoolteacher. I closed the door behind her, and she sat on the opposite side from me.

"What the hell was that?" She blurted out looking like she had been crying.

"Shiiiit…" I replied.

"Seriously. Has everybody lost their ever-loving minds? You and Mommy out here fighting with Linda and our damn brother at our father's freaking funeral; some big chested floozy just gave me daddy's watch and said he left it at her place the last time she saw him…" she said holding out one of my father's chrome plated watches between us before dropping it into her purse. "Pastor Johns is acting like he doesn't even want to go to the burial site now because of the ruckus you two caused, and now Uncle Tony and Linda are outside arguing. This is exhausting. I'm ready to say F all of y'all and get in my car and go home!"

I don't know why Brenda always called Aunt Linda, Linda instead of "Aunt Linda" but even as kids she never put the "Aunt" in it.

"Well fuck it then let's roll out," I said leaning toward her.

"I'm serious as cancer Brian," she said looking distraught and fingering the latch on her purse. "This is too much to take in for one day. It was hard enough for me to put my feelings aside for him and show up at the damn funeral and now it's turned into some kind of circus of dark secrets or something. Then when I asked mommy about Julian, she said she already knew?"

"When did you get a chance to ask her?"

"When I went in the bathroom to talk to her. She admitted that she's always known about him. It's like we were the only jack asses that didn't know we had another brother floating around Atlanta."

"Floating around is right. I'm mad he's a fucking flame."

"So, what Brian. Is that really all you care about? I wonder how many more we got around here. I got bitches walking up to me and handing me his stuff like they expect me to know them or something," she complained. "Our stupid ass mother had the nerve to tell me that no matter whether daddy had other kids out there or not she was always the queen and she could never be replaced in his heart. You should have seen how proud she looked saying it."

The limo door opened again, and Aunt Charlene helped the two kids climb in before she stepped up with a little of my aid.

"Tony is coming in a second he had to go to the bathroom," she said as she situated herself and the children in a seat on my side of the limo. "Scoot over a little closer to me kids."

I was both restless and anxious waiting for the rest of the clan to get in so we could go.

"Did everybody but us know about Julian?" Brenda began to probe her.

Charlene threw her hands up in surrender. "Listen this is a family matter between y'all, and I don't want to get involved in it. Especially with my children in here," she said. She was a short brown skin woman with neatly curled short black hair and cat slit eyes. The dress she wore was probably a size too big and the children's clothes looked like the iron at the house had gone on the fritz. Aunt Charlene and I always got along okay but I would never invite her to anything that required she display any style. She was clearly devoid of that.

"It's a simple yes or no question. Did you and Uncle Tony know about him before today?"

"Like I said Brenda, I don't want to get involved. I can't speak to what my husband knows or didn't know. I'm sorry for your loss and I understand that this is a big issue for you right now, but I don't want to be in this."

Brenda sucked her teeth, shook her head and said, "Let me out," as she immediately started shuffling her way over everyone to the door. "I'm done."

"I'm sorry," Charlene muttered almost inaudibly.

"Yeah, everybody's sorry," Brenda grumbled.

I opened the car door, helped her to get out and exited right behind her.

This was for the birds and we were flying the coup.

9

Brenda

THE SAGA CONTINUES

I intended to drive to my house, take off my funeral clothes and crawl in the bed, but I didn't. I didn't want to be alone and I didn't want to be in the company of my screwed-up family at my father's funeral. I was glad my mother had the funeral late because it was only a little past 6:00pm and Happy Hour was going on at most places around Atlanta. I needed a drink...bad.

I put the Bluetooth in my ear and voice called my BFF Rhonda.

"Hello," she answered with a sizzling sound in the background.

"You cookin'?" I asked driving the highway towards her house.

"Yes. Is the funeral service over already? I'm sorry I couldn't be there girl. You know they wouldn't let me out of that regional meeting if my life depended on it. I just got home about 20 minutes ago."

"No, the funeral is not over and believe me, you didn't need to be present for that hot ghetto mess. I didn't even want to be there anymore, so I left. Too much crap for me to digest in one day."

"What happened? Did your mother throw herself on the casket or something?"

"Hell, she probably did but I missed it if she did. I skipped before we actually went to the burial site. Those fools started fighting...at the funeral," I proclaimed leaning my elbow against the driver's door.

"Get the hell outta here! What happened?" She exclaimed.

I sighed and swallowed hard, "Damn I don't even know where to start. First my Aunt Linda snuck our illegitimate brother, named Julian, into the family row at the church. Then we find out he's probably a gay version of Brian." I said as Rhonda gasped. "Then Brian, my aunt and Julian got into an argument and the next thing I knew people were in a tizzy and Brian and Julian were fighting in the church lobby."

"Oh-My-God! Un-be-freakin-lievable!"

"Oh yeah but it gets better. I corner my mother in the bathroom and found out she's known about the kid for years. I didn't get a lot of details, but she knew. Then before I can wrap my mind around that, my mother and Aunt Linda were scrapping in the lobby."

"Get the H-E double hockey sticks outta here! Your mother?"

"Girl...it was a mad house in there and you know Pastor Johns was not ready," I chuckled a little. "I just couldn't take it anymore. Me and Brian were in the limo ready to go to the cemetery and I just changed my mind. I felt like everybody but me and my brother knew about Julian, plus there were too many of my father's ho's that had the nerve to show up like they were welcome," I complained.

"This sounds like an episode of GOSSIP GIRL or out of a LIFE-TIME movie or something. Unreal. I'm just shocked that Brian and your mother would be fighting people. As style conscious as she is and as conceited as Brian is, I thought he only fought girls," she said with a slight laugh.

Sad but true. My brother did have a bad reputation for chopping it up with women. He was pretty ruthless to both men and women, but he rarely pushed the envelope as far with men as he did with a female. I wouldn't call him a woman beater, because I knew what a woman beater was like after dealing with my father all of my life; but he would push and shove a woman without hesitation.

He didn't like to mess up his clothes or his face though, so fights were usually not his aim...although he threatened a lot. I don't know who won the fight between Brian and Julian, but Julian looked pretty disheveled when I saw him and Brian had cuts on his face that I was sure he didn't know about immediately. He really would have lost it if he had.

Brian distrusted pretty much everyone and sometimes even I didn't feel exempt. Unfortunately, my brother inherited a lot of my father's qualities, if you can call them qualities. Handsome...check. Arrogant...check. Cynical...check. Sarcastic...check. Merciless...check. Womanizer...check. Vain...check, check, and check.

I'd seen him go off before, yes, but it was usually just verbal, and I only knew of him hitting his college sweetheart who cheated on him. Whenever Brian bothered to discuss his romps with me, the disdain he expressed for the women at times was a little unnerving, however. His remorseless attitude reminded me a lot of the degrading way my father talked to me and my mom.

Now my mother's fight on the other hand was really the biggest shocker. My Aunt Linda and my mother had been brewing that fight for years already and I think my mom was glad she finally got a piece of that evil trick. I felt like she always handled me with a cold hand, so I refused to call her Aunt Linda and I rarely spoke to her.

From the looks of the two of them after the fight, I think my mom got the best of my father's little witch of a sister. Linda's poorly secured wig was ripped off of her head in the tussle and my mother made sure to toss it across the room. The slapping and scratching I saw was vicious but neither of them showed any visible injuries.

"Anyway, I need a good friend and a good drink away from my crazed family. Can you get out? I'm only about 5 minutes from your place," I coaxed.

"Yeah of course I can get out for you girl. I'm almost done with this fried chicken I was making for Paul. I'll put it in the warmer and be down in a hot second."

"Alright. I'll honk when I'm downstairs."

"Okay," Rhonda said hanging up.

When I arrived in front of Rhonda's apartment building, I parked in one of the visitor's spots by the entrance, honked my horn and moved my purse from the passenger's seat to the backseat. I hoped she wouldn't take too long to come down...I felt like a crack head needing a hit. I was all too ready to drown my sorrows away with alcohol and I was additionally agitated because I couldn't call Teddy for a late-night appointment. We hadn't spoken since he left for his appointment Sunday morning which was what I wanted; but there was still a part of me that was hurt he hadn't tried to.

Beyoncé's song "ME MYSELF AND I" started playing on the radio and I sang along like I'd written it myself. Eyes closed, belting out my best notes and shifting back and forth to the beat, I was startled when Rhonda opened the car door.

"Sorry to interrupt your performance Bey," she joked getting in.

I smirked and started the car back up. "Is FORK IN THE ROAD cool?" I asked pulling out of the spot and heading back to the street.

"Yeah, that's good. You remember Phil we met at Myrtle Beach? He's a bartender there so we might be able to get a little hook up," she answered while applying a fresh coat of lipstick. I nodded and flipped the stations on the radio once Beyoncé's song went off and an ignorant sounding booty shaking rap song replaced it.

"So, where's Brian?"

"I don't know. We didn't discuss it. You know he's a hot mess; probably went to go screw some miscellaneous girl he met at the club. I swear Rhonda, if you saw Julian you would think Brian was in disguise."

"Oh yeah? Well, I hope he doesn't act like him too, "she frowned.

"Too early to know but he's definitely more ready to fight than Brian is. They were saying he hit Brian first and you know how my brother is about his face."

Rhonda was shaking her head, "No offense, but I'm sorry I missed it. I still can't believe Miss Olivia was opening a can of whoop ass. I never would have seen that one coming."

"Yeah... my mother is full of surprises, isn't she?"

***

Rhonda and I found 2 open stools and sat down, but before I could put my purse on the bar, I felt a tap on my shoulder.

"Wow! I thought that was you," Alan said with a big white toothed smile hugging me.

Alan was a plastic surgeon in his late 30's that I'd met on the plane coming back from visiting my grandmother last summer. He was dark chocolate with a military style fade, two dimples and a muscular build. When he first started talking to me, all I could think of was how much he looked like an older version of the R&B singer Tyrese Gibson. He was an on and off thing while I pined for Teddy and he boasted about his practice or how he "took 'em to the hole" playing basketball at the gym.

We'd slept together a few times and I let him wine and dine me when I needed company, but Alan, was boring as hell. His conversation was boring, his breath was horrible, and the sex almost put me to sleep before it was over. Besides, he made me feel uncomfortable with myself every time he commented on one of my features or touched me. I felt like he was sizing me up for flaws that needed plastic surgery. I only did it more than once as a courtesy payment for expensive nights out. This dude and I were not on the same page, and I was turning the page on him now.

I managed a phony grin and fluttered my eyes to Rhonda when he hugged me.

"Heyyy" I feigned the same excitement.

"Hi, I'm Alan," he introduced himself to Rhonda.

"Hi. Rhonda," she replied looking behind the bar for the bartender.

"What's cookin' good lookin'?" Alan said diverting his attention back to me. "Funny running into you like this. You look amazing!"

Oh brother. His compliments always seemed contrived, but I figured it was a habit he picked up in his profession.

"Thank you."

"I'm here with a couple of colleagues for some shop talk. Would you and your friend care to join us?"

"No, but thank you," I answered hoping that would be the end of the conversation and he'd go away to buzz in their ears instead of mine.

"No? Okay then let me at least get you 2 lovely ladies a drink?"

"Thank you," Rhonda answered a little overzealously. Not that I wouldn't have accepted the drinks, but she almost answered before he finished his sentence.

A decent looking coco-brown bartender with her hair in natural curls finally noticed Rhonda and came over. "What can I get you?"

"Vodka Cranberry. What you want Bren?" She quickly replied.

I shifted my bottom jaw a little in aggravation at how thirsty she was acting and said, "Rum Runner please. Thank you, Alan."

"A Corona for me please," Alan said with his eyes still focused on me.

The bartender went to make our drinks when Rhonda pulled her cell phone from her bag.

"Hello?... Oh, hey baby. I'm at FORK IN THE ROAD with Brenda... I'll be home in a couple of hours...Paul says hello and he's sorry for your loss," she said to me.

"Hi and thank you," I replied as Alan conveniently stepped between our stools partially blocking Rhonda from my view.

"So again, you look lovely. You're not gonna break my heart by telling me you're here to meet up for a double date or something are you?" He questioned with a sly grin.

"No, I'm not gonna tell you that," I answered nonchalantly.

He paused with a frozen smile and looked past me at what I assumed was the table where his colleagues sat.

"Well, where are you headed when you leave here? Maybe we can...catch up," he asked running one finger across my thigh.

I laughed inside. As out of touch as he was with me, he couldn't catch up if I gave him a head start.

"Not tonight."

"Why not? You have other plans or are you just playing hard to get this evening? You know it's not often that our schedules mesh where we can actually get in some good quality time together," he said with a Cheshire cats grin as the bartender brought our drinks and he paid. "You know you gotta give me more time with you to figure out where this thing is really headed."

I couldn't bare that comment and actually laughed aloud. So now he was under the impression that this "thing" was headed somewhere and that he had control of it eh? Hilarious!

"You find that funny?"

"Alan I just came from my father's funeral and I have no desire to be around anymore dead bodies tonight."

Rhonda nearly spit out the swig she'd just taken and quickly grabbed a napkin to her mouth. Alan's blank expression with his plastered grin showed that he clearly didn't understand what I was saying...but Rhonda did. I'd told her about his snoozable sex game before.

"Are you being serious? You just came from your father's funeral?" He asked skeptically.

"Dead serious," I replied not being able to resist the pun.

"Oh, Brenda I'm sorry. I clearly had no idea," he began with his eyes darting back and forth between Rhonda and I. "Was it expected?"

"He drowned in the pool. Long story I'd rather not get in to."

He leaned in and hugged me before I took a huge gulp of the Rum Runner I ordered. "Listen sweetheart, if you need to talk or need me for anything just call me. I'm really sorry to hear about your father's passing. I'm gonna get back over there to my colleagues but..." he attempted to rub the back of his hand against my cheek, but I jerked away. "You know I mean what I'm saying right?"

I nodded and he turned to Rhonda. "Nice meeting you," he said. She smiled; he patted my free hand and walked over to his table.

I was so glad he'd bounced back over to his colleagues and out of my face. I downed the rest of my drink and quickly ordered 2 more from the bartender. No need in pretending I wasn't going to have at least that many.

"Whoa Nelly. Don't over-do the drinks or you're gonna have a killer headache to remind you of your mistake in the morning. I guess my 1 drink is the only one I'm having since you are clearly not planning on being in any condition to drive," Rhonda announced. "He's a lot cuter than I thought he'd be though Bren."

"Who is?"

"Alan."

I sucked my teeth. "Don't let the good looks fool you. He's probably his own most profitable patient. I started looking at him real close once when he was sleeping in my bed and I'm sure I saw some small scars where he probably had a face lift and maybe even a nose job."

"You're crazy. That man did not have a face lift. Did he? Naw, stop playing. I know he's a plastic surgeon and everything, but he doesn't look like he had any work done to me."

"Ooookay. Don't believe me then," I said shaking my head. "The point is for you not to be able to tell he had plastic surgery, if he did his job right."

"You find something wrong with almost every guy you date... except for Teddy that is. Old king ding-a-ling has your head all messed up. Plastic surgery or not, that man is fine."

The bartender was back with my drinks; I paid for them and took one to the head. When I put the glass down, Rhonda was glaring at me. "Brenda. I know you got a lot on your mind right now but if you keep chugging those drinks like apple juice...you're gonna regret it."

I doubted it. My tolerance level was a lot higher than she was giving me credit for. I rolled my neck in an attempt to relieve the tension in it and looked at the picture flashing on my cell phone as it began to vibrate. Teddy was calling.

I picked up my second drink and held it up for an air toast to Rhonda.

"Girl I can't believe you just talked that Negro up. It's cool though. Voicemail!" I exclaimed pushing the ignore button on my phone with a huge grin. "Don't underestimate me woman!"

* * *

Rhonda and I sat at the bar talking about what happened at the funeral in more detail, my thoughts about my mother's possible hand in my father's death and then onto Rhonda's ideas for her wedding next year. By the time 9:00pm rolled around, we were nearly talked out and I... was pretty wasted.

"Well alright girly. It's getting late and I told Paul I'd be home like 2 hours ago. Not to mention that you are lit," Rhonda proclaimed.

"Ok okay. Well let me just finish my fries and this last drink then," I pled.

"Alright. Hey, is that Lane over at the pool table?"

"Where?" I asked almost losing my balance as I turned toward the direction she was looking. "Yes, it is," I confirmed as my eyes soaked him in.

Lane was my brother's best friend Ike's cousin. We'd met at Ike's birthday party nearly a year ago and had gone on a few dates. He was 6'4" with an athletic physique, dark brown skin, low fade, a neatly cropped goatee. He reminded me of a finer and slightly darker version of Alonzo Mourning from the Miami HEAT. Interestingly enough, Lane played basketball overseas for 3 years but got injured and wasn't able to get back in condition to play.

He told me on one of our dates how he and his father would fix cars together and that he'd consequently become a skilled auto repairman. When he came back to the states, he opened up what had now become a very successful auto repair franchise throughout the Atlanta area.

"See now that is who you need to be dating instead of chasing after Teddy's worn-out ass," Rhonda said as she looked Lane up and down like the juicy stick of candy he was. I couldn't help but cosign with a nod. When she was right, she was right.

"Girl you ain't never lie. I'm about to go get my man right now," I proclaimed with a smile as my alcohol induced balls inflated.

I hopped off the bar stool, straightened my dress and strutted over to Lane who's back was to me, while he stood in conversation with another man.

"Lane?" I said tentatively resting my hand on his shoulder while I inserted myself slightly between him and the other man.

"Brenda," he replied with a broad smile and a hug.

"Oh, excuse me for interrupting," I apologized to his friend who seemed unusually amused.

"No problem," the other man said politely.

"Brenda this is my boy Doug."

Doug and I both nodded hello with a smile.

"It's been a minute pretty lady. Who are you here with?"

"Rhonda. She's over at the bar," I said gesturing towards her. Lane and Rhonda waved at each other and he turned back to me with his eyes scanning me from my shoes to my eyes where they remained.

"Well big boy I'm gonna get outta here," Doug interjected as he and Lane exchanged hand clasps. "I can't stay out like I used to anymore with the new baby. You know Viv don't play that. Nice meeting you Brenda."

I smiled and Lane replied, "I believe it. Alright well tell your brother to bring his ride to the shop on Peachtree and I'll have my guys check it out."

Doug nodded and made his way to the exit leaving me and Lane standing face to face. Or rather, face to chest.

"So how long have you two been in here? Or are there more of you?" He asked.

"No this was an impromptu sort of get together so it's just us tonight. We've been here for a few hours. What about you?"

"I've been here about an hour. I used to play ball with Doug in Spain, so we met up for a few drinks while he's in town to catch up. You look like you've been getting your drink on pretty good tonight young lady," he scolded jokingly.

I guess that would explain why he and Doug's smiles looked more amused than I expected. I wondered if I was looking like a pissy drunk hot mess, or a sexy drunk vixen?

"Oh-my-God," I replied biting my bottom lip. "You can see that huh?"

"Yeah, just a little bit," he chuckled. "Let me go say hello to Rhonda too. I don't want to be rude with her sitting over there all by herself and everything."

He put his hand in the small of my back and escorted me back over to the bar. I silently kicked myself for drinking so much. Although we'd only been on a few dates, Lane and I talked on the phone a few other times and exchanged emails. We seemed to be jelling well and I was never annoyed to see his number in my caller ID... which was not common.

"Hey," Rhonda said smiling and hugging Lane as he leaned into her sitting on the bar stool. She took her bag off of the stool for me to sit. Rhonda and Lane had also met at Ike's party, but she saw him more frequently than I did since her fiancé had become an employee at one of Lane's shops a few months ago.

"So, did you two set a date yet or are you still planning?" Lane asked her.

"Well, you know I've already got some dates in mind but we're still trying to settle on one," she joked.

"Oh okay. So, your girl here is a busy lady who rarely has her cell phone with her...or is that just what she tells all the guys?" He asked slyly gazing at me.

"Don't even get me started on her and that useless relic of a cell phone she has. Believe me, it's not just the guys that can't get her on it," she answered rolling her eyes at me and looking at her watch. "I hate to have to cut this short, but I told Paul we were getting ready to leave and I gotta get some things ready for work tomorrow Bren."

Uh...sorry but leaving a fine, sexy, virile man to drop my BFF off at home was not on my agenda.

"Girl you already know I'm in no condition to drive anybody-anywhere-except crazy," I answered with my eyes sensually fixed on Lane before looking at her. "So, if you drive us in my car to your house, how am I gonna get home? Even though I don't have to go to work tomorrow, I still need to get back to the house and I know you and Paul are not going to feel like getting your car, him following you driving me home, blah blah blah. Seriously...I'm not really ready to go yet."

Rhonda cut her eyes at me, looked at Lane and then back to me. We'd been friends long enough for her to understand my tricks, so she played along. "Okay so then what are you saying? I need to take a cab?"

"Well, if you want to let Rhonda take your car, I can take you home," Lane proposed rubbing his hand across his goatee as he returned my previous sensual gaze.

"How are you gonna get your car back then?" She asked.

"Just tell Paul to drive Brenda's car to work tomorrow and whenever she calls the shop for it, he can drive it to her house, and she can drop him back at your house to get his. If that's okay with you I mean," Lane replied. "I'm the boss so I guarantee he will have the time to do it whenever she calls tomorrow."

Rhonda twisted her mouth and laughed mockingly. "Hey if that works for you, it works for me. Hand me the keys so I can burn rubber outta here." I handed her the keys and she winked at me as I did. "Hot ass," she whispered in my ear before she hopped off of the stool.

"Alright well it was good seeing you Rhonda," Lane said as they exchanged hugs.

"Call me," Rhonda said to me before she headed toward the door.

Lane replaced Rhonda on the stool and I coyly licked my lips as the bartender asked, "Can I get you 2 another round?"

"Another Rum Runner for me please," I told him with a smile.

I definitely planned on taking Lane for more than 2 rounds after we left the bar.

***

We sat at FORK IN THE ROAD for another hour or so...maybe more, maybe less. I can only remember seeing him drink 1 beer, while I had 2 or 3 more Rum Runners. Hell, I didn't have to work the next day and all I wanted to do was drown my sorrows in an alcohol filled glass before getting some ass. Lane and I were debating the words to THE JEFFERSON'S T.V. show as he walked me up the flights to my apartment.

"I'm telling you she's saying 'took a lot of tryin' just to get up that hill'," I debated.

"She's saying 'tera-hein'... like terrain but she's stretching it out. I'm telling you, I watched that show all the time woman," he joked.

"Lane...seriously...tera-hein? Uh uh," I mocked while unlocking my front door and turning on the lights in my apartment.

Zeus came running out of my bedroom barking, wagging his tail and leaping in the air.

"Oh yeah I forgot you had a little rat dog. He's cute," Lane said rubbing Zeus's head.

"Rat dog? My baby is not a rat dog thank you very much. He is a miniature pincher. Don't make me sic him on you."

"I'm shaking in my shoes," he replied laughing. "This is a nice place you have."

"Thank you. And thank you for taking me home too," I continued walking over to him and passionately kissing him.

He was definitely caught off guard, but his lips quickly responded as he pulled me into his arms. I felt one of his hands caressing my back while the other slowly found its way to my butt cheek. It wasn't long before his third leg was also making his presence known beneath his pants. I slowly peeled myself from his embrace and brushed the hair out of my face slinking backwards towards my bedroom.

"You look so good right now baby," he said in a quiet whisper.

"I bet I taste even better," I teased.

A smile drew across his face and I could hear him lightly panting. "Is that the alcohol talking or you?" he asked slowly walking towards me with the focused eyes of a panther stalking its prey. "You're just saying whatever you feel tonight huh?"

"Both probably. You're looking too good tonight for me to beat around the bush," I replied stepping out of my heels one at a time and kicking them to the side. My panties were getting wet just thinking about how sexy his body probably looked underneath those clothes and what he was going to use it to do to me. None of our previous dates had gone past second base kissing but tonight he was going to hit a home run.

When I reached my bed, I began to unzip my dress from the back and he started unbuttoning his shirt as he approached. Once we were face to face, we started kissing again while getting out of our clothes. It was hurried but not frantic; and I was probably a little alcohol induced clumsy. I had barely removed my bra when I felt the warm sensation of his soft lips on one nipple and his hands cupping both my breasts in his hands.

"Oh God," I cried out tossing my head back and dropping my bra to the floor where my dress laid.

He continued to suck and caress as I slowly opened my eyes and looked at his now nude physique. His muscular arms were flexed, his abs were chiseled, his legs were large and toned, and his third leg was long and thick. Aye! His lips and tongue began to travel up to my neck and I felt the invisible hairs on my back stand up with excitement while I squirmed away to my bedside table to get a condom.

"I've wanted you for a long time," he breathed, now kissing my lower back and tugging my panties half off with his teeth while his hands scaled my body.

I rotated around to face him and pressed the condom inside one of his hands while I let my tongue and lips explore his inner neck. The enticing smell of his cologne fueled my thoughts while I worked my panties the rest of the way off with one hand, and began to stroke his erect muscle with the other. We started the passionate dance of kissing, rubbing and pressing against each other. We continued through heavy breathing and moan until Lane finally got the condom on and laid me down on the bed.

He stood up straight for a moment between my legs looking down at me and ran one hand over my stomach just as he slowly guided himself inside me with his other hand. I let out a series of deep, bliss filled breaths as my sopping box adjusted itself to fit his size inch by inch. Soon he was thrusting inside me and kissing me deeply with his arms pinning me down on the bed, and my legs wrapped around his back.

"Yes! Yes! Right there! Oh oh..." I cried out after maybe 20 minutes of our bodies snaking together like synchronized swimmers. I don't know if it was an effect of the alcohol or simply the euphoria the sex brought, but my orgasm was so powerful that my vision was temporarily blurred. I hadn't had a climax that deep with anyone other than Teddy in years.

Lane seemed to be trying to go even deeper inside once he heard my cries. His heavy moaning and the multitude of expressions on his face showed that he wasn't far behind me. Sweat dripped from his brow as his closed eyes slowly opened to gaze at me. "You feel sooo good baby. I don't want to stop," he said kissing me again as my heart began strangely fluttering like a moth under glass.

"I don't want you to stop," I whispered into his ear lifting up under him, kissing and moving so that I'd repositioned our bodies where I was now on top. He was long and hard as a rock and I was definitely going to have to put my back into it if I was going to ride this cowboy.

He kept his hands on my waist and breasts while his eyes followed my rhythmic movements with meticulous focus. It wasn't long before the control he had over his lower body was lost between the magic walls of my pulsating puss and he was groaning with pleasure.

"Umph..." he began between heavy breathes. "I thought...you said you didn't...want me to stop," he almost whimpered.

"I don't," I answered as he grasped me tightly and I felt his love muscle fill the condom inside me.

I'd collapsed on top of him for a few minutes afterwards, still kissing and caressing him until he decided to grab another condom from my bedside table. Round 2 was even more exciting and lasted nearly a half hour longer than the First. When we finished, my bed sheets were drenched and I was feeling like I might have missed my calling as a contortionist. We lay intertwined in each other's arms; exhausted and spent, looking up at the ceiling.

"Wow," he said between pants. "I don't know how you can still do everything you just did after all of those drinks you put away. You must drink like this a lot."

"Not at all. I've just had a hard day. Hell, I've had a hard week. I swear if I hadn't left...my father wouldn't have been the only Andrews getting buried today," I snickered as I brushed a wet lock from my forehead.

"What?" Lane asked with a disturbing jolt. "You were coming from your father's funeral...tonight?" His expression was a mixture of confusion and pity. "I'm sorry, I didn't know."

"Hell...don't be sorry, I'm trying to forget."

10

Brian

I woke up with a hangover that superseded any I could remember. My ribs were still aching like I had been a substitute body bag for Floyd Mayweather. I lifted the leopard skin sheets and saw that my beautifully naked body was still bruise free. That faggot ass Julian must've gotten better blows in than I originally thought.

"Hey brotha you finally rising from the dead huh?" Black Fox said leaping on the bed in an open space beside me.

I grunted as the screeching sound of her voice was making my headache even more. I sat up in the bed and eyed the room for my clothes.

"Boy you were tore up last night. Not too tore up for me to handle you though. Your head hurting?" she asked.

"You must be a genius on your day off huh?" I said getting out of bed and finding my pants in a pile beside it. "Get me some water or orange juice."

"Uh… you must be smoking crack or something. You didn't just get up all crabby talking crazy to me and then give me an order, did you?" she asked with an attitude. I could almost hear her neck rolling in her voice. "Because I don't get down like that. Look around asshole. You're in my spot."

I turned and gave her a hard look before picking up my pants and underwear and starting to dress. I wasn't in the mood for a whore to be acting like a princess or to argue the point.

"Now if you ask me nicely, I might get up and make you something to get rid of your headache."

"Nicely then. Can I get some orange juice?" I mumbled.

"That's better. Yeah, I'll get you some," she said getting back out of the bed and heading out of the room. "You're lucky I like you because your ungrateful ass should be thanking me instead of waking up with an attitude."

I turned and looked at her confused. When she returned a few minutes later with a glass of orange juice I must've still had the expression on my face.

"You don't know what I'm talking about do you?" she asked standing in a long housecoat which she let freely hang open to expose her naked body.

I shook my head no, as I sipped my liquid pain reliever.

She left me scanning the floor for my things and went into the master bedroom's bathroom. I heard her making noises around the sink and then she emerged with a tooth pasted toothbrush in hand.

"So, you don't remember showing up all pissy drunk at my doorstep last night?"

I paused, threw my head back and closed my eyes. Damn. Now I did.

I had the limo driver drop me off at my favorite bar ANDRETTI's in Midtown and hadn't thought about how I was going to get home until after I had already gone through a dozen or more beers. I remembered Black Fox saying she didn't have to work so I gambled on the fact that she'd be home. Given my waking situation, my gamble had paid off.

"Yeah... now I see it's all coming back to you," she chuckled going back into the bathroom.

"I remember coming here after I left the bar, but I don't remember anything I should be thanking you for. Not unless you're talking about your head game. Cause although I don't remember it specifically, I do know it's worthy of a 'Thank you'," I said smiling as I buttoned up my shirt and slid my feet into my shoes at the same time."

She took a few minutes to finish brushing her teeth and then emerge from the bathroom with a sassy strut over to sit on the bed. "I wasn't exactly here alone at that time of night and when I opened the door you didn't want to take 'No' for an answer. I had your boy over getting ready to relax and then you pop up at my door uninvited." Black Fox kept an even tone, so I didn't feel like she was upset I had come by; maybe not ecstatic, but not upset.

"My boy?" I mimicked as I stood looking at her, vague memories of the night's events came back to me.

She'd tried to turn me away, saying I should have called first and looking all half-crazy with her door cracked open. I wanted a warm body to take my mind off of the family drama I couldn't seem to shake from my thoughts and when I want something, I usually get it. I was determined not to be turned away no matter what motherfucker she had in her place, so I pushed her door open, grabbed her by the back of her head and kissed her deeply the way she liked it on nights we sexed each other.

She had her hair lazily piled in a clip above her head and was barefoot wearing loose fitting boy shorts & a sports bra. I used my free hand to probe her inner thigh and slid my fingers under her shorts and into her bare box. She started to pull away until 2 of my fingers found a sweet spot inside her that prevented her from doing anything but melting in my hand.

"Whoever you have in here can't get you off and make you wet like I do," I whispered in her ear looking deep into her eyes and licking my lips in the same motion I was moving my fingers inside of her.

"Oh... my ... GOD," she said slowly and dazed while her body jellied to my touch.

"Make him leave and let me spend the night tasting you," I continued pulling my fingers from her shorts, putting them in my mouth and sucking her juices off of them.

Her eyes widened like I'd just shown her the number key to the winning Lottery numbers and she quickly left me and went upstairs to her TV room. I heard talking between her and another man, the man making a plea in as macho of a way as he could muster, and her essentially shutting him down. Shortly afterwards I heard their footsteps coming back down to my level and I immediately recognized the 5'11", light skin guy in a sweat suit accompanying her. Tyler. One of Ike's groomsmen. Coincidentally, we'd butt heads before over a woman some years ago when I first met him at Ike's place and we'd never really gotten along since then.

"Yo', are you serious right now Fox?" He immediately said to her when he saw me. "I know this dude. We're about to be in a wedding tomorrow."

Her expression was callous, and she grabbed him by the hand and struggled to pull him past me towards the front door. "Well, that's nice. So, then I know you can leave without startin' no mess on the way out."

"What up player?" I said in a jovial tone. "What's a nigga' like you doing in a place like this?" I asked continuing to make myself laugh. Once again, I was going to get the girl, much like I had on our first meeting when I found out the side piece I'd brought with me to Ike's place was Tyler's current girlfriend. They'd gotten into a huge argument then; he broke up with her and she'd left out crying. I didn't follow, cause hell she wasn't my girl, but did continue to bang her out for months after the incident.

"I'm tellin' you, that dude ain't no God Damn Cop," he was saying as she hurried him out.

"I didn't say he was a Cop. I said he can help me get out of my problem with a Cop. Look don't sweat it baby. I'll see you tomorrow night at the bachelor party then." I heard a kissing sound, (likely on the cheek) and then him saying, "No baby, come on. We were just really getting to know each other and..." The door closed and Black Fox came walking briskly back to me.

"Look you better be ready to make this pink box scream for the next few hours for all that drama you just caused me Brian," she said grabbing my hand and pulling me through the house into her bedroom.

"So, what was he doing here? And what did you tell him?" I asked while I stepped out of my shoes at her bedroom doorway.

"He's just a dude I met at a party my friend Lex was doing a while back. We been talking on the phone and tonight he was coming over to prove he wasn't just talking. Until you showed up that is," she chuckled getting completely naked. "I didn't want to waste time with a new dude when I had a sure thing at my door. P.S... don't do this mess again."

"What reason did you give him for letting me stay over him? Something about me being a Cop?" I asked unbuttoning my shirt as I stumblingly approached her.

"What's with the damn interrogation? Talk to this pussy!" She demanded lying back onto her bed and spreading her legs open. "Since when did you start caring what I'm doing or what I'm talking about? Shut up and let's fuck!"

Hell, when she was right, she was right. So, I just shut up and did what she ordered.

***

Friday was going to be a busy day for me. First, I had to get back to my crib, relax for a minute, go to work, and then hit THE MAN TRAP with the fellas for Ike's bachelor party. After I got myself together, thanked Black Fox for her hospitality with a kiss & a hug and left out to head to my crib. While I walked from Black Fox's apartment and turned onto Piedmont Rd. I pulled my cell phone from my pocket and called Ike.

"Hello," Tara answered on the first ring.

"Hey this is Brian. Le'me speak to Ike," I replied.

There was an annoyed sigh and she said, "Hold on a minute. He's in the shower." Then I heard her call his name out loudly away from the phone.

"Why you gotta sound all annoyed that I'm even calling? You still mad I don't call to speak to you after all these years? I know it's hard to forget about the dick that got away and move on, but you're getting married tomorrow. You should be over it by now," I jibed.

"Go to hell Brian. You're a sleazy slime ball. You're a dick all day," she replied without missing a beat.

"So, you still think about my dick every day is what you're saying?"

"Shut up idiot. You can..." she began but then quieted quickly.

I heard the shuffling of the phone and then Ike's voice on the other end picking up. "Yo what's up man? I don't know what you said but stop riling up my baby. Where you been? I tried to call you last night after the funeral."

Ike was used to me and Tara bickering. We had an ongoing love/hate relationship. More love on her side and hate on mine, but I had to show him love for coming to my pop's funeral.

"Yeah, well I wasn't really in the mood to talk after that circus. Me and Brenda left outta' there early and I rolled over to Black Fox's place to get a little stress relief. Coincidentally, I ran into your boy Tyler. I guess he was about to get in her panties before boy wonder showed up and she chose door number 2 instead."

There was a long pause. "God Damn Brian. Black Fox from THE MAN TRAP?"

"Idiot you know more than one?" I asked sarcastically as I reached my destination.

"Aiight so what happened? I'm not gonna have to pull y'all off of each other tonight or at the wedding, am I?"

"Not me. I'm good. Your boy's the one who got kicked out the house. She told him some stupid story about me being a cop, or helping her with a cop, or something. I don't know she was too anxious to get at my magic stick to give details."

He chuckled. "Of all the people in the city you 2 bastards always end up trying to get with the same chicks. So y'all just dapped, and he left?"

"Hell no. She was walking him out the door and he was trying to plead his case. That was it. We barely spoke. I don't know why that dude is always trying to wife hoe's up, but he might need to reevaluate his dating plan."

We both laughed. Tyler was always bragging about his exploits whenever we were in same company, but so far, he was 0 for 2 that I could see.

"Alright well as long as there's no beef about it I'm good. Seriously though. You okay? Y'all were fighting pretty hard," Ike asked concerned.

"I'm a little sore and that faggot fighter scratched me, but you know I always bounce back. I'm just pissed off that we got exposed to his fruity tooty ass at the funeral like that. My Aunt Linda is messed up in the head."

"Yeah, your mom fighting her was definitely out of the blue," he said.

"Right!" I said in agreement. She'd shocked me too with the ferocity that she went after my aunt. "But kill it; I didn't call you to talk about the fight, I called to make sure we got our schedules on point. We got the tux shop, rehearsal dinner tonight and we got a bunch of VIP areas and drinks covered at THE MAN TRAP from 1am-3am thanks to my hook up with Black Fox. After that we gonna have to move to general population."

"Now that's what I'm saying. You gonna be into it? I don't wanna be insensitive about your dad passing and all."

"Man, I'm good. Don't worry about that. I'm ready to party."

"My best man takes his duties serious as a heart attack," Ike responded with an audible grin.

"I bet he does," Tara said snidely leaning into the phone to get her comment in.

"And that's the hag you're gonna marry huh?" I joked.

"Watch your mouth talking about my future wife motherfucker," he joked back.

"You know I'll have the Navigator gassed up if you need a getaway driver. Just say the words and I'll screech off out of there like NASCAR."

"Nah man I'm ready to get all of this stuff over with and make my queen my wife for life."

I grimaced while crossing the street to my STARBUCKS destination. "Cut that mushy bull out while you're talking to me. Sittin' here talking about, 'I wanna make my queen my wife for life'," I mocked. Shut that shit up. I'm taking you out to forget about that one pink kitty to experience a pleasure palace of pussies tonight. Don't bring that punk ass girly talk out with you."

"Boy you a fool. Hold on," he told me as I heard him briefly mincing words with Tara. "See now you starting some bull over here for me because you know she's standing right here and can practically hear everything you say," he returned complaining.

"Whatever. She about to get her bachelorette freak on too so tell her to shut up and sit down."

"Sounds like you trying to get me divorced before I get married," he partially joked.

I wished. "Alright man well I'm on my way into this STARBUCKS & then I'm gonna take my ass home. What time we gotta be to the tux shop?"

"2 o'clock," he replied.

"Alright," I answered.

"Later," he said as we mutually hung up.

***

When I got home, I went straight to the bathroom and looked in the mirror at the cut by my eye. It was already starting to heal but I could see I'd have to make sure I put Vitamin C on it regularly to ensure there was no scarring. I was sure that cat bastard Julian had intentionally gone for my face. I searched around under my bathroom sink for the liquid Vitamin C and put it out on top of the toilet seat. I'd put some on after I took a shower and let the grime from yesterdays and last night's events wash down the drain. When I got out the shower, I heard the faint sound of a Faith Evans song playing through the wall.

I guess Halle Berry next door was home too. I pulled some sweat shorts from the laundry basket of folded clothes near my bed. After I dried off and was about to go knock on the beauty with a booty's door when my cell phone rang. I saw Tyler's name on the Caller ID and my neck tensed. "What the hell does he want?" I said to myself. "Hello?" I said answering the phone.

"Hey what's up Brian, this is Tyler."

"What's up," I replied dryly.

"Umm..." he paused clearing his throat. "Yeah... I was umm... I was calling to check what time we're supposed to come to JAGUARS and be at THE MAN TRAP."

"Whenever you feel like it, I guess. Any time after 9pm for JAGUARS, your name is on the list; and we're going to the strip club afterwards."

"Oh okay," he said with a pregnant pause. "Hey man that was a little awkward last night huh?" He said with a phony laugh.

"I guess."

"Oh, by the way, my condolences on the loss of your father."

"Thank you," I answered with a bit of ice in my tone. I don't do small talk and if this punkass was beating around the bush about something, I needed him to spit it out so I could get off the phone.

"Umm...." he paused clearing his throat again! "So, what was that all about with you and B Fox last night? I mean I don't want to step on any toes, but I have been kinda moving in on that."

"I don't dick and tell, but if you wanna hit that and she's open to it, do you. We're not an item so my toes aren't even in walking distance for you to step on them homeboy," I chuckled cynically. I'm sure in Tyler's dreams he was man enough to frustrate my dating life but in reality... I didn't give that dude any thought.

"Nah man I didn't think y'all were a couple or anything, but I'm just making sure there won't be no hard feelings tonight if me and her cut somethin'," he also had a laugh of sorts.

I got the feeling he was hoping to upset me. He was probably still bitter about how his girl played him out to be with me. Too bad he could never get revenge on me for it either because there wasn't a woman alive he could sleep with that would upset me, except my sister, and even that might not do the trick.

"Alright well I'll see you tonight man. Do what you want. Believe me, I won't give a damn. Peace," I said hanging up before he could respond. Jealous guys are pitiful.

That brief call full of crap had already exhausted me so I decided against going next door and opted for a nap instead. As I lay down, I thought about what was to come in the future for my boy Ike.

My best boy was getting ready to be the latest lost in the battle. He was going to marry The Wicked Bitch of the South, Tara, and I was going to be expected to stand on the front lines while my boy laid down his weapon to be shot...but fuck it...who was I to tell somebody who wants to die not to commit suicide?

Tara's been Ike's girl on and off since college until he popped the question to her last year. I was surprised he'd want her to be Mrs. Ike Stringer after their history of drama...but he did.

Ike proposed to Tara during intermission at the play "A GOOD MAN IS HARD TO FIND" last year. He had to pull some major strings to make that happen and that bitch ate the public display of affection up like Jaws in a kitty pool. She cried, screamed and kept saying, "Oh my God, Oh my God, I can't believe it! This is such a dream come true! I can't believe it!"

I wanted to say, "Believe me bitch, neither can I."

Ike met Tara our junior year in college at the bookstore and his nose has been open for her ever since. She was a pretty Holly Robinson Pete looking, chocolate brown, long legged, 5'6" glass of water with an A-symmetrical style haircut and big gold bangle earrings. Fresh out of Brooklyn, New York with the shitty attitude to match. She used to be all up in my face just as much as she was up in Ike's face and I told him, "She's just a hood rat with big titties." But he didn't listen. She was always too loud, bossy and aggressive whenever I saw her, and I never liked the mouthy type. I was always tempted to put my hand over their mouths and smother them until they were quiet.

Somewhere during our senior year, he started dating Tara exclusively, but she was constantly flirting with me and I couldn't understand how Ike missed the disrespect. He always claimed I was taking her "playfulness" the wrong way. Yeah right. Of all people, I knew what a bitch looked like when she was throwing her pussy at me, and Tara...she had her pussy glued to a fast ball. I was dating Gabby back then, back when I was a lame, so besides the fact that Ike was my closest home boy and had only been dating her for 3 months, I wasn't interested. I thought I was in love with Gabby during our nearly 2-year relationship, but the weekend we broke up I decided to take Tara up on her offer to drown my sorrows.

I was still hot as embers about finding Gabby cheating on me, and Ike and I had gotten into a big argument earlier in the day when I made more accusations that Tara was making advances to me. Ike had left for an away game with the track team but when I got back to our apartment Tara was lying half-dressed watching T.V. on the couch.

I felt angry at the world and wanted to do something to show I was in control, so I chose Tara as exhibit number 1. All it took was a few compliments, me sitting next to her on the couch, and it was on like a light switch. We spent almost the whole weekend fucking in different places around the apartment and if I had to say anything good about her, I will say she's a good lay. I realized that weekend why Ike kept going back to her.

She worked her hips, mouth, and hands like a professional and she was definitely sexy...until she opened her mouth that is. I tried to keep her tired and spent that weekend so I wouldn't have to talk to her loud ass. She made sure she was up and out of the apartment before Ike got back that Sunday, but little did she know she was still... there in spirit so to speak.

When I heard Ike's '96 Volvo pulling up I sat on the couch and turned on a video I had in the VCR and drank a beer in my underwear. He came in the house, dropped his bags at the door and went into the kitchen without a word. I snickered and continued watching my tape, turning the volume up.

"So, you just up in here blasting porno movies at 3 o'clock in the afternoon huh dude?" He asked mocking me as he passed by on his way to his room. I could almost feel him stopping behind me once he realized what I was watching. What dude would be able to walk by a porno movie without taking at least one glance at it? Not many!

"What the… What the fuck is that? Oh shit!" He exclaimed rushing me from behind the couch and we began scuffling. "You been fuckin my girl mother fucker!" He yelled as we fought.

Me and Gabby used to tape ourselves having sex, and one of the times me and Tara were getting down in my room, I turned on the camera beside my television and filmed it.

"I told you that bitch was a whore and she wanted to fuck me you stupid ass bastard! I told you that from day one!" I yelled back just before he tried to put me in a sleeper hold.

We rolled around the apartment punching, kicking, elbowing and destroying things with our antics. We eventually got too tired to swing another fist, but I don't know exactly when the physical stopped. Either way, we kept slinging insults and curses at each other until he stormed out. It got really ugly to the point where we'd had another fight when he came back, and they called the police. I ended up moving out within a week and we almost got into it one other time at a campus party a few weeks later. It was hard for us to socialize because nearly all of our friends were mutual, and we could barely be in the same room together.

There was a lot of drama around campus and in our friend groups for months, much of which was not lost on Tara. Ike's sister Jackie caught Tara at the mall one day and beat her like a runaway slave on his behalf. It took about 6 months for me and Ike to be able to hang out with our boys without fighting and eventually we talked about what happened. There was a lot of machismo and one-sided logic at first, but ultimately I apologized and over time he forgave me. A real man always chooses 'Bro's before Ho's' and he did…back then.

Of course, that didn't stop him from rekindling his relationship with her 4 years later after he saw her at a Braves game. I don't get how a dude could ever forgive a chick who fucked his best friend while they were supposed to be together…but apparently Ike was cut from a different cloth. He forgave me because I was just showing him who she was, and he knew I was still gonna be his boy forever; but her? Something about her made him a glutton for punishment.

Dudes need to take notes from me on how to get what you want without having to give up your manhood.

***

I came outside to find my truck had been keyed on the driver's side and it read HERE'S YOUR AWARD BASTARD in jagged letters. Fuck! It didn't take a rocket scientist to figure out that the little red-headed bitch was the culprit. I really needed to start being more careful about these bitches because I hadn't bothered to save her number in my phone, and it was a good chance that it had been erased by now. I wanted to beat the freckles off that tramp, and I thought about how I was gonna find a way to do it the entire drive to the tuxedo shop. When I arrived, I trotted into the store because I was almost ½ an hour late for my fitting.

"Yo where were you driving from again? Siberia?" Doe-boy asked as I began talking to the seamstress.

"Aw get off my nuts fat boy," I responded.

"I'll be right back with your Tux," the seamstress said as she went to the back of the store.

After she'd gone, I said to the fella's, which consisted of Doe-boy, Ike, Nate, Fred, Mitch, Kyle, Tyler and Benny, "What's with the chick fitting us? They would never let a man be in the fitting room with a woman. They'd swear dude was trying to cop a feel or sneak a look."

Fred replied, "I was thinking the same thing because everybody else in here is a dude. Maybe she's really a dude. She's looking kind of masculine around the ankles."

"That's what I'm saying," Mitch said laughing. "I keep looking for the Adam's apple. Wait a minute...did you say the ankles? Who in the hell looks at ankles as a sign of womanhood?"

"No but it is," Fred protested. "Women have a... like a... like an hourglass kind of shape and men just have a thick sausage kind of thing. See like..." Fred said lifting up one pant leg and attempting to show what he meant.

We all stood looking at him in bewilderment as he went on to explain his ankle philosophy. The seamstress walked back in with my Tuxedo and a huge smile. "Okay now handsome; here's your Tux. You can change in here," she said opening a dressing room door for me.

"Thanks," I replied staring at her as I went in. I couldn't help but look at her ankles, thanks to Fred. Damn if they weren't some thick son-of-a-bitches. Maybe she was a man.

The fellas continued talking and joking with each other as I changed, and when I stepped out from the dressing room in my Tuxedo; I stood and posed in front of the mirrors.

"I don't know how you cats are gonna handle it; especially you Ike," I said.

"Handle what?" Benny asked.

"Being overshadowed by this fine ass specimen at your own wedding," I said flexing my muscles as all the guys moaned in disagreement. "You lame asses aren't even gonna exist once I get at the altar. Only reason Ike's gonna get any attention is because his Tux is white and mine is black like you numb nuts."

The guys let out a roar of laughter and Kyle pushed me playfully in the back. "Motherfucker you are delusional. Ain't nobody lookin' at your conceited ass. I'm sorry to tell you but you are not that fine. Last time I checked that modeling thing had fallen through. I got you beat on every level accept them female eyes dude," he said laughing as he and Doe-boy smacked hands.

Kyle was a little less than 6 feet tall with a dark brown complexion and a bald head. He worked as a personal trainer, so he was extremely buffed up. Anyway, you looked at it though, he couldn't look better than me if I lent him my face for the night.

"You wish Magilla Gorilla! I'm surprised you can talk without a neck anyway. Does RIPLEY'S BELIEVE IT OR NOT know you can do that?" I clowned as I posed at different angles admiring how handsome I looked in my Tux.

"Yo' you always on some bullshit," Tyler said laughing and patting me on my shoulder playfully.

"Yeah whatever," I said converting my smile back to a straight face.

Tyler removed the smirk he'd previously been wearing as well. "Oh, it's like that?"

"Like what? Like you're on my dick?" I replied.

"Man, to hell with you," Tyler answered with a finger pointed my way.

The seamstress came briskly into our area, "Uh gentlemen, can you hold the noise and the language down a little please?" She was grimacing as if it was hurting her to speak and she truly deserved to be smacked upside her head for the dramatics.

"Yeah, I'm sorry; we'll keep it down," Ike replied looking at all of us.

As I turned back to look at myself in the mirror, I tugged at the coat tail and smoothed some stray hairs in my fade down.

Tyler said in a lower voice, "Yo Brian you got a lot of nerve acting like you got a reason to be raw with me. You're the one who was doing my girl, not the other way around. Why every time we in the same room, you acting like..."

"Oprah! Oprah! I don't want to discuss it. Back up off me and pick your balls up man. We don't need to talk it out," I said cutting him off.

"Alright y'all calm the hell down now before we get kicked out. Can't take y'all no-damn-where," Doe-boy said looking like a sausage about to burst out of its wrapping. "We're here for Ike. Whatever this is, let it go."

"You need to have them let that jacket out so your stomach can let it go and your bellybutton won't leave an imprint on it."

The guys all laughed, except Tyler. "That's dirty man," Doe-boy replied. "I'm gettin' it let out damn it. Chump!"

"None of y'all asses could fight your way out of a paper bag so y'all all better chill out for my boys wedding," Mitch said buttoning his shirt.

"Shut up!" All the rest of us said in unison.

"Alright children cut the crap and let's get to the important stuff. What time y'all coming to get me for my bachelor party? You know it's the last night out for mini-Ike! But ain't nothin" mini about him." Ike said as the tension swayed and all the fellas began laughing again.

"You know we got Geronimo driving the limo again so it's every-body's night to get fucked up!" Mitch shouted.

"Shh," the seamstress said loudly as she came rushing into the room. "Gentlemen please. What else can I do for you?"

"Listen I'm sorry, we're pretty much done. My boy here needs you to let out this jacket a little though… right here," Ike said demonstrating on Doe.

"Yes, I'll handle that today and we'll have it ready for him by 10 tomorrow morning. So, nothing else?" the waif thin Chinese woman asked in a pleasant but hurrying tone.

"Well, I look fabulous so I can't think of anything that needs to be changed. Can you?" I asked sarcastically. I knew she couldn't have improved perfection.

She smiled, "Yes you do look very nice. I can't think of anything that could improve it. Well gentlemen, when you're finished changing, if you'll meet me at the desk, I'd appreciate it. Sir, if you'll leave your tuxedo at the Alterations Desk, we will have it fitted for you by 10 am like I said. Will that be all gentlemen?"

"Yeah, that's it. Thank you," Ike said as she walked away.

"Man, I don't think I've ever seen you so excited before," Benny said to Ike.

"Yeah, especially for somebody who's about to put a padlock on his nuts for life." Nate joked.

"Aw whatever. I've got a good woman and I'm gonna put her on lock while I have the chance. Mitch, I know you not getting in on this," Ike said as he walked into a dressing room booth.

"Naw man I ain't say nothin'. I'm happily married; it's these lonely ass single faggots that's hatin' on you."

"Who's lonely? I'm never alone unless I want to be, and I ain't a fag-got, punk!" Benny said laughing.

"My reputation speaks for itself. I've had half of them women y'all deal with as it is. If I haven't, it's because I either spared you or they weren't up to par," I said as I went in a booth to change.

There was a resounding sound of "What?!" from all of the guys.

"Negro please!" Benny said.

"You wish," Mitch said.

"You takin' this conceited business too far," Kyle followed.

"Bitch ass!" Nate followed.

"Gentlemen!" The seamstress shouted.

11

Brenda

FRIDAY'S CHILD

I woke up with my head in a corner at the bottom of the bed, my hair looking like I'd stuck my finger in a light socket, and one leg hanging halfway off of the bed. I sat up in the bed, rubbed my eyes, blinked away my blurry vision and tried to recompose my faculties.

Not only had the funeral turned into a battle ground yesterday but now I'd brought Lane home and humiliated myself. Lord only knew what he was thinking about me after I'd said and done everything. I got up to go to the bathroom and Lane nearly scared the piss out of me when he walked out.

"Whoa baby," he said stepping back. "I didn't mean to scare you. Good morning."

I chuckled nervously pushing past him and closing the bathroom door behind me. "Oh my God you're gonna make me pee myself," I said sitting hurriedly on the toilet.

"My bad sleeping beauty. By the way, your car's out front. I had Paul come pick me up this morning and I drove him to work so you're all set," he said leaning against the door.

When I finished my bathroom business, I washed my hands and opened the door to meet his gaze. "Thank you," I said while we stood face to face. "You gonna let me pass or are we at a stalemate?" I joked.

He smirked and let me past him. I was glad to see he had stuck around. He'd either had a change of clothes in his car or he'd gone home because he was now wearing jeans, a black buttoned-down shirt, black Dock Martens and smelled like an ocean breeze.

"I stopped at my crib on the way back and picked up a change of clothes and a toothbrush," he said displaying the toothbrush in his hand almost on cue. "You feeling up for some company today since you're off? Or do you have plans?"

I was stunned into silence. Wasn't it usually the woman who was trying to lock the guy's time down after a spontaneous romp? Not that I was complaining, just surprised.

"Uh, yeah," I replied finger combing my hair and pulling my bathrobe from behind my bedroom door. "I would like your company."

"No pressure if you're not up to it Brenda. I just thought..." he trailed looking around self-consciously. "Were you really coming from your father's funeral last night? You were kind of incoherently talking to me after we did our thang."

"Our thang huh," I said smiling sitting back down on the bed where he joined me. I cleared my throat and looked him in the eyes. "Yes, I had just left the funeral of my asshole father, discovered I have a half-brother, upon whence my other brother commenced to whoopin' his ass while my mother fought my father's sister. It was quite the Jerry Springer episode, so I went out for some drinks with Rhonda."

I was sure this kind of talk wasn't giving Lane visions of wedding bells in his head, but he asked and I told.

His staggered expression quickly turned into a huge smile exposing his freshly brushed pearly whites. "Wow girl. You have a comical comeback for everything. I don't really know what to say to that. So, do you even remember what happened here last night or did you drink enough to forget everything?"

"Of course, I remember what happened last night Lane. There were plenty of unforgettable things about it. Although I may have been drunk..." I started.

"May have?"

"Okay, I was drunk, but I knew exactly what I was doing and who I was doing it with. Although the timing might have been a little crazy, it's not like we didn't already have some previous chemistry. Don't you agree?" I asked nervously brushing an out of place hair from my forehead.

Zeus was jumping up and down by my feet at the end of the bed wagging his nub so hard that his entire backside moved with it. "Get down," I scolded.

"Yeah, I think we do. It's just rare that we've been able to catch up with each other. Me with my business; you with work and whatever other extracurricular activities you've been occupying your time with."

"Seriously Lane? So, you're gonna act like I'm the one who's always busy?"

"Are you still seeing that guy Freddy?" He asked to the point.

I jerked my head back a bit, surprised by his question. "You probably mean Teddy and... what in the world...why...who told you about him? Ike?" I could barely get my question out.

"You didn't think my cousin would fill me in on going out with his best boy's sister?" he asked stroking his goatee and looking me in the eyes.

"No, it's not that. It's just that everybody doesn't always know what they're talking about," I replied a bit defensively.

"Alright so then you tell me what the deal is. I heard you've been on and off with him for some years and you fill the void with random dudes like myself while y'all figure out if you want to be together."

"Well damn, Ike said all that? What's he been reading my diary or something? 'I've been filling the void with random dudes while we figure it out.' Really?" I mimicked with an attitude. Not because Ike wasn't right, but because I didn't appreciate him analyzing and relaying my dating disposition to Lane in that way. No telling what bullshit Brian had told him about what he thought of Teddy and me dating.

"Hey, I'm not judging you Brenda. As you can see, I must've been asking about you though right? I just wanna make sure I know my position before I accept the challenge. I'm a straightforward type of guy if you haven't figured that out yet. I like what I see to be what I get, just like what you see is what you get. If last night and today is as elevated as we're gonna get because of that dude or somebody else, I'm good with that. I just want it to be clear," he said kissing my lips softly.

The sweet touch of his lips to mine quickly lightened my attitude along with my bewilderment at his straightforward approach. I wasn't even sure how to deal with such an unusual animal.

"Okay well the facts are that I've been dating whomever I want to whenever I want to. Me and Teddy don't see each other anymore because I'm ready for a relationship that's going to lead to marriage and he's not. What about you? Any females waiting in the wings for you?" I was halfway expecting him to spontaneously combust when I mentioned marriage, but he didn't flinch.

"I date when there's a woman I'm interested in, but I don't have anybody special that I've been seeing regularly."

"Really," I said skeptically. "So, there's nobody that's gonna be blowing up your phone if you don't call them while we hang out all day?"

He smirked and lay back on the bed. "You used to dudes playing games huh?"

I looked back at him and felt self-consciously transparent. Didn't they all?

"What you gotta Google me or get references to believe what I'm telling you or something? I'm free as a bird to do what I want whenever and with whomever..." he began grabbing me and pulling me on top of him. "I choose. I'm not so sure about you though. You got a little touchy when I brought up Freddy."

"Teddy," I said giggling. "And no, I didn't."

"Well, whatever his name is," he replied sliding his hands under my robe and cupping both butt cheeks.

"It doesn't matter."

"Prove it," he said kissing me deeply as I brought my hands around holding his face.

I planned to.

***

Lane and I were connecting like we'd known each other since childhood. After our morning romp we showered together, made brunch and talked about everything from my aversion to men with hairy knuckles to his fear of dating a woman who he'd later discover was born with an Adam's apple. We took Zeus for a walk in PIEDMONT PARK and broke out the lawn chairs he had in his trunk to enjoy the weather. We spent most of the time laughing, kissing and digging into each other's history. I felt a comfort level with him that I hadn't felt for a man in a long time. He seemed to be an open book, but that, for some reason, made me even more uneasy than typically having to decipher the Morris Code of men's intentions.

"So, you said you and Brian just discovered you have a brother? What's the story with that?" Lane asked.

I took a deep breath before answering. "Hell, if I know. We didn't know he existed until we saw him at the funeral. My father was quite the ladies' man when he was alive. Brian actually got a lot of his looks and attitude from him."

"Oh yeah? Brian is definitely a character. I've only met him a few times but he's definitely a confident kind of guy. I don't know how Ike is marrying Tara after his best boy has been with her but... he's in love."

"Yeah, I gotta cosign with you on that one. I couldn't forgive that either if I was Ike. She must have that Fiya' kitty action."

"What?" he exclaimed playfully nudging me. "Chicks be thinking like that too?"

"Hell yeah," I said nudging him back. "Women can spot a tramp and her antics way before a guy can."

"Are you calling Tara a tramp?"

"No... I mean... no," I said feeling caught. I guess I was.

Zeus was chained to a stake in the ground in back of us and when he started barking, Lane and I both turned to see why and saw Edwin approaching.

"Hey! What are you doing here?" He said approaching with a huge creepy grin. The hairs on the back of my neck stood up and I cringed to see him.

"Chillin' with the dog," I mumbled rolling my eyes.

"Yeah okay. I see that. What's up bruh, I'm Edwin," he said to Lane extending his hand which Lane shook.

"Well, this is interesting," he continued awkwardly shifting from one plaid pants leg to another along with his eye contact. "Is this a date?"

Lane's eyebrow raised and he kneaded my thigh, "Yes, it is Edwin. Don't let us keep you from anything."

"Oh no you're not keeping me from anything. In fact, I was meaning to check up on you. Wasn't your father's funeral yesterday? Wow, you really seem to be handling his death well. I bet Lane here is helping you get through this hard time huh?" Edwin answered eyeballing Lane.

"Yo' my man, I'm not really sure what's up here but..." Lane said in a posture which looked like he was ready to pounce. "I'm not sure I really like how you're approaching us right now."

"Edwin, I think you know you're interrupting, and you and I have already discussed you giving me my space soo..." I said leaning forward myself.

"So now I'm just supposed to ignore that you're out with another guy right in my face? It's one thing to cheat on me behind my back, but now that I see it up close and personal... Wow, this hurts!" He said clutching his chest and pacing in front of us.

I couldn't believe the theatrics and I could only imagine what Lane was thinking. He wore an aggravated expression and said, "Brenda you need to let me know what's up here cause..."

"No, I don't!" I cut him off exasperatedly. "I've been telling this dude to leave me alone for weeks now and he keeps popping up every-damn-where I am talking crazy like we're Ashford and Simpson! Edwin c'mon with the bullshit already!"

Zeus started barking when my voice raised, and Lane stood up making the height difference between him and Edwin extremely noticeable. Edwin abruptly stopped pacing and said, "It's okay Brenda. I see what's going on now. I see how you are. You're just gonna toss me to the side like an old banana peel, right? To hell with my feelings and to hell with everything we could have had right?" he proclaimed chronically nodding his head.

"What?" I replied with a confused scowl. "What world are you living in?"

Edwin didn't respond he just stormed away still clutching his chest and mumbling what were probably derogatory statements about me under his breath.

Lane turned his attention to me with a vexed expression, "Alright so what the hell was that all about?"

"Listen," I said pulling him back down to sit in his chair. "Edwin doesn't have all of his marbles. We dated a few times till he started getting too obsessive, like pulling stunts like today with me. He was showing up places, calling me all the time, just ridiculous stuff. I cut him off and apparently, he was making way more of what we had than what existed. I've told him the last 3 times I've seen him that I want nothing more to do with him and it goes in one ear and out the other. Seriously," I pled.

"Brenda don't have me out here looking like some kind of idiot with dudes you fuckin' wit' steppin' up like he's got balls of steel on me. I told you I'm not about playing games and if this is the type of stuff you're used to then..."

"It's not the type of stuff I'm used to dealing with Lane. Maybe he went off his meds or something. I don't know but c'mon now. You can't be mad at me for what the next man does."

We sat with our eyes locked for a few seconds and then he said, "Alright. Let's get out of here. I think it's pretty clear the picnic is over."

I wanted to yell, "Before it even started!"

***

Lane wasn't particularly talkative on the way back to my place and although I did make a few attempts to draw him back out of his shell, I started to become aggravated the longer he brushed me off. Once we were back by my place, I definitely was a little huffy when we got out the car. As I was gathering Zeus and my bag from Lane's Aston Martin, Kelly was on her way up the stairs to her apartment.

"Hey Bren," she said stopping midway and turning to face me. "Girl! Your brother better slow his roll cause these women are starting to close in on his ass. Oh, excuse me, hi," she said acknowledging Lane.

Lane nodded with a faint smile and I put Zeus down as I approached the stairs and we both started walking up with Lane behind us. "What's that mean?"

"It means some chick keyed his car, which his neighbor Nadia saw was some white chick, and Gwen keeps showing up, waiting in her car for him and crazy stuff like that. He's been slipping because he usually doesn't let these freaks know where he stays but lately... oooh child they have been showing up and showing out!" She said as we reached our floors landing.

"Oh boy," I said rolling my eyes. "Must be a family curse. You didn't see Edwin hanging around here today, did you?"

"Edwin?" She asked with a raised eyebrow. "Oh wait, the bald headed dude? No, I didn't see him today. Hey, I'm Kelly," she said putting her hand out to Lane when we all reached my apartment.

"Lane," he said smiling politely.

"Alright Cuz, I'll check you later. I might have a date!" she said excitedly as I waved goodbye.

Once we were inside, I sat down on the couch and Lane stalled a bit at the door before following suit.

"It's okay if you changed your mind about hanging out for the rest of the day. It was nice. Thank you for spending time with me," I said drably grabbing the remote and cutting on the television.

"What? Is that your way of sending me home?" Lane asked with furrowed eyebrows.

I didn't respond, I just rolled my eyes as he came in and went into the kitchen and played my messages as I went to the refrigerator to pour myself some water.

"You have one message.

"First message 2:39pm:

"(Sound of someone clearing their throat) Uh yeah, Brenda, this is Edwin, but you probably know that since you're still not answering the phone. Umm, I wanted to apologize for the scene at the park. I was caught off guard, maybe a little jealous. I know you wanted some space for a minute, but I still don't think I deserved to be treated the way you did me. Now that I'm thinking about it, I guess I was a little out of line. I need you to call me so we can discuss where we are now because I'm a little confused and I don't want to break up with you without giving you a chance to explain your side of things. (Pause) You know I hate talking to these machines."

All I could think about was what a psycho I had gotten myself wrapped up with. He didn't like talking on machines? I sure as hell couldn't tell! I had already told this moron I didn't want to see him anymore. Why couldn't he just leave me alone!

He continued, "I came to your place this morning, but your car wasn't there. I was thinking you might want a comforting arm around you after the funeral. You know I would have come with you if you had asked. But then I guess it's hard to ask someone to come somewhere with you when you want space huh? (Chuckling) You know sometimes..." the machine cut him off.

That long winded imbecile was annoying, and when I looked at Lane, he had a stern expression.

"I told you he's crazy," I said walking over to the couch he was now sitting on. "So now you're mad at me huh?"

"Why would you think that?"

"Because you seem to have flipped a switch since that whole thing at the park. I don't know how to turn it back on since I didn't have any control over it anyway. Honestly, between my father's dying, the funeral, this damn guy stalking me and all of the other stuff I have ahead of me to do, I'm not up for being on the defensive today."

"I don't know what guy wouldn't have been upset by that bullshit today, or what guy wouldn't be wondering what lies ahead for the future if we continued to see each other, but I'm the guy that does these things. We've been out before and you've always been a little bit unattainable which I was cool with. I like your style; I like your personality and I like you. But..." he paused sighing and clasping his hands in his lap. "I gotta make sure I know what I'm getting myself into here."

"Getting yourself into? Really? Listen I'm not a project and..."

"Don't go taking it all sideways Brenda. I'm just saying that I've had feelings for you for a while now and last night we took it to another level. You know I used to play professional sports, done a lot of traveling and I'm working hard on my businesses now so I'm sure it's no secret I've got a past just like you do. I just gotta know I'm not gonna be willing to put all of that aside to see where things go with you, only to get played for that Teddy dude you keep flip flopping with or some other guy."

I had mixed emotions. On one hand I was excited to hear him admit that he really liked me because I was feeling the same way; but on the other hand, I was irritated that he was acting like I'd damn near cheated on him after only one day of the freaky sneaky.

"Well, I don't know what I can say to reassure you that I'm free. We did just start seeing each other last night so I haven't exactly had enough time to set my little black book on fire but neither have you," I said wiping a small bead of sweat from my brow as I crane necked at Lane.

A slight smile began to spread across his face. He leaned in and kissed me deeply. I was confused and pleasantly surprised all at the same time.

"What's that all about?" I said breaking space between us.

"You got me over here feeling like I'm switching rolls with you. I'm the one trying to get our status clear all quickly and you're the one being all nonchalant about it. I'm humbled just a little bit by you girl, but I'm gonna go out on a limb and just take it day by day. What I know today, is that I want you and I think you want me too," he said with his beautiful face inches from mine and his fingers on my cheeks.

"That I do," I said melting in his hands. Just as our kissing was getting more passionate... the phone rang. We continued our tongue tag session until it went to voicemail, but the caller hung up and called right back.

"Sounds like somebody is really anxious to speak to you," Lane said slowly letting me up for air. "Maybe you should get that."

I sighed, pushed an out of place hair from my face and picked up the cordless from its cradle by the couch just as the caller hung up and Edwin's cell phone number stopped flashing on my caller ID.

"Oh well," I said smiling slyly at Lane, intending to continue where we left off. He smiled back at me but got up from the couch.

"I'm sorry girl. We been out all afternoon and nature's calling," he said leaving me and going into the half bathroom near my dining room.

I inhaled a deep breath of relief and allowed myself to hope that things with Lane and I would eventually blossom into the relationship I used to dream of having with Teddy. Zeus jumped up onto the couch and lay in the spot where Lane had been sitting with a guilty wag. He knew better, but I suppose he wanted some love too.

When Lane came out of the bathroom he playfully glared at Zeus. "Oh, so I've lost my seat huh?" He asked as Zeus wagged his tail but didn't move. "What time you about to start getting ready for the bachelorette party?"

"Damn I almost forgot about that," I said honestly. I was enjoying my time with Lane so much that I was already planning the rest of our evening in my head. "I guess in a couple of hours or so."

"Okay that sounds like enough time then," he said approaching me.

"Enough time for what?" I asked as he picked me up from the couch and headed towards my bedroom.

"For me to reiterate how much I like you," he replied with a seductive grin.

"Show me!" I yelled excitedly.

12

Brian

HERE COMES THE BITCH

THE MAN TRAP was ridiculously full when we arrived with the groom to be. At least half of the guys there were friends of mine and Ike's; and we were going to make his bachelor party the best one anyone had ever been to. Ike's face lit up when he saw all the people who were there and the banner, they let us put up which read, GOOD LUCK ON YOUR JOURNEY TO HELL! My idea of course. The women knew who Ike was and they knew that he was supposed to get special attention all night long. I already took up a collection from the fellas and I'd paid 5 of the girls working $200 a piece to make it worth his wild. They would of course still get tips all night long, but that was just to make sure that they gave it their best.

Black Fox had gotten us hooked up with 2 bottles of Grey Goose and we got 1 large VIP club room exclusively. I was looking dapper as ever in a black stretch muscle shirt and black slacks with black alligator shoes. Everybody else tried to compare, but obviously they fell short. Black Fox was also one of the dancers getting paid to entertain us; of course, I already knew what she could do. We made up pretty easily after our little argument a while back. Shanghai was the most popular dancer at the club, and she was selected especially for Ike. She was a tall busty Chinese and Black chick with an ass that could hypnotize a thousand men. She was most famous for popping that ass on a handstand while she sucked a beer bottle with both sets of lips. Ike always talked about it nonstop whenever we saw her do it.

I went to the DJ booth and got on the microphone. "Alright, alright, alright! Tonight, is my boys last night of freedom before he ties the knot. We brought him here tonight so he can have one last memory of all the beautiful women he's gonna be giving up. Now this is my best friend in the whole world, and I want y'all to show my man the best time he has ever had tonight. Pussy poppin' and all that!" I said as I gave the microphone back to the DJ and everybody in our group roared. I got down from the DJ booth and gave a few pounds to my boys who were standing near the door. I saw Ike getting a glass of Grey Goose from the large, reserved table in the middle of the VIP room. TaTa, known for her bodacious tata's, was dancing on the table when I got there, and dudes were sticking dollar bills in her G-string like it was a money machine.

"Yo' man, enjoy," I said in Ike's ear as I pat his back. He turned around with the biggest smile on his face I ever remember seeing and hugged me. "You are my brotha," he said. I wished.

I pushed my way through the crowd of dudes and some women scattered about and got closer to the stage. This was one of the times where it paid to know some ex and current professional athletes because the dancers were scrambling to get in here and show off their best pole work to get the big dollars. I was glad Ike and I had always stayed close with dudes from college cause many of them went pro.

Black Fox and another chick I didn't know with caramel skin and long curly blonde braids down to her ass were sliding down the pole together with their legs locked. I envied the huge panther tattoo that traveled from one large ass cheek down "Blondie's" thigh. Damn they could come up with some creative moves on that pole! "That's what I'm talking about," I said as I stood in between Doe-boy and my boy Carl.

"Hell yeah!" Carl said holding out a $20 bill. The girl came slithering over to us and took the bill in her mouth. She rolled over and did some provocative moves and then shook her ass on turbo speed in Carl's face.

He stuck his face in between her butt cheeks and made a blowing bubbles sound with his lips.

"Hey! No touching the girls!" Security yelled to him.

Carl jumped back laughing with hands in the air. "My bad, my bad. I just had to do it once though bruh. I know you know what I'm sayin."

That brotha was too wrapped up. Me and Doe-boy looked at each other and cracked up laughing.

"Dude now yo' face smells like straight bu-dussy!" Doe-boy yelled. When the stripper moved to the next dude holding bills out, Carl turned to us with a big Cheshire cat smile and said, "Sweet!"

We shook our heads.

I worked my way through the club all night getting lap dances and such, passing money to Ike to give to the strippers and laughing it up with my boys. It was a mad house and Ike was so pissy drunk that I could barely understand anything he said. On my way to a private VIP room with a stripper, one of the groomsmen, Kyle, came up and grabbed me by the shoulder. "Hey B., your boy Tyler is drunk off his ass and he drove himself here. I tried to get him to give me his keys, but I don't really know him that well and he wasn't trying to hear me. I don't want to bother Ike with all of this, but somebody needs to look after him. You wanna see if you can get him to hand the keys over or get him a cab? Maybe one of us should let him have our spot in the limo?" he asked.

"Man Kyle, he's a grown ass man. If he doesn't have the sense not to drink and drive, I can't make him. Don't be fuckin up Ike's night with that guy's problems either. Tell him he can ride with us in the limo if he's willing to wait a couple of hours because we're not ready to go yet. If he doesn't wanna do that, I don't know what else to tell you. I don't babysit grown men," I said as Porsche, a white double D cupped brunette began tugging my arm.

"Aiight well, I'll see what he's gonna do. I got him to sit down for a minute while I was looking for you & Ike," Kyle said looking disturbed.

I threw the 2-finger peace sign up behind me as I followed the sway of Porsche's hips into the other room.

After I got some head and paid her a mint for a job well done, I stumbled out and went to join everybody & Ike. He was lying with his head down on the table at one of the booths and Fred was sitting next to him with his head back passed out. Damn these brotha's was getting too old to hang, I chuckled to myself. After releasing all my kids into Porsche's gut, I was starved, so I ordered some chicken fingers and a beer to wash them down. I ate and watched the strippers along with the rest of my boys while Ike and Fred drunk-snored in unison. I was happy the wedding wasn't until late afternoon the next day. I went around the club rounding up everybody who came with us in the limo and let Ike lean on my shoulder to walk his drunk ass out to the car.

The fresh air seemed to revive the dead and suddenly everybody had a lot to say. "Did you see how that bitch was all over me? She wanted me man. You can't tell me she was suckin' it like that just for the money," Benny, another groomsman told Doe-boy.

"Man whatever. That ho was suckin' dicks like they were oxygen sticks. You ain't anything special. If you had the money, she had the Jaws of Life. I can't understand y'all idiots letting these skanks suck on your dicks. For money at that!" Doe-boy said laughing.

"Hell yeah I do. All of them need to be at the head of the class! I'll pay for it if it's gonna be that good," Fred said cracking himself up laughing as he fell sideways on the seat.

"Some of those women in there make you wanna drink their bath-water. That Black Fox...umm umm...she was love-ly," Kyle homed in with a Cheshire cat grin.

"Man, I've never seen so many big titties in one place in my life! I love Atlanta!" Mitch proclaimed. "I might have to get my wife a pair."

"Y'all lame asses," I joked. I had been drinking but I was starting to sober up.

Ike said something incoherent and we all burst out laughing at his slurred drunken vernacular. Fred was gonna be the first drop off but as the driver got closer to the street where his house was, there were 2 police cars with flashing lights on the side of the road.

"Yo' what's the deal?" Fred said rolling down the window and sticking his head out. "Looks like a crash or something," Mitch said hunching overlooking out the same window.

We all rubber necked while what little traffic there was moved slowly.

"Hey that looks like Tyler's car," Doe-boy said squinting. "Is that a red Mustang?"

"Yo' driver! Stop the car my man!" Mitch yelled out to the limo driver as the car came to a complete halt. "Yeah, that does look like his car," Mitch cosigned.

"Ike is that...never mind he's passed out. Brian is that Tyler's car?" Fred asked turning toward me.

I shrugged since I hadn't actually seen the car yet.

"What? Tyler's car?" Kyle repeated as he moved Ike's passed out mass out of his way to get a better look.

I leaned so that I could see past Doe-boy and Mitch who were crowding the window nearest me and saw two Paramedics taking an obviously mangled body from the driver's side of the crashed Mustang and lifting it onto a gurney.

"What the hell?" Doe-boy exclaimed almost like a question. "That's not Tyler, right? That's not his car, right?" He asked looking around the limo for confirmation.

Kyle's face turned ghost white and he said, "Oh my God."

I was silent. I recognized the car, and I knew the answer as well as everybody else did. It was his car. He must've driven drunk after all.

"Excuse me officer! Officer!" Mitch called rolling down the window. An officer walked over to the car with a lit wand.

"Sir we're trying to secure an accident with fatalities here."

"Officer I know but I think that's our friend. Is that Tyler...Tyler umm...what's his last name?" Mitch looked around the car for some help.

"Sir I'm not at liberty to give any information at this time. If..." the officer continued to talk but I was no longer listening to him, I was listening to Kyle.

"That's his license plate," Kyle said in a barely audible voice. "KAP-PAMAN. He had the same thing on his keychain."

From the looks on the guy's faces, the officer must have said something that confirmed their thoughts as well and everyone looked crushed.

Benny cupped his hands to his mouth and exhaled hard. Everyone but Ike, who was still passed out, seemed to be in a state of disbelief.

I felt the heat of glaring eyes on the back of my neck and I turned to my left to see Kyle…staring intensely at me.

***

My alarm clock went off at 11:00am and I woke up still groggy from the night before. I sat up in the bed and ran my fingers over my hair as I let out a big loud yawn. The day was going to be a trial after the night be fore's events. After we pulled all of the pieces together, it turned out that Tyler left with a stripper and most likely lost control of his car going too fast around the curb. Originally, all of the groomsmen were supposed to be in the limo, but he said he'd had too many errands to meet us in time to ride.

I did feel a little bit sorry for the cat since he didn't have the common sense not to drive drunk, but I damn sure didn't feel like I was to blame. Kyle kept staring at me the rest of the ride and I could see the blame in his eyes. Not that I really gave a damn what he thought; but Tyler was a grown man and I'm not his mother. It wasn't my job to make sure he got home safely. At any rate, Tyler was Ike and Benny's boy, not mine. Benny was silent the rest of the ride, but he looked like a shell of the man he was before we found out about the accident when he got out of the car.

I remembered that I'd turned the ringer off on my phone when I came in, so I turned the ringer back on and picked up the phone to see if I had any messages. Six messages; four from miscellaneous girls last night, one from my boy who couldn't find the club, but who did later, because I saw him there, and one from Brenda around 10am. I clicked the END button and sat on the bed a while longer getting my faculties together. I decided it was a better idea to take a shower and get dressed before I called Brenda back.

The phone rang a couple of times while I was in the shower and when I got out, I reviewed the caller ID. One was from an unknown caller and the other was from Ike's house. I immediately recalled Ike's number.

"Hello," Ike answered sounding horrible.

"What's up man. You called?" I said.

"Yeah man," he replied. He let out a deep sigh and then a sniffle. "Man, I don't know if I'm coming or going. This isn't the way my wedding day is supposed to be starting off. My head feels like hamburger meat and one of my groomsmen is dead."

"Aiight man. What can I do?" I asked. There were only a handful of people in the world that I would do almost anything for, and Ike was one of them.

"Man, we're supposed to go pick up the tuxes by noon and I don't even feel like leaving the house. I can't believe my boy Tyler is dead. I knew he drank like a fish; I should have made sure he was gonna leave with us." Ike said.

"Naw man. Don't beat yourself up. It was your night, and you shouldn't have had to worry about anybody else. He was supposed to come with us, but he chose not to. I'm sorry for what happened and everything, but he was a grown man and he knew the risk he was taking when he got behind the wheel. I'm a bartender; some people are hardheaded like that. Kyle tried to get his keys and he turned him down. You can't baby sit a grown man. Listen this is your wedding day. You and Tara have been planning this for almost a year and we're gonna make it happy. Even if you are marrying the wrong chick," I joked.

"Damn I sure hope this day turns out better than it's starting off man. I'm trying to be happy, but I just can't seem to get there right now," he said with a slight chuckle. "Damn whenever they have the funeral, I'm gonna be on my honeymoon. What kind of a friend am I gonna look like if I skip the man's funeral?"

"Everybody will understand. It's not like you're just blowing him off. Don't beat yourself up over it. Life has to go on dude. I mean really, you weren't even that close to the dude Ike. As for the hangover, yeah you should have one since you were drinking like it was going out of style. I'll come over there and get you out of this funk in a minute."

"Did I do anything I'd regret last night?"

"I don't know. If you regret getting a blow job, at least 5 lap dances, and an hour in the VIP room; where I don't know what the hell went on by the way...then you might. I know I wouldn't regret it, but Tara will make you regret it if she finds out." I joked.

"Tara made me promise I wouldn't get a blow job after that J-Lo and Ben Affleck thing. Damn I'm starting this marriage off wrong already."

"The what? Forget it; I don't even wanna know what kind of stupidness that is about. Nobody's gonna tell her about it man," I said as I put my keys in my jeans pocket and checked my hair again in the mirror over my dresser. "Relax baby boy. What you gotta do today before the wedding? You got your hair cut yesterday and everybody's gotta get their tuxes I know, but what else?"

"I gotta pick up the rings," he replied.

"Aiight I'm about to roll out now and I'm on my way to get you. Get all the stuff you need to bring to the church because we're not coming back to your place." I said as a matter of fact. "I got it covered."

"Okay. Damn man: I appreciate you looking out for your boy like this. That's why you're my best man. I'll see you in a minute." Ike said hanging up.

I hung up, grabbed the shoes I was going to wear at the wedding from my closet and put my cell phone in my pocket on the way out of the house.

The phone rang again, and I saw that it was Brenda on her cell phone on the caller ID. I let it ring and started calling her from my cell on my way to my truck.

"I was just calling you," Brenda said when she answered her cell.

"I know," I said as I got into my Navigator and started the ignition.

"You already getting ready for the wedding?" she asked.

"Yeah, I'm going to pick up Ike and run errands." I answered.

"Oh okay. So how was the bachelor party last night? Did Ike behave?"

I let out a deep sigh. "It was all good until the end."

"What happened at the end?"

"This lame ass groomsman was driving drunk last night and killed himself."

"What?! Oh my God, that's horrible, who?" she asked.

"He was a stand in for Ike's brother. Tyler." I replied.

She gasped. "Oh wow. I know that guy… That's some rough stuff to deal with the night before Ike's wedding. How is everybody taking it? Why wasn't there a designated driver for the guy or something?"

What the hell? Did people really expect grown men to baby-sit other men? I didn't answer her question as I began on my drive to Ike's place.

"Hello?"

"What is this, an interrogation or something? Why do you need all of the details and the background story? Are you writing a paper?"

"You are such a jerk sometimes Brian." Brenda said sucking her teeth. "So, who's gonna take the guys place in the wedding party? Maybe his cousin Lane."

Lane? That was out of left field, "I don't know who's taking his place but why you asking about him? You doing Lane now on a regular, or you still got him following you around with his nose open?"

She sighed annoyed, "Brian he *is* his cousin, you freaking jerk. That's not a crazy assumption. Why you gotta be such an asshole Brian? I swear!"

I chuckled, "Yeah okay. So, you are fuckin him then. Old' Teddy finally got the 86, or is he just another sub? Are you bringing Lane with you to the wedding?"

"Dick head. See that's what I get for calling your silly butt. So anyway, what happened to your car? Kells told me she saw it all scratched up."

"Listen Matlock, I'm on my way to run errands for Ike and help him get on point for the funeral...I mean wedding," I said chuckling. "Aren't you supposed be getting your own shit together instead of worrying about everybody else's business?"

"Alright punkass. I was calling to tell you about that guy Edwin I was seeing. I think he might be stalking me now so if you see him around, run his ass off. Oh, and umm...I was gonna see if you could try to come to dinner at my place on a day next week?"

I was immediately suspicious. "First off, don't get me all hyped about this dude stalking you because I will put a bullet in his ass. Secondly, why you inviting me to dinner? I know it's not to meet Lane because you know I've already met him. Who's coming? The new Andrews fruit? Don't play."

She sighed. Busted! "What is your problem Brian? I mean don't you wanna know anything about this guy? What kind of contact daddy had with him, what he knew about us, and how many other people knew about him, stuff like that? Cause I do. No telling how many other little rat bastards are gonna crawl out the woodworks now that he's died. I know y'all didn't start off on a good foot, but I was gonna call Linda and see if I could get Julian's contact information and..."

"Knock it off," I interrupted. "Just leave it alone. You know that faggot scratched my face, right? We didn't know about his ass for almost 3 decades. What's knowing his history gonna do for us now? Daddy's dead. There's no point in making ties with this guy now."

"Who sounds like a faggot now?" She replied in a snotty tone.

"Fuck that. You know that faggot was bitch fighting me Brenda! What you got his back all the sudden?"

"Seriously? Are you asking me that? Can you grow up already and stop just thinking about yourself for a change? Our father just died, possibly by the hands of our own mother, we just found out we have a half-brother older than me, and you got a pregnant stalker on your ass worse than my stalker is on mine. Maybe it's time to focus on more important things than fighting, partying and sleeping around."

"Well obviously this convo has crossed the city limits to 'getting on my fucking nerves ville'; so, I'll see you at the wedding." I said hanging up on her as I pulled into the gas station. Who the hell did she think she was to try to run down my situation when her shit stank just as bad?

Women.

***

The wedding started as scheduled, and save the flower girl trying to sprinkle rose petals on some of the guests as well as the carpet, it went off without a hitch. After the ceremony and 30 minutes to an hour of taking pictures in the bridal party, we finally went to the reception hall and started partying the night away.

"Alright now I'd like everybody's attention," I said as I tapped my wine glass with a spoon once everyone had settled down for dinner. "It's time for the handsome best man to toast the not quite as handsome, but dapper groom; and his lovely new wife Tara," I said as the reception hall filled with polite laughter. The entire bridal party sat at a long white table in front of 50 or so round tables filled with wedding guests.

I turned to Ike and said, "We've been through a lot together and you are the closest thing I've ever had to a brother. You've always been my boy and I think the only fight we've ever had was over your new bride." People looked around nervously waiting to see what I'd say next.

"But alas... the best man for her, won. When we first met Tara, he thought she was too high post for him; and of course, she agreed," I said as Tara feigned a smile while cutting her eyes at me and the guests laughed. "They've been dating for a lot of years and some said it wouldn't last. Well, I guess those of us who didn't believe are eating our words, along with wedding cake, today. Much love and many blessings to you both. To Tara I say, you've got a great man there; treat him well. To my man Ike, for lack of anything more positive to say about a man cashing in his player card for one woman... all I can say is; more women for me!" I said laughing as I air clinked my glass in a toast and sat down.

There were some uneasy laughs and some groans but... ask me if I really cared. Ike smiled while sipping from his glass but Tara however...

not so much. She turned to me and said between a clinched teeth smile, "Can you stop being an asshole for one freaking day?"

"I'll try," I grinned back.

"Yo' chill out B. It's our wedding day," Ike said in a relaxed tone. I was just happy he'd stopped moping about Tyler for a change.

I put my hands up defenselessly and replied, "I said okay. I haven't even done anything."

Tara huffed and rolled her eyes while Ike playfully shoved me and laughed.

Given his earlier state of mind, he was becoming the epitome of the happy groom. Of course, I had to perk him up with some beers and some jokes; but his sorrow over Tyler's death was soon overshadowed by what I assumed were normal wedding day jitters. Ike's 19-year-old cousin Danny ultimately substituted in Tyler's place because he still had his tuxedo from his high school prom. The wedding had gone off without a hitch and now that we were about 45 minutes into the reception, the anxiety was probably replaced by relief, eating, and drinking for most of us.

"So, Brian, that was some toast you gave there," the bridesmaid I'd escorted said as she took a bite of salmon from her plate. "I'm not sure how many people raised their glasses to it though," she said smirking.

"What's your name again?" I asked indifferently.

She paused and raised an eyebrow as if she was trying to determine whether I was serious or not. "Drusilla. I guess you really don't remember me then huh? You were acting kind of strange at the rehearsal dinner, but I just thought you might have been preoccupied."

"I was acting strange?"

"Well, I mean like you didn't know me when we'd talk. It's been a long time though I guess. I live in Santa Monica now. California," she said as if I didn't know where Santa Monica was. "We dated briefly some years back."

I tried to pull her up in my memory, but it was a no go. "We dated?" I said doubtfully. Women had a real low opinion of what dating was considered to be these days, so it was more likely that I'd fucked her more than once and she'd categorized it as "dating."

"Well, we went out a few times. We had a little fun, but it didn't go anywhere," the plump brown skin woman with a slight West Indian accent said.

"You must have changed a lot from when we kicked it," I said looking her up and down. I knew I never kicked it with any mediocre fat chicks.

"Well yeah I've put on a few pounds. I just had twins 2 summers ago." She said bashfully.

"Yeah, I figured something must have run a-muck," I chuckled. "I thought it only took a year to lose baby weight. Is that different when you have twins?" I asked before I finished off the last morsel on my plate.

She looked wounded, then insulted. "Wow. So, you really are just as big of an asshole as Tara says. I barely remembered you accept that you were cute, and we slept together once; but wow. Somebody really needs to give you a wakeup call my brother. Your poop stinks like everybody else's." she said frowning.

I laughed out loud. Somehow poop doesn't have the same effect as shit does when you're supposed to be telling someone off.

"Asshole, jerk, people got a lot of jacked up names for me today. So, you're a little sensitive about your weight I guess. No harm intended."

"Regardless you need to watch what you say to people. I'm sure you're intelligent enough to know what's not appropriate," she scolded.

"I don't recall asking for a conversation. You started talking to me. Don't blame me for your lack of self-discipline. I'm sure I'm not the only person who's wondering what you did with your gym membership money."

She sucked her teeth and pushed away from the table knocking a glass of water over on me as she stormed off. I wasn't fazed. Water dries. I spotted Brenda at a table in the middle and went to speak to her and Lane.

"What's up girl?" I said putting my hand on her shoulder when I reached her.

"What's up big head?" She said looking up at me as Lane and I gave each other a pound and a nod greeting.

"Nothing. I just came to check on you. Hey Rhonda, Paul," I said noticing and acknowledging them at the table. There were 2 empty seats near Brenda's side of the round table where the occupants had probably gone to dance so I sat in the one nearest to her.

"Hey! Brian what's up boy?" Someone yelled grabbing my shoulder from behind.

When I turned around, I saw Mario Peters; my arch rival from my college basketball team. We'd had a fight my freshman year on the team because I was making him look like the scrub he was. Just my luck he was Gabby's brother's dorm roommate all the years we were in school, so he gloated like a motherfucker once news got out about me and her breaking up.

I turned and looked at Mario with a smirk, but I didn't respond.

"I see you're the same old arrogant Brian. What's happening man? I was looking for Gabby, but I didn't see her anywhere. I know her and Tara used to hang tight back in the day. Are you two still together?" He said with a stupid grin on his face. I wanted to stuff my fist down his throat, but I had no intention of messing up my boy's wedding day.

"Yeah, whatever dude. I'm talking to my sister; go sit down some-where."

Mario looked taken aback. "Aw man; you still holding a grudge from college? Man, I'm over that. You not still harping on that rivalry, are you?"

I looked him up and down like the lame he still was and turned back around to my sister. I heard him sigh deeply and walk away.

Brenda shook her head. "My brother never lets anything go," she said to Lane.

"Fuck that dude," I reiterated. "Bumbling idiot knows me and Gabby ain't been together since forever."

"Brian are you drunk already?" Brenda asked looking at me accusingly.

"Maybe. Who are you now; my sponsor?" I asked laughing while spotting a long legged, dark skin, pretty woman with a ponytail dressed in a long, slinky blue dress at the same time. My favorite color. As expected, she was already eyeing me while trying to pretend she wasn't. She had a muscular but feminine build and I imagined she could get a good cardio work out in my hotel suite after the reception.

"I'm just asking smart ass. You must have been drinking for a while to be drunk already at…" Brenda paused to look at her watch. "…at 7:15 in the evening."

"Again…do you have a part time gig as an AA sponsor I don't know about? Damn drink Gestapo. You need to be getting drunk. I'm sure your boy Lane would be happy if you did," I said nodding at Lane for him to cosign. He smirked but put his arm around the back of Brenda's chair and looked off into the crowd gathering on the dance floor. Pussy whipped. I chuckled and shook my head at his weak ass reaction and went over to the pretty woman in blue.

"Come on sexy let's dance," I said to her as I took her hand and pulled her to the dance floor. She couldn't have been more thrilled to be in my presence.

***

Fred caught the garter after wrestling with at least 20 other guys for it and jumped around like he'd scored a touchdown. It always baffled me that dudes who don't want to be monogamous, let alone married, would fight for possession of something that would symbolize both. I don't fake the funk, so I just stood back and watched these lames push and shove for a little piece of material like it was a money clip full of hundreds.

Kyle came and stood next to me with his hands in his pants pockets. His clothes looked ruffled and he was definitely drunk. "So, what's up man?" He asked.

I looked him up and down and sighed. I knew he was about to bring up the whole Tyler thing because he had been sulking and giving me 'I know what you did last summer' stares all day.

"Nothin' man. You look like shit," I said.

He gave me a harsh look and replied, "Yeah well I've been going over and over in my head whether there was something I could have done to save Tyler. It's really messin' with my conscience. Can you say the same? Do you even have a conscience?" He asked.

"I save it for important stuff; not sulking over someone I barely knew and something I didn't have any control over."

"What? You could have at least tried to stop him Brian. I mean damn, he was our boy? God forbid it was me like that," he said taking his hands out of his pockets and gesturing. "I know you act like a son-of-a-bitch most of the time, but you can't really be that fucked up."

"First of all, Tyler was Ike's friend, not mine. Secondly, I don't try to stop grown men from doing what they want to do. I don't expect anybody to baby-sit me and I don't do it for no other cats either. And if you really want to know, if it was you, and you were stupid enough not to know when you're too drunk to drive; you'd be right where Tyler is. I'm not anybody's momma."

"Yo' that's fucked up. You are a messed up dude, man. I don't know if you didn't get enough titty when you were a child or what; but you messed up in the head. Somebody is dead man! Dead cause of you!" Kyle said as his voice got louder, and his words began to slur. He was about to get his drunk ass whooped.

"Aiight man keep it movin'," I said waving my hand from right to left to show him the way to walk. "You on some bullshit tonight and I'm done talking about this with you. This is a wedding not a talk show. Nothing's getting resolved here dude."

"Don't tell me to keep it movin'. I really want to know why you so fucked up in the head? You don't care about nobody but yourself and you are the most arrogant motherfucker I know. I think you might be a sociopath or something like that. Like that Ted Bundy dude. No fuckin' emotions." He said stepping in front of me and becoming even more animated.

I bit my lips in and took a deep breath while scratching the back of my head. "Kyle, you had too much to drink and you about to really get hurt up in here talking all this bullshit." I said as I began to walk away before it got out of control.

The music was loud and most of the people at the reception were focused on the garter and bouquet rituals. Of course, there were still people who noticed the small commotion and were now looking our way.

"Yeah, walk away asshole! I don't know why I bother with a punk ass like you anyway! I can tell you one thing though…" he yelled getting louder the further I got away and the more people paid attention. "…that's over man! I will never be friends with you again knowing you'd let a brotha ride off to his death just so you can get some head from a Ho! You're always talking about what a grown fuckin' man you are!" He continued to yell as Mitch came over to him and tried to calm him down. "You ain't no man though! You a bitch!"

People gasped in the crowd and others looked to their neighbor to try and find out what the commotion was all about. I was steaming. Not only did Kyle try and embarrass me in front of 250 plus people, but that faggot had the nerve to call me a bitch! Damn near to my face!

As I continued across the room, I saw Tara with an even greater scowl on her face arguing with Ike and pointing in my direction. I busted through the reception hall doors which lead to the hallway and went into the men's bathroom. Kyle's lucky I didn't punch his teeth out. I was trying not to make a scene at Ike's wedding, but Kyle had seen to it that it wouldn't be possible.

I went over to the urinals and took a much-needed piss as I closed my eyes and enjoyed the release. I hadn't been able to have one day, not turn to shit in weeks; my luck had gone as sour as lemons lately. I heard the door swing open and I turned my head to the side to see who it was.

"What the hell is going on Brian?" Ike asked angrily.

I shook, put the long dong back into my pants and zipped up before turning to respond. "Look man, Kyle had too much to drink. Hell, I walked away so why you coming at me? You need to give me some credit because you know I usually would have handled his ass." I said as I went over to wash my hands.

"Tell me this…what's he talking about? You could have stopped Tyler from driving drunk?"

"When did I become captain save-a-ho? I'm not his momma and I didn't give him the keys either. I couldn't have stopped him from doing anything anymore than Kyle could when he tried. How the fuck is all of this about what I could have done for a little jealous brotha I barely knew?" I said turning to Ike after I finished washing my hands. "Kyle tried to take his keys from him, and he refused. He asked me to try and I said if he didn't get them then it wasn't anything for me to do because Tyler's a grown man, and I went back in VIP. What did you want me to do?"

"You could have told somebody to watch him. Hell, you could have told him to ride with us in the limo and he could have come and got his car in the morning. Brian man…you let a man die over some petty fucking bullshit with women?" Ike said looking wounded as he leaned his back up against the wall.

"Man, damn that! Since when have you ever known me to hold another man's hand? If he wasn't smart enough to know when to say when, how the hell is it my fault? I stop telling people how much to drink as soon as I clock out from behind the bar. And anyway, I did tell Kyle to tell him to ride in the limo with us but Tyler's ass didn't want to wait! It's not like I knew he was gonna drive off and kill himself. Why all of the sudden are y'all expecting me to look out for motherfucker's? Be real man! He was trying to kick it with one of the strippers that night dude. She died in the car with him. You think he was gonna let us drive him home? Tyler is dead because he was an idiot who didn't know his limits; not because I wasn't a good friend. I've never been his friend."

Ike looked at me with almost the identical scowl Tara was wearing earlier; I guess they were meant to be together after all. "Damn man.

How have we stayed this close for so long? When did you become this heartless self-centered motherfucker you are? Would you do that to me? You don't even feel any guilt. None. Tyler was my friend; and maybe because of your callous ass, he's dead. This is my wedding day and I'm supposed to be spending it with my wife and family and friends enjoying ourselves; instead, I'm in the John with you talking about a friend who should be here with us."

I didn't even know what to say to that. I mean Ike was my boy and everything, but he was really getting too sentimental over a brotha he only kicked it with on occasion. I guess Tara was lending him some of her bitch faculties too.

"I don't know what else to say to you man because you don't even get it. I'm lookin' you in the face right now and I can see that you don't get it. I'm about to get back in here to my lovely new wife, and try to enjoy the rest of my reception; but this changes things wit' us man. I knew you weren't the most caring cat I knew, but for you to let a dude drive to his death? A cat you knew was my friend? Some stuff you're just supposed to grow out of man," Ike said as he turned to walk out of the bathroom.

"You gotta be kidding me. I've always been there for you when you needed me. I don't treat you like these other lames out here. Didn't you hear me say you're like my brother? Even your wife's betrayed you more times than I have, and this is how you do me? This shit is making you question our friendship? Who I am?" I asked becoming annoyed. "What the hell does one thing have to do with another?"

"Like your brother huh? I bet your real brother doesn't think much of that title and I probably shouldn't either after some of the things you've done to me. Listen man, if you can't figure out what's wrong here, I can't tell you and I don't have the time to try right now," Ike said walking out of the bathroom.

Well God damn it... that wasn't an answer to my question!

13

Brenda

Lane and I were enjoying ourselves dancing like we were features on SOUL TRAIN before they stopped the music and gathered everyone for the garter and bouquet toss. We managed to get through the garter toss but just as the ladies started to gather to catch the bouquet, we heard Brian and Kyle getting into a commotion. I shot Rhonda an exasperated look and she rolled her eyes and sighed at Brian as well. Wherever there was trouble, there was likely my brother. To my surprise though, he was actually the one walking away from the drama instead of antagonizing his opponent.

Ike and Tara exchanged what looked like unpleasant words and then he left out behind Brian as Tara pasted a smile on her face and got ready to throw the bouquet to us desperate single chicks.

"Trouble in paradise already, courtesy of my brother," I said to Rhonda who was standing beside me texting.

"Yeah, he seems to be the center of everybody's attention today," she said back, rolling her eyes.

"Huh?"

"Gwen keeps texting me asking where the wedding is, if he came with a date, Yadda," she answered with a sigh and shoving her phone back into her purse. "I'm like, really? Give it a rest for a day for Christ's sake."

"I swear I need to set her up with Edwin so they can swap stalking stories and smother each other to death," I replied with a scowl as we both prepped to catch the bouquet.

Tara threw it and we all rushed forward with hands grabbing for a flint of hope at matrimony. Both Rhonda and I came back empty handed but at least she was already engaged. My options were still sketchy. Some frumpy looking average girl caught the bouquet and was whooping and hollering like she'd just scored a touchdown. Pathetic.

Lane was standing on the outskirts of the bouquet circle and when I got to him, he leaned in and gave me an unexpected kiss. Okay! He was so tall and looked so sexy and sleek in his dark gray suit that I was already wet just from looking at him, but if he kept putting those lips on me, I was going to drench my panties.

He took my hand and began leading me to a table filled with people I didn't know. I could see myself really falling for this guy if things progressed the way they were going. When we got to the table he leaned in and hugged and kissed an older woman with her salt and pepper hair in a bun and a bright pink dress suit, then hugged the balding older man in a brown suit seated next to her.

"Mom and dad, this is Brenda," he introduced.

"Oh," his mother said with a big smile with eyes darting back and forth between Lane and I. "Well, she's a pretty one. Irma."

"Roland," his father said nodding hello to me.

"Hi, nice to meet you I said," with an instant smile. His parents? I might have been reading more into things than were intended, but either way, it had to be a sign that he liked me as much as I wanted him to. I think.

After a brief conversation with his parents and a few other introductions to his family, we made our way over to Ike and Tara who were sitting back at the wedding table.

"Congrats cousin!" Lane said smacking Ike's hand across the table. "And congrats to Tara, my new cousin."

They smiled and I also offered my congratulations, but I honestly felt like Ike was too good of a guy for Tara. She was a snotty dictator who'd already proven she was a disloyal tramp once; I just hoped she wouldn't do it a second time. Ike and Lane exchanged a little more banter while Tara and I exchanged some phony conversation. When Lane grabbed me around the waist to head back to our table, I couldn't have been happier to go.

"So, you're really not a big fan of Tara at all huh?" He asked smirking when we sat back down.

"Why, was it that obvious? We were pleasant, weren't we?"

"Yeah, in the phoniest way as possible. She always plasters a smile on her face when she's bullshitting, which is way too damn much if you ask me. You though... now you have a different kind of phony. Your facial expressions say 'nice' but the tone of your voice says, 'blah blah blah.' Just so you know, I'm gonna be watching you for that phony stuff when you're talking to me."

I giggled, "Don't worry about it. You haven't lost my interest yet."

"Let's keep it that way," he said leaning in for a kiss yet again.

Damn I loved his aggressiveness and the fact that he wasn't shy about showing me affection in public. Teddy was a beast in the bedroom but in public, I might as well have been his sister.

"I'll be right back," I said as I got up and went to the lady's room. My phone started ringing in my bag when I was in the process of washing my hands and startled me a bit. I rarely brought my cell phone with me, so people usually didn't bother to call it. I hurried and dried my hands before answering it on the first ring without looking at the number first.

"Hello?"

"Holy mother of God did you just answer your cell phone?" Teddy laughed on the other end. "It was a long shot, but I didn't actually expect you to answer."

What the double fuck! Why was he calling me now? "What Teddy," I answered drably.

"What? Why are you acting like that? You mad about me not coming to Ike's wedding? I just figured..."

"I'm not even thinking about you Teddy. Don't even worry about it. You weren't hard to replace."

"I wasn't huh? One of your many late-night phone calls take my spot? You know I do miss you?"

I was silent. That wasn't what I wanted to hear cause every time I heard his silky voice, I melted like ice cream in a microwave.

"Brenda?" He questioned.

"What?" I answered again in a monotone voice.

"So, you don't miss me?" Silence. "Brenda baby I miss you. I'm sorry about how we ended things last week. I was really just stressed out about the closing I had to do in the morning and... and you know. It just wasn't a good time to talk about "us", but we can talk later tonight if you want to. If you still want to baby," he said quietly.

I thought about it for a minute when a couple of laughing guests came into the bathroom and went into 2 stalls.

"Listen Teddy I don't have time for this anymore. Like you said before, we've done this time and time again. I don't want to meet up with you tonight so you can fuck me into believing you'll eventually marry me and then get up the next day acting all brand new. I've gotta go," I said opening the bathroom door and walking toward my table.

"Brenda don't be like that. You know I love you but...I just gotta get some things straight in my own house first before I can even think of making our house. I just need a little more time to..." he was saying before I hung up on him.

His time was up.

"You ready to go yet baby?" I asked Lane when I reached the table putting the phone back in my bag.

"Uh...yeah," he said surprised and drinking the rest of his glass of wine.

"Call you later Rhonda. Good night Paul," I said and waved good night to the other 2 people at our table as I led Lane away and toward the reception hall doors.

It was time for a change.

***

It took us less than 25 minutes to get to Lane's huge, gated home and park in his 4-car garage next to 2 other cars. Impressive. He'd invited me to his house for the night and promised to get me back home in time to feed Zeus his breakfast on time, so I agreed. I was curious to see what it looked like since Paul had told Rhonda it was a mansion. Lane got out of the car before I'd even unlocked my door and came around to the passenger's side to let me out.

"Such a gentleman," I said smiling as he walked me to his garage door and inside.

"My momma raised me right. What did you expect?" He answered returning the smile.

Entering from the garage you are immediately in a huge foyer. It had a high vaulted ceiling, and the room was terracotta orange with huge, framed pictures on each wall. The living room wasn't too cluttered with furniture or pictures and it too was terracotta orange. He had a huge black sectional couch that took up most of the room and of course a huge, big screen TV. A man's must have accessory. There was a large circular table in the middle of the room with an African mask on a stand and a lot of African art adorning the walls. He was stylish too.

"I love this living room. Did you decorate it yourself?" I asked.

"No, my brother has an interior decorating company that decorates the models for the apartment buildings he owns," he said leading me through the living room and up the spiral staircase.

The first room we came to was an office. The walls were covered with plaques of things I couldn't read too well from the door and I saw a lot of trophy's in a cabinet on the wall. There was a big oak desk by a large window with an executive looking chair behind it.

"My home office," he said as we passed it.

The next room was his. "Okay now this is the Lion's den. Don't get too excited."

"Yeah, I'll be sure to contain myself," I said playfully.

It was another huge room with a black chase in front of a picture window. Everything in it was black, emerald green or close to it. There was a big king-sized bed with long black bed posts and a grand dark emerald rug covered a hardwood floor. There was only one picture in the room, and it hung over his bed. It was of a green trumpet surrounded by black rose petals. There were full length mirrors all around the room and I gave Lane an eyebrow raised look.

"You sure do have a lot of mirrors in here," I said.

"Closets. Obviously, this was also the work of a woman," he said walking over to 2 of the full-length mirrors and pulling slim handles between them to reveal a huge walk in closet.

"I think I'm in love," I said walking over to the closet. "How deep does this go?" I asked looking around inside it. It was very wide and long, yet he seemed to have enough clothes and shoes to fill it nearly to capacity.

"With me or the closet?" He asked.

"The closet. Slow your roll buddy," I replied chuckling.

"That's messed up," he said walking over to a dresser inside the closet, putting his wallet on it and taking his watch off. "I like to dress up a little bit." he said as he pulled open a draw in a dresser inside the closet. He pulled out a blue checkered pajama top with matching pants and handed them to me. "I'm sure these will be big on you, but you should be comfortable. They're my favorites so don't steal 'em. I know how women are with confiscating clothes."

His favorite pajamas? I liked that he would give me his favorite pajamas to wear, but then I wondered how many other women he'd let wear these same favorites?

"Thank you but, is this your go to pajama outfit for all of your chicks or what?" I asked.

"You're pretty skeptical huh? I don't have any go to pajamas for your information. I'm not gonna say no other woman has ever worn them before but I can say that the one that did wasn't just a fling.

I rolled my eyes with a frown and pursed lips. "Can I get your second favorite pair then? Or has that also had other women's vaginas in it before?"

He shook his head and exchanged the pajamas for a red cotton tank top and grey cotton sweatpants. "You worry a lot about other women, don't you?"

I thought about his question for a second and wasn't sure if I should be offended or not. "What do you mean?"

"I mean you're constantly trying to find out if some other chick is waiting in the wings or has been in your spot before. What's that all about? You used to other women being a factor when you're seeing a man?"

"I'm used to men trying to make things look better than they are, so I like to nip it in the bud at the beginning and get to the reality of a situation. I'm not worried about other women, but I know other women exist and are probably still a factor so I can't just ignore it," I answered defensively.

"Look, I know other dudes exist too, but I'm not compelled to speak on it at every turn. It comes off as being insecure and I don't think that's what you want to portray.

"Insecure? Listen I am very secure within myself for your information," I informed him with my neck rolling. "What I'm not secure about is how much of what men usually say is true and how much is phony. You and I have been out a few times before this and talked and enjoyed each other but until recently, my possibly staying at your house wasn't even on the table. I think it makes perfect sense that I'm..."

"Alright well hold up now. Slow it down a minute. You got a hot temper girl," he said with a slight smirk. "Say the wrong thing to you and its fireworks huh?"

"It's not about the wrong thing or the right thing Lane. I'm just..." I suddenly felt a little embarrassed. Was I acting like some overly jealous and defensive chick? Probably. When I thought about it again, I probably was blowing things out of proportion. "You know what... you're right. I have had a lot of experience with dishonest men down from my father, to my brother, to most of the men I've dated. I might be a little wound tightly about that subject, so I apologize. I told you the whole thing with me and Teddy was still fresh," I finished deflated.

"I know that about you and Teddy. And I know a lot of women have known a lot of cheating men; and I'm not pretending like I've never been the dude you're talking about either. All I'm saying is that I'm not looking to be that guy anymore and you and I are just starting to date so we shouldn't be starting off with a cloak of distrust already. Don't you agree?" He asked approaching me and pulling me close to him.

In his arms I didn't feel like I could have said anything else but, "Right."

***

When I awakened Sunday morning, I smelled breakfast cooking and the sun seemed to be shining directly on my face. I sat up in the bed and wiped the slobber from my mouth as I combed through my hair with my fingers. I'd hoped I was minimizing the monstrosity it had probably become. I got out of bed and went to the bathroom to brush my teeth and relieve myself before embarking on my tour of Lane's house. I double checked myself in the mirror and I thought I still looked pretty good for first thing in the morning. My curls were still fluffy and though my makeup had been washed off in the shower the night before, my skin and face still looked in pretty good condition, I thought.

At first, I intended to look at the other rooms and give myself a complete tour of his mansion but then I thought better after our conversation in the closet. If I was caught it might look like I was snooping. And I would be. I made my way downstairs to the kitchen instead and saw Lane standing in front of the stove flipping pieces of bacon wearing pajama pants and no shirt. Oh, how I'd have loved to sop that up with a biscuit! He had a tattoo of a long sword down the middle of his back and with the word WARRIOR written down the blade. Sexy.

"Nothing sexier than a half-naked man cooking," I said as I sat in the nearest chair at the kitchen table.

He turned his head slightly towards me with a smirk and went back to cooking; now stirring scrambled eggs with a spatula. "Ah, so you like?" He responded as he grabbed some pepper from an overhead cabinet and sprinkled a little in the pan. "Well, I'm no Martha Stewart, but I get by. I hope you like what I'm making. I don't eat pork, so I have turkey bacon, scrambled eggs, grits and some toast waiting for me to press the heat."

"Sounds good to me. I really need to be getting out of here though," I said as I looked at my watch. It was 9:30 in the morning already and I hadn't taken care of Zeus.

"Girl I'm slaving in the kitchen to make you a superb breakfast and you trying to jet on me? We're gonna get to your dog. Believe me baby. But I don't miss breakfast and today, neither will you," he said as a matter of fact.

"No for real. I gotta let him out to pee too," I said laughing as I playfully banged the table in protest.

"Listen woman, I'm not gonna be neglected because of your dog. I've been slaving over this breakfast for at least 15 minutes. Now..." he said leaving the stove and grabbing a cordless phone from its holster on the wall and putting it down on the table in front of me. "I don't know who you can call for bladder control for your dog, but get the digits going." He walked back over to the stove and flipped the bacon over in the frying pan.

"Bossy," I said taking his advice with a smile. At least he knew what he wanted, and if that was me, I was glad to oblige. I called Kelly because she had an extra key and was already familiar with Zeus. After a brief conversation she agreed, and I hung up resting the phone down on the table.

"See how easy that was?" He asked as he brought some plates filled with food to the table. "Listen to me. I'm a hell of a problem solver."

I rolled my eyes at him and eyed the food on the plate in front of me. It did look pretty good I must say.

"Orange Juice?" Lane asked standing in front of the refrigerator.

"Yeah, with ice please," I said admiring the curves of his muscular hips into his pajama pants. When he turned to bring me my orange juice, he caught my stare and returned a look that said he wanted to eat more than just breakfast.

"What you lookin at?" He asked slyly putting my drink on the table in front of me and sitting.

I just smiled and said nothing. We exchanged short conversations as we ate but we spent more time flirting across the table and making suggestive comments than anything else. I actually was hoping we could spend the day together again, but I dared not ask unless I wanted to look as desperate as he probably had already started to think I was.

"Well thank you for this delicious breakfast and the great company last night. I almost hate I have to leave you," I said getting up from the table.

"I enjoyed myself too," he replied putting our dishes in the sink. "If I didn't have some things to do today, you might not have had to leave me."

I smiled to that but didn't say anything as I walked upstairs to his room. He lingered downstairs for another 5 minutes or so doing who knows what else while I was changing back into my wedding clothes and just as I was about to zip up the back of my dress, I felt his hand unzipping it down.

"What are you doing?" I said half turning to face him.

"I'm helping you get dressed," he whispered in my ear with his tongue as I felt his erection pressing against my bottom and my dress falling down to the floor.

I closed my eyes, reached my arm around and caressed the back of his head.

"I think this is the reverse of getting dressed," I muttered as his tongue, now on my neck brought tingles to my body.

"Now that I've tasted you..." he said in a sultry voice as he slowly kissed my shoulders, then my back, then my waist. "I want to taste all of you," he continued pulling my panties to the side and letting his tongue probe into my pink walls.

He began to lick, suck and kiss my lower lips like a delicious 5 course meal. Before I knew it, I was whimpering like a puppy and holding his ears like handlebars on a motorcycle going 100 miles an hour.

"Oh my God!" I yelled after a few more minutes as my body erupted into a pleasure that can only be achieved when you are at the peak of arousal. The more I whimpered, the more his tongue massaged every pleasure filled nerve of my pink box. I felt him kissing his way up my calves, to my thighs, to my waist and then he turned me to face him while he removed my bra and journeyed up to seduce my breasts.

It didn't look like I was leaving anytime soon.

***

We spent the next hour exploring each other's bodies like Raider's in a lost Ark and now my jaws, back and thighs were aching from our acrobatic performance. We lay naked on the sweat soaked sheets in each other's arms until he reached a single finger under my chin and lifted it to gently kiss my lips. It felt so good to not feel like my man had to rush off to do something or someone that was taking precedence over me. Even though we weren't officially a couple, I could see it in our future.

Lane got up and led me to his bathroom where we showered and fornicated together. When we got out, he handed me a towel from the linen closet, and I stood staring at him drying himself off through the wide bathroom mirror over the sink.

"Why you looking at me like that?" He asked with a grin.

"I'm just wondering what took us so long to get to this point? It seems like time is moving so fast all of the sudden... but I like it," I answered toweling my hair.

"Timing is everything. Maybe neither one of us was in the right place in our minds to be where we're at right now. Speaking for myself, I've been feeling you for a good minute, which you know, but I can't say I was actually ready to lock any one woman down until a few months ago."

"What happened a few months ago to change that?"

He went over to the sink and put toothpaste on his toothbrush. "Life. My best homeboy and his wife had a son and made me the godfather. Holding him in my arms and seeing how much he looked like my boy and his wife just reminded me that I had no legacy. I had no woman to love me and hold me down like Malcolm, that's the guy, and Sherri, his wife. I wasn't getting the same thrill from going to the clubs and having no one to answer to or care what I did on my days off."

I nodded, watching as he began to brush his teeth. "I can understand that. I guess every guy has to come around in his own time. I've been ready to end this dating game for a long time myself, but the person I wanted to end up with was never on the same page with me. Sometimes you just gotta stop blocking your blessings with space fillers. I just hate that it took me so long to follow that."

We freshened up, got dressed and he cooked me a quick bacon, egg and cheese sandwich on his George Foreman Grill as we sat conversing about things in our lives and where we wanted to be in the coming years. I was mesmerized listening to him talk about the plans he had for his business, for the family he wanted and even for his house which I discovered he'd designed himself.

Just as it seemed we were getting deeper into each other, again, my cell phone was ringing inside my bag. I rolled my eyes and sighed deeply. "This is why I don't carry my cell phone with me. I don't like feeling obligated to talk to people whenever they want no matter what I'm doing and having my daily life interrupted."

"Might be important," Lane said pouring more orange juice into my nearly empty glass without me asking.

I smiled and reached inside my purse and saw my mother's name and number flashing on my cell phone screen. She'd attempted to contact me a few times since the funeral, but I'd declined to answer. Why I answered this time was a question even I couldn't answer, but I felt compelled to. "Hello?"

"Brenda why have you been ignoring my calls? You have no idea what I've been going through and since the funeral you children haven't even bothered to check on me here or see how I was doing after that horrid Linda started..." my mother instantly began babbling.

"Mom!" I interrupted. "Slow down. I'm not at home right now and this isn't really a good time to talk so I'll call you later."

"Oh. Well, you need to call me back this time Brenda. Really. Don't just say you will and don't call back. Have you talked to your brother? He's been ignoring my calls too. I don't understand you kids. I could have been dying for all you know. I mean here I am grieving over the loss of my husband and your father and neither of you even has the decency to call or check on me? And that damn Linda. I swear that woman is out to put me in the grave right beside her two-timing brother. Who comes to a funeral with the illegitimate child of the deceased? Only a tacky bitch is who. I mean is that the time to parade him around in front of all the family to try and humiliate me? She thought she was making me look like a fool, but she ended up being the one looking stupid cause..."

"Mom...Ma! I just said I can't talk right now," I said slamming my hand on the table. "I'll-call-you-later."

"Okay okay. Well what time is later? What are you doing right now that you can't take time to talk to me while I'm grieving? It's been less than 2 weeks and already you and your brother are just moving on with your lives like nothing happened? This is not the way mourning children should behave."

"Stop lumping what me and Brian do into one thing and no I am not just going on like nothing happened. Anyway, you're one to talk about how we're behaving. You aren't exactly the most consistent grieving widow I've ever seen either," I spat.

She gasped. "Me? How dare you question my authenticity! After all of the years of betrayal and abuse I've endured from your father and from you and your brother, I think I'm entitled to have a few mixed feelings during this time. You and Brian are so unappreciative of the sacrifices I've made for you and you're so...so arrogant and judgmental! I know you say you can't talk right now when I'm sure you really can, but you listen to me miss high and mighty" she said in a guttural tone. "I am your mother. I need to talk to you about things that you need to know, and you need to hear. I expect you to call me back tonight. I don't plan on leaving to go anywhere so if you call, I will answer. Call-me-back!" She hollered before hanging up in my ear.

Oh no she didn't! I looked around in disbelief at Lane who wore a perplexed expression. "Please excuse that conversation. My mother is a bit of a drama queen and... I'm sure you heard most of that since she was yelling loud as hell in my ear," I said embarrassed as I put my phone back in my purse and stood up. "It's actually time for me to go now anyway. I need to be getting back to the house so I can change my clothes and…"

"I understand," he broke in. "I do," he continued moving in front of me and planting a sweet kiss on my lips. "Call me later when you get a minute."

14

Brian

STALKER CHANNING

"Ohhhh," Blue Dress from the wedding yelled as I thrust inside her in my hotel room. I knew I'd be too drunk to drive after the wedding, so I had Tara (reluctantly) book me a room along with her wedding guests in the hotel where the reception was when she made the arrangements.

"Ummm," I moaned as my jizm flowed into the condom. I stopped thrusting and started pulling out when she said, "Wait, wait baby. I was right there."

I was feeling a little charitable, so I lay on my back and said, "It's your show." She seemed unfazed and straddled me with the skill of a jockey.

After Blue Dress climaxed, she fell limp onto my chest.

"Oh my God," she said kissing me on the side of my lips. "Oh my God," she repeated before rolling over on her back and lying beside me. "Damn I'm glad you let me get on top cause every time I was about to come, you'd move or something."

What? Who the hell was she talking to? I'm a master fuck bitch! Get it straight! I turned and looked at her face illuminated by the light from the bedside lamp in the dimly lit room with a frown.

"Whew," she said getting up and going into the bathroom. When she turned on the light, I could see her nicely toned body glistening with sweat. She checked her perfectly laid ponytail, looked at her teeth, and proceeded to sit on the toilet and pee, with the door open and the light on!

"Uh, hey chick I can see you, you know?" I said sitting up in bed.

"Well, what the hell are you looking for then? You don't have to see me. What did you think I came in here to do?" she said with a sassy attitude. What the fuck?

"Yo that's just nasty!" I yelled out as I got up and closed the bathroom door. I put on my boxers and flipped on the television.

I heard the toilet flush and then the sound of running water. Soon the bathroom door opened, and she walked out just as confident and as naked as she'd walked in. She searched around the bed for her clothes and shoes and got dressed. I like a woman who knows when the party's over.

When she was done dressing, she came over to where I sat watching TV and said, "Alright then. You take care," and kissed me on the forehead as she headed toward the door.

"Yeah, I'll do that. I'll say one thing for you; you know when it's time to go. Most women never know when to leave." I said to myself more so than to her.

She turned and looked at me with a huge smile. "You're serious huh?"

I was confused. "Serious about what?"

"Sweetheart I hope you're not fooling yourself into thinking I'm leaving as a favor to you," she said pausing. When I didn't say anything, she continued. "Baby you're really handsome and your body is gorgeous; but your personality leaves a lot to be desired. And the sex..." she said looking over at the bed and then back to me. "It's mediocre at best if tonight was your normal. I'm leaving because there isn't anything for me to stay for. I'm about to catch up with my girls and go out to MAN TRAP and enjoy myself. You enjoy yourself." She said opening the door and leaving before I could respond.

I sat there with a confused look on my face before busting out in laughter. "Ain't that about a bitch," I said aloud. I guess she felt like she was Mighty Aphrodite in bed or something but whatever. LAW AND ORDER was on TV, so I let it play while I laid back on the bed thinking about what Ike said to me.

My cell phone was ringing in my pants pocket and I got up and retrieved it. I looked on the screen and PRIVATE popped up. I usually didn't answer unknown numbers on my home or cell phone; but what the hell. I didn't have anything better to do.

"Hello?" I answered.

"Um, hey Brian. It's Nadia. I hope you don't mind but Kelly gave me your number," the other voice said.

"My neighbor?" I asked sitting on the edge of the bed facing the television.

"Yes," she said tentatively. "Is this a bad time to call?"

After the day I'd had, and frankly the week I'd had, it was actually welcomed. "Naw it's cool. I'm just relaxing after coming from my boys wedding and chillin' in my hotel suite. You wanna come join me?"

"Uh... I think not. I'm calling because I wanted to tell you that I saw the person that scratched your car in case you didn't already know who it was. I was on my way out at the time, so I didn't have time to stop and let you know but I think it was the same girl you had at your place last week."

"Wait a minute. Three things you said are disturbing me right now. One, you saw somebody scratching my ride and you couldn't take a minute to tell me; Two, how did you know it was my ride she was scratching? And Three, how do you know who's in and out of my place?"

She cleared her throat nervously, "Okay well I know it sounds crazy when you say it out loud but it's not how it sounds. I saw you and the girl getting out of your truck last week when I was bringing my trash to the dumpster, so that's two in one right there, and I didn't tell you because I was running late for an appointment. She was hopping back into whoever's car that drove her when I was coming down the steps, so I didn't see it until I pulled out of my parking space and passed your driver's side. I got the plate for you. That's why I'm calling."

I knew it was that bitch, but I was glad it was now definite. I thought that trick said she was gonna be in Cali, but I guess she came back sooner than I expected.

"Well, I appreciate you looking out for me like that. Are you sure you don't know about that chick from playing ear hockey on my walls?" I joked.

She chuckled back, "For your information, I have better things to do than crack my ear up on your wall. Do you want the plate number or what mister conceited?"

"Yeah shoot," I said readying to write with the pen and paper the hotel had on the bedside table.

"The plate was a Georgia plate number AS4577. You definitely got a lot of traffic at your place, that's for sure. Some other chick was banging on your door a few hours ago like the police in a drug raid. Woke me up from my nap," she complained.

These tricks popping up at my house were really trying to throw salt in my chances with Hot Halle next door. Damn!

"What did the banger look like?" I asked.

"I don't know. I didn't look out to check or ask her for her driver's license," she taunted as I got up and went over to the table in the room and grabbed the ice bucket.

"Okay Nancy Drew. My bad, I thought you were on the case, but I guess not."

"You always got jokes huh?" She asked giggling. "I don't know what you're doing to these women to get them this pissed off at you, but you might want to tone it down a bit."

"What that chick did to my truck was inconsciencious. I'm a nice guy," I said looking for my room card and finding it on the floor by the bed.

"Inconsciencious you say? That's not a word?" she laughed. "You might need a library card in addition to a visit to the psychiatrist. I believe the word is unconscionable."

"Oh, so you're the new JEOPARDY champion now? You'll be using that word tomorrow. Watch," I replied leaving my room and heading toward the elevators in my boxers to go to the ice machine one floor up.

"Yeah, I wouldn't hold my breath on that one mister," she shot back playfully.

"So why are you in the house on a Saturday night?"

"I'm still getting my place together. Once that's done, I can start getting out and about."

"What about tomorrow? You got time to grab some brunch, lunch, or dinner? All three?" I asked pushing the lobby button by the elevator door.

She paused for a moment, but I could almost hear her smiling.

"I might. Why don't you call me tomorrow morning after ten and we can talk about it?"

I smiled to myself. My charm was never failing. "I'll do that. Good night."

"Good night," she replied as we both ended the call.

Just as I pressed the elevator button again, I heard its movement coming to a halt at my floor and when the doors opened, Gwen stood inside glaring at me with her arms crossed. I don't know what bitch put roots on me but whoever it was, her curse was on overtime.

***

"We need to talk Brian. Face to face and get this thing together. I'm not gonna be brushed off anymore," she said standing with her hands on her hips. She had her blonde weave up in a ponytail and she was wearing jeans, flip flops and a white shirt that read BABY ON BOARD.

"You damn mega-stalker," I uttered as she stepped out of the elevator and the doors closed behind her. "How did you know where I was?"

"I have my ways of finding out things. Especially when my cousin works here. Believe it or not, you get around more than a taxicab; you're not hard to locate and I knew you were at the wedding. Anyway, I didn't come here to fight with you. I want to talk, if you're capable of doing that without being a complete jerk."

Batting a thousand with the females. "There's nothing to talk about. If you're pregnant and you think it's my baby, have an abortion. If you wanna have it, which it looks like you do, then do it and call me when I gotta show up to court for the paternity test." I said pushing the elevator button again.

"You cannot be serious. I know your mother raised you better than this." She said stepping into my space.

"Shows how much you know me or my mother," I said snidely. "And back the hell up. You're all up on me."

"Listen I don't want to make a scene, but I will if you make me. I just want to talk to you like 2 adults. All you wanna do is go around telling everybody I'm a freak and this isn't your baby, and I don't know who the father is. It's like you're in high school or something."

I sneered at her and replied, "Aiight you got 10 minutes to speak."

Gwen followed behind me back to my room and once the door closed, she sat on the bed while I sat in the chair by the table.

"Okay look; I'm gonna have the baby. I'm getting older and I've got some medical history that makes it a bad idea for me to have an abortion. I know you don't want me to have it and I'm not thrilled about having a baby with you either based on the way you've been acting. You've made it clear that you don't give a damn about me or the baby, but I just had to make one last try. This baby is gonna be for life Brian and since it's gonna happen either way, can't you just try to be civil with me? I mean you have barely gotten a chance to know me and I can be really easy going. We got along so well the night at the party. It just takes a little effort." She pled.

I turned the television to ESPN and sat looking at her in silence. I was not going to be like my father and have some little bastard running around. Especially with some two-dollar Ho.

"I really don't think this has to be as ugly as it has been. I'm sorry for all of the things I said to you on the phone too. Can you at least consider being an active father when the baby is born? Maybe even trying to see if there's a way to work things out with me? I mean you had to feel some kind of way about me to have slept with me at all right?" She continued.

"Gwen, I don't want any children. Point blank. You and I never had anything but a night of fun and fucking. If you respected yourself you wouldn't want to have a baby conceived that way," I said fingering my cell phone which was ringing. She remained silent as I looked at the caller ID on my phone. It was from Donald. I'd call him back later.

"Brian, feel this baby. Your baby," she said approaching me and trying to put my hand on her stomach. I snatched my hand away and stood pushing past her.

"Woman please. I'm sure your 10 minutes is up by now. You said what you came to say and there's nothing more to be said; bounce," I said starting to move toward the door. Gwen blocked my way and stood glaring at me.

"Get out of the way," I told her.

"No, I will not get out of the way! You made this baby with me Brian and you're gonna take responsibility if it's the last thing you do!" She suddenly began yelling in my face.

"You better get your psycho ass up outta here before I flip out on you." I said angrily as I grabbed her by her arm and began pulling her toward the door.

"Get the hell off of me!" she yelled pulling loose. "You're not gonna ignore me! You and your fucking sister are not going to ignore me! I'm carrying your baby! A living thing of yours! You're gonna acknowledge me God damn it! This is a real life, and you can't just brush me up under the rug."

She was hysterical; like someone turned on a psycho switch. I grabbed for her, but she snatched her arm away and tossed the ice bucket from the table hitting me in the shoulder. "Put your hands on me again and I'll bash your head in!"

"What? Bitch, get the fuck out of my room! I barely even touched your ass!" I yelled back.

She stood like a cat with its back up and then suddenly, she lunged at me with her claws out. I immediately brought my hands up, grabbed her and backhanded her in the face. She fell up against the wall and I slammed her up against it again.

She began whimpering and screaming for me to stop and proclaiming that she was sorry. She was flailing around with tears coming down her cheeks and a few of her swipes caught me across the face. I flinched and came back with an even harder left-handed back slap and pinned her up against the wall. She was lucky she was pregnant, or they wouldn't have been open handed.

"You gonna leave peacefully?" I asked through clinched teeth.

"I'm gonna leave! I'm gonna leave!" she cried. "You're hurting me! You're hurting the baby! Please! Get off of me!"

I didn't want an instant replay of the Gabrielle incident, so I eased up on her and let her up off of the wall crying and heaving heavily. She grabbed her stomach and ripped the room door open quickly within an instant before disappearing out in a hurry as it shut behind her.

Sweat beads dripped from my forehead as I wiped them from my face and looked around the room. I hadn't intended to put my hands on her, but she wouldn't back down until I did.

Women. Sometimes words weren't enough.

***

The next morning when I woke up, I had a slight hangover and sour memories of the night's events. I got up, showered and got myself together before digitally checking out on the TV in my room. Once I was sure I'd packed all of my overnight stuff back into my duffle and suit bag, I left my room and went downstairs to eat lunch in the hotel since I didn't get up until nearly 1 O'clock. I had until 2pm to get to the gym and meet up with the fellas for our usual Sunday basketball games. Because Ike's wedding was the day before, we changed our normal time to a couple of hours later.

When I got there, Mitch and Doe-boy were standing against the wall talking and waiting for the court to free up.

"What's up playa," Mitch said smacking my hand.

"Sup," I said to him and exchanged the same greeting with Doe-boy. "We got next right?"

"Yeah, they probably got about 10 minutes left. Fred's running late and Kyle's...umm...not gonna be able to make it." Doe-boy answered. "You good?"

"Never better," I replied blandly.

"You and Ike straighten things out before they left this morning?" Mitch questioned.

I swallowed, annoyed. "Work what things out? There's nothing for us to work out."

I saw Mitch and Doe-boy exchange a disconcerted glance from the corner of my eye.

"Why y'all over there giving each other goo goo eyes? I said everything is gravy with me and Ike. You know something I don't know?"

"Hell no, we know the same thing you know, and you know everything is not gravy with y'all," Mitch had declared in an agitated tone. "It's not all good between you and Kyle either. Is what they're saying about what happened with Tyler true?"

I groaned and kicked the basketball that was on the floor in anticipation of our game down the sideline.

"I swear to God if I have to talk about this one more time, I'm about to snap off on somebody. Ike and I talked about what happened at his bachelor party. Tyler was in control of his own destiny. I told Kyle to offer him to ride with us in the limo, he chose to drive himself. I feel like I'm stuck in a TIVO remote or something. I can't even believe all y'all dudes are acting like I fed him alcohol and then handed him the keys to his car. Why is everybody comin' at me about it? Why aren't all of y'all up Kyle's ass for letting him leave with the keys since he knew so damn much about it?" I ranted.

Various people at the gym and even on the 2 separate courts paused to look our way. Doe-boy shook his head and looked away towards the teams on the court without a word. Mitch had his mouth open like he was in shock and then went to retrieve the basketball. Fred was entering the Gym door on the opposite side from where we stood and threw one hand up in greeting as he walked towards us just as the court was freeing up and we all started to walk on.

"What's up fam?" He said smacking hands with me and Doe-boy as Mitch returned with the ball and followed up with the same greeting. "Yo' Brian your alarm on your truck is going off and it looks like somebody keyed and bust the windows out your car."

As Fred told me the news there was a call over the gym speakers, "Will the person driving a black Navigator with license plate number 2-G-O-O-D-4-U please report to the front desk immediately."

I fumbled for my keys in my shorts pocket as I rushed out of the gym to get to my truck in the parking lot. The alarm continued blaring until I shut it off with the remote on my key chain. There wasn't anything new keyed on it, but some son-of-a-bitch had definitely bricked out my back window after I'd gone inside.

"Come on!" I yelled to no one in particular. "This is some bullshit!"

"Brian, I called the cops already. We got video camera's here so they're gonna be on tape," I heard Matt the gym's manager saying behind me. "Did anybody see who did this?!" He asked loudly to the forming crowd.

There was a lot of mumbling and snickering but nobody admitting to seeing the culprit. I felt helpless and angry as hell that these sniveling bitches were trying to destroy my truck because they couldn't get me. I knew it couldn't have been The Little Red Headed girl because she wouldn't know I'd be at the gym or what gym I went to. It had to be Gwen. She's the only psycho who'd been showing up here on a regular looking for me and after last night, she was probably still hot with me.

"Damn!" Mitch said coming over to me. "Gwen?"

"Probably," I said through clenched teeth.

"Wow," Doe-boy chimed in. "You on everybody's shit list right now."

I looked at him with steam practically coming out of my ears and walked over to my truck to inspect it and see what else she might have done to it. Glass was shattered all over the pavement around the back of my car and on the inside backseat where a single brick laid to rest.

When the police came, they took my report and Matt took us to a back room to look at the security footage. It was clearly a woman, but it wasn't clear what woman. She was wearing a black ski mask, black gloves, black pants and a black turtleneck shirt.

"You mean to tell me that nobody thought it was strange to see some chick dressed up like a damn cat burglar approaching my truck as hot as it is outside right now?" I questioned angrily. "Come on!"

I told the cops who I thought it was and why, but I omitted a few details from the previous night; mainly the part about me shoving Gwen into the wall. It was gonna have to be my word against hers if it ever came up.

***

I was steaming with anger about the new scratches on my truck and the police weren't much help once they came on the scene. One of the officers seemed to think he was Billy Crystal or something with all of the lame jokes he cracked while taking the report. 'Made some lady really mad I see. Maybe the sex will be hotter when you make up,' he joked with a cackle. What a riot he was... NOT!

I called Nate on my way home to tell him about my truck, but his cell phone went to voicemail. I thought about calling Brenda but decided a root canal would've been less painful.

"You bitches stop messing with my truck!" I yelled to the air. It had to have been Gwen. She was obviously a slow learner. Some mother she was gonna turn out to be. Her stalking ass had better pray I didn't get my hands on her. I should have choked that bitch out when I had the chance. I needed to think about moving.

After I parked in my apartment complex lot, I grabbed my bags from my truck and went to my door. For some reason I was having a hard time unlocking it with my keys and spewed a bunch of cusses jiggling the lock until it eventually gave way and let me in. I'd barely entered the door when I felt a sharp stab in my neck and my knees instantly buckled beneath me.

When I came to, my head was throbbing, and I was finding it hard to focus. I was propped up against the wall by the kitchen, sitting on the floor with my wrists taped together behind my back. I looked down at my stretched-out legs and saw that they were taped together around the ankles with electrical tape. I knew it was gonna hurt to rip the tape off of my hairy ankles. I blinked several times, hoping to clear up my vision and just as my focus became clear, I saw Gwen sitting in a chair pointing my 9-millimeter gun with a silencer I didn't recognize at me. She was wearing a black velour sweat suit with her hair back in a pony-tail and she was holding the gun lackadaisically in her right hand with her elbow resting on her knee.

"You're gonna pay you know that? I bet you thought you were gonna get away with what you did to me didn't you motherfucker? Just beat me up and treat me like a whore right," she continued as she began tapping one foot on the floor.

"You're not God. You're nobody to judge me. Not you and not your uppity bitch sister either. You and her think you can just keep doing people wrong and nothing is gonna happen to you? Nobody's gonna pay your pretty boy..." she said leaning forward and two-finger shoving my forehead. "...ass back?"

I was too angry to speak and too busy trying to figure out how she got into my apartment, let alone how I was gonna get out of this. I shook my hands around trying to untie myself. This deranged whore had me at gun point in my own damn crib!

"Oh what? You don't have anything to say now? You always have something smart to say, why not now?" She taunted as she approached and hovered over me. "Funny thing is I was just going to settle for bust-ing the windows out your car and messing up your place since some other woman obviously beat me to keying your car. Lucky for me your sister is as big of a bitch as you are."

What did that mean? What did my sister have to do with what she was doing in my place or doing to me now? I wasn't gonna ask her the question though. I'd be damn if I was going to give her the satisfaction of showing her the slightest bit of weakness. I knew for a fact I'd choke the life out of her if I got loose though.

"Say something you bastard! You better start talking when I tell you to or I'm gonna make you scream," she screamed kicking my legs send-ing a sharp pain to my calves.

I grunted in agony but didn't respond otherwise. I simply glared at her and thought of the many ways I'd pistol whip her till she passed out when I was free.

Why-the-fuck-aren't-you-talking?!" She screamed turning beet red, getting deep in my face and hitting me in the side of the head with the butt of the gun. I could feel the blood gushing from the aching area where she hit me, and I screamed out in pain and anger. "You scared? I bet your punk ass is scared now, huh? You got all the balls in the world to beat up a woman but now that I got the upper hand you've gone silent?"

She glared at me, spat in my face and smacked me hard as hell with her left hand. The ambidextrous fucking bitch!

"So, you're trying to be mister macho now? You trying to act like you're not ready to piss in your pants? I bet you don't like that spit in your eyes now do you? Let me tell you something mister you're too good for everybody. You think you're sooooo fucking superior and you don't have to answer to anybody right? Well, you're gonna answer to me today. And before it's over, you're gonna answer to God."

I pressed my bleeding forehead flat up against the wall thinking it would stop the bleeding and relieve some of the pain. Wrong!

"So, you're gonna kill me because you forced me to stop you from stalking me?"

"Oh, you wanna speak now?!" She yelled theatrically. "That's not even the half of why I'm gonna kill you. And I am going to kill you if there is any question in your mind." Gwen said with a long pause afterward.

In her damn dreams! I figured if she was gonna kill me no matter what, I wasn't going out like a punk.

"You notice anything different about me Brian?" She asked menacingly staring down into my face again.

"I never noticed you enough to notice anything different about you," I answered dryly.

She drew a deep breath, looked at the gun in her hand and then looked back at me with eyes full of hate. "You should have noticed that my stomach isn't as big anymore. You know why that is Brian? Huh? Do you Brian? Guess! Guess why!"

I didn't answer but I completely understood. She'd lost the baby. A twinge of fear suddenly began to enter my thoughts. She wasn't just angry I hit her; she was angry she'd lost the baby because of it. Or so she says.

"Yeah, let it sink in," she said watching me intently. "Now you know I'm not playing with your monkey ass. So, is that what you wanted? Is that what you were trying to do when you were slamming me and the baby up against the wall? No, you wouldn't have done something so despicable to me on purpose would you? Would you!" She asked aiming the gun at me in her best Nancy Drew pose.

"I didn't even plan on seeing you. How could I have planned to make you lose the baby?" I sighed shifting and leaning the back of my head on the wall. "Anyway, it's not like you haven't had a truck load of abortions already. Why you so choked up over losing this one? You killed the others in the doctor's office and this one died by an unfortunate accident. Maybe it was God's will."

"An unfortunate accident! You bastard snake! What kind of man are you that you don't even feel anything for causing the death of my baby? Our baby! You know I might not even be able to have any more babies now because of you? You know that?" She questioned with tears streaming down her cheeks before she quickly spun around to wipe them from her eyes.

"So, what if I had a couple of abortions before," she said gutturally. "I was keeping this one!" She shrieked spinning around and pulling the trigger. I saw her fingers moving, but I didn't hear anything. I just felt an instant pain in my shoulder and the butt of the gun coming down on my head again as I began to howl. Everything went black.

15

Brenda

GETTING IT TOGETHER

It was already late in the afternoon and I'd taken most of the day to frolic with Lane. Driving home, there went my cell phone ringing again and I reached into my purse searching for it frantically while I drove.

"Hello?" I said grabbing it just in time and putting it to my ear.

"Girl, where are you? I've called you twice this morning on your cell and at the house," Rhonda asked with a slight attitude.

"What you looking for me so hard for? I stayed over Lane's last night," I answered with a similar 'tude.

"Oh. Y'all getting really close now huh? I saw all that lovey dovey kissing and caressing y'all were doing at the wedding reception." She teased.

"I'm not complaining."

"Alright well that's not what I called for. Have you talked to your brother since last night?"

I sighed dreading whatever news she was about to hand me. "No. What he do now?"

"Girl he roughed Gwen up last night. She went to the hospital because she saw blood dripping when she went to the bathroom this morning. I think she's losing the baby and..."

"Hold up, hold up, hold up!" I shrieked. "How do you know she didn't just make that up? Brian had a room at the hotel last night. When exactly was he supposed to have beaten the broad up? Is she trying to say Brian sent her to the hospital?" That bitch Gwen was really out of control.

"Wait a minute now, listen. She went to the hotel last night and she said they talked in his room and then he started slamming her up against the wall because he didn't like what she was saying. She sounded believable to me. Why would she make that up anyway? She went to the hospital and everything. She sounded mad as hell when I talked to her on the phone and if he did it.," Rhonda warned.

Although I was nervous about the possibility of what she was saying being true, I didn't want it to be and I knew Rhonda had already leaked the fact that Brian had inheritance money from our grandfather. This could all be some kind of set up. "How do you know she didn't do this to herself? Go home and make her injuries more than what they really were, if he hit her at all?" I questioned. "I wouldn't trust that lying hooker as far as I could throw her. I know Brian can't stand her, but I don't believe he'd beat up a pregnant woman. She needs to stop fucking with him and just get the baby tested when it's born."

"Really Brenda? Get your damn head out the clouds. Whether you like her or not, he had no right putting his hands on her and it's not like it's so farfetched that he would do something like that. Get real. What kind of pussy puts his hands on a pregnant woman? You gonna stick up for him regardless of what he does?" She hammered.

"Whatever Rhonda," I replied feeling cornered. "There's nothing I can do about it either way. That's not my fight and I don't want to even put that on my plate if I don't have to. That's between Gwen and Brian."

She was panting and I imagined her pacing her apartment hallway as she often did when she was having a heated phone conversation. "You need to talk to your brother. You need to tell him to get down to the hospital and see about Gwen and make sure that he didn't make her lose that baby. He better pray to God he doesn't walk out in handcuffs! That's your potential niece or nephew so it should be your fight."

"Rhonda I'm getting off the phone cause I'm getting upset and my battery is damn near dead anyway because it's been off the charger all night. I'll talk to you tomorrow," I said hanging up abruptly.

I wasn't lying about my phone battery dying but I also wanted to get off the phone with her before I said something I couldn't take back. I was pissed that she would side with Gwen under the circumstances. Yes, Gwen was also her friend, but so what! She also knew that Gwen was a Ho and a stalker. I rolled my eyes and scowled at the thought of Brian beating her up. How would she have even known what room he was in?

I rolled my eyes as I pulled into the parking spot in front of my building and grabbed my purse before getting out. Briefly scanning the lot for Brian's Navigator in any of his usual spots, I didn't see it, so I assumed he was still in, or leaving the hotel.

As I was locking the door behind me, Amanda yelled from a lower-level apartment window, "Hey chick!"

"Hey girl what's up?" I said heading towards the stairs.

"Merchandise. Come here for a minute"

I truly didn't feel like it, but I felt obligated. "Okay," I answered.

Amanda opened her apartment door before I got there, and I closed it behind me. "Girrrrrl come back here!" she yelled from her bedroom in the back.

When I got to her room, she was standing in her closet dressed in a red jogging suit. Amanda stood 5'4" with dark brown skin and shoulder length brown hair. She was from the Philippians and I envied her beauty and her figure. She was a mother of 3 girls and a boy, all 2 years apart; but her shape looked like that of a 20-year-old model. She was 26 and her oldest child was 8 years old.

"My boy Anthony…" she said pulling a bunch of clothes on hangers in long bags from her closet. "…he works at Nordstrom's and he has the major hook up. He just hit me off with an ass of clothes and I'm about to sell 'em and get some change." She said with a huge grin as she loaded more piles of clothes onto her bed. "So, you being my home girl and everything…" she said pausing and putting her hands on her hips. "I'm a let you get a couple of outfits before I get my sale going."

"What?" I said smiling. I wasn't condoning the sale of stolen goods, but I'll be damned if I was going to pass up the opportunity to get some clothes for free 99!

"Girl I owe you for helping me get my car out of the impound last month and plus you're my friend. So, like I said, grab a couple of outfits. Looks like you need some since you wearing the same thing 2 days in a row!" She said laughing and playfully pushing me as I looked through the clothes to select some outfits I wanted.

"Damn what you spying on me or something? How you know I had this outfit on yesterday? Maybe I have something similar," I said knowing it sounded ridiculous.

"You know I don't miss a beat around here. Another late night with your Teddy bear huh?" She joked.

"No miss know-it-all. That playboy brother has been dismissed. I had a good date with a good brother and good riddance to bad rubbish," I said as I selected 2 Armani pantsuits from the pile.

"Yeah... surrrreeee. I've heard that a million times girl," Amanda said as she sat on the edge of her bed. "That's the same thing I said about Clyde and look how that turned out," she said laying back on her bed and laughing. "Two kids later."

I was really starting to get tired of people with their skepticism when I told them I'd curbed Teddy.

Clyde was the father of one of her 4 children as well as the man she'd been living with.

"Girl I hear you but it's really over this time but anyway, can I come check these out later? I need to get upstairs and wash up and what not now that you mention it."

"I hear you girl. I know how it feels wearing the same outfit 2 days in a row," she snickered. "That Edwin dude you told me about was knocking on your door this morning too. He's creepy. I was gonna call you, but I know you don't keep your cell usually anyway."

"Damn," I replied walking toward the front door.

"No problem. Let any of your friends know that I got some stuff if they're looking though. I'll give them a good price for it." She answered.

I nodded and headed upstairs to my apartment.

When I came into my place, I saw Zeus out on the patio scratching at the glass door and noticed Kelly's keys on my coffee table. But where was she? And why did she put him outside? 'He must've torn something up and she put him out there as punishment or something,' I thought to myself. "Kelly why you got my baby..." I began to call walking toward my bedroom. I short stopped in the doorway when I saw Kelly's motionless body lying on the floor at the bottom of my bed and Edwin sitting in the armchair across from her pointing a handgun at me. I froze.

"Don't move. I don't want to hurt you now," he said standing. "Finally made it home did you? I got tired of waiting for you, so I had to use your cousin here to get in," he said in a sinister tone stepping over Kelly toward me. "Okay I can barely even look at you in those same clothes from yesterday knowing you're in them because you've just come from giving yourself to that other guy. Go take a shower," he ordered waving me towards the bathroom with the gun in his hand.

Tears scurried down my face and my legs felt like planted two-by-fours. I didn't know if Kelly was dead or not, but I was paralyzed with fear to find out. "Doesn't she need help?" I asked in a mousey voice.

"No, she doesn't," he replied without explanation. "Now go take a shower before I start getting mad."

That's when I noticed the silencer on the gun. I couldn't decipher what caliber it was, but I knew what a silencer looked like. My gaze fell to where Kelly lay, and it wasn't until then that I spotted the pool of blood she was sprawled out in on my carpet. I gingerly walked towards the bathroom which was on the side of the room where I stood. Once inside I began to close the door. No such luck. Edwin obstructed the closing with his foot and pushed the door wide open with his free hand.

"We've already seen each other naked so there's no need for modesty anymore. We can leave this door open," he instructed.

I was now sobbing more heavily while I disrobed, and my vision was blurred with tears and disbelief. Edwin kept his gun pointing at me as I turned the water on in the shower and stepped into the stream of warm water without closing the curtains.

"Wash him off you. I want to know every trace of him is down the drain. You have a deuce...douche...whatever that thing is called to squash up inside of you?" He asked opening the cabinet under my bathroom sink.

I closed my eyes and silently prayed this was all a terrible nightmare I'd wake up from as soon as I opened my eyes, but Edwin shoving a SUMMER'S EVE bottle at me quickly dashed that hope. I swallowed the huge lump in my throat as I used the product for its intended purpose and let my cries and tears penetrate the water now drenching my body.

***

My mind raced in 20 different directions as I sat on the edge of the bed facing Edwin who was seated back in the chair he occupied when I came home. I was only allowed to put my robe on, and my wet hair dripped down my back as quickly as tears still fell down my face.

"What are you gonna do with me?" I finally asked.

"Why did you choose that guy over me? Why do you choose all the other guys over me when I've been so open for you?" He asked ignoring my question.

"We weren't working out."

"But why? What else could I have done? You obviously liked me at first, right? I mean we went out, we even had sex, but then you just started pulling away. I brought flowers, wanted to spend time with you, I called...what did you want that I didn't try to give?" He chastised.

"It was too much too soon. I just wanted you to slow down but you kept speeding up," I said through sobs.

"Oh, but that guy from last night was just in the right pace for you right? Why was he so special? You never even invited me in your place before, but you go and get him and let him spend the night, you spend the day together and everything!" He complained becoming animated and pacing in front of me with his gun still on alert. "Within a couple of days, he's all the sudden the most important man in the world? Just when I'd gotten Teddy out the picture?"

"Gotten Teddy out the picture?" I asked confused. Had he killed him too?

"Yeah, you broke up with him because of me, right? I heard you on the phone with your friend at work saying how you'd had it with him."

Oh, I understood. He hadn't harmed Teddy. He was just delusional and crazy as hell! "So why can't I get dressed? Are you going to rape me?"

He looked shocked and hurt at first. "Rape you? What kind of guy do you think I am? Besides, it's not rape when it's consensual, and you gave that to me when we made love before. You should be flattered that I'd even still want to touch you knowing how easily you give it up," he replied changing to a disgusted expression.

"Why did you kill my cousin?"

Edwin was silent for a moment. He ran his hand over his face, looked up to the ceiling, down at his gun and then at me again. "I didn't intend to at first. I saw her walking your dog and I knew she must've had a key, so when she was going back in, I tried to talk my way in but she... she was mean. Mean for no reason like how you get sometimes when we talk. She started trying to close the door on me and she kept threatening to call the cops and I just lost it. I pulled the gun from my waist and shot through the crack in the door before I even thought about it."

He began pacing but never took his eyes off me or his finger off the trigger. "She let the door go and ran to the bedroom. When I came in, she was lying on the floor where you saw her. I couldn't get her any help because then... well I couldn't get her any help."

I hadn't stopped crying to begin with but now my tears were more for my cousin than for me. Kelly didn't deserve to be shot down like an animal and it hurt my heart to know it was a favor she was doing for me that caused her death.

"I don't think it was that painful anyway. She was dead pretty quick so it's not like she suffered or anything," he said looking me up and down as I tightened my grip on my closed robe. "You know I never planned for this to go this far but now that it has, I just gotta follow through. As soon as Gwen gives me the signal that your brother's home, we're gonna go downstairs."

I almost stopped breathing when he mentioned Gwen and my brother. I began to silently pray again for me and for Brian. Zeus was barking incessantly and scratching on the balcony door and Edwin said, "Your dog is lucky I'm an animal lover cause all that noise he's making is driving me crazy."

"You and Gwen planned this together? I didn't even know you knew each other," I questioned.

"I wouldn't say we planned it together, but we just came to an understanding. We became acquainted a little while back and discovered we had you and Brian in common. She's the one who convinced me to bring you flowers last week, but you were so wrapped up in yourself that you didn't care. Well actually, I guess that's not fair since your father did die but...whatever. You might say you two were the catalyst for our chance friendship."

"So, you met while you were stalking us?"

"Stalking? I was just trying to get your attention. How was I supposed to know you were the type to sleep around and then discard a man so freely? I'm not saying Gwen wasn't stalking, because she was showing up places and talking to people, but I just sat in my car and watched. I was just trying to figure you out. You know, so I could be the kind of man you needed in your life. That's all down the drain now," he said fixing his glasses and nervously cracking his neck from side to side. "But that's your fault, not mine."

"So, you're doing all of this because I lost interest in you? That seriously makes sense in your mind?" I asked shaking my head in disgust.

"Hell yeah, that makes sense to me. You can't just lead a person to think you're gonna be together and then change your mind because another guy likes you," he scolded.

"Edwin I already knew Lane. We've gone out before this, before you and I even went out. That's why he and I click more. Anyway, why even continue to pursue me if I'm so slutty and shady? What is all of this supposed to do for you now?"

"Give me closure. I still love you and I still want you. But you're right. I can't make you love me back or want to be with me. I just wanted to make you feel some of the pain I feel for you but...things got more out of hand than I thought. Brenda, you have no idea how much of a good, loyal man you've missed out on with me. And now you'll go to your grave knowing that. Regretting it."

'Go to my grave knowing that,' rang in my head loud as my tears began to dry. It was apparent now that tears weren't going to get me out of this and honestly, my sorrow was beginning to turn into anger. Who the hell did this judgmental, delusional, stalking bastard think he was to come into my life and tell me about my life? Trying to tell me that if I wasn't with him, I deserved to die? I wasn't going to give into whatever he was planning for me or for Brian. He wanted me to bow down to him but there was only one way that was going to happen...

Over my dead body!

***

Edwin took a deep breath and ran both of his hands over his face to try and regain his composure. If you can call it that. He allowed me to get dressed in a tank top, shorts and socks, under his watch, and then scanned my bedroom floor before picking up my Nike sneakers and putting them down by my feet.

"Are these the ones you were gonna wear?" He asked.

I didn't answer I just began putting my feet in them. All I could think about were ways I was going to get past him to get out of the house; or get him to leave. The look in his eyes said that he was not the harmless putz I'd taken him for previously. I doubted the reverse psychology thing that usually works on TV was going to work on him.

He grabbed me roughly by the arm and released me with a shove like I was a rag doll.

"Okay so do I have your attention now?" He asked.

"Yes," I said wincing in pain and grabbing my arm where his fingerprints were starting to appear.

"Sit on the bed!" He commanded taking a deep breath. "Like I was saying... I realize I didn't play my cards right because of my timing.

Sometimes a beautiful woman can throw a brotha off of his game, you know what I mean?" He paused for my response, but it was only met by my blank stare. "But when we made love…"

"We had sex Edwin. We did not make love! Stop romanticizing it!" I screamed.

"You better lower your damn voice before I put a bullet in your voice box!" He responded waving the gun at me.

I cowered into the corner by the wall between my bathroom and bedroom as he continued," We had sex? Stop romanticizing it? You're really a broken woman Brenda. No normal woman is so callous and gives away her womanhood like government cheese. So, what we had didn't mean anything to you? Is that what you're telling me?" He asked splaying his hands above his head. "You fucked with my head."

"I didn't fuck with your head. You must've been fucked in the head long before I came into the picture. You're the one who's got me here at gunpoint and won't leave me alone. You stop fucking with me!" I yelled and then flinched in anticipation of him shooting me as promised for my loudness.

"Selfish bitch!" He scowled. "You're making me crazy. You're turning me into somebody I don't-want-to be and for Christ's sake, will that dog shut the hell up!" He exclaimed storming out of my room and into the living room facing the glass doors where Zeus was locked out.

"Don't hurt him!" I cried peeling myself from the corner and running towards him. He was pointing the gun towards Zeus and was in the process of turning it towards me when I rushed him. Between the shock of my charge and his pure lack of coordination, he'd lost the upper hand.

The combination of fear and anger I'd built inside rumbled out through my fists. I swung as he stumbled backwards trying to avoid my blows causing him to trip over his feet and go crashing to the floor. I nearly fell with him, but managed to keep my balance as the gun flew across the room and I turned toward the front door. This was my chance to get away and I didn't want to waste it grappling for the gun.

I fumbled with the locks, opened the door and ran smack into a police officer who was just about to knock. I was startled and screamed as we collided and the officer grabbed me by both arms out of reflex, and quickly put one hand on his gun belt.

"Whoa, whoa," he yelped almost equally startled.

"He's got a gun! He killed my cousin!" I hollered with momentum pulling us both farther outside the doorway.

"What?" The officer asked shaken a bit with his gun now pointing inside my apartment. "Who is this in your apartment ma'am?"

"Edwin Ward! He's a stalker! And he has a gun!" I exclaimed frantically looking around as Zeus suddenly came running out of the door. The officer almost shot him but pulled back realizing the dog was not on the attack or heading for him.

"This is Officer Sanchez code 11-99, 246 possible 187 and a 417. Officer proceeding with caution," he said pushing a button on a microphone device on his shoulder as the dispatcher said back, "Repeat, officer needs back up, residential shooting, possible homicide in pursuit with armed assailant."

He proceeded cautiously into my apartment after telling me to stay where I was. Hell...not in this lifetime! As soon as the officer disappeared into my apartment, I took off down the hall and down the steps with Zeus in toe. Once I got to the First-floor landing, I started to run towards my car but then I realized I didn't have my keys with me. Damn! Then I remembered what Edwin had said about us going downstairs to Brian's apartment to meet with Gwen and when I saw Brian's truck I turned back around, ran down to my brother's door and started banging on it.

"Brian! Brian!" I yelled banging on the door with Zeus barking loudly behind me and running in circles. I thought I might have heard Brian's voice, but I couldn't make out what he said, and no one came to the door. "Brian, open the door!" I hollered. Now it was silent, so I ran back upstairs to my apartment intending on getting my keys from the house so I could open the door. I heard sirens blaring as multiple police cars screeched into the lot and the officer exited my apartment.

"He must've gone out the patio door because he's not in there," he said grabbing hold of me and pushing me back towards the stairway. "You need to come with me for your own protection and for questioning."

"You got him?!" Another uniformed officer yelled up from the bottom of the stairway.

"No. He climbed over the balcony or something. What does he look like miss?" Officer Sanchez asked me.

"He's dark skin, bald with glasses, wearing blue jeans and a blue shirt. His name is Edwin Ward. We need to go check on my brother though," I said hysterically. "He said him and my brother's stalker Gwen were going to kill us both downstairs in his apartment, and nobody answered when I banged on the door, but I think I heard him, and I know he's there cause his car is there. If you let me get my keys, we can get in."

The officer at the bottom of the stairs called in the description and he and some other officers scattered looking for Edwin. My neighbor Lina opened up her door in a robe with her blonde hair piled all over her head and wiping her eyes. "What the hell is happening?" She asked.

"Ma'am please go back inside your apartment and lock the door," Officer Sanchez ordered.

"God damn it while I'm paying to live here somebody needs to tell me what's going on when I open my door and it looks like an episode of NYPD BLUE," she responded with a frown.

"Ma'am! Go back inside your apartment I said!" he yelled more forcefully causing her to jump and rush back inside quickly. "Okay let's get the keys," he then said to me.

As I rushed into my apartment to grab my keys, I let a prayer slip from my lips, "GOD please let my brother be okay."

16

Brian

NOW WHAT

When I came to, Gwen was kneeling down beside me sneering like a dog with rabies.

"I wasn't sure if you were dead or not. Wishful thinking, I guess," she said monotonically getting up beginning to pace a few feet away in front of me. I know Edwin better hurry up and bring that bitch down here before my trigger finger gets too itchy to wait to put a bullet in you."

What the hell was going on with this crazy bitch? Her and my sister's bumfucked stalker had this planned together? This had to be a dream.

Gwen cackled. "You're starting to get scared now huh? I see it on your face. "

"How'd you get my gun?" I asked weakly.

She eyed the gun in her hand and then looked back at me with furrowed eyebrows and a smirk. "This isn't your gun idiot. You think I'd come in here unarmed and search your pansy apartment for a gun to torture you with? Your brain must've already started dying with that stupid ass question," she scowled rolling her eyes.

It looks just like my gun you evil bitch! I yelled in my head. I'd at least wizened up to the fact that taunting her would only expedite her eagerness to carry out her plans and I had to come up with something before she could.

Then she stopped pacing and focused on me. "Wait a minute. So, you have a gun in here? Where?"

I felt hot as an oven and blood or sweat (because I couldn't tell which one it was with my eyes tightly clinched together) was dripping down my forehead. Apparently, I wasn't the only one who's brain might have been going dead cause hers was definitely in need of CPR if she thought I was going to tell her where my gun was.

"Somebody stole it out my car last week. I thought that was how you got it," I lied.

She squinted contemplating whether to believe me or not and checked her watch before addressing me again.

"You wanna know how you're gonna die or do you want it to be a surprise? Or...do you want me just to tell you how your sister is gonna die?" Gwen taunted with a nasty smirk finally sitting her raggedy ass down on the couch.

I glared at her, murmuring in pain as the bullet in my shoulder continued to make its presence known. I inched myself upright so that I was again sitting with my back against the wall facing her. Even though it probably took a minute or more in my position to do, Gwen said nothing while she watched me struggle.

"Comfy?" She asked sarcastically. "So, which do you want to know? Cause he's probably gonna be down here with your sister any minute now and I bet it will all go so fast that I won't have time to tell you then. At least you won't die confused right?"

"Why can't you just let it go? We were never even seriously dating," I asked.

"Let it go? Negro please. I'm gonna let it go alright. One cap in your ass at a time," she chuckled menacingly. "See the plan is to make it look like a burglary gone wrong where your nosey ass sister walks in while it's in progress and ends up getting popped too. She's gonna get it as soon as she opens the door so you can watch her die, and then you'll get yours."

That's when I started to really look at her. Gwen was wearing clear rubber gloves, black jeans, black sneakers, and a black long-sleeved hoody. That bitch was fast as hell. She was the one who broke my car window too! It must have been a stall tactic to slow me up at getting home. I also noticed that my flat screen was gone, and my stereo was missing. Amateur bitch hadn't even checked my dresser drawer for my gun. But how would I get to it?

"Why are you waiting for them to get here first if you plan on killing me anyway?" I asked.

"Because in case they check time of death or whatever we want them to be the same time. You know, to tell the story basically. Punk ass Edwin said he doesn't think he can shoot her himself, but I know I can. Hell, I'm dying to crack your head open right now," she said with her eyes closed as if basking in the thought. "You know they said it was a boy. The baby." Gwen stated out of the blue. "You could've had a son."

"I didn't want a son."

"You didn't want a son, or you didn't want a son with me?" She asked with an attitude.

"Both."

"Well then maybe you should've been wrapping it up every time you had sex with somebody because that's how babies are made idiot. If you don't like me so much, then why the hell did you sleep with me anyway? You were always all standoff-ish until that night. You should've just left me alone then," Gwen Scowled.

"Nobody forced you. Maybe you should've learned not to spread your legs for every guy that shows you some attention."

"You knew I always liked you, although I don't know why the hell that was anymore, but you took advantage of the fact."

I laughed but was interrupted by a sharp pain in the wound on my head. "Took advantage of you," I mocked. "Ok."

"You want another bullet?" She threatened pointing the gun at me again.

"Nobody's gonna buy this was a robbery. How are y'all gonna get away? Y'all have some serious flaws in your plan. Is my life really worth spending the rest of your life in jail?"

She stared at me blankly for a moment and then began to chuckle. "You watching too much LAW AND ORDER with that mess Brian. I already shot you and pistol whipped your black ass, so I think I've pretty much crossed the point of no return already, yes? Now shut up. I'm sick of talking to you now and I just want to wait for them to get here in silence. Feel free to die if you can't wait," she growled. "And anyway, we have a failsafe getaway plan."

That's when I started laughing again. Partly because I was satisfied that she'd be caught if she succeeded in murdering me, judging from the sloppy way she was holding me captive, but mostly because I knew that would irritate her. She needed to get it over with if she was going to do it because it was becoming harder for me to stand the pain.

"Fuck you laughing for? Believe me; you don't have anything to be happy about.

I was starting to slip out of consciousness...I prayed it wasn't for good.

***

"Do you know how humiliating it is to have to call somebody off the hook and track them down wherever they go just to get them to have a conversation with you? Huh? Do you know how low you made me feel every time you said something nasty to me? I never did anything to you but let you make love to me. Why did you have to be so damn mean?" Gwen angrily begged with tears starting to well in her eyes.

My shoulder and left arm felt like it had already died, and I was extremely weak; but not too weak to respond.

"We had sex in a pool. That's not making love. Let it go." I answered leaning my head up against the side of the wall I had my back to.

My mind started drifting off to the day I let my dick and the alcohol seal my destiny. Gwen was hawking me (along with all of the other women) from the time I hit the door at Rhonda's pool party. She was looking considerably better than she'd looked any other time I saw her and for a moment I almost didn't recognize her until someone said her name. Gwen made sure to linger around me posturing all night long to ensure I got an eyeful of her see through dress that cloaked her string bikini like a piece of tissue paper.

"So, you still bartending at the club?" She asked leaning on the wall near the portable bar where I was getting a drink to add to the four I had earlier, hanging with my boys at Ike's place.

"Amongst other things," I replied stirring my drink before gulping it down.

"Can you make me one too then? Something hot, sexy and strong," she said emphasizing her words while leaning into me.

I was never a fan of black women with blonde hair, but Gwen seemed to be pulling it off well; or so my drunken eyeballs said.

"What do you want me to make? Looks like they only have Vodka and Hennessey left."

"Give me what you think I need," she continued grinning and pushing her breasts up against my arm.

Mini-me was starting to stretch himself awake and the smell of her perfume was pleasantly accompanying my thoughts to get between her and that bikini. "If you keep rubbing your tits up against me like that, I'm gonna give you what you really want," I answered letting the alcohol drive my words.

She grinned slyly traced the outline of her right areola with her index finger, which immediately made her nipple stand at attention, and then dipped her finger in the drink I was making before licking the mix off of it.

"What the hell was that?" I laughed nearly spilling her drink before handing it to her. "Something you saw in a porno? Girl stop playing," I teased.

She forced a smile through her broken ego and whipped her blonde hair around like Farrah Faucet's ghetto hair double. "You're always trying to be a funny guy Brian. Don't talk yourself out of this pussy trying to be funny."

"It would seem to be impossible to talk myself out of getting something you've been trying to give to me now wouldn't it?" I played along.

"Don't be so certain pretty eyes. Now come and get in the pool with me. All these birds around here trying to act like they're too good to get in the pool at a pool party," she said rolling her eyes and grabbing my hand. "It's too hot to just stand around and my bikini is too cute to keep it covered up all day."

She was looking mighty fine and I certainly appreciated the sight of her plump butt jiggling with the sway of her hips as I followed behind. I left my glass on the bar, since I drank it at once but Gwen put her drink down on a poolside table after taking a huge sip.

"Woooo!" She said squinting her eyes and flapping her hands like a falling baby bird. "That drink is way too strong man."

I cracked my neck from side to side and noticed my sister with sunglasses on her head in a red one-piece bathing suit with big holes strategically placed around her torso headed my way.

"You wanna be my spades partner?" Brenda asked side eyeing Gwen and turning so that the back of her head was in Gwen's eye view.

"Later. I'm about to get in the pool," I answered slipping out of my mandal's and taking my tank top off up over my head so the ladies could get a glimpse of my 6 pack in swim trunks.

"Uh... Hi Brenda," Gwen said with a phony smile and a bitter tone as she slipped her dress cover up off and put it on the lawn chair by the pool.

Damn! Her body was definitely looking ripe. Why had I been ignoring her before again? I couldn't remember.

"Give me your shirt baby," she said taking my tank and laying it over the top of her dress.

Brenda didn't reply to Gwen's hello and instead pulled the sunglasses from the top of her head onto her face. "Alright well come get me when you're done in the pool. Rhonda plays like she just learned yesterday, and you know I don't like to lose."

"Shiiit, don't wait for me. With all the drinks I had today I'm not gonna be paying attention either."

"Yeah, it's too nice to be inside. It's a pool party! You should get in with us. Your swimsuit looks really cute too." Gwen exclaimed smiling at Brenda and walking backwards slowly toward the pool.

"Thanks," Brenda answered coldly and sashayed her merciless ass back through a crowd of people by the sliding glass doors and back into the house.

There were maybe 20 people at most in the backyard of Rhonda's mom's house while the rest of the 50 or so guests occupied the house and/or the front yard. Rhonda's small apartment couldn't have held everybody she invited to her birthday party, so her parents let her use their mansion sized crib instead.

Gwen and I stayed in the pool for a long time talking; joking and half-ass swimming because it was dark, and I'd had at least 2 more drinks to her 4 when I noticed the skimpy amount of stragglers in the pool with us. The in-house deejay was blasting the remix to The Notorious BIG's song "GIVE ME ONE MORE CHANCE" and Gwen started bouncing up and down in the water like a buoy on speed.

"Oooohhhh that's my jam!" She slurred as her left breast bounced deathly close to popping completely out of her bikini top.

"Here, let me help you put that back in where it belongs," I said cunningly wading over to her and using my tongue to lick and suckle her exposed breast.

She moaned and thrust her head back pulling me closer into her and letting her blonde locks dip into the water. "Oh yeah baby. Kiss me all over. Baaaaby give me oneeeee more chance..." she said and sung grasping me and wrapping her legs around my waist under water.

I pulled both of her breasts free and began breastfeeding like I was expecting milk to come out at any moment. She was grinding her body against my rock-hard wood and supporting herself by leaning her back against the edge of the pool with her elbows on the side of it. I wasn't sure who else was around to notice what we were doing but if she didn't care, neither did I. Her body was calling me, and my body was ready to bust the doors to her inner circle wide open.

Gwen slid her bikini bottom to the side and unleashed the dragon from my swim trunks as she descended onto the rod she'd practically been begging for since the day I met her. There were a lot of things you could call what we did in the pool that night, but "making love" is not one of them.

***

"I'm bleeding too much," I said more to myself than to her noticing the puddle of blood forming around me from my injured shoulder and head as I opened my eyes.

"Bleeding too much for what? To die? I hope you don't expect me to help you."

"So, if I die before my sister gets here it's not gonna mess up your little plan?" I asked weakly.

Gwen frowned and looked around as though she was possibly considering what I said and self-consciously touched her hair.

"Listen Brian, you can try your little mind tricks trying to scare me about getting caught if you want to but you wanna know something? I don't give a damn if I get caught or not. I'm willing to risk going to jail if it means I'm gonna get the satisfaction of slowly snuffing the life out of you the way you snuffed the life out of me."

"So, because you're mad at me, mad I've been ignoring you, you let some other crazy lunatic talk you into a double murder for revenge? You that naive and jealous of my sister?"

"Jealous of your sister? Jealous of what? Of herself righteous attitude? Of her trying to turn one of my closest friends against me because she doesn't approve of some of the things I've done in my past? Who the hell is she supposed to be to judge me? Ain't nobody jealous of her man hoppin' ass. She's just as wishy washy with guys as you're saying I am. She had sex with Edwin, lead him to think they could have a relationship and then out of the blue she just started ignoring him. That smug bitch didn't even have the common courtesy to tell him to his face that she didn't want to date him anymore even though they work in the same building. Y'all are definitely two of a kind," she said shaking her head in disgust.

"And that's enough to kill her for?" I asked judgmentally feeling like the wounded half of my body was falling asleep.

"Apparently it is for him. Now you and me, that's another situation all together. You can't just go around fucking everything that moves and then if you end up getting somebody pregnant you just ignore them. You had a responsibility to see it through with me and do your part as the father. I see now you would've been a horrible father anyway, but you didn't have any right to take my baby from me," she paused as though she was thinking about what could have been. "Or to put your hands on me," she glared.

"You weren't giving me any choice," I feebly attempted to assert. "You been stalking me and busting out my God damn car windows too. What about the other guy that could be the baby daddy? You been running up on him and talking to people where he plays ball like you've been doing me? Staking out where he lives and showing up uninvited to get at him? I dicked you down once at a party. Nothing more and nothing less. You're acting like I promised you a ring. Why can't you just let it go?"

"Let it go. Let it go! That's all you keep saying to me. Let it go. You got me pregnant, you beat me up and you murdered my baby! Don't tell me to fucking get over it! No, I haven't been talking to the other guy cause in all probability it was yours!" She screamed. "Now I got your black ass begging me to let it go," she mumbled eyeing the gun.

"I'm not…begging," I replied feeling as though I was about to pass out again.

The fire in her eyes could have set my apartment ablaze had she the power Drew Barrymore had in FIRE STARTER.

"You know what Brian? I'm tired of waiting for Edwin to bring your bitchy sister down here. Change of plans. How about you come with me into the bedroom…" she said lunging out of her seat and coming towards me just as there was a loud pounding on the door stopping her in her tracks.

"Brian, Brian!" I heard Brenda yelling and banging on my door.

Gwen's eyes widened to the size of golf balls and a spark of hope and energy scampered back into my spirit.

"Brenda call the police! Gwen's got a..." my feeble voiced warning was cut short as I ducked to dodge a bullet that lodged itself inches away from my head into the wall behind me. Gwen's eyes narrowed with hatred and she shook her head.

I closed my eyes tightly expecting to feel a bullet enter my skull next.

She scrambled to the door and looked out the peep hole frantically saying in a low grumble, "This isn't the plan. This isn't the plan. Where the hell is Edwin?" She pushed random strands of hair from her face and paced in front of the door when the banging stopped.

Gwen looked out the peep hole again and seemed confused by what she saw. She shot a wild-eyed glance back at me and then looked out the peephole again from different angles which lead me to believe she couldn't see where Brenda had gone.

I could hear the sirens announcing the police's arrival. My inner voice was screaming, 'Were they having donuts in front of our complex? How did they get here so damn fast? Get this bitch out of here and get me to the hospital!'

"Holy shit!" She exclaimed scurrying around the apartment like a mouse in a cage. "What the hell did he do? I know that motherfucker didn't rat me out to the cops? But this was his fucking idea! Oh my God." She panicked. "Your bitch of a sister must've turned him against me! Fuck!" She howled looking up at the ceiling as tears erupted from her eyes.

Suddenly she seemed intensely focused and began approaching me with the slow prowess of a lion about to devour its prey. She stopped a few feet in front of me pointing the gun at my face as her eyes darted between the front door and my sweaty pain staked face.

"The only way you're going out of here is in a body bag," she advised.

I heard keys turning in the lock and a struggle to open it just before I felt something whirr past my temple and felt an unbearable burning pain in my right cheek.

The door abruptly burst open and a clamor of male voices filled the room yelling… and maybe Brenda's voice too as Gwen shrieked, "No!" before I heard a loud explosion, and everything went black.

17

Brenda

THIS TOO... MIGHT PASS

Edwin hadn't gotten far when he jumped from my balcony because he'd broken his ankle during the landing and police swarmed him like bees to honey providing him with a few additional blows to keep him down. Everything afterwards that day is a hazy blur of surreal events. I remember seeing Brian slumped and bloody against the wall and feeling like we were too late to save him, Gwen's bullet riddled body lying face down in the middle of his apartment while the paramedics rushed past me, and then my uncle Donovan.

He'd walked from the entrance down to our units because the police cars blocked any other way of entry. Carrying a plastic bag full of CHINESE PANDA Chinese food in his big brawny hands, he looked confused and concerned. A couple of officers stopped him at the landing of our apartments, and he made several motions that I interpreted as him explaining who he was and why he needed to know what was going on. Then he locked eyes with me as they were carrying Brian out on a gurney.

"Brenda!" He exclaimed with worry in his eyes as I approached with tears in mine and feeling like I was walking on a waterbed.

"I... I think he's dead," I murmured as the pavement seemed to rise up and smack me in the face.

The next thing I remembered I was in the back of an ambulance being taken to the hospital. Everything after that was a whirlwind of me telling and re-telling the police what happened, checking on Brian's condition, crying dealing with my mother and her antics while dealing with the overwhelming grief I saw on my aunt and uncle's faces at the hospital mourning their daughter's death and waiting to see if Brian would be next.

Even Uncle Donovan couldn't hold back sobs as he embraced my Aunt Tonya in the hallway at the hospital. Apparently, they'd brought the body to the morgue and they'd identified Kelly's body at some point the same night when Brian was admitted although I'd told the officers who she was from the beginning. They weren't able to stay long afterwards because my aunt was inconsolable.

As I curled up in a chair in the ICU waiting room, I saw Rhonda approaching who looked like she was a few steps from bursting into tears and when she reached me, she did just that.

"Oh my God Brenda I'm soo soo sorry baby," she wept embracing me as I stood to return the hug.

I wasn't really sure what to say back since my mind was racing and I didn't think I had enough water in left in my body to shed another tear.

"Has there been an update on Brian's condition yet?" She asked.

I shook my head no and replied, "Not since they took him back to surgery. He stopped breathing when they first brought him in, so they had to bring him back and now they're doing emergency surgery to remove one of the bullets and a kidney. He's got so much internal damage that I think they said it nicked his lung too and they're trying to stop the bleeding." I sat down and covered my face with both hands. "She was really going to kill him Rhonda, and God help me I don't know what I'm gonna do if they come out here and tell me that she did. I can't get the visual of him leaning up against the wall all bloody and beat up out of my head. I thought he was dead, Rhonda. He looked dead," I continued lifting my head to look up at her.

She took a seat next to me and put her hands lovingly on both my arms. "He's gonna be alright. Just think positive Bren. He's a strong guy and they know what they're doing," she consoled. "Did Edwin hurt you?"

I shook my head sideways. "Not physically. He was planning to though. They were gonna kill me and Brian. Did Gwen tell you what she was gonna do?" I asked remembering Rhonda's call to me earlier. "Did you know she was gonna come to murder us?"

"No! For God sake Brenda you think she would tell me something like that and I wouldn't tell you or call the police?" She screeched clasping her hands to her chest. "I swear to you I didn't know she had gotten this far gone. I mean I knew she was really mad, and she kept saying that he thought he was above the law and how he wasn't gonna get away with doing whatever he wanted to do to her, but I didn't think she was gonna do anything like that. Not even remotely. I definitely didn't think she was going to try to do anything to you."

"Well, what were you saying back to her when she was talking to you? I know you weren't just stoically sitting there and listening. Were you agreeing that he needed to pay? The way you sounded on the phone was like you felt like I was responsible for looking out for her too," I badgered feeling my anger overtaking me. Rhonda was supposed to be my best friend and there she was consorting with the motherfucking enemy who tried to kill me and my brother!

"I wasn't saying anything to encourage it!" She exclaimed. "I didn't think she was gonna do anything above maybe scratching up his car like the other chicks did. I never thought in a million year she was gonna try to kill him though Brenda...or do anything to hurt you. I'm sorry about how we got off the phone before, but you know me and you know I would never say anything like that."

I stared at her momentarily reading her face for any signs of deceit. I saw none. "Yeah ok," I said sitting back in the chair and inhaling deeply to calm myself down.

"I just can't believe they had to kill her though..." Rhonda's words trailed as I leaned forward, and we drew eye to eye again.

"I'm not sorry they had to kill her. She was a crazy chick with a damn weapon. Were they supposed to come in with a negotiator and try to talk her out of blowing our heads off? Get the fuck outta here with all the damn sympathy for that bitch," I said defensively getting angry again.

"No I... I didn't mean it that way," Rhonda stuttered. "I'm just...just thinking out loud. I know they had to do it, it's just crazy that she's dead I meant. I'm sorry," she pled looking like a cornered mouse in front of a lion.

"Forgive me if I don't have any sympathy for the dead bitch who tried to body bag my brother," I reiterated coldly.

Rhonda looked away and nervously fidgeted with her cell phone. If she said one more word in defense of Gwen, I felt like I might haul off and punch her in the face.

"I'm sorry Brenda. I swear I didn't mean it how it sounded. It was a stupid thing to say, especially right now." Rhonda apologized just as I saw another headache coming down the corridor.

Just what I needed, my mother.

***

"Mrs. Andrews, hi," Rhonda said standing and hugging my mother who leaned into it while holding 2 bags of chips in one hand as her Louis Vuitton bang hanging from her wrist and 2 soda cans in the other hand.

"Rhonda, hello," my mother replied with a June Cleaver smile and then stepping around her to sit in the chair on the other side of me. "I was going to bring you something from the cafeteria on my way up, but they didn't have anything worth putting in our mouths down there Brenda," my mother said handing me a bag of Doritos and a Sprite. "So, I just stopped at the vending machine and got us these for now. I called Avis and he's going to bring us some food from the fridge in the house later since there's still so much left from the funeral. Any updates about Brian?"

"And how is Avis getting in the house?" I asked with a piercing stare.

My mother looked flustered and caught off guard, "Is that all you heard? I asked if there was an update on my son," she replied with an equally curt tone.

"No update. Does he live there now?" I continued still feeling confrontational after my conversation with Rhonda. Olivia Andrews needed to start explaining how she got over my father's death so quickly and moved onto some idiot with a car company name.

"I left him in the house when I ran out to come to the hospital. Unlike you, he took the time out of his busy life to try and comfort me. Do you have a problem with that?" She asked idly straightening her perfectly creased slacks and switching one crossed leg for another.

"Umm hmm," I replied rolling my eyes. "Funny how this man who I've never heard about until today and just happened to be at the house the night daddy drowned is suddenly comforting you in his spare time. Oh no... that's not suspicious at all. No there's nothing out of the ordinary about that," I mocked.

Not appreciating my candor, she said, "Brenda, this is not the time or the place for you to interrogate me and furthermore you have no right to speak to me about anything I'm doing when neither you nor your brother have taken an interest in it previously. You fail to understand who the mother is in this situation so clearly I have to remind you."

"I don't fail to know who the mother fucker is in the situation though," I stated snidely. Who the hell did she think she was fooling with these cock-a-mamee stories? My mother was having an affair with this Avis dude who was everywhere she was lately and no doubt he was her accomplice the night my father's body met the bottom of the pool.

"Watch your mouth Brenda! I will not be spoken to like that and...and who are you to judge what may or may not be going on in my life anyway? You've got your own skeletons to tend to as is evident by this mess you and your brother have gotten yourselves into. And who's here to help you pick up the pieces? Me, your mother. Have you or Brian been there for me during this time? Even bothered a phone call? No! But look who is right here, front and center when you two need me," she said sternly. "Just as selfish as Robert was. Always thinking about yourselves and ridiculing everyone else. We can discuss this in further detail when we go home after we know your brother is stable if you can stand to hold off your interrogation until then? This is not the right place."

"Home? Home where? I'm not going home with you, if that's what you mean," I frowned swiveling my neck to turn and face her. I'm staying with Rhonda and plus I wouldn't want to cramp you and Abel's style," I said intentionally screwing up the man's name and looking at Rhonda (even though I hadn't exactly cleared it with her beforehand).

Rhonda's dumb founded expression turned to reassurance, "Yes Mrs. Andrews Brenda is staying with me."

All of the blood rushed to my mother's face and she shuffled in her seat uncomfortably. "His name is Avis, and you're a grown woman so if you'd rather stay with a friend, that's your prerogative. I thought you might want to be in the company of family during this time and to try to reconnect considering that you've just lost your father, your brother is touch and go, your cousin has been killed and you've been victimized as well; but I guess I was wrong. I suppose you feel more comfortable staying at your friend's house and running away from your problems as you always do.

I'm not going to try to force you to do anything because I have my own grieving and concerns about my son to worry about. If you're content consoling yourself, that's fine. I also have to console my sister who has just lost her child because of the carelessness of my children and I'm sure your grandmother isn't taking it well either. No one sees the sacrifices that I have to make or the struggle I have, but it's okay. I guess it's just the plight God wants me to have as a mother," Olivia whined looking solemnly and yet again straining to force tears to her eyes.

I rolled my eyes and exhaled some of the hot air she'd apparently been trying to blow up my ass. "Mother Teresa, I'm sure we all realize all of the sacrifice's you've made and are making for us all," I said blatantly feigning sincerity. "But personally, the last thing I need right now is to be trapped in a house with you playing Scarlet O'Hara the whole time. Why can't you just be real for once? Seriously ma! I can't believe even with Brian in surgery and everything going on right now that you're still in character. What is that phony side of you on autopilot or something?"

My mother pursed her lips, swallowed hard and returned a ferocious stare. Admittedly, it was momentarily paralyzing and remembering how quickly she pounced onto my aunt at the funeral, I was beginning to second guess my prodding.

"Shut your mouth Brenda before I shut it for you," she'd said in a guttural tone I'd never heard before.

And I did.

***

Brian had been in and out of consciousness (mostly out) since he was admitted and was on a breathing tube. They'd successfully removed the kidney and he looked like he'd been in a car wreck with all of the bandages and bruising he'd sustained from multiple gunshot wounds and Gwen's fury. He'd been in stable condition for the last 24 hours and after sitting in his room for most of the day I'd gone back to Rhonda's. One thing I knew for sure was that I was moving out of my own apartment as soon as I knew where I was going. In addition to the terrifying memories my apartment held for me, I didn't want to look down at my cousin's now vacant apartment and remember that I was the reason she was no longer with us. Kelly didn't deserve that, and I'd have to look her in the face in a couple of days for the last time ever, at her funeral, and know that.

I sat on the couch with my legs folded under me and my chin resting in my hand as I leaned on the arm of the couch. I had been getting very little sleep due to nightmares, guilt, and the fear that some fluke would afford Edwin the ability to be back out on the streets to finish me off. When I'd called Rhonda a few hours earlier and said I'd be back to her place by 6 o'clock she'd told me some of the girls were coming by to see me.

"Girl don't even sweat it," Belinda said to Yvette as she popped a cheese puff in her mouth while lying on her stomach on the floor. "I mean some brotha's just take longer than others to realize when they have a good woman."

"Longer than others for what? We been together for almost a year and he's always the one talking about taking me to California to meet his family and stuff. Now his mother comes to town and it doesn't even occur to him to introduce us? What does that say about how he feels about me?" Yvette whined raking her fingers through her curly black tresses.

"It just says he's a typical man," Rhonda said on the other side of the couch. "They don't think the way we think. When we fall in love, we want the whole world to know. We tell our girls, our family, we talk at work, we on cloud 9. Men, they might big you up to their boys in the beginning; or brag about your skills in bed; but the commonsense stuff? Pu-lease. Common sense is not common for those morons. Believe it. We're in a whole 'nother zone than they even think about," she said taking a sip from her Margarita.

"Preach sista!" Belinda said playfully as she rolled onto her back. "Take it from me. Before me and Corey got married, he was a virtual pile of clay. I had to mold him into the man he is now. He didn't come that way." They all laughed; I smiled. "We dated for six years before he proposed to me, so I know about their bullshit way of thinking. What used to drive me crazy the most is how he'd do stuff without even attempting to include me. Even after we moved in together; someone would invite him to a party or something and I'd only find out about it because he'd be like, 'Yeah I got invited to a birthday party by some people at work, so I'll be home later.'" She said in her impression of a man's voice. "Did the buzzard check if I wanted to go? Hell no!"

"Yvette, do not listen to these old bitter biddies. Men are not as out of touch as some of them would have you believe and if he's doing something raggedy that you feel contradicts previous words or actions, go with your intuition. Just because these chicks put up with the games doesn't mean it's the norm or that you have to. Quame' tried that foolishness when we first started dating and when he got shut down, he learned. Don't play around with my emotions or you can play with yourself because I'm out!" Athena said rolling her eyes and leaning forward to eat a cheese puff from the bowl Belinda ate from.

"Exactly Athena. I don't care what y'all chickens are cluckin' over there because I know the man and something ain't right if his mom is in town and doesn't introduce us. We're supposed to be moving in together in January but I'm not good enough to meet his mother in May? He said she has a problem with Yankee girls but so freakin' what? He knew I wasn't Jamaican when he first started dating me, so if he loves me, he needs to stand by that. We eat over at my family's house all the time and hang out with my friends all the time. How can he play me out like this?"

"Ooh girl this is just the beginning of the drama with the Yankee thing. You left out the part about his momma being Jamaican born," Rhonda chimed in. "Take it from someone who is also dating a Jamaican born and bred man. Luckily his mother and I get along pretty decent but me and his sister...not so much. She sucks her teeth at me on sight and she's always quizzing him on what I've been cooking for him and comparing it to how she or her mother cooks. I want to say, 'Damn bitch are you dating him, or am I?'"

We all chuckled at Rhonda's frowny faced reenactment of how she wished she could address his sister. "You wait till after the year is up. He's just now getting ready to show you who he really is. They hide all of their bullshit personality traits until you're in love with them; that's when they spring the flaws you wouldn't touch with a yard stick. That's when they stop putting the toilet seat back down, stop opening your car door for you, stop calling you to tell you they're on their way," Belinda said as we all nodded. "That's when they stop cooking breakfast for you; stop watching television with you, and most importantly, when they stop eating the punany like a RITZ cracker to a starving Ethiopian! Now if you can handle that, then he's your soul mate."

We burst into howls of laughter again and Yvette's face turned as red as her brown skin could manage with embarrassment while she leaked tears of laughter.

"That mouth on you!" Yvette said as she wiped the drops from her eyes.

"I can't speak for the rest of you, but I'm still a RITZ cracker," I interjected and suddenly everyone was looking at me. "What?" I asked frowning with confusion.

"That might be the first thing you've said since we got here," Athena said leaning over and love tapping me on my thigh. "Plus, y'all are still new so it doesn't count. He hasn't even seen you in your period panties yet," she said as Belinda yelled "EWWW," and the rest of us chuckled again.

"Damn I'm sorry girl. We're all supposed to be here cheering you up and instead we're talking about my problems. How you doing?" Yvette said as she shuffled in the lazy boy chair she was sitting in.

"No, it's cool. Actually, I'm sick of thinking about it so the last thing I want to do is talk about anything that's going on as far as that's concerned right now. It's like I'm replaying everything in my head all day when I'm supposed to be being strong for my brother. My father's dead, my cousin's dead, my brother's shot, I'm a basket case, and that doesn't even include all of the mini spawn problems that are included. I just wanna be back to normal for a minute," I explained as I watched my hand flick some imaginary lint from the couch.

"I hear you," Belinda replied pulling her micro-braids back into a ponytail. "But can we talk about it for a little while? I don't mean to be the one who's getting on your nerves; especially after that speech you just gave but, I don't want to end up asking you about it later down the line and get screamed on either."

Both Rhonda, Athena and Yvette gave her a piercing stare. "Y'all know you got some questions too!" She retorted.

18

Brian

CONSEQUENCES

When I woke up, there were a bunch of tubes up my nose. I felt like I'd been hit by a Mack truck. I was disoriented, although it was clear I was in the hospital, I wasn't sure how bad off I was. I turned my head to the left and saw the hooked up IV & monitor. When I looked to the right, Brenda was curled into a ball, asleep in a big, cushioned chair. I tried to say something, but I couldn't because I could feel the tubes down my throat although I did manage a moan, but it hurt like hell.

Brenda's eyes sprung open and she came rushing over to my bedside.

"Brian," she said with fresh tears in her eyes touching my head. "Oh my God thank you," she said looking up to the ceiling.

I looked around the room and then back to her, hoping she'd elaborate on what the hell was going on. She removed her hand from my head and inched further down so that she was looking into my eyes. "You're in Piedmont Hospital. Do you remember what happened to you?"

I tried to nod but every movement, including breathing, hurt. She apparently understood my motion though and continued.

"I can't believe this crap really happened to us Brian. I'm so glad we got to you in time. Oh my God you had me so scared when they had to revive you in the ambulance. You've been in here almost 4 days now,"

Brenda paused briefly wiping tears from her eyes then resting her hand lightly on my leg.

A tall burly white man with dark hair cut in a 70's mullet and an equally outdated thick mustache entered the room in a lab coat holding a chart in his hand. He smiled gently at my sister and pulled out a pen light as he approached my bed and shined it in my face as he neared.

"Ahh...Mr. Andrews we're glad to see you're awake. Excellent," he stated while simultaneously pushing a call button by my bed. "Mr. Andrews I'm Dr. Frasier and we'll have that breathing tube removed momentarily. You've had severe trauma to your body, lost a lot of blood initially and you'd stopped breathing once when you first arrived so that's why we have you on this device."

The tubes up my nose and down my throat felt awkward and horrible when I attempted to turn my head and my entire body felt like it was wrapped in electrical tape. The doctor began looking at the IV in my left arm, inspecting bandages wrapped around my torso and over my entire arm which was also in a sling. I felt stiffness in my right cheek, and I could see that it was bandaged up in my peripheral.

That spiteful bitch had scarred my face!

The room door opened again and an average looking 20 something Hispanic nurse with her hair in a ponytail and thin rimmed glasses entered quickly holding some type of breathing apparatus in her hands. She excused herself past my sister, who moved back out of the way, and attached it to something else on the wall behind me where I couldn't see. Suddenly Dr. Magnum P.I. had his hands on my face removing the tape that supported my breathing tube from around my neck.

"Be still a moment Mr. Andrews. I'm going to remove your breathing tube. This may feel very uncomfortable and may hurt a bit, but please do your best to remain immobile and exhale as I'm extracting it from your nose. It will be very quick. Okay, here we go. One...two...three," he counted as he pulled a plastic cork that held the tube in place from my nostril, which felt like a smoothie straw, from my throat while I tried not to gag.

The nurse quickly inserted 2 soft plastic prongs just inside my nose and instructed, "Breathe deeply and cough please Mr. Andrews."

I did so painstakingly and was hit with an uncontrollable bout of coughing as Dr. Frasier elevated my bed remotely and my sister rushed within view to see what was happening. After a few minutes of breathing through the oxygen device, taking a few sips of water and clearing my throat, the nurse removed the prongs from my nose.

"Your throat will probably feel raw for the next few hours and it may be a strain for you to speak so, at least for the next 2 to 3 hours, I'd recommend minimal talking, limited mobility and that you communicate primarily via hand and eye signals. Drink some fluids," Dr. Frasier said gesturing to the cup of water on the bedside table. "I'm not sure of how much you know about your current condition, but I'm prepared to fill in any medical blanks there may be for you. Please blink once or nod if you'd like me to continue speaking about your medical condition in the presence of your sister and blink twice or shake your head if the answer is no."

Ignoring his request, I attempted to verbally respond to him and found that not only did I sound like a talking chalk board, but my throat felt like I'd swallowed a mouth full of dirt. The nurse brought the cup of water to my mouth again and helped me drink what little I could manage before I pulled back. Dr. Frasier shot me a "What did I just tell yo' ass to do?" look.

"Nod or blink yes or no for your response," he reiterated. I blinked once and glanced at Brenda who looked like she hadn't slept in a month of Sundays dressed in sweats, her hair in a messy ponytail and no makeup. I wondered what had happened with Edwin that she was able to get the cops to my place instead of being bound and kidnapped like I was.

The room door opened abruptly and in walked my mother with Aunt Tonya. My aunt looked as raggedy as Brenda did with her grayed shoulder length hair unkempt and a haphazardly thrown together outfit framing her sunken eyes. She wasn't as much of a diva as my mother was, but I'd certainly never seen her look that run down in my life. I almost shed a tear to see how unraveled she'd become over me.

My mother on the other hand, never failed the mirror test. Olivia Andrews wore a gray jumpsuit with 6-inch pumps, her salt and pepper hair nicely curled and a full face of makeup. Nobody but a psychic could have guessed her son was in a hospital bed half dead.

"Oh, he's awake!" My mother exclaimed handing my sister a brown paper McDonald's sack and a drink as she scurried over to my bedside. "Oh my lord, baby I was so worried about you. Brian baby can you see mommy? I'm here baby. Mommy is here," she said waving her hand back and forth in front of my face."

I glared; aggravated at her ridiculous antics. What the hell was her crazy ass smokin' before she came to the hospital? I wanted to scream out, 'Hell fucking yeah I can see you! I'm not blind bitch! Mommy is here? I'm not a 10-year-old! Who are you putting on this show for lady?'

Lucky for her I could barely utter a steady word yet anyway, so I turned my head slightly away from her and toward the doctor.

"Is he going to be okay doctor?" my mother continued giving Dr. Magnum P.I. her best Sally Field's heartfelt performance as she rushed to the head of my bed and put her hand on the top of my forehead lovingly.

My right shoulder was throbbing now underneath the bandages and all I wanted was something to manage the pain.

"Pain," I squeaked to the doctor.

"Yes, I'm about to give you some morphine now," he answered pulling a needle from his coat pocket and injecting it into a tube connected to my IV. We've got some challenges ahead but I'm optimistic about your recovery," he answered looking at me and then to the nurse who went over to the door and grabbed my chart from the holder.

Optimistic? Why did he have any doubts?

***

"Hi Aunt T," Brenda said hugging her with tears welling in her eyes.

My aunt pat Brenda lovingly on the back as they hugged and then pulled away. "Don't start me back up crying Brenda. It was hard enough for me to stop crying for a second and get up the strength to leave the house and make it here," she replied looking down to the ground somberly.

Man, she was really taking me being shot up and in the hospital hard. I was surprised Kelly didn't have her dramatic behind up here crying and asking a bunch of questions like a little gnat.

Dr. Frasier looked at me and I mumbled in a ratchet sounding voice, "Tell me...injuries info."

"Well, I see you're determined to speak," he frowned. "You sustained some rather serious gunshot wounds in addition to some lacerations from blows to the head with the butt of the gun," he continued looking through the notes in my chart and then back to me. "One shot had a clean exit through your right scapula and exited the other side, that's why your shoulder has been completely immobilized while it's healing."

"Scapula?" My mother questioned.

"Yes. It's a bone in the upper right shoulder," Dr. Frasier clarified. "It will be touch and go with the healing process for your shoulder because the majority of your upper arm mobility relies on that area. I'm optimistic that with the right physical therapy, medication and relaxation you will be relatively as capable as you were previously. You were also shot in your right cheek where the bullet lodged into your jaw. I was able to remove the bullet without incident and repair as much of the damage as possible. It also took about 12 stitches to close the gash on the top of your head."

He paused, took a deep breath and turned to another page in my chart before continuing.

"There was another shot on the left side of your abdomen where the bullet traveled and nicked just under your diaphragm, entered your kidney and broke 2 ribs. This was the most severe of your injuries. The kidney was completely ruptured and un-repairable, so we had to perform a full Nephrectomy, which is removal of the kidney, about 12 hours after your arrival..."

"Yeah, Brian we had to give consent because they said you would die of internal bleeding and that it was a bad organ and if we left it..." my mother interrupted with a pleading stare as she reached out to grab my leg.

Brenda's expression tightened and she spoke through clenched teeth. "Mom just let him finish telling Brian everything and stop cutting him off."

My mother brushed a hair self-consciously from her face and nervously swept imaginary lent from her jumpsuit. "Yes, Brenda well I'm just trying to make sure that he's informed about what has happened while he wasn't capable of making decisions for himself. This is still hard to hear and it's hard to look at my son this way. I mean I've already been in such a state after losing my husband so recently, then you and Brian get...held hostage," she stammered wiping a tear that was barely forming in her eye. "Then I find out my niece has been killed and my son has been shot and is in critical condition..."

"Killed?" I exclaimed as loudly as my voice allowed and inadvertently moved too much which caused a barrage of pain to prick me everywhere, I could feel. Tears automatically rushed from my face and I looked toward my Aunt Tonya who sat in a chair with her head leaned back against the wall with her tightly shut eyes unable to prevent the waterfall from escaping them.

Brenda cleared her throat and edged in closer to me beside my mother. "Kelly was...Edwin..." she started but then wiped her own crying eyes before clearing her throat again and speaking. "Edwin shot her when she wouldn't let him into my apartment. He and Gwen planned to get us together and do God knows what to us before they killed us. Turns out that Lina called the cops with a noise complaint because she sleeps during the day and Edwin had put Zeus out on the balcony. When I made a break for it there was an officer already at the door and I told him what was going on, he called for backup, Edwin jumped off the balcony and we ran downstairs to you," she said like she was in a speed talking contest through heaving tears.

"Funeral already?" I asked with tears in my eyes as well.

My aunt began audibly crying at that point and my mother answered, "It's going to be tomorrow morning."

Too much death. Brenda went and sat in the chair by my aunt and pat her back as Aunt Tonya tried to re-compose herself through sniffles and butterfly blinks.

Dr. Frasier looked on wide eyed and anxious as I'm sure he wasn't privy to the back story that landed me there as his patient. After a few moments of silence, he spoke up. "Would you like me to continue or would you rather hold off while you and your family have a moment?"

"Continue," I said as my voice seemed to be attempting to get back a little bit to normal.

"Although you've got another kidney, removal of one will force the remaining one to work twice as hard. Many people live a long healthy life with a singular kidney, but you will need to make some dietary changes. Believe it or not, most of the pain you're feeling is from the broken ribs because unfortunately, those will have to heal on their own although I can provide you with pain medication. Are you following what I'm saying so far Mr. Andrews?" He asked with a concerned frown.

I was listening but my mind was churning at the same time. What kind of lifestyle changes did I need to make? How long was I going to be in the hospital with all of these injuries? That bitch better not have made bail either because she needed to pay for what she did to me.

"Mr. Andrews? Did you understand what I was saying to you?" Dr. Frasier repeated.

"Yes," I answered.

My mother asked him, "When can we take him home?"

"Take him home?" He replied dumbfounded. "Ma'am he's gonna need to stay here for treatment and observation at least another week. Depending on the rate of his recovery, he may be released sooner but don't hold me to that. He's been through a lot and his body has been severely traumatized."

Just then Dr. Frasier's pager went off. He looked at the numbers on it and said, "I'm sorry, you'll have to excuse me for a moment please, this is an emergency. Mr. Andrews, I'll be back to answer any other questions you might have as soon as possible and if you need anything else nurse Stephanie should be able to assist you with that including pain management," he said as he rushed out of my room.

I wanted to say that I was in more pain than he could possibly imagine, but there wasn't any medication that would deaden it. I closed my eyes and wished this was all just a really bad dream, but I knew it wasn't.

"Did you need anything else Mr. Andrews," the nurse asked.

"No" I replied not opening my eyes.

I heard her exit the room and I wished everyone else would too.

∗∗∗

"Oh lord Brian…I told you to stop your whorish ways with these women. It never did your father any good and now look what it's gotten you. They tell me the girl was pregnant and you beat her until she lost the baby so that's why she was so angry? My God I hope that's not true," My mother harped. I heard Brenda gasp.

"Mom!" Brenda yelled angrily.

"That's what your kidnapper told them," my mother continued as she turned to Brenda defiantly. "He said she was the one who decided to do all this to get back at you and Brian for treating them badly and because Brian made her lose their child."

"Since we're on the topic, Brenda did you know about Brian's love child with this girl?" my mother inquired.

"Nobody's love child," I eked out. "Maybe not even mine."

"Well did you beat her up while she was pregnant?" My mother questioned.

"I didn't make her…" I cleared my throat and reached over for the cup of water. My cheek and jaw were beginning to hurt, and I was guessing the meds that were numbing the pain were starting to wear off.

Brenda picked the cup up and assisted me in drinking it before I turned my head away. "I didn't make her lose the baby," I continued.

"You didn't answer my question," my mother insisted. "Did you beat her up?"

There was silence in the room, and I was pissed at the interrogation and insinuations coming my way when I was the one laid up in the hospital with bullet wounds and a missing kidney.

"She got physical with me and I stopped her. I didn't beat her up. She's a crazy stalker and they better put that bitch under the jail."

"She's already been sentenced to a box six feet under," Brenda said.

"What?" I questioned not sure I understood.

"The police shot her when they broke in to get you. She died on the scene."

"I swear I don't know how things got this bad. One child is hopping from man to man and got one so angry he kidnapped her and the other one is so full of himself and so much like his father that he's beating up women and making them want to kill him. Lord I just..." Olivia began her monologue.

"Mom what the hell are you talking about? Do you think me and Brian need to hear your holier than thou mess right now? We were both nearly killed, and you want to stand here blaming us? If anyone is to blame for how we act it's you and your shallow ass parenting!" Brenda shouted.

Nurse Stephanie stuck her head in the room door and asked softly, "I'm sorry to interrupt but can you please lower your voices a bit? We can hear you at the end of the hall."

"We're sorry," Brenda said rubbing her forehead with her hand agitatedly.

Nurse Stephanie smiled and withdrew letting the door close softly behind her.

"So much pain and hurt in this family right now, let's not get into that and just be happy Brian is alive instead," my aunt sobbed. "Cause my Kelly isn't."

Brenda and my mother quickly entered into a stare down.

"Well, I'm going to take your Aunt Tonya home and I'll be back later tonight to check on you Brian," my mother said without taking her eyes off of Brenda.

"Don't," I said knowing I'd had enough of her ignorance for the day.

"I'm picking up your grandmother from the airport tonight and I know she's gonna want to see you Brian. This is too serious for you to behave this way towards me. You'd think with the passing of your father and everything the two of you have been through that your hearts would have softened. You are so hateful. Even with all of this going on, and you know I've been having a hard time myself you're still being your selfish, hateful self."

"Hateful? I'm hateful?" Brenda protested. "Mommy please. Did you get a job on ALL MY CHILDREN or something? Cause you're acting is really over the top right now and you need to knock it off. If you wanna talk about being hateful why don't you explain how daddy died to us all again? Cause something with your story just ain't right," Brenda stated with her hands on her hips.

My Aunt Tonya's face turned ghost white and not only did her tears momentarily cease, but it appeared her breathing did too.

"Okay oh my God. This is all too much for me to deal with right now," Aunt Tonya said standing and grabbing her purse. "Olivia I'm gonna meet you at the car. Brian, I love you and I'll be back to see you soon but I can't right now. I can't stop thinking about my baby and how scared she was, and I can't keep talking about all of this death and drama with y'all."

If my mother had darts in her eyes, they would have bulls eyed Brenda a thousand times. "You don't want to let that go huh? You know what? If you two want me out of your lives so badly, maybe I'll just let you all handle yourselves and I'll stop worrying and being here for you when nobody else has been. You've obviously been doing such a superb job already judging from the situations you've gotten yourselves into. Talking to me any kind of way, accusing me of murder. Is that what you're doing Brenda? Are you saying I killed your father?" she asked with both hands on her hips.

"I'm not accusing you of anything. I'm asking you if you did it or not. It's that damn simple. What's your answer?" Brenda shot back.

"Unbelievable," my mother said before storming out of the room without another word.

Brenda turned and approached my bedside as the angry fire in her eyes mixed with sorrow.

"I feel like we're stuck inside a bad LIFETIME MOVIE CHANNEL movie," she said as she laid a hand on top of mine and gently pat. "But we have each other's back like always."

That, we did.

***

I was glad my mother had left, and happy that Brenda had my back, but I needed to be alone with my thoughts…and my anger. I feigned like I was dozing off not long after Olivia's exit so Brenda would also leave me but before I knew it, I had actually fallen asleep. When I awoke Brenda had gone but when I tried to take a deep breath, not only did it hurt like hell, but it made me cough and feel queasy. I imagined if I were to look under the bandages on my torso that it would be black and blue, and I'd look like something out of an autopsy report; except I wasn't dead. I couldn't believe that my perfect body had been mangled by bullets and I almost wished Stalker Channing hadn't died so I could kill her.

I needed something to dull the pain and some beer to make me forget it; but I knew I only had a chance of getting one of them. I buzzed the nurse with the button on my bedside and hoped I'd at least get some eye candy for my patience. About 30 seconds later an old as dirt Asian woman with a nurse hatchet frown, too much make up and way too many pounds, came rumbling into my room.

"You need something Mr. Andrews?" She asked witching up her expression to a wide, ill grilled smile. I'd expected her to have an Asian accent but her southern twang took me by surprise. "Mr. Andrews?" She repeated as I stared at her dumb founded for a moment.

"My chest hurts, face hurts when I talk and my side is starting to hurt too," I finally answered.

She reviewed the chart she was holding in her hand and then glanced at me as she removed a needle from her pocket. "It has been a few hours since your last dose. I think they're planning on giving you either a self-medication line so you can release it yourself or one that's on an automatic timer now that you're able to communicate with us on your needs," she advised smiling warmly coming over to me and injecting it as painlessly and smooth as butter. "Do you need anything else?"

The TV was off. "The remote?" I uttered.

"The remote for the TV is attached on the arm of your bed," she said removing it from a side pocket I hadn't seen. "This is the power, channels, etc. We have cable too. If…" she began as the room door opened.

Doe-boy and Mitch walked in dressed in sweats and baseball caps. They looked like twins from the ghetto basketball league except they weren't wearing the same colors.

"What's up man," Doe-boy said to me with a huge grin.

"Hello gentlemen," the nurse said to them before turning back to me as they returned the greeting. "Okay well just buzz if you need us," she said leaving.

"Didn't expect to see you awake and off the tubes my dude," Doe exclaimed.

"Damn man, I hope you feel better than you look," Mitch said with a sarcastic smile. I rolled my eyes, but I was smiling and happy to see my boys cared to check on me. "Nate's on his way up here too."

"That chick finally hit you with the kryptonite huh?" Doe-boy said pulling up a chair from the wall and sitting near the end of my bed. I nodded and pressed the button on the bed to raise me higher into a sitting position.

"Bitch's can't kill me," I answered with a half grin since it hurt to smile.

"I see that. I'm glad to see they can't. Did anybody say when you can get out of here?" Doe asked.

"We came up here when we first found out, but you weren't conscious then," Mitch added.

I shook my head no with a subtle shrug which actually hurt a bit. Mitch and Doe-boy exchanged looks and then they both looked back at me.

"Well anyway, I thought they might let you get out of here before my birthday bash next month, so I paid for your spot on the trip. You got a little over 45 days since the month just started. We're going to Br-rrraaaazil," Doe-boy said rolling his r's in an attempt to mimic a Spanish accent. "Where the natives are beautiful, sexy and friendly."

"For a price they are," Mitch said smirking and stationery by my bedside.

"Whatever man. You know if wifey number 2 didn't get in that ass about you going you would have booked your suite before the rest of us did."

I was glad to have something to look forward to while I healed.

"Yeah, we're flying to D.C. first," Doe-boy said walking over to my bed side. "We got a party boat and we're gonna have a big joint like in that Jay-z BIG PIMPIN' video for 2 days with lots of women, drinking, crab legs and fun."

"You off..." I started before clearing my throat. "You off the leash now?"

"Yeah, you gotta hurry up and get better man. This shit don't even seem real with you laid up in the hospital like this. I knew she was off her rocker but to take it this far...and with some psycho dude after your sister too? I swear I couldn't make this up if I wanted to." Mitch spoke nervously rubbing his 5 o'clock shadow. "Brenda looks like she's holding up well though from what I saw the other day. It's bad enough we already lost one of our boys in a car crash, we didn't need to lose another; especially not the nigga' we all love to hate."

One of our boys? Tyler wasn't one of our boys like Mitch was talking. He was never that chummy with all of us like that because he was mostly Ike's friend; but whatever. Dudes get sentimental sometimes when a cat dies.

Talk about a brotha being fucked! This was definitely some soap opera mess. Shot by a crazy bitch, lost a kidney, scarred my beautiful face and body; this was for the birds. I flipped channels on the television until I got to ESPN. The room door swung open and in walked Ike and Tara with flowers.

"What's up home skillet?" Ike said with a big smile as he approached, and Tara hung back by the door.

I would be a liar if I didn't say I was happiest to see him.

19

Brenda

When I left Brian's hospital room, I drove back to Rhonda's place feeling exhausted. I was happy that he was now awake and stable, but I was still unsettled about the situation with my mother. That old biddy was hiding something about that night, and I knew that Avis guy was in on it. Judging from the way my aunt reacted, she knew something I didn't. There'd be no surprise there just like mommy and my mother's sister knew all about Julian but never said anything to us until we were putting my father into the ground. That was one more chapter I was gonna need to get more information on later on when I could focus.

Rhonda was letting me stay in their second bedroom with Zeus, but I was gonna have to find another place to rest my head soon because she'd already said Paul wasn't a dog person but was willing to tolerate Zeus's presence until I was gone. Luckily Paul's 12-year-old daughter who visited frequently loved Zeus and spent every moment she could up in his face, which Zeus seemed to be perfectly happy with.

Rhonda was in the kitchen cooking when I came in around 5:30pm.

"Hello," I called out as I entered and locked the door behind me.

"Hey B," she said sticking her head out around the corner towards me. "Trenice took Zeus out for a walk. He was getting antsy."

"Oh, okay that's cool," I answered putting my pocketbook down in the second bedroom and then coming into the kitchen where she was.

"So, how's Brian?" She asked stirring the ground beef she'd made to go with the huge pot of spaghetti on the stove.

"Better. They took the breathing tubes out and he's awake and talking and everything."

"Wow! That's a big change in 24 hours' time. Does he remember what happened to him?" She inquired turning slightly my way brushing some strands of hair from her face with the back of her hand.

"I don't think so. We didn't really ask him a lot about what he remembers, just kind of gave him the run down on his condition. The doctor did I mean. Then of course my mother had to bring her Hollywood Diva ass up in there with my Aunt Tonya who could barely keep it together long enough to sit in the room with us," I answered hanging my head low and feeling more guilt about causing my aunt such pain. I was truly dreading having to go to another funeral tomorrow. Ugh!

"Oh man. I bet she is taking it really hard. Was Kelly her only child?"

"Yeah, she was. I just feel so guilty about its Rho. I can't sleep at night thinking about how she looked laying on my floor with that blank stare. Thinking about how Edwin said he killed her. She was only in my apartment because she was doing a favor for me," I whined.

"Brenda you had no idea what he was planning to do and from what you said he told you, it all just happened out of the blue. I'm sorry he killed your cousin, but you could have been lying right there next to her and I'm glad we weren't going to be going to your funeral tomorrow too. Think about it, if it wasn't for you, Brian probably wouldn't be alive today. You're a hero actually," Rhonda said now stirring the spaghetti in the pot.

"Hero? I'm definitely not a hero. I was almost scared shitless. To make it worse, when I look at Brian all shot up, I feel like I got off easy. Yeah, I'm traumatized by what I saw, but I'm untouched. Nobody shot me or even shot my way."

Rhonda's eyes dropped sympathetically for a moment as the doorbell rang. Her eyebrows rose. I looked at my watch and gave Rhonda a confused look. Lane was supposed to pick me up in another hour and a half, but he hadn't called, which he said he'd do first, so I didn't think it was him.

"Are you expecting somebody?" I asked.

"Nope. Maybe it's someone for Paul," she said turning off the fire under the pot and walking past me toward the door.

"Oh-my-God," she said looking through the peep hole and then back at me. "It's Teddy."

My heart immediately began to pound against my chest like a prisoner trying to escape and I was a ball of excitement, surprise, and confusion.

'What the fuck?' I mouthed without sound towards her as he rang the bell again.

She motioned towards the door with a questioning look on her face as if asking what I wanted to do and... I nodded.

Rhonda opened the door and there stood Teddy in a dark grey business suit looking sharp and crisp as always.

"Hey Rhonda. Uh...I heard Brenda has been staying with you?" He asked tentatively.

She didn't respond she just let out an unfriendly sigh.

"Why are you looking for me?" I asked trying not to look and sound uninterested.

"I heard about everything that happened with you and Brian. It was all over the news and I've been calling to try to talk to you, but you haven't been answering your cell phone," Teddy answered with that boyishly handsome grin I'd loved for so long.

"Well, I'm fine. Thanks for checking," I replied with my hands on my hips. I'd had my cell with me and working for a change, but I assumed the private id calls I'd received and ignored multiple times in the past couple of days had been his.

"You gonna make me talk to you standing in the doorway?" He asked glancing at Rhonda and then at me with pleading eyes.

Rhonda scoffed at him and rolled her eyes swiveling her neck as she turned to me.

"I'll talk to you outside for a minute, but I don't have a lot of time," I told him as I strutted nonchalantly towards him. "If you need me for anything I'll be right here."

Rhonda's eyes got wide and she whispered before I went out, "What about...you know who coming?"

'I know' I mouthed waving her off as she closed the door behind us.

***

I walked over to the staircase that led from Rhonda's third floor apartment to the fourth floor ones and sat down. Teddy followed but leaned against the railing facing me instead of sitting.

"First, let me apologize for stopping by without asking you if it was okay. I know you hate pop ups and after all of the stalking business that has gone on, the last thing I wanted to do was make you uncomfortable. I talked to Amanda one of those times I came by and she told me you were staying with Rhonda," Teddy said as he took my left hand and held it in his.

"How did you know where Rhonda lived though?" I asked.

Teddy paused and nervously scratched his eyebrow. "Umm...I was doing some real estate stuff in this area once before and I think I ran into her and her guy once....you know how I always run into people. Anyway, I can't remember really, it's not important."

I knew he wasn't being truthful. I'd become particularly astute at recognizing his lies given the abundance of them that he saved for me. I should have been able to work his mouth like a ventriloquist by now. Why lie about knowing where Rhonda lived? This was one mystery I simply didn't have the strength to try to solve.

"Uh huh... Okay. And you knew the exact apartment," I said drably.

"I got lucky," he said licking his lips nervously but still managing to look sexy. "I wanted to come see you since your dad passed. When I called before I didn't know how to approach the topic with you given that we were supposed to be taking a break. Not that you really let me stay on the phone with you long enough to break the ice..." he trailed off. "You know I still love you and worry about you baby. I can't believe you didn't even call me or anything during any of this. I always thought we were better than that. How you holding up?"

"I'm holding up fine," I said feeling uneasy butterflies fluttering as I dropped my eyes to my fidgeting hand. I hated his effect on me.

"Just the thought of what could have happened to you…I can't even stand it. When I was watching the report on the news and I saw your place, and they said your name…" he paused and kissed the hand he held in his. "I can say I was genuinely afraid to hear what was coming next. You've been right this whole-time baby. I was taking you for granted and I don't want to ever make that mistake again. I haven't been able to sleep at night thinking about how you're doing. Thinking about how I messed up and almost lost you for good."

I shook my head slowly in disbelief at what I was hearing. Was this the same Teddy who always put his work above my feelings finally putting me first? Some brothas never ceased to amaze me and before today I wouldn't have thought he could. Was I being punked?

"Teddy, what am I supposed to say to all of this? You were pretty clear that your career comes first, and you haven't wavered for nearly 2 years. Now all of the sudden you've rearranged your priorities?" I questioned trying not to let his words melt the ice I was protecting my heart from him with.

"I know I've messed up in the past and played a lot of games; but that's all done now. Maybe it was fear of finding what I was looking for. None of these women out here can take your place and no matter how successful I become, it's not gonna be anything without the woman I love by my side. We've weathered good and bad times and we always gravitate back to each other. I know you've been seeing some guy or whatever. You can't find anybody that can fill my shoes in or out of the bedroom Brenda. You know it and I know it. There's nobody for you but me. And here I am."

"Oh, so you think of yourself as being irreplaceable? Because you sure seemed pretty willing to let it all die when I was pressing you for a commitment before. Am I supposed to think I'm your everything now?" I asked rolling my neck and noticing the similarities in Teddy's and Brian's arrogance.

He flashed his Colgate smile and looked away briefly. "I have never tried to replace you Brenda. I just had other priorities that you didn't understand and, in the meanwhile, when we were having our lapses in communication I filled it with a few substitutes. My career is very important to me, but it was never because of another woman and honestly, I always saw you at the end of the tunnel with me."

"I'm the same me now that I was the last time you left me crying in my apartment. Listen, I appreciate you coming to show your concern for me and trying to give me another chance or whatever it is you're trying to do but I'm fine. I'm getting over this slowly but surely and contrary to what you may think, you're not irreplaceable for me anymore. In fact, you've already been replaced. Take care," I said attempting to get up. Teddy grabbed both my wrists and pulled me back down to sit directly in front of him.

"Wait Brenda. I know I've been careless with your feelings before sometimes, but I realize that now. I've had an epiphany or something; I don't know. I...I...I don't know baby don't make me grovel to put us back together. I know you want to get back with me and miss me just as much as I miss you. Work is great for a change; even in this economy I'm doing well. In fact, I just closed the biggest deal of my life 2 days ago and if I don't sell another property in the next 6 months, I'll still be comfortable," his smile brightened.

I didn't react. Did this fool really think that I was supposed to keep pining over him until he decided he felt like giving me another shot?

"But it's missing something," he continued turning to look into my eyes and holding my face in both his hands. "You. I'm missing you. I know you're seeing somebody but where was he when that guy tried to rape you? Where was he when..."

"Teddy you don't know what happened or what you're talking about," I warned pushing his hands away from my face and leaning back against the steps. "Yes, I am seeing someone and there isn't anything anybody else could have done because nobody else was there but me. He couldn't have saved my cousin Kelly, me or Brian and neither could you, so don't talk like you would have arrived in the bat mobile and saved the day if we were together. That's your oversized ego and furthermore, you're the one who decided I wasn't what you wanted." I scowled.

"What you have now will never completely satisfy you Brenda. You know I can't just sit idly by while you give your love to some other man when we both have clarity that we should be together. We wasted enough time. Well...I wasted enough time. Like Lorenz Tate said in LOVE JONES, 'I love you and it's urgent like a motherfucker.' Teddy leaned in and kissed me deeply.

My mind was telling me to pull away and slap his face but everything else responded to the familiar touch of his soft lips like he had the owner's manual to my emotions.

Sucked into the abyss again.

***

When he set my lips free, I was stunned into silence by his proclamations. It was as though I'd entered the twilight zone and my worst nightmare and deepest desire had morphed into the same thing. Why now? Why when I'd finally gotten him out of my system? Why when I'd finally found someone that was on the same page as I was, did Teddy decide to give me everything I'd been wanting for all these years?

"It's too late for all of this now." I said wiping the sweet taste of his kiss from my lips. "You can't just keep me as number 2 to your career and never fully give yourself to me, break up and then come back into my life to pick back up where we left off. I'm seeing someone else and that's where my heart is now. I can't do the seesaw thing with you anymore. Today you're saying all of this to me and then tomorrow you'll feel some other kind of way. No."

"It's obviously not too late because if it was, you wouldn't have let me kiss you or kissed me back. The new guy can't have your heart when your heart is with me." He said turning so that he was now kneeling on the ground in front of me.

"Well, you're wrong. It is too late for us. That ship has sailed, and you missed the boat. I was just caught off guard by your kiss, but this is over Teddy … and can you get up? You're making me nervous." I said as tears welled in my eyes.

For Christ's sake! 'Stop crying Brenda!' my mind shouted to me. 'It's just the same old bullshit on a different day from him!'

"I know this guy can't love you the way that I do. You know you don't love him the way you love me either. It's not even possible in such a short time. I just wasn't ready to give up the life that I've been used to and risk it all for a life of love and happiness with only one woman. You know my background, my family life Brenda. You know my father never settled down with one woman, and you know my mother kept an influx of "step daddy's". You're right, I was putting my career first because I'm in control of that but I'm not gonna do that now. I'm ready to put everything into us and give you what you want…me and you."

"Well, I don't want that anymore. You had me wrapped around your finger and look how you treated me. Now that I've moved on you've suddenly had a…a…what did you say? An epiphany that I'm the one? If that's the case, then I've been the one all of this time. I don't believe it. Get off your knee because it looks like you're about to propose," I said nervously agitated.

"I'm not perfect; I don't always do the right thing and sometimes I need more than a kick in the ass to do the right thing. I've never missed any woman in my life as much as I've missed you. Not being able to talk to you all the time and come see you…hold you in my arms. It eats at me. My pride prevented me from coming clean sooner, but this whole…this whole thing with you being attacked and nearly killed…I can't risk it again. I can't risk the chance that my silence could lose you to me for good. I need you Brenda. Plain and simple. I love you and I need you. There isn't much more than a period that I could add to that. Nothing except a period made of diamonds. Will you marry me?" He said pulling a black velvet box from his jacket pocket.

My heart was beating ten thousand times a minute. This could not be happening. Why was this happening now?!

"I knew before I came over here that I was going to have to really bring it on for you to believe I was serious. I'm as serious as a heart attack Brenda. I love you with every-single-solitary-ounce of my being. I'm ready to be a better man; but I can't do that without my better half." He declared opening the box with a flip of his thumb. Inside was a beautiful diamond princess cut engagement ring with tiny diamonds on the band accentuating its gleam. My eyes grew wide as I stared at the offering and back at him with tears streaming down my face. Oh my God!

I sat staring at him with my mouth agape. Here was my chance. The thing I'd prayed to God about the entire time we dated. It was more than just exclusivity, it was marriage. But I was with Lane now and this was not supposed to be happening!

"Marry you? Why now? I can't..."

Teddy was shaking his head in protest and cut me short. "It's because right now, at this moment I don't want to spend my life with anyone else, but you and you want to be with me. Don't let some miscellaneous relationship destroy your chance for the love you've been waiting for all this time. You got me where you want me and I'm here. Here proposing that you marry me. Proposing that you be my wife!"

Dazed and temporarily brain dead, I stared at him with my heart fluttering inside my chest. Where were my wits now? Be strong! Do not give into his sexy brown eyes, soft lips and charming pleas that I once desperately prayed for. It was what I wanted for myself. I wasn't getting any younger and the time I'd put in jockeying to get the ring from him had now paid off.

"That kiss did not say you wanted me to leave Brenda. I know what you want; what you need. This new guy doesn't have a clue. I don't dispute that I've done some...I don't know, insensitive things in the past. But that's what it is, the past. The future can be all about you and me if you let it. Now, will-you-marry-me?" He repeated slowly.

I wiped the tears from my eyes and sniffled as he took the ring from its box and held it just above my hand. So many things were running through my mind that I was beginning to feel dizzy.

"Yeah, will you?" Lane asked as standing at the top of the stairway landing.

20

Brian

Tara gave me a "chin up" hello with a fake smile as she leaned back against the wall just inside the doorway.

I guessed she wasn't too thrilled to have cut her honeymoon short for the likes of me.

"Oh God Damn Brian! Wow my man, what's good?" is all he could say as he approached my bed and tentatively put a hand out to touch mine while leaning forward to smack the hands of Mitch and Doe-Boy.

"I'm alive. That's about the only thing I can say that's good about this feeling. Aren't you supposed to be on your honeymoon?" I asked.

"Man, I go away for a second and look what kinda shit you get yourself into. You know I had to come back and check on you dude. They told me you were on a breathing tube and in ICU," he replied with a bit of bewilderment.

I couldn't front, I was glad that he wasn't holding a grudge because of everything that went down at his wedding. The last time we talked I wasn't sure if he was ever planning on talking to me again, but I guess given the circumstances, he was letting all of that be water under the bridge.

"We left Barbados 2 days early," Tara chimed in doing a miserable job of masking her repugnant expression.

"Tara," I said with a smirk in my eyes as she moved to stand next to Ike. Fuck Barbados bitch! I almost died! My boy should've came back to check on me! But then what would she know about loyalty with her shady past?

"I'm sorry to hear about what happened," she replied with concern struggling from her throat.

It was funny that none of the fellas said anything to her, nor she to them. Ike was too good for her snooty ass.

"Thanks," I said starting to feel drowsy. "These drugs got me a little numb and dizzy like Ike when he's playing basketball."

The fellas chuckled and Tara forced a smile.

"Negro has jokes even when he's laying up in here with a tube in his dick," Ike said looking towards the guys.

I laughed again but then I started to cough a little and the coughing really made my face hurt. Ike looked concerned and Tara's eyes got wide, but they sort of looked...pleased.

"You okay?" Doe-boy asked rushing up from his chair as they all bore panic-stricken expressions.

"I'm cool people, I'm cool." I said as the coughing subsided.

"So how long do you have to stay in here?" Tara asked blandly.

"I don't know. I might end up being the boy in the bubble the way the doctor's been talking. Why were you going to invite me to come stay with you?"

"Yeah right," Tara replied. "When hell freezes over and Flavor Flav wins a spelling bee."

"Tara," Ike said frowning at her and then turning back to me. "So, what are the damages? Seems like you're out the woods now, right?"

"You see my face, right? Bitch shot me in my shoulder, I got a bruised lung, they took my left kidney and I got broken ribs," I complained. "She hit me with the gun in my head too. She had me tied up though because you know it would not have gone down like that if I wasn't."

Tara grunted quietly without much of an expression and the guys mostly looked dumb founded. "Damn dude," he said almost inaudibly.

"One day I'm the life of the party and the next day I almost lose my life."

"Sometimes karma is a bitch," Tara said with piercing eyes.

"Or a bitch is a bitch," I retorted wishing Ike would muzzle his bitch. Fuck karma: this didn't happen because of some damn karma.

"Tara, baby," Ike said almost as if "baby" was a cuss word. "Can you go get me something to drink from the vending machine please? I really don't want to spoil our honeymoon vibe already."

Finally, the emotionless cunt showed a glimpse of shame, "I didn't mean…"

"Naw we all got what you meant," Doe-Boy, who was not a fan of Tara's said.

Tara gave him a hard glance, "Actually, I have a few phone calls to make since we're back in the states earlier than expected. How about I just meet you in the car? You don't have to rush or anything. I have a lot to say.

"Alright baby," Ike said as they both leaned in for a superficial peck on the lips.

"Speedy recovery to ya' Brian. Fellas," Tara said to me and then to the guys before walking slowly out of the room.

We all gave her the 'Good bye' head nod which simultaneously meant, 'Fuck off' without another word.

"There's one person who probably isn't thrilled I made it out alive," I said glimpsing at the instant replay of Saturday's basketball game on ESPN. Once you scorn a bitch, they never recover, I thought to myself. Why Ike would sentence himself to life with that witch was beyond my comprehension, but at the moment I didn't care.

Ike shook his head no, "It's not like that B. She's just still a little upset about having to cut our trip short. When last I heard, you weren't even breathing on your own though. I had to come back and check on my boy."

"Aww ain't y'all so cute. The bro-mance is still alive," Mitch said in a mock baby voice.

"Shut up man!" Ike said playfully kicking Mitch's chair.

"I'm sorry you cut your honeymoon short for me bruh," I said knowing it was a sacrifice on his part.

All 3 of them looked at me like I had 3 heads. "What?" I asked.

"You're sorry?" Doe-Boy said sounding bewildered.

"Damn we might need to get the doctor back in here because clearly his head injuries are way more severe than we originally thought," Mitch said.

"For real. Brian would never apologize or expect anything less than the world stopping to cater to his needs. Dude how many fingers do I have up?" Ike asked holding up 4 fingers as all 3 of them began chuckling.

"I got a finger for all y'all asses," I said managing to lift my middle finger up to them with my left hand.

"I didn't realize you could even move them things," Doe-Boy clowned.

"My homeboy is awake?!" Nate exclaimed coming into my hospital room with a big bright smile.

My smile was probably as big as his was.

Who needs bitches when you got your boys?

***

My face, my ribs and every other place that could ache on me was beginning to supersede all conversations with the fellas after a while and I was also getting drowsy so they'd left after about another hour. I hated having to piss inside a catheter and I'd woken up several times in the night thinking I was back at my apartment and almost fell out of the bed when I jerked out of my troubled rest.

At about 10:00am I got a phone call on the cordless room phone and I struggled to pick it up before it stopped to no avail. Whoever it was called right back though, and I was able to reach it.

"Hi this is Nadia, is this Brian?" the voice on the other end said.

"Yeah. Nadia from the building?" I asked surprised.

"Yes. I was on a site check today and I saw your patient information on the nurse's rounds list. Is it okay if I come visit you?" she asked.

So, my new neighbor wanted to come visit me. She was doing a site check? What did that mean? She wanted to see how I was?

"Site check? You work here?" I replied moving my neck from side to side to relieve a crick in it.

"Well, sort of. I'm the Nursing Service Manager for the hospital group so I have to periodically go on site to ensure everyone and everything is in compliance with hospital, federal and medical regulations," she said sounding a bit amused at my ignorance of what she meant.

"You know what room I'm in already?"

"Yes, I do."

"Come see me," I said hanging up without another word. Holding the phone was starting to hurt and my cheek felt inflamed.

They'd finally hooked me up to a self-releasing medication line last night that would only release a given dose 4 hours from the last dosage. I pressed the button on the device they gave me which released the drugs into my system and prayed they'd start working quickly.

A few minutes later Halle Berry came into the room with a subtle knock dressed in dark blue dress pants, a silver short sleeve blouse and 4-inch dark blue heels. Her hair was slicked back, and her makeup was enough to let you see that she had some on, but light enough so that you could tell she was naturally beautiful. Something about this chick I was really digging.

"Hey there," she greeted with a quaint smile.

"Hey," I answered feeling the areas of pain begin to numb.

"I heard what happened to you and your family at the complex and I just wanted to give my condolences for the loss of your cousin and to...to I guess just come by and see how you were since I was going to be up here. How are you feeling?" Nadia asked furrowing her nose at the last part which I assumed was her reaction to seeing me all bandaged.

"Thank you. Probably about the same as how I look," I said trying to smile on my left side only. "Pretty good despite the circumstances."

She chuckled. "That is not what I thought you were going to say." Revealing a dimple. "I'm glad you still have a sense of humor. I doubt I would still have one after being shot."

"She's dead now so at least I have one thing to be happy about. I'm betting that pussy that killed my cousin is gonna get the maximum," I replied without a smile.

Nadia looked uncertain about how to respond to that, so she diverted her eyes away and fiddled with some paperwork she was holding momentarily.

"So, do you know when you'll be discharged yet?" She asked changing the subject.

"In a week or 2 is what they're saying."

"Oh okay. Your wounds must be pretty severe for you to have to stay that long."

"You didn't look at my chart?" I asked not believing she didn't know exactly what injuries I had.

"No, the rounds list doesn't give specifics and it wouldn't have been appropriate for me to look into your chart unless I was evaluating nursing procedures, which I wasn't. I know from the news that you had multiple gun shots though," she responded coming a little closer to my bedside.

"Yeah. I feel like I'm on instant replay as much as I keep running down my injuries to everyone," I told her, not masking the agitation.

"I'm sorry, I..." she started.

"Naw it's cool," I retracted. "Shot in my side, 2 broken ribs, shot in my cheek and my shoulder and I got hit in the head with the gun. She was serious about trying to take me out."

"I saw her picture on the news. It was crazy because I'd seen her around the complex before, but I thought she was somebody's pregnant girlfriend or something. I didn't know she was your...your girl..."

"She was not my girlfriend," I said sternly cutting her off. "She was a delusional girl I used to date who wanted me to be the father of a baby she wasn't even sure was mine."

I couldn't read the expression on Nadia's face completely but the caring look she'd had was replaced with something less sympathetic. What was that about?

"What's that look mean?" I asked in the same tone.

"What look? I was just listening to what you said," she answered in that voice that my sister and my mother both used. It sounded pleasant but really meant there was a thunderstorm brewing.

"You didn't like my answer?"

"It's not about whether I like your answer or not. It's not my place or my concern as to what or who you do in your private life. I just wanted to stop in and say hello since we're neighbors. I'll let you get back to resting. I've got to get back to work myself anyway," she said as if she were about to exit.

Really? Just like that she was gonna be out? Well, I wasn't ready for her to leave yet!

"So, you not gonna tell me what I said that's got you ready to leave my handsome ass all alone to fend for myself?" I prodded throwing on what charm I could muster.

Her eyes darkened and she tilted her head to the side with a "Negro pu-lease!" expression on her face.

"That's exactly what I'm going to do. I guess it's a good thing you didn't call me to go to brunch, lunch or dinner like we planned on Sunday or else I could have been in here with you or worse. It was obvious you were a ladies' man when we met, but you clearly like to play with some dangerous ladies...and that's not my scene," she stated with a smug look on that beautiful face.

Challenge!

***

I was enjoying Nadia's feisty show, but it was already too late for her to pull away from my web. Oddly enough, she intrigued me enough to want to dig deeper. Not that I was in any condition to waste time with her right now.

"Yeah, well I can't argue with you there. I'm taking a hiatus from seducing deadly women; unless you're one of them. You do seem like you might have a bad temper. Is that why you don't wanna tell me what I said that changed your temperature from warm to cold?" I asked pushing the remote to raise the head of my bed up to a sitting position.

She rolled her eyes but smiled. Got her!

"I haven't turned cold," she protested. "Why do you care what I think anyway? You basically just met me."

"So. I can't want to get to know you better? Don't you deserve some consideration for coming to visit me in my hospital bed when I 'basically just met you'?" I countered.

Her smile grew a little bigger and she playfully batted her now softened eyes at me.

"Brian, you really have a strong ego, don't you?" She asked resting her weight on one leg.

"Even from my hospital bed, yes. When I see something or someone I like, I pursue. Isn't that a good quality?"

"It can be, but in your case, it looks like I'd be setting myself up for getting my property destroyed and a bevy of stalkers jumping out at me. Not to make light of your situation or anything because I know it's serious, but the more I talk to you, the more I hear red flags."

I didn't like that, and I really didn't know what to say to turn things back around to my favor.

"As good as I am, there's no bevy of women that I deal with. I don't have a girlfriend or anyone who's even close to that title if that's what you're worried about. I admit I might have made some bad decisions in dating or misleading some of them until I was no longer interested, but seeing as I'm gonna need to focus on recovery in the next couple of weeks to a month, I doubt I'll have much time for that. Even if I did, that's not really where my focus is right now. This is the first time I've ever heard of someone hearing red flags," I said truthfully.

What the hell was happening here? What was it about this girl that made me want to open up and speak unabridged? Hell, I even surprised myself with how forthcoming I was being with her. She was beautiful, but her beauty wasn't enough, it was...it was something else. Not that I was planning on settling down with anybody, but I really wasn't interested in the juggling act I'd been doing right now. "I can be a good dude when you get to know me Nadia. Don't let my good looks and my confidence, intimidate you. I'm approachable and a good conversationalist for a beautiful woman such as yourself."

As much as I didn't want to admit it, Stalker's behavior and consequent torture of me may have in fact had an impact on me after all.

"Wow. Are you trying to be funny with some of this arrogant, over the top stuff you're saying? I'm beginning to feel like I stopped by Kanye West's room to ask him about his music and he can't stop telling me how underrated he is," she said with a sarcastic chuckle. "But seriously, I did only stop by for a quick hello. I've got to get back to work," Nadia said turning on her heels and walking slowly towards the door.

"So, when they send me home can I call on you for some nursing? You are a nurse, right? Because I do live by myself," I threw in hastily.

She paused at the door for a moment, looked down at the floor and then back at me.

"Uh... yes I am a certified nurse, but I don't think I can commit to being available when I'm off duty," she answered softly.

"Commit? I'm not asking you to commit, because we're still getting to know each other; but can you at least promise to come over and check on me from time to time and maybe help a brother out if I need it? I'm a good cook you know. If I'll be able to stand long enough once they discharge me, I'll pay you kindly in a gourmet meal," I coaxed trying to smile.

"I might be able to do that. I mean you do owe me a meal anyway, don't you?" She said smiling flirtatiously at me and opening the hospital room door.

"Can you come back for lunch today? Or after you finish your evaluation or whatever it is, you're doing for work? I enjoyed our brief conversation, but I want to know more and I have nothing but time to kill in here."

"We'll see," she said exiting my room without looking back.

Oh yeah! This woman had my antenna up and for some reason I couldn't and didn't want to ignore it.

I had been dozing in and out since Nadia left and was visited by the doctor and a nurse for a check and redress of some bandages around noon. The pain was constant in most areas and the medication was helping to numb the pain, but I was always aware of where I was injured. Just as I was about to drift back off to sleep, there was a knock at the door and Nadia slowly opened it.

"You up for company?" She asked softly.

The sight of her dulled my aches and I managed a slight grin. She closed the door behind her, pulled a chair up to the side of my bed and sat. She rested a small coach purse and a brown paper bag with a WENDY'S logo on her lap.

"I grabbed a little lunch and thought I'd come eat it with you," she smiled.

"Couldn't even check to see if I wanted an apple pie or a burger huh?" I joked.

"Nope. Neither of those are on your dietary foods list buddy. Especially after a kidney removal with all the salts in fast food," she replied pulling out what looked like a carton of salt with fries dipped in it. "Don't be eyeballing my fries either. I work out very hard to be able to afford a couple of vices per week and this is one of them," she chuckled noticing my expression.

"You barely have any fries in that salt miss," I said turning more towards her in my bed.

"I'm sweet enough to absorb it," she flirted.

"I bet you are," I replied with other things in mind.

21

Brenda

OR GET OFF THE POST

Things got ugly. Lane approached us with cinders burning in his eyes and Teddy turned to confront with his chin lifted defiantly. This was a hell of a lot more than I'd bargained for!

"No! No!" I said stepping between them facing Lane with my back to Teddy.

"No don't fight or is your answer no?" Teddy asked frowning down at me but holding his position.

"No to you clown! She's moved on!" Lane argued for me.

Oh my God! As much as I didn't want them fighting over me, I had to admit that it was kinda' hot knowing that two fine Mandingos were willing to battle it out for me. At least in the heat of the moment they were.

"Ain't nobody talking to you punk! She can answer for her fuckin self. She doesn't need you trying to put words in her mouth. You better play your position playboy," Teddy hollered back at Lane.

I heard a few apartment doors open as neighbors attempted to get a better listen.

"The answer is no. No, I can't marry you," I said to Teddy as sternly as I could manage although I wasn't 100% sure my heart agreed.

There was a momentary calm until Lane boasted back up, "Okay so you got your answer now bounce!"

"Motherfucka you bounce!" Teddy responded reaching his hands above my head and gesturing to Lane to go. "Brenda don't let this dude's presence intimidate you away from the answer you wanna give. When his number's up, it's up! You don't owe him anything."

"Open your ears motherfucka'! She said 'No!' What part of that didn't you understand? You can't be using her like a revolving door. Now the door is shut so take your fuckin ring and…" Lane started.

"You my man…you better shut up and go home. You don't know me, and I guarantee you don't know me and Brenda's history. You're a benchwarmer; but I'm back in the game now," Teddy asserted.

Lane was a couple of inches taller but apparently that didn't faze Teddy.

"Hey! Hey! Hey! What the hell is going on out here?!" Rhonda yelled at us rushing out of her apartment.

"Dude you don't know me," Lane continued ignoring Rhonda. "And you'd better stop talking crazy before I bust your ass out here. Don't let the fact that I haven't beaten you down yet fool you into believing it can't happen." Then he turned to me. "What your answer to this lame?" He demanded.

"I chose you," I said timidly flinching a bit from the hard air Lane spat at me as he spoke.

"Brenda…" Teddy said astonished. "Don't let him pressure you into making a choice you'll regret."

As much as I wanted to yell that I knew exactly what I was doing and wasn't making a mistake, I wasn't sure. I was sure that my feelings were not clear enough to accept anybody's proposal though.

"Now take it like a man instead of a pussy and step!" Lane ordered Teddy.

"Alright cut it out!" Rhonda interjected looking frustrated at me.

"Fuck you!" Teddy yelled at Lane putting the ring back in the box and closing it with a scow before turning to me. "I hope you're gonna be able to live with your decision baby. Cause it was the wrong one."

With that, he exited down the staircase.

I wiped the developing tears from my eyes and noticed both Rhonda and Lane staring at me, although Lane's was more of a glare. His face still flushed with sweat beads forming around his forehead, he wiped them away with the back of his hand and descended the steps as well.

Oh lord! I hoped he wasn't going after Teddy to finish what they started.

I soft sprinted after him, but quickly realized he was only headed to his car. He got in on the driver's side as I approached and quickly stood in the open doorway before he could close it.

"Lane..." I wasn't sure what I wanted to say but I knew I didn't want him to leave.

He was fuming. "What Brenda?"

"I had no idea he was coming over here, or that he was going to do that," I answered weakly.

He looked away from me as he put his key in the ignition. "What am I supposed to think when I go to pick up a woman and her ex is standing there proposing? Yet you claim y'all aren't together?"

"Yes! I haven't kept any secrets from you Lane. Don't you think I'm going through enough drama not to add more to it? I didn't even know that he knew where Rhonda lived. I swear to you," I pled taking my left hand and attempting to pull his chin to face me; but he pulled away. "Baby I swear that's the truth."

He frowned and shook his head.

"Don't drive off angry like this. Please. Talk to me," I appealed.

"Keep it real with me Brenda. Are you still in love with that man? Yes or no?" He asked looking me straight in the eyes.

"Not anymore," I answered softly.

He sighed heavily and turned the ignition off.

***

"Can you wait for me while I go get my stuff?" I asked. He nodded without looking at me.

I knew that I'd better hurry up before he changed his mind and drove away. It was a good thing I'd already loosely packed my overnight bag because I didn't want to take too long. I ran past Rhonda who was standing at the entrance to her apartment stairs watching us, and she followed me inside the apartment.

"What's going on? Are you okay?" She asked stopping in the kitchen as I rushed into the spare bedroom to get my things together.

"I don't know. Right now, I'm just trying to keep my head on straight and keep my man," I replied tossing deodorant, perfume, my comb and brush and a few other things in my overnight bag.

"I can't believe Teddy proposed. And damn if Lane didn't stand his ground! Paul said he can be a tyrant when he wants something done, but the look he had on his face tonight...OOOOhhh girl. He was not letting Teddy have his new woman!" She yelled from the kitchen.

"Girl I hope I can keep the title as mad as he is. I still can't believe Teddy just proposed to me though," I said getting my shoes and grabbing a pair of socks from my suitcase to shove in my bag.

"Me either," she cosigned.

"I'll call you later," I sputtered running back past her in a hurry not to keep Lane waiting.

"Your phone!" Rhonda called out handing me my cell phone just as I was leaving. When I looked at it, I saw the missed call from Lane earlier. It was so stupid of me not to have brought my phone out there with me when I was talking to Teddy. At least I would have known to wrap it up with him long before Lane walked up on us out there.

He didn't get out and open my door as he'd done before but I didn't dare mention it. I'd barely closed the door before he sped off. I locked my seatbelt and leaned back into my chair, wishing I could disappear. The tense look on his face made me tentative to speak, but I was compelled to clarify where I stood with Teddy before we got to the house.

"Lane, again, I'm sorry this happened. I had no intentions on getting back with Teddy. Especially since we got serious and..." I started.

"Since we got serious? When was that? Yesterday? The day before that? A dude doesn't just come to somebody's house... no my bad, somebody's best-friend's house, and propose. I don't believe that," he said smugly.

"Well, that's the truth. It's not hard for anybody who knows me to guess that I'd be at Rhonda's. I was just as shocked as you were to see him and for him," I answered clutching my chest in as I plead my case.

"Oh, I doubt you were as shocked as I was," he said looking at me with disgust. "I doubt anybody was as surprised as I was to walk up while some dude was proposing to my woman. First Edwin thought you were an item and you say you weren't; now this guy pops up with a ring. Shit seems out of whack to me."

"Lane that is not fair," I argued. "The situation with Edwin didn't have anything to do with today and I told you what kind of relationship I had with Teddy. Hell, your own cousin told you about that according to you. That's a low blow to bring up Edwin after what he just did to me and Brian too. I know you're mad right now but you're going too far. This isn't my fault."

"Yeah, a whole lot of stuff happens to you that isn't your fault doesn't it?" He replied coldly.

I was silent. Insinuating I was a false victim was more hurtful than anything else.

"Just let me out," I said. "Obviously I made a fucking mistake in choosing you since all you want to do is attack me and my character. I don't need to take your shit. Let me out."

"What?" He asked as we pulled up to a stop light.

"Let-me-out. I'm not gonna sit here and listen to you talking to me like this if you've already got your mind made up. I understand why you're mad, but I'm not about to deal with this crap from you. I have bigger problems than your ego. Let me out here and you can go your way and I'll go mine so we can both be done with the drama."

He continued looking straight ahead and took the ramp getting onto the highway. I stared at him, waiting for a response, but he didn't say anything. He made no motion as though he were planning to pull over, but he didn't say anything either. What the hell?

When he got on the highway I said, "Did you hear what I said? I'd appreciate it if you didn't wait until we were in west bubble fuck before you let me out."

"I heard what you said. I'm calming myself down. I'm not letting you out the car unless you really want to get out that badly. I took it too far, and I'm sorry. I'm calming myself down," he repeated.

Admittedly I was a little relieved that he wasn't letting me get out. I didn't really want to go, but I wasn't gonna let him down talk me either. The fact that he didn't want me to go and was calming himself down was a good thing. I leaned back in my seat again and gazed out the passenger side window for the 20-minute drive until we drove up into Lane's driveway. When he turned off the ignition, we both sat there in silence, not moving.

After a few minutes of waiting, he grabbed my bag from the backseat, opened the door for me and headed into the house without waiting for me to get out. When I followed him in, he was walking upstairs, and I followed his lead into the spare bedroom where he put my overnight bag down on the bed. Spare bedroom eh? Somebody clearly hadn't calmed all the way down yet. Damn! I didn't come over here to sleep in the spare room.

Obviously, I was going to have to pull out the big guns to change things.

***

I sat on the edge of the bed watching Lane. "Wait a minute," I said before he could exit the room.

He stood looking up at the ceiling like I was annoying him. "What."

"What?" I said rolling my neck again. "Listen, I know you didn't bring me over here to have me sleep in the spare bedroom and have an attitude with me tonight. I told you to let me out 20 minutes ago and you decided not to so you could 'calm down.' Okay well you apparently haven't calmed down just yet, but we need to be working towards that because I'm not about to be left off in isolation while you walk around here mad and ignoring me," I demanded.

He smiled subtly and looked at me sideways. "We've been in the house all of 2 minutes and you've already determined that I'm gonna walk around the house mad and ignoring you?"

"That's what you're doing right now," I said with raised eyebrows.

He was silent, dropped his head down, turned towards me, walked over and sat on the bed beside me. "Brenda baby you gotta understand that I can't just move on and pretend nothing happened right? I mean this dude came into our newly started relationship and basically pissed all over it. You and I talked about what we want, opened up to each other and I'm trying to be here for you while all of this crazy stuff is going on in your life, but I'm not gonna compete for you. There are too many other options in Atlanta for me to have to compete once we've established we're together. You said..."

"Hold on, hold on, hold on. I know you don't have to compete because you're a big-time car shop repair owning, fine ex-ball player and I'm not trying to make you compete. Like I said in the car, I understand that you're mad and why; but Lane I swear to you that Teddy did not give me any inclination that he was coming to Rhonda's or going to propose...ever for that matter. He was dodging commitment the whole time we were together, which I told you before. I said 'No.' Does that count for anything? I chose you," I rebutted.

"Yeah, it counts for a lot, but..." he started.

"No buts," I said leaning over and kissing him deeply.

For a second he felt as though he was going to pull away, but instead he leaned in closer and put his hands behind my head. We kissed more deeply and then he separated his soft, plump lips from mine.

"You're not playing fair," he said softly pecking my lips once more. I smiled and let my hands rest on his hips. "I'm possessive with the ones I love Brenda. I don't smother, I let you do what you want and have to do; but you will have enough rope to hang yourself if you're not being real with me. I'm human and I can be hurt. Seeing another man propose to a woman that I'm trying to make a future with and not knowing 100% that she wouldn't consider it, is not a place I'm comfortable in. I love you."

His eyes were sparkling as he gazed deeply into mine and all I wanted to do...was whatever he wanted me to do. He loved me. And truth be told, I loved him too. My heart and soul were telling me that I made the right choice. For once, things might just turn out the way I'd hoped.

"I love you too," I echoed softly. "I want you."

The gazes lingered a bit longer and then we were back to kissing.

Yes! Love does conquer all! At least it would tonight.

Our lips quickly found their ways to each other's necks and our hands were on undress-autopilot. We fell backwards on the bed and began pulling our underwear off. The warmth of his breath and his tongue danced over my nipples while his hands held my breasts in place for the feast.

I moaned and felt his fingers caressing, then strategically exploring my vagina. The girth and stiffness of his penis rubbed against my leg as he massaged and tasted my breasts. My body cried out for him because I was surely in need of pleasurable. He was so sexy and smelled like the kiwi scented shower gel I'd noticed the other morning. I hoped he'd taste as good as he smelled when it was my turn.

I worked my legs around his so as to signal that I wanted him to move up further on me and he did.

"All the way," I directed as my hands scaled down his body like a rope.

Soon my hands were on his thighs and his large, beautiful love muscle hung before my awaiting lips. My hands cupped the back of his thighs as I slid as much of him into my mouth as I could take. He moaned and tensed his butt cheeks. "Oh yes baby, take it all," he mumbled thrusting slowly in and out.

I swirled my tongue around his thickness while he worked the walls of mouth like slave laborers. When I felt him expanding and heard his moans turn into whimpers, I reached up and tapped the hand he was holding the condom in. He was oblivious to what I was doing at first, but came out of his trance long enough to place the condom into my hand. I ripped it open with both hands and slowly worked him out of my mouth.

His rod at attention, I slid the condom on and tugged on his hips as he again followed my lead, descending down to my wet box and inserting himself.

"Your mouth felt sooo good," he moaned into my ear as he stroked in and out. "I'm trying so hard not to cum right now cause your tongue has me ready to blow already."

"We have all night for you to cum wherever you want," I replied working my kegel exercises on his hot rod.

With that he couldn't hold it anymore. "Oh, shit baby!" He cried out. "No, not yet..."

I was pleased with the control I had over his body as he collapsed on top of me and pushed his arms under my body.

"Damn girl you got me losing control," he said with a sweaty smile. I smiled and kissed his neck while I basked in his embrace.

These were the arms I wanted to be in.

22

Brian

LARGE AND DISCHARGED

Because I was such a healthy stallion before Stalker Channing put a few in me, my recovery time was actually a lot quicker than Dr. Frasier had initially predicted. He'd expected me to remain in the hospital for at least another 2 weeks. My gunshot wounds and bruised lung added to the damages I'd suffered by losing my kidney, but I'd beat his prediction by being discharged in 8 days.

My maternal grandmother had come to visit me every day for a week while she was in town for the funeral. I was actually glad to see her though I wasn't so thrilled to see her chauffeur so frequently (my mother). They did as much as they could to try and help my recovery and arrange things like getting the door of my apartment fixed, etc. My Aunt Tonya and Uncle Donavan managed one visit a couple of days after Kelly's funeral. My uncle was his typical strong self on the outside, but his eyes looked weak and my aunt appeared to have aged a number of years in the days since she'd lost her daughter.

Three months had passed now and in that time both of them had lost complete interest in the apartment building. My uncle once confided that they'd intended on passing ownership down to Kelly so that she would always have an income. I'd been trying to convince my aunt to go into the restaurant business with me prior to "the incident" but recently she'd offered to sell me and Brenda the complex. That was an investment I hadn't previously considered, but it was a good way to make steady money with the prime area it was in and frankly, I didn't plan on going back to bartending.

Brenda had since resigned from her position and received a pretty hefty severance package from what she told me and was open to the purchase since she also had inheritance money in the bank like I did. She did however make it clear that she would never live in the building again because the memories traumatized her too much. I was still considering opening the restaurant in the space I'd been looking at, but it had to be on hold a moment until I was at 100% and could figure out if I wanted to embark on the venture alone.

I spent the first couple of months recuperating in my same apartment with help from Brenda, my boys, my mother (since she was the main one available to be at my beck and call regardless of how much I liked her) and Nadia. Yes, my lovely next-door neighbor had let her guard down even further and mysteriously found the time to tend to my ailing needs.

Four days after I was discharged and Nadia was at my place bringing me Chinese takeout food and toting my remote control from the one room to another, she let me into that plush place I was seeking. She was propped up in the bed beside me eating her Chinese food out of the carton as I was while we watched CSI on television.

"Hey girl, don't spill any of that on my bed. I'm not like those other hood dudes you're used to dating, I'm neat," I joked but was serious.

She frowned and rolled her eyes at me, "You don't know jack shit about what kind of guys I'm used to dating Mr. Mom. I haven't eaten since breakfast this morning so please believe that any food missing my mouth and making it to your bed will be a total anomaly."

"Mr. Mom?"

"Yeah! You sound like somebody's momma with all that 'Don't spill your food now baby,'" Nadia replied mocking me with an old woman's voice.

"Okay smart ass," I retorted smiling and elbowing her playfully. "Let me find a fried rice up my ass when I go to bed tonight and I'm gonna make you lick it out."

"You wish!" She said animatedly rolling her neck and looking me up and down. "Sorry bruh, you got the wrong girl."

"What, you don't lick ass? Quit lying. I know ass lickin' lips when I see them," I joked.

Nadia's face went cold, and she put her Chinese food down on the night stand on her side. Aww hell! Now she had an attitude! She then reached over and grabbed my carton of food out of my hand and put it down on the nightstand beside hers. I wasn't sure what she was doing so I didn't say anything or move, but I was hoping she wasn't about to turn my developing feelings for her into anger.

"You sir, have been making sexual innuendos about my lips, my tits and my hips damn near every day that I have been over here this week. Do you want me so badly that you can't concentrate on anything else?" She said now straddling me with a mischievous look on her face.

I smiled. I'd been on the receiving end of female seductresses enough to know when one about to spread 'em like butter. My dick got instantly hard and she lifted a little in response.

"Oh!" she chirped. "I think you just answered my question for me."

I reached out and put my left hand on her face, as my right shoulder was still tricky while it was healing. She raised both of her hands and brought them to my face, pulling me closer so that our lips could touch. We were immediately in a passionate dance of lips and tongue as my "mini me" begged to be released in my jogging shorts.

I hadn't been one to waste too much time kissing since I'd broken up with Gabrielle years before because I found the girls read into it more than I intended; but this time, I almost didn't want to stop kissing her.

Almost.

I dropped my hand from her face to her ass and brought my right hand up to get equal playing time on her other butt cheek. It felt soft, yet firm, and she was either wearing a thong or going commando. That only meant one thing; she was planning on giving me the pink before she got over here.

Your boy was back in action!

***

"Wait a minute," Nadia said grabbing the remote control and changing the channel to the Jazz music station. "I don't want to...do it to the sound of people being killed and police sirens."

I shook my head and grinned. "You need theme music? You sure you haven't stripped before?" I joked with a wink.

"Boy! Shut up," she chuckled blushing red and pulling me in tightly to kiss me.

I winced a bit because my side was still healing from the bullet wounds, the removal and most of all, my broken ribs. Because ribs have to naturally heal on their own, I definitely experienced some pain daily, and trouble breathing periodically.

"Oh, did I hurt you?" She asked jumping back a bit.

"Don't worry about it," I said keeping my grasp on her butt cheek with my left arm. "I'm bruised but not broken baby," I responded before my lips found her neck and I inhaled the sweet smell of her perfume. A woman that smelled good enticed me to want to find out how she tasted.

Nadia's head lulled back as my tongue traced over her throat and my lips danced behind it. Her waist was small, but her hips and butt were wide, just how I like it. Her hands caressed my head, which thankfully had healed from the gun butt that scarred it and continued to straddle me as she gently fell back and I maneuvered myself above her.

The red silk shirt she was wearing was clinging to her ample breasts and I couldn't wait to get them in my mouth. It had been almost 3 weeks since I'd had sex with anyone other than my left hand and my body was impatiently yearning for her in my underwear. Just as my kisses and sucking reached her collarbone, I felt her hand caressing my erection and God knows I had to mentally road block the explosion waiting to erupt.

"Oh, baby you can't do that right now. You know it's been a long time for me; you liable to set off a bomb in my pants before I get to the target," I murmured in her ear.

"Well let's stop playing around then because it's been longer than that for me," Nadia replied tugging on my shorts so that they were sliding down my legs. "I'm assuming you have condoms nearby?"

Aggressive and not afraid to say it. Sexy...coming from her.

"Yeah, in the night stand," I answered.

"I'll get them since you're not as mobile as you once were," she said sliding from under me as I rolled over onto my back.

Them? Somebody had big plans for me, I thought.

She returned straddling me yet again, kissing me more passionately this time though, and she'd already slipped her shirt off between reaching for the condom in my nightstand and coming back to me. This girl was quick. She was wearing a pretty light blue lace bra that cupped her breasts just right. I guessed they were somewhere between C and D cups, just the right size for my mouth.

We both worked our clothes off between kissing necks, arms, chests, breasts and stomachs while I slid the Magnum condom over my hard-on. I remained lying on my back as she lowered herself down letting my dick slide smoothly into the plush wetness she'd been keeping from me. We both called out with moans of pleasure before she began to rock her him back and forth milking my muscle.

I grabbed her shoulders and pulled her down closer so that I could put her beautiful breasts in my mouth at the same time. Oh, she must have liked that because she sped up her hip action and I immediately had to start thinking about the time I saw my grandmother changing bras when I was 10 years old so that I would lose some of my erection and not bust a nut in the condom right then. She was feeling so good though and I didn't want to stop. My God I loved the feeling of being inside a woman while she road me to ecstasy. After what was probably about 5 minutes of that, she yelled out that she was cuming and I saw, as well as felt, her body follow suit.

She then turned her body around without letting me slide outside of her and began the same cowgirl like motions she had when she was facing me. It only took a few minutes of that before the vision of her beautifully sculpted body and lower back, accented by her taking me deeper and deeper into her love cushion, forced me to explode inside the condom like a scud missile filled with sperm.

"Oh!" I yelled feeling uncontrollable convulsions of pleasure pulsating through my dick causing the rest of my body to lock up.

Once they'd subsided, I laid lightheaded and sweaty on my side gazing at Nadia who'd lain down beside me with her head on my left shoulder looking at me too. I was in turmoil. I felt feelings I hadn't felt, or wanted to feel since I'd caught Gabby on her knees in her apartment, but there was something good about it this time that I couldn't shake. Something sincere and beautiful in Nadia overrode my typical and ingrained cynicism. I was still on the fence about how I would handle it though.

"Why are you looking at me like that?" Nadia asked with a slight grin as she snuggled closer to me.

"Like what?" I replied brushing a loose strand of hair away from her sweaty face.

"Like, I don't know, that's why I'm asking. What are you thinking about?"

I hesitated to say what I was thinking, and then rolled over on my back with her still laying in my embrace on her side.

"You're different," I finally managed.

She wrinkled her nose and said, "Different than whom?"

"Not who. Different than I thought you were. Than what I thought this was gonna be when I first met you," I said honestly.

"What did you think when you first met me?"

I turned and looked at her with a mocking expression and then looked back up at the ceiling. "I don't think you want me to say."

"Really? Why not? Was it that bad?" She asked raising herself up on one elbow with her hand to her head.

"Not good or bad. I just didn't think it...being with you, was gonna be any different than being with any of the other women I... umm... entertain," I said closing my eyes in anticipation that she would fly off the handle and start going off on me; but she was silent. In fact, she didn't say anything until I opened my eyes again and looked at her.

"So why am I different?" She asked.

"Because I actually care about you," I said before I had time to re-think my words.

Nadia smiled warmly and lay back down inside my embrace.

"I care about you too," she said.

And now 3 months later...we were in love.

***

It was still strange living in the apartment building without Kelly barging in at will or being able to walk upstairs and shoot the shit with my little sister. Amanda and Nadia were still here but Lina was planning on moving at the end of the month, no one was living in Kelly's old place and Brenda had only come back to move all of her stuff out to storage or Lane's house. Those two were inseparable since Teddy brought the big guns out with the proposal and I hadn't seen her this happy with a dude since...since never.

What was even crazier is that I was seeing my mother more than she was. In fact, with my mother periodically checking in on my recovery, Brenda would either leave when she came over, or make sure she wasn't here when she came over. Brenda said they'd had some words at Kelly's funeral, but my grandmother put an end to the bickering in light of the circumstances. My Aunt Tonya wasn't in any condition to mediate that catty shit anyway, so I was glad to hear nothing had come of it.

On a better note, that sorry mother fucker Edwin waived his rights to a trial and plead guilty to all charges. They found out that Brenda wasn't the first person he'd stalked and in fact there'd been 2 other women at his company that reported his unwanted attentions previously. Unfortunately for my sister, she'd been the only numb nut that gave him a taste, so he'd have a reason to become more attached. How he was able to keep his job with all of the time he spent following and keeping up with my sister, I can't understand. Stalker Channing just escalated the level of crazy he was willing to go to.

Police said he had pictures of her shopping at the mall, walking her dog, leaving Lane's place, at my father's funeral...the guy was sick in the head. Brenda saw the photos at the police department, and she was pretty shaken about the quantity of them. I had to sign some paperwork and answer some police questions while I was in the hospital but for the most part, the nigga'd given up trying to fight anything before we even started to prosecute him. It was a good thing too cause if he got out, I was gonna see to it that he was dead and buried soon enough.

Nadia had just left a few minutes earlier to go to work since she was doing some site visits today instead of working from home. We still had separate apartments, but we had keys to each other's places now and rarely spent a night alone. This was another crazy thing that took adjusting for me to do. I was constantly resisting the urge to say things I normally would to the girls I dealt with and to think the worst when things didn't turn out the way I expected. My grandmother said something to me while she was visiting me at the hospital that put things into perspective for me.

"Brian, I know you're a young and handsome virile man, but let me tell you something…everybody dies. Now you came closer to it than I ever have in my 82 years of living and what I want you to think about is this," she said clearing her throat and touching my hand gently. "Would the life you'd lived already have been good enough? Would all of that womanizing and pimping you done have been so good that you would have been okay with signing off? Is your life right with God? Are you the man you've always wanted to be yet? Cause all of these are very important questions.

I know you have a hard shell, and I know why you do, but just like you're keeping the bad out, can't nothing good get in. I know my daughter has not been everything she should have been, and I know your daddy has really…scarred y'all chil'ren. But baby, you don't want to grow up and be like your daddy. Handsome like him, maybe, but not just like him. He wasn't loved by many and I don't even think he loved himself. He was mean and mean will eat you from the inside out. Trust me when I tell you this," she said pushing the thin rims of her glasses down over her wrinkled nose exposing her cataract infested eyes.

There might as well have been a vacancy sign flashing above my head as she was talking because I'd already decided that I wasn't open for anything she was saying to me until she said one other thing.

"They say the good die young but the despised do too except they don't just die…they're killed." Grandma's face was as serious as a heart attack and she stood her 4'11" self up, long gray hair tied up in a bun, dressed in grandma jeans and a flower shirt with orthopedic shoes on and walked over towards my mother who was sleeping across 2 chairs in my room. "C'mon now Livvy let's go. You exhausted and me too and I know this boy needs some rest to keep up that healin'," grandma said turning towards me with a wink.

My mother got up stretching, came over to where I sat up in my hospital bed and gave me a kiss on the cheek which I promptly side eyed her for.

"I'll be back tomorrow Mister Grinch," she said walking away slowly.

"Good night baby. Now you remember what I said to you and let that light that I knew of you when you were a young boy shine out again. I miss that fun child that used to come and hug his granny and sit with me for hours talking about Scooby Doo," she said with a slight chuckle as she approached and kissed me lightly on the cheek as well. I was considerably warmer to my grandmother as I recalled some of those fun times when she still lived in Atlanta and we'd spent most of our days in her care. "And treat that girl that's been nursing on you good too. She's a pretty one and I like how she don't take your crap like your momma," Grandma added as my mother rolled her eyes and held the door for the both of them to walk out of my room.

I let what she'd said marinate for a moment as much as I wanted to ignore it. I certainly wasn't enthusiastic about having anymore psycho bitches trying to kill me or bust the windows out of my car. The last couple of months had been nothing but a gauntlet of running from, to, and over women and as unfortunate as the circumstances were for why I was in the hospital, it was actually a welcomed break from the dram. I'd almost lost my best friend behind my usual ways.

As I thought of that night, I ran my fingers over the side of the bed where Nadia had laid a little while earlier, put my head down on the spot and prayed aloud, "God please don't make me be making a mistake trusting this one cause if this doesn't work out, nothing will."

23

Brenda

THE TRUTH & NOTHING BUT

I parked in the newly renovated stone winding driveway that led to the front door of my mother's house which she'd apparently wasted no time in overhauling. Either the insurance money from my father's "accident" had come in or she simply didn't give a damn about spending the money now.

I stepped out of my car wearing beige 3-inch sandals, brown Capri pants and a beige off the shoulder shirt. My sunglasses were on the top of my head and my hair was brushed back into a neat, but bushy ponytail. I saw her glance out her front room window as I approached the door and she met me on the walkway.

"Just take your time Brenda. No need to rush to see me huh?" She said with a frown. For some reason my usual lackadaisical pace always made her feel like I wasn't in enough of a hurry to do anything. Well too bad bitch!

My mother was wearing loose fitting designer jeans with a crisp white tank top and no shoes. I guess today was dress down day for her alter ego.

"Ma please; can I get in the door before you start with the drama?" I replied.

She eyed me as I passed her and walked down the hallway to the front room. It was only partially decorated but the new color scheme was an obvious champagne and white décor. I suspected it would turn out nicely. Flopping down on the posh champagne colored couch which faced toward the huge front window allowed me to see how dirty my car had gotten which made me wrinkle my nose at the revelation and I threw my arms back on the couch.

"The house looks nice so far Ma," I said to her as she took a seat in a champagne cushioned straight chair. "Not wasting anytime moving on I see."

"Thank you. No time like the present now is there? So, you're looking good. How do you feel?" She asked fingering the arm of the chair and glossing over my jab about moving on.

"I'm fine. Time is healing it all. How are you?"

Her eyebrow lifted. "I'm surprised you asked. But...I'm doing well considering everything. I tried to see if your brother would come but he...well you know how he is. He's not coming."

I laughed. "I don't even know why you tried that one. I could have told you he wasn't coming. Must be something big if you were trying to get him here too then huh? Are you finally about to drop the bomb about how my father really died?" I prodded.

Her eyes got wide and she crossed and uncrossed her legs uncomfortably. "We can talk about that later if we must Brenda. What I want to talk to you about is...different. Something that should have been said years ago."

"Okay."

"Have you already moved into a new apartment or a home? I'm sure you haven't been staying with Rhonda and her fiancé' this long," my mother asked tapping the chair arms with her nails.

What, was she bi-polar now? "Mom, how many subjects are you gonna get on at once? You're all over the place. I've been staying with Lane for now."

"Lane. Okay well I never thought that Teddy guy was right for you anyway. He reminded me a lot of your father and how I got in the predicament that I'm in now," my mother said looking off into nowhere. Then she snapped back and continued. "I just wanted to let you know that my door is always open because there's plenty of room for you here. Shacking up doesn't lead to anything accept sharing bills and babies. If he loves you enough to live with you, he should love you enough to marry you."

I smirked and brushed a loose hair away from my forehead. "I don't recall asking you for an opinion on how I'm living my life mommy. Thanks for your advice, but no thanks."

She glared at me and pursed her lips. "I will always love you and your brother no matter what kind of venom you spit at me, but I never thought my own children would talk to me like this. I guess the serpent is everywhere no matter what you do," she replied sounding wounded.

"So, you're still taking those acting classes?" I joked frostily.

She looked confused for a moment; then I almost literally saw the light bulb come on in her head. Her expression changed from wounded to one of annoyance.

"Don't be disrespectful Brenda. You're beginning to sound a lot like Robert used to," she warned.

"Why did you call me over here Ma?" I asked becoming aggravated with this drawn-out song and dance. She always went to the father characteristics in me or in my brother when she wanted to make us feel ashamed.

And it did.

"Brenda do you love me?" She asked leaning forward.

"What? Why are you dying or something? Do you have cancer?" I asked shifting in my seat.

"I just need to know that you love me and won't cut me off entirely when I say what I have to say because we're all we have left now."

I tensed up thinking, 'This is it. She's gonna tell me that she held daddy down in the water or something and killed him.'

"Yes, I love you Ma. Please spit it out already," I answered.

"I realize that I could have been a better mother at times, and I know that is why you and Brian are sometimes ugly towards me. What I am though is the only mother God gave you, and I love you and would die for you. Regardless of the mistakes I've made with you, you know I tried to be a good mother to you," she was saying.

Her words were beginning to sound like background noise because she was simply rambling about nothing as far as I was concerned.

"I'm sorry that I didn't protect you better from your father, but I wasn't always in my right mind either," she continued. "But...did you ever notice how Brian looks like your dad and you just look like me? Brian has Hazel eyes, and you don't?"

"Yeah, I also noticed that both he and Julian look just like daddy too but nobody bothered to tell us about Julian," I replied sarcastically. "Even now you haven't sat us down and talked about daddy's illegitimate bastard with us," I said coarsely.

She swallowed hard. "I found out about him the same year your brother was born. It was a very difficult time for me; I was still virtually a newlywed and your father promised he'd never cheat on me again." She laughed an uneasy laugh. "Well, we know that was a crock of crap now, but I didn't know that then. I'm sure you kids thought I was stupid for always taking him back when I knew he was cheating and I know you didn't understand why I stayed with him when he hit me sometimes, but some things are just not that easy. Sometimes you have to walk in someone else's shoes to understand what they're going through."

"Where's this going Ma?" I asked impatiently, fearing she'd ramble on for hours like usual.

She took a deep breath and said, "I wasn't always faithful to your father either." She was silent and then looked at me for a reaction. I had none. I'd never assumed she would let him cheat on her for almost 30 years and never stray. So, was this supposed to be her big secret? Don't tell me this woman is about to tell me she was having an affair with Avis all this time and now she was gonna marry him?! Oh brother.

"I never assumed you were Ma. Is this your secret?" I answered.

"I want you to know that I didn't keep this from you to be malicious or deceitful, but, Robert is not your real father."

What the holy hell?!

***

My mother went on explaining how sorry she was for keeping it a secret all of these years with tears running from her eyes. She moved next to me on the couch and kept making attempts to touch my hand or my knee in the process of her explaining. I was stunned to silence, but I didn't let her touch me.

"Brenda you have to understand. I found out that he'd still been seeing Julian's mom on and off when Brian was 2 and I was always finding phone numbers and, I was tired of being cheated on. I got tired of sitting home while he flew all over the world; having sex with other women and making more babies for all I knew." She was crying hysterically, and I was sobbing now too, but without sound.

"I went to a lawyer to file for divorce and he told me to get a private investigator first. He referred me to a guy and after all of the meetings, over so many months and all," she paused to grab a tissue from a box conveniently placed near the couch. "We got really close. He understood what I was going through, and he was there for me when Robert wasn't. I didn't plan for it to happen Brenda. I didn't plan to sleep with him or to get pregnant or anything. Besides that, I was drinking a lot in those days too. I was unhappy and he made me feel happy for a while."

"So, the investigator is my real father?" I asked in a mousy and tearful voice.

My mother nodded and blew her nose into the tissue. "When I found out I was pregnant I knew it was his. I don't believe in abortion and I knew your father would know it wasn't his because of the timing. Hell, he probably spent more time screwing his crew then he did me. I was lost. My case had gone to hell because meanwhile I was going to accuse him of cheating; here I was pregnant by another man."

"So why didn't you leave daddy and be with him?"

"I couldn't," she said shaking her head from left to right. "He was already married, and he didn't want to leave his wife. He loved me Brenda; he really did," she plead. "But he was in a hard spot too. His wife was the kind that would never let him see his kids if he left her and they had a 3-year-old daughter. I already had Brian and I knew Robert would try to hurt me physically and financially if I left him and you know how he was. He was possessive like that, even if he didn't really want you. I, I wanted to keep you Brenda." She sniffled and wiped her eyes with a fresh tissue before she handed me a new one as well.

"Your father and I fought nearly every day for about 3 months when I told him I was pregnant and how it happened. I mean how mad could he be when he had a son while we were married and was still cheating? I stayed with him and he had to stay with me. He tried to convince me to have an abortion and even threatened to beat you out of me one night when we were arguing. It was the worst time of my life baby, but I fought for you.

I've always fought for you; even when you didn't know it. We decided that no one had to know, and we went to counseling for the rest of my pregnancy to try and work it out. Counseling didn't help a whole lot because he was still violent when he was drunk, but I think he tried to treat you the same way he did Brian. You never knew any different right?" The drinking and violence that followed increased too but on a much cleverer level, my mother claimed. He wouldn't hit her in places that visible bruises would show in public places; but he would choke her, throw things at her, spit on her, push her and poke her with his index finger in the temple.

I couldn't control my blubbering and I heard myself sounding like a wounded animal as I buried my head in my hands. So, my whole existence was a lie? My real father was a married cheating bastard too? I had an older sister? The man I'd known as my father was not my father? I'd suffered through mental and physical abuse by a man who wasn't even my real fucking father?

My brother and I usually suffered verbal abuse or neglect as opposed to being hit, but we were not immune. My father hit me more often than my brother, but Brian's beatings always seemed to be more severe. As time went on, the alcohol wasn't always the indicator that abuse was ahead. A bad day at work would almost certainly lead to a bad day at home, if he came home.

"Brenda. Baby I'm so sorry. I just didn't think there was ever a good time to tell you. I didn't think there was ever a good reason to tell you."

"Right cause everything was so perfect in our house already! That's your fucking problem Ma!" I screamed, lifting my head up. "You don't think! You didn't think I'd want to know that the man who kicked my ass and taught me that men aren't shit for most of my life wasn't my real father? You didn't think I'd want to know who my real father was? Maybe see him sometime? How could you not think I needed to know? Honestly, so what the hell's the point in you telling me this now? The asshole I knew as my father is dead. Why tell me at all?"

My mother flinched at each harsh word and she nervously rubbed her left arm with the ball of her wrist. "I didn't know if Julian knew and, well things have changed, and all secrets come out eventually. I wanted you to hear it from me rather than finding out on accident."

"So, where is he? My father?"

She licked her lips nervously and dropped her eyes to her hands. "That's another thing I needed to tell you. Avis, Avis is your father."

I suddenly felt as though I couldn't breathe. I began gasping for air and dry heaving. I held my stomach and stood up looking frantically around for the bathroom.

"Oh my GOD are you okay?" my mother asked jumping up to try to assist me anyway she could.

Even as it seemed I was having some sort of a panic attack, I managed to push her hands off of me and rushed hunched over to the first-floor bathroom. I immediately began throwing up and it felt like all of my feelings had congregated in my stomach, decided it was time to exit, and did just that.

When I finally stopped retching, I flushed the toilet, got up and washed my mouth out as best I could and stood looking at myself in the mirror.

This woman had actually managed to tell me something worse than what I was ready for.

Now I wished I hadn't pushed.

***

"Are you okay?" My mother asked watching me from the doorway.

"Hell no," I responded wiping my mouth with a hand towel. I turned and looked at her as I put the towel on the edge of the sink.

"So, you've been fucking my real father and you had him all up in daddy's...daddy's face the night he died?" I said stumbling over calling my deceased father 'daddy' as I always had.

She turned her eyes away from me. "Robert didn't know who he was. I told him your father was someone else who I knew he couldn't track down back then. He thought Avis was Jenny's friend."

"You two really belonged together with your sneaky conniving asses. I can't get a good man because you showed me how to accept a bad one. I thought I learned the opposite by never dating a man who would hit me or who drank too much or who called me names; but that's a bunch of bull. I just chose the less abusive bastards. Same shit, different level. They didn't lie to my face; they just cheated behind my back. They led me to believe we'd have long, loving, committed relationships together; instead, they ménage-á-trois-ed their asses to obscurity. I'm as fucked up as you! You let that motherfucker who is not my daddy beat me and talk down to me and humiliate me all my life! Does my real father know that? Or is he too busy kissing the ground you walk on?" I said shaking my head in disgust.

"It wasn't like that Brenda."

"Oh, it wasn't? And why the hell would you bring the man you cheated on him with up in his house with him and even now you're seeing him? Where's his wife now? Or did y'all off her too?" I screamed.

"His wife died a few years ago of lung cancer and Avis didn't have anything to do with your father's death. Absolutely nothing."

"Then why was he coincidentally there that night Ma? Huh? You think I'm stupid or something?" I scolded walking past her back into the living room but standing with my hands on my hips instead and stopping to set my icy gaze on her.

"Brenda, I don't think you're stupid," she stated walking closer to me shaking her head. "But...he wants to get to know you."

I stared at her without a word. I knew how cunning this bitch could be when she had to be and changing the subject from them conspiring to kill my father, to old dude wanting to get to know his long-lost daughter was a pretty blatant subject toss.

"Well, I don't know how you killed him but I'm sure the police don't know this side of the story and since you won't share, maybe I'll just let them figure it out," I threatened.

"No! Just...just hold on a minute," my mother said running her hands anxiously through her short locks. "Just, just sit down for a minute and let me talk to you."

"Yeah, let you talk to me right now because I want all of my God damn questions answered today and right now!" I hollered at my mother.

"Okay okay I'm gonna talk. Just calm down please. Sit down Brenda...please," my mother plead as she walked around the couch and sat down.

I took her original seat in the solo chair because the last thing on earth I wanted to do at that moment was sit next to her!

"Alright," she began, inhaling deeply, and then looking me directly in the eyes. "You know my best friend Jenny," she said pausing. I just stared at her. This bitch knew I knew who Jenny was.

"Get on with the story Ma because I'm ready to leave and if you wanna waste anymore of my time bullshitting..." I started.

"I'm talking! Damn it!" She said sitting up stiffly. "Okay so Jenny still models and hangs out on the club scene. She was telling me about this drug, GHB, that some of the younger models have been using to get high that also keeps their weight down. She was saying that she'd seen something in the news about guys slipping that same drug into people's drinks and then raping them and a few of those girls died. Jenny and I started talking about it a little more, I researched it and found out it was colorless, liquid, odorless, and it's virtually undetectable unless they are specifically looking for it."

"So, you put GHB in his drink?" I asked.

My mother nodded and tears, possibly genuine ones, fell from her eyes. "Brenda you know how miserable he was. When Avis got back in contact with me, I was ready to leave Robert, but he promised me

I wouldn't get a dime and that he was gonna drag the divorce out until we were old and dead. I earned my share of everything we owned Brenda. I took beatings for it, I was humiliated for it, and I was miserable for years to keep it. I wasn't going to leave here with nothing, and I was tired of living the life I was living. He should have drunk himself to death years ago anyway, but that mother fucker just wouldn't die! Crashed his car 7 years ago on the DUI, you remember that?" She asked.

I nodded.

"Yeah, well that car looked like a can of sardines but Robert...Robert walked away with nothing more than a bruised hip," she sobbed. "It was time for his ass to go. No way in hell was he gonna give everything I'd earned away to that new bitch he started dating that he was blatantly talking to in my presence on the phone. Whatever she was putting on him, he was willing to do anything to keep it. He even learned how to swim for her. Robert Andrews, who was scared of the water; learned how to swim for a piece of young pussy. So, I convinced him to stay home that night and play Bid Whist with me and Jenny and Avis. That's your father's favorite game and I knew he'd jump at the chance to play since it had been so long, and I'd heard him talking to his little girlfriend the week before on the phone. She was gonna be out of town that weekend."

My mother looked like a mad woman in a trance as she spoke, and I was getting a sinking feeling in my stomach hearing how the plot unfolded.

"He thought Avis was Jenny's date, and he was drinking that pitcher of Long Island Iced Tea I made for him like a fish at the same time he was drinking his beers. He made it easy. I put about 40 ml of GHB in it, we sat and played Whist, and soon he was slurring his words, becoming incoherent, and finally he blacked out. Me and Avis picked him up and put him on the float and pushed it in the middle of the pool hoping he'd flop off and drown," she shook her head visualizing the events with a snarl. "But the mother fucker barely moved so we knew we had to...help him. I used the pole part of the pool cleaning net and kept nudging him until he rolled off into the water. He was down there for maybe 20 seconds and then he started flailing in the water. I guess he was too disoriented to save himself though, because he went back down pretty quickly, and then he was still."

She began to refocus and look into my eyes again with tears still streaming down her cheeks, yet her expression was calm.

"It was for the better good," she stated.

24

Brian

CURRENT EVENTS

After I showered, I stood looking at myself in the bathroom mirror. My shoulder was still badly scarred, but the mobility was much better in it now thanks to physical therapy twice a week. The area on my torso where I was shot and had my kidney removed was also healing decently although it was still tender. My ribs were seemingly healed completely judging from the ease with which I'd been able to breathe and the extra stroke moves I put on Nadia the night before without any chest pains.

The gash on my head had healed weeks ago but the hair hadn't grown back around the wound at all, giving me a permanent part in my hairline. What bothered me most was the mark on my right cheek that could have disfigured a lesser man. My good genes and genetics luckily overpowered the affects an ugly scar could have on the average man's face, because I was obviously above average. The few times I'd ventured out since the shooting without a bandage covering it, women seemed to use it as an in to talk to me.

"So, who tried to harm that beautiful face? They don't want me to come from behind this counter on them," One big busted Spanish chick with thick eyebrows and thighs to match asked when I was down at HOME DEPOT. Any other time I would have taken her up on her offer and made her "cum from behind" that counter like she wanted to, but I didn't have any desire to mess things up with Nadia by playing games, so I just smiled and said, "Long story," instead.

The scar actually gave me an edge I might have been missing with my chiseled good looks and now I was feeling like Tupac or the rapper 50 Cent after surviving 3-gun shots. In fact, my severely underworked modeling agent had called recently about some bookings who wanted a handsome but rugged looking guy, and I was gonna be headed down to her offices to see what the offers were. I wasn't at 100% at the moment, but I was definitely hovering around 97%.

My cell rang and I took my time walking over to the dresser where my phone was to answer it since it was just my general ring tone which made me assume it was a "jump off." Plies song BUST IT BABY blared for the last time before I answered as I looked at the name that popped up on the ID: Jaws-o-life.

"Hello," I said pulling out the top draw in the dresser to pull out some boxer briefs to wear.

"Hey sexy. It's Lyla. How have you been?" She said on the other end.

She'd acquired the name "Jaws-o-life" because she'd blown so good one night after an Usher concert that it felt like she'd sucked all of the life out of me. I vaguely remembered what she looked like. Slender, milk chocolate, 5 foot something female with huge soup cooler sized lips that she used to bring me to pleasures only a chick with lips that large could do.

"What's up sweetheart I'm doing as expected, and yourself?" I replied nonchalantly.

"Not surprised to hear from me? It's been what...like," she paused thinking. "Maybe 9 or 10 months since we last saw each other right? Did I catch you in the middle of something?"

"Maybe that long. I'm getting dressed," I offered as I continued shuffling around my room pulling out brown linen pants and a beige linen shirt from my closet.

"Dressed? I think I like you better un-dressed," she chuckled. "I'm gonna be in town on business for the next 4 days and I'm trying to see you."

Business? What did this bitch do again? I had to find out before I set fire to the bridge.

"Oh yeah? What kind of business?"

She sighed. "I sell high end antique furniture, remember? I've got a big client that wanted some pieces from Alaska so I..."

"Uh huh. Yeah I forgot what it was you did," I interrupted. "But I'm kinda in the middle of something right now and I don't really have the time to talk to you."

I thought I might have heard her gasp. "Oh. Okay. Are you off the market now or something? Cause this is a first," she stated sounding a bit irritated.

I'd torn it out the frame maybe 10 times in various places since meeting her at JAGUARS one night if I remembered correctly and I suppose she'd been spoiled by the ease at which it had previously come about. Oh well J.O.L! I laughed internally to myself.

"Yeah something like that. It was nice talking to you. Take care," I said hanging up abruptly before she began to speak again.

No need in prolonging the pain. I'd already decided that I would simply rip the band aids off quickly and cut the convo's short on any of my old flings that called me from here on out. I was staying away from THE MAN TRAP and since I didn't work at JAGUARS any longer the temptation of young tender-roni's on a daily basis would no longer be an option. Of course the daily pressures of women throwing themselves at me would be the same, and maybe even more with my new "thug" appeal, but I was up for the challenge as long as Nadia stayed on top of her game.

My distaste for monogamous relationships wasn't because I didn't think they were possible, but mainly because I didn't think one woman could hold my attention and I'd yet to run across a chick with two X chromosomes that could hold my attention and respect long enough to do it. Of course I was a little jaded after Gabby took my heart and shit on it, but something about Nadia told me to give this a shot. She and I had been sharing a lot of personal information during my recuperation and besides my sister, there hadn't been another woman I'd ever felt so comfortable and vulnerable with.

My grandmother's words, coupled with my near-death experience had made me reevaluate some of things and despite the ribbing I knew I'd eventually get from my boys, I was up for that challenge too. My heart hadn't beat for a woman like this in almost 10 years.

I hoped she was worth it.

***

"I'll be down in a minute," I told Ike on the phone before hanging up. I picked up my wallet from the top of my dresser and grabbed the house keys. Now when I locked up, I had 2 new sturdy locks to turn. When I reached Ike's Audi, he popped the automatic locks to let me in. I hadn't been driving myself too often these days unless it was necessary since my shoulder sometimes gave me trouble and sitting for long periods had previously been agitating my healing ribs.

"What up dude," Ike said to me pulling off.

"Everything is everything. Thanks for driving me," I said adjusting my seat back further and tilting the head rest. Tara's short ass liked to sit too close to the dashboard.

"No problem dude. So, are you thinking about buying the restaurant from this guy?" Ike asked checking his rearview mirror.

"Nah, I'm thinking about going into business with him. Have you ever been to EAT YOUR ART OUT?"

"Oh, that's where they draw portraits of you while you dine or something right?"

"Yeah, yeah something like that. It's got an art gallery feel to it and they sketch romantic or custom portraits of you either while you eat or at various spots in the restaurant. It has a live band too," I explained shuffling in my seat.

"Sounds nice. So, what's the plan then?" He asked.

"Right now, they basically just have tapas food and deserts but I have some ideas of how to revamp their menu and add my special chef's touch to it. I've eaten there a few times and I like it, but I'd love it if it was done with my added touch," I said smiling.

The owner was the son of a friend of Jimmy, the owner of JAGUAR'S. Jimmy knew I was looking to become the chef of my own restaurant and he'd even tasted some of my leftovers before and praised my skill. When he found out Trent Sheppard was potentially looking for a partner to enhance his restaurant and financially invest, he called me at home and told me. That was one thing I could say about Jimmy, he was an all-around good guy. He seemed like a redneck on the outside, but he was actually a cool boss and a decent acquaintance. He was sorry to hear that I wasn't coming back to work for him, but sent me a get-well basket and visited me in the hospital more than once while I was there.

The meeting was set for 10:30am and though we were about 15 minutes early, the restaurant only opened for patrons after 5:00pm anyway.

Ike parked in a lone spot in front of the entrance and said, "Looks like we're the first one's here."

I nodded and sat with my elbow leaning against the window and my fingers propping up my chin staring at the doorway. Ike had left his honeymoon early, visited me in the hospital, came by my crib to see me while I was healing and had picked me up to take me to this appointment, all while never mentioning our argument at the reception. Despite the fact that his bitch ass wife couldn't stand the air I breathed and probably huffed and puffed at the mention of my name, he'd maintained a friendship with me, though he'd threatened to end it before. I was grateful for that. Him and Nate were my oldest and truest friends and when I looked around at my father's funeral, I didn't see anybody that he called a best friend or vs. vs.

Don't get me wrong, I wasn't planning on turning into some Theo Huxtable nice guy type or anything, but I was beginning to see the benefits of giving people a chance. I was even starting to get a soft spot for my bird-brained mother while I was recovering. It was almost impossible for me to continue my grudge and treating her like dirt while she was trading off time with Nadia in seeing to it that I got the things I needed. Almost. She made it easier on the days she couldn't help but dwell on her own insignificant issues rather than tending to me though.

Anyway, I felt it was a good time for me to say something to Ike about our...incident.

"Hey man, I been meaning to tell you how much I appreciate you looking out for your boy even though I know it may not be exactly what Tara would have you do," I said continuing to look straight ahead although I could see him through my peripheral.

He didn't immediately reply, but then he said, "You always been my boy."

"I know but, I know we ended things in a fucked up way when I left the reception and... I know you were mad about how I handled stuff with Kyle so..."

"Let that go man," Ike said raising a hand and shaking his head. "It is what it is and it's already over. I know you aren't responsible for what happened to Kyle and everything just got out of hand at the reception. I had been drinking, I was still wound up from the night before and knowing I was gonna miss his funeral. We don't even have to talk about it. I'm good with it."

I looked at him and studied his face to see whether he was scratching his head or scratching his chin. He had a habit of going to his head when he was lying and scratching his five o'clock shadow when he was being honest. Tell tales like that got him busted with many a woman in school, but he was scratching his chin. Since he was willing to let it go, so was I then. I certainly wasn't getting any kind of a rush by having to apologize.

A burgundy Range Rover pulled up and parked next to our car on the driver's side and I could see the driver bopping his head to whatever loud music he was playing.

"I guess this is him," I said to Ike.

"Aiight dude. Call me when you're ready for me to come get you. I'm gonna go over to the mall and get my watch fixed," he replied.

"Will do," I answered as I got out of the car a few seconds after Trent had gotten out of his.

"Brian Andrews? Trent Sheppard." The 6 foot plus dark brown skinned man said to me holding his hand out.

"How you doin' Trent?" I replied shaking his hand.

* * *

Trent led me inside, showed me around the restaurant's dining areas, kitchen, restrooms and everything while explaining the concept of it and why he was looking for a partner. We'd already spoken on the phone on a couple of occasions and he'd sent me some basic contract paperwork to look over with my attorney to get the ball rolling. I hadn't mentioned it to anyone other than Nadia, but I was leaning more towards partnering with him on this than I was in doing anything else. I loved the theme of the place, I liked the decor, the area, and I liked that my menu items and cooking ability would give me the opportunity to shine and to ramp the place up a notch.

Eventually, he brought me into the modernly decorated management office in the back of the restaurant. He sat in a black leather chair behind a tall glass desk and offered me a seat in a less plush leather chair on the opposite end of the desk.

"So, what do you think?" Trent asked in a baritone voice that reminded me of Barry White. His voice didn't fit his looks in my opinion, but whatever, I would get used to it.

"I'm liking what I see. I do have some concerns about the size of the tables though if we're gonna expand the menu. People will need more space to put their food and eat," I answered leaning back in the chair.

Trent nodded, slid a piece of paper in front of him and began writing on it. "I can agree with that. So, what type of menu items were you thinking about adding? You know, just so I can get a rough idea."

"I'm thinking, Steak Tar Tar, Fettuccini Alfredo with shrimp or chicken, Vegetable Lasagna, Honey Braised Pork Chops and Sweet and Sour Tilapia to start," I said crossing my legs.

This dude wasn't ready for the chef-tastic cooking skills and ideas I had.

"Honey Braised Pork Chops and Sweet and Sour Tilapia? Damn that's got my taste buds ready for a sample already. I don't think I've had those before," he replied with a smile.

"Yeah, I would want to put some of the general favorites on there for the less adventurous patron but I'd say those two are my signature surprise dishes. What do you think?" I asked as if I didn't already know he would love them.

"Yeah, those do sound great. So, listen," he said leaning forward and putting his hands down on the desk. "Everything looks good to me as far as the offer for partnership our attorneys agreed on and I think this would be a great partnership if we can work out the minor kinks in office space. How are you feeling about it?"

"I'm feeling like this would be a great collaboration for us both also," I said as I thought that we damn sure would need to make sure my office was at least this big and better than his.

"How did you like the Lobster Meatballs and Mango Mousse dishes I had brought to you yesterday?"

He leaned back in his chair and rubbed his stomach with one hand. "Woo! I can't tell you how happy I was you had it delivered at lunch time because I scarfed it down like I'd been starving for days..." He was saying as we heard a doorbell sound buzz through the intercom. "Oh, that's probably just my wife coming in. I have a walkway doorbell that rings in here set up for off hours, so I'll know if someone comes in. Hell, she'll tell you how great your food was too because she tried to eat what I had left," he smiled looking behind me in anticipation of her entry.

I heard her enter behind me and instinctually turned my chair and stood to greet her, but I suddenly felt like I was in an episode of the TWILIGHT ZONE when the camera would zoom in around your face and the spinning coils would start revolving.

"Baby you..." she said breaking off her words once she saw me. "Oh, I'm sorry. I didn't know you were in a meeting. Good morning," she said with a half-smile and holding out her hand.

"Good morning," I said shaking her hand with a blank expression.

"I knew you were gonna be by here ASAP as soon as I saw your iPad on the arm rest in the truck," Trent chuckled. "Brian Andrews, this is my wife Gabrielle. Gabby this is my new partner in crime Brian."

"Your new partner?" She said trying to keep her level of surprise cordial. "Oh... okay. Great," she said feigning a smile.

Gabrielle hadn't aged much. She'd chopped her shoulder length mane into a curly cut that framed her face just below her ears and was wearing mauve dress pants with a white ruffled shirt and white heels that made her look 5'6" instead of 5'2".

What the hell was going on here? How could my luck be so bad that I would end up partnering with the one bitch I never wanted to see again in my life's husband? Fuck!

Trent pulled the iPad from a leather bag on the side of his desk and walked over to hand it to her. "Since I bought her this thing last month, she hasn't been able to function right without it," he said to be jokingly. "I thought you might even beat me here trying to get to it," he said to her as he leaned forward and planted a kiss on her cheek.

I wanted to yell, 'Oh hell fucking no! This deal is off if I'm gonna be seeing this bitch in here!'

But I didn't say anything. I just stood there looking like a pawn in a game of chess thinking about my next move.

"Okay baby well I'm gone. I just had to grab this. Good day Brian," she said with a quick glance and phony smile in my direction before turning to leave. Something about the way she said baby to him cut me like a knife.

What the hell had I gotten myself into?

25

Brenda

NEXT SUBJECT

Be careful what you ask for or you just might get it. I wanted to know for certain whether my mother had anything to do with my "father's" death and now I know. The crazy thing is that even though I already suspected it, I never truly thought about what I'd do if she had killed him. Now, as I sat here leering at her and thinking about all of the years, I suffered at the hands of a man I thought was my father, who resented me for something totally out of my control. My mother sat teary eyed, looking away from me and then nervously back into my eyes. I really saw the fear in her face now.

"Are...are you going to report it?" She asked softly.

"Why did you tell me if you thought I'd report it?" I asked holding back the frog that was steadily rising in my throat.

"Because you already knew anyway. I was just gonna tell you about Avis, but you just strong armed me into telling you everything and I didn't want you to go and get the police started back looking if I could stop it. Brenda you know he wasn't just an innocent victim. He deserved what he got, and I deserve what I have. I believe that," my mother said posturing.

Really mom? That's her excuse? She deserves what she has, and he deserved what he got? She might have even been right but...what did I know at this point. Everything I thought I knew about myself was now in question.

"So, what did you want to happen now?" I asked.

"I wanted you to get to know Avis and forgive me," she responded brightening and wiping a tear from her eye. "He's always wanted to know you really. We kept in touch on and off over the years. He even has your high school and college graduation pictures that I sent him," she said smiling lamely.

"So, he knows you were telling me all of this today?" I said coldly.

"He knew I was going to tell you about him being your father. Not the...the other thing," she said patting her now dry face with her palms.

"Well," I said wiping my own tears away and grabbing my keys off of the coffee table and standing. "I gotta go."

She stood instantly with me. "Where...where are you going?" she asked panic stricken.

"I'm not going to the police if that's what you're worried about," I glared. "I just need to get away from here and think for a minute."

"Oh," she replied immediately softening. "I'm just asking because I'm worried about you. I don't want you to run out of here all emotional and hurt yourself. We can talk this through Brenda. If you really look at it, this is better news than what you actually..."

I cut her off abruptly, "Don't you fucking dare. Don't even try to spin it in your favor right now after you not only admitted that you are an adulterous liar, but a conniving liar. Really mom? Do you really want to keep standing here and talking to me about the many trifling and fucked up things you've done?"

She flinched. "Okay, alright, you don't have to use such harsh language Brenda. Just be careful going home or wherever you're going then," she said turning and trotting up away and up the stairs as her voice cracked with tears again.

What the hell?! Why was she crying so hard when I was the one who had been blindsided? This trick knew all along I was not Robert Andrews's daughter! She knew she'd murdered a man and was hiding it with her best friend and her ex, now current lover! Why the hell was she so upset when I simply regurgitated the facts?

I let myself out and strutted down the walkway fiercely, almost twisting my ankle halfway when my heel got caught between one of the stones. Regaining my balance before actually falling, I slowed my pace and cussed the ground for attempting to sabotage my dignified exit. Once in the car I turned the car on and sat in the driveway while Mary J. Blige sang the lyrics to her MY LIFE song almost on cue. "If you looked at my liiiife, you'd see what I seeeee, la da la la la," she sang.

"If you looked at my life, you'd see that I don't know anything," I said aloud clicking my seatbelt on before pulling off.

I had been semi-prepared to hear that my mother had been involved in my fa... her husband's death since the time I arrived at the house and heard what was supposed to be the full details of it all. The truth was that I never planned on doing anything about it one way or another; I just wanted to know the truth. Not that he deserved to be killed in the way that he was, or at all for that matter, but I certainly understood how a man who'd done the things he had, and treated people the way he had could end up 6 feet under by a plan not ordained by GOD.

To be honest, I was impressed at the method and research she'd put into executing her plan. I was a bit surprised that Jenny was involved in helping her commit it, but then I shouldn't have been. She and my mother had been best friends since Junior High School, and she liked my father about as much as Don King liked barbers. I had no idea that GHB could be used like that and had only heard about it as a "date rape drug."

I guess the mouse finally got the cat in my dad's case. Now my mom was free to date the man she wanted and thus far it looked like they had gotten away with it all. Since I'd done everything in my power to avoid her since Kelly's funeral, we'd barely exchanged more than 5 words until she called me a few days ago asking if I could come by today. Now I almost wished I hadn't agreed.

I drove at the pace of a woman with nowhere to go and no reason to get there. I was having a hard time keeping my composure as I wiped periodic tears from my eyes and my runny nose as Mary J. continued to sing, "Life can be, only what you make iiiiit. When you're feeling down, you can never fake iiiittt..."

***

So many things ran through my head now that I knew Robert Andrews wasn't my real father and a one situation instantly came to mind. 15 was the age of the ass whoopin' for me in the Andrew's house. Once while my father had been out of town for work and my mother and brother were out of the house, I decided to have a little male company over for a make out session in the living room. I was still a virgin and hadn't planned anything more than some kissing and heavy groping so consequently, that's what we engaged in.

I was lying on the couch with Carmello lip locked on top of me. Suddenly he was flung off and I was smacked in the face. My father was cursing and struggling to maintain his grasp on Carmello; but the boy was quick and managed to escape his grip and get out of the house all in a flash.

I wasn't so lucky.

"What the hell is going on here? Is this what you do while I'm out of town!" my father shouted.

"No daddy I...we were just kissing..." I tried to explain with tears rushing down my cheeks and the heat from the smack on my face beginning to increase its sting.

"You were just kissing? With his hands all up your clothes? You were just kissing!" He continued to yell.

"I wasn't even doing anything!" I yelled back.

"Are you yelling at me in my house little girl? You feeling pretty grown right now? You must've forgotten who the hell I am," he said approaching me as I backed up and navigated around any furniture I could keep between us.

My father's hazel eyes blazed angrily at me as he took off the jacket to his blue pinstriped suit and maneuvered the furniture out of the pathway, he thought I was moving toward.

"Okay! I'm sorry. I wasn't doing anything though. We were just kissing." I said as my crying became chest heaving, hysterical fit.

"Brenda I was not born yesterday. I know you weren't doing anything yet, but that's because I walked in on you. You need to be focusing on school not letting boys get into your pants!" He yelled at a blood curling volume that made me jump.

Carmello escaped through the door to the garage, which was how my father had come in, but I would have had to pass by him to get to it. I took off running through the house and got the front door open, but he was quick behind me and slammed it back shut. I squealed and he grabbed me by my neck and pushed me down on the floor.

"I understand! I understand!" I yelled scooting away from him with my hands raised defensively. "Okay! Okay!"

"Okay? What the hell is that supposed to mean? You don't tell me when it's okay. I stop the punishment when I feel you understand. You don't manipulate me! I'm your damn daddy girl! I'm the all-seeing God of this domain!" He picked me up from the floor, grabbing me under my left arm and forced me into the living room before twisting me around and letting go as I fell onto the couch.

My right calf hit the table and I shrieked in pain, immediately grabbing at the source.

"I don't care if you hurt yourself. That's not gonna get you out of this beating." My father said through clenched teeth as he hovered over me.

The door to the garage opened again in the foyer and my mother came rushing into the living room dressed in tight jeans, a form fitting sequin white shirt and white pumps, with her then long hair cascading down to her shoulders.

"What's going on? I could hear this entire ruckus outside! Robert what are you doing?" my mother asked stepping between us.

"Oh, so what… you came to save her? No wonder why she's starting to act like a whore; look how you're dressed when I'm not here. What the hell are you dressing like this for if I'm not even home? And you always up my ass about what I do when I'm gone?" My father scolded.

"Act like a whore? What are you talking about?" She asked glancing at me quickly and then turning to face my father. "And I'm not dressed any different than what I wear all the time. You used to like it before you started in with all your side-whores. What is wrong with you? The first thing you do when you come home is start in on us?" My mother said before she turned around to face me.

"Who the hell are you talking to like that? I told you about contradicting me in front of the kids too! I ought to back smack you!" he yelled shoving her from behind onto me. "She's your daughter anyway, right? You want her to grow up to be a whore who sleeps around on her husband and can't stand on her own feet?"

"Robert!" My mother cried out lifting herself off of me and putting her arms around my shoulders for comfort. "You're so mean."

"Mean? I come home and find her about to spread her legs with some little nappy headed boy from the hood and I'm the bad parent? You're missing in action and coming home dressed like a street walker but I'm the bad guy!" He yelled storming out of the living room and up the stairs.

My mother and I sat on the couch in tears as she attempted to console me, "I'm sorry baby, I don't know what is wrong with him sometimes."

I leaned on my mother's shoulder and cried as I held my aching calf.

"Were you having sex in here Brenda?" My mother asked softly.

"No! We were just kissing!" I yelled with fresh tears developing in my eyes.

"Okay, okay. I just had to ask. We'll talk about it later."

Now, I understood what he meant by, 'She's your daughter anyway right? You do what you want to do with her if it's like that. You let her grow up to be a whore who sleeps around on her husband and can't stand on her own feet'. I wasn't his daughter; I was her daughter.

I cried harder as I pulled onto the expressway and headed toward Lane's shop.

I needed a shoulder to cry on...and Lane's were the biggest one's I could think of.

***

I'd regained my composure by the time I reached Lane's shop. The twisted emotions of anger and confusion I was feeling, now suppressed so that my life's woes wouldn't be apparent by anyone else when I arrived. I parked in a space in front of the entrance, took a deep breath, and sat for a moment. There was a beautiful lavender purple Benz parked in the spot next to me and I speculated that whatever they were bringing that in for it was gonna cost them an arm and 2 legs.

I brushed my hair back with my hand and grabbed my purse from the seat before getting out and walking into the shop. I'd been in a few times since Lane and I started dating and now he had a picture of us on his office desk from the Maxwell concert we'd been to a few weeks earlier.

"Hey Donna," I said leaning on the counter where the pretty slim receptionist took refuge.

"Hey Brenda," she said smiling and flinging her convincingly real black weave to one side. "Lane stepped out for a minute to get lunch at Fellini's. It's kind of a ghost town right now here anyway. You could probably wait in his office if you want to, or you can sit out here and keep me company."

"Girl my mind is too messed up right now to be social but thank you. I'm gonna go wait in his office," I said forcing a smile and walking toward the door that said EMPLOYEES ONLY. Once I opened it, I walked down a narrow hallway to his office and put my purse on his desk and glanced at the picture of us embracing and smiling like Cheshire cats. I was so glad I'd chosen him over Teddy, or I'd probably be headed towards a similarly miserable life like my mother's.

My stomach was queasy, and I felt the urge to hurl rising up to my throat. It seemed like I had been throwing up at even the thought of drama lately and sometimes even when I didn't. I left Lane's office and headed past the supply closet to the bathroom next door to it. I barely made it to the toilet before I was throwing up into it and dry heaving shortly afterwards. As I hovered over the toilet hoping I'd puked the last of my insides out, I noticed the animalistic sounds coming through the walls. What the hell?

I wiped my mouth with toilet tissue and paused to listen more intently. Oh yeah, somebody was fucking or getting fucked and I could hear their moans through the walls. I started rinsing my mouth out in the sink and wiped it with a paper towel and I prayed to GOD that it was not what I thought it was.

"GOD help me if I find out Lane is fucking some bitch in here, all hell is about to break loose," I uttered aloud to myself wiping my hands dry with a paper towel before I opened the bathroom door and stormed out into the hallway ready to battle.

I stood in front of the doorway looking both ways down the short hallway and listening for where the sounds were coming from. The supply closet! I thought I could still hear the faint sound of moans coming from behind the door next door to the bathroom. I put my hand on the doorknob, heart pounding through my chest, beads of sweat developing on my forehead, as my neck tensed at the idea of what I was about to see. Brian's words when I spoke to him about how he felt when he caught Gabrielle cheating came to mind, "It felt like my eyes were on fire and my heart was melting to see the woman I loved turned into an instant conniving bitch. I could never forgive or forget that B."

I closed my eyes in silent prayer, and turned the doorknob slowly and softly so as not to interrupt the potential moment of betrayal happening on the other side. As the door slowly crept open, I saw the long straight black hair of the chick on the receiving end draped down over her face as she tried to muffle her moans of pleasure. The more the door slid open, the more of them I could see and clearly, they were too engulfed in what they were doing to notice my uninvited interruption. The chick was bent over with her large hands grasping what looked like a box full of parts and that box was definitely shaking from the doggy style thrusting she was getting from...

"Oh my GOD!" I shouted in shock as Paul's startled eyes widened and he inadvertently stumbled backwards with his pants down.

That's when the girl getting pounded lifted her head up and I thought I was going to faint.

"Oh my fucking GOD!" I yelled again gazing into Julian's bewildered hazel eyes. "Holy shit!" I exclaimed yet again.

There stood my best friend's fiancé' who was not only fucking someone other than my best friend, but he was fucking my brother! Well actually given my latest family dynamic discovery, Julian isn't my brother, he's Brian's. Regardless of the fact, I'd just walked in on yet another situation that I was completely not ready for.

"Brenda!" They both shouted in unison as they scrambled to pull their clothes up.

"Please! Please! Wait a minute now!" Paul begged in his Jamaican accent while he buckled his pants. "It's not how it looks. I... I just had a moment of weakness and...I just," he tried unsuccessfully to explain.

It was obvious he didn't really have a good one and Lord knew there was no way in hell I wasn't going to tell Rhonda, my best friend in the world that I'd just found her fiancé, dick deep inside another man. No way in hell!

Julian flung his hair back and straightened his all too tight purple t-shirt and tucked it into his purple pants. Purple! I bet that was his Mercedes Benz out front!

Wow. Out of the pot and into the frying pan.

Enjoyed This Book?

Please leave a review on Amazon and Goodreads to share!
Other releases by K.F. Johnson:
LIAR'S BALL: BEHIND CLOSED DOORS 2
WHEN I'M BAD I'M BETTER
WHEN I'M BAD I'M BETTER 2
WHAT I'D DO FOR LOVE
WHAT I'D DO FOR LOVE 2
LOVE HURTS: SERIES COMPILATION
WHEN I'M BAD I'M BETTER FOREVER: SERIES COMPILATION
STABBED THIS CHRISTMAS: A NOVELLA

Join my mailing list!
http://www.kfjohnsonbooks.com

"The Empress of romantic, murder, suspense", **K.F. Johnson** is a Queens, New York native residing in Atlanta, Georgia. As a child, habitually failing to make curfew before the streetlights lit, earned her numerous occasions on restriction where reading & writing became her main form of escape. Later, K.F continued to develop her talent while obtaining a B.A. in Psychology at Spelman College & acquiring an MBA. In 2012, she published her 1st book for her social media friends & family to see. To her delight, it went viral, repeatedly reaching #1 on Amazon's top 100 for its genre. Since then, K.F. has published multiple books, started One Ironwoman Publishing, been featured in magazines & nominated for numerous awards, both for her books & as an author. With her fan base cheering for more, this mother & wife has blossomed into a witty & cunning author, penning spicy, realistic & deadly tales of African American life to remember.